THE GOLDEN GRYPHON AND THE BEAR PRINCE

HEIRS OF MAGIC
BOOK ONE

BY

JEFFE KENNEDY

A Legacy of Honor

Crown Prince Astar has only ever wanted to do the right thing: be a credit to his late father's legacy, live up to his duties as heir to the high throne of the Thirteen Kingdoms, and cleave to the principles of honor and integrity that give his life structure—and that contain the ferocious grizzly bear inside. Nowhere in those guiding principles is there room for the fierce-hearted, wildly free-spirited, and dizzyingly beautiful shapeshifter, Zephyr. Still, even though they've been friends most of their lives, Astar is able to keep Zephyr safely at arm's length. He's already received a list of potential princess brides who will make a suitable queen, and Zephyr is not on it.

A Longtime Obsession

Zeph has wanted the gorgeous, charming, and too-good-for-his-own-good Astar for as long as she can remember. Not that her longing for him—and his perfectly sculpted and muscular body—has stopped her from enjoying any number of lovers. Astar might be honorably (and foolishly) intent on remaining chaste until marriage, but Zeph is Tala, and they have no such rules. Still, she loves Astar—as a friend—and she wants him to at least taste life before he chains himself to a wife he didn't choose. There's no harm in him having a bit of fun with her. But the man remains stubbornly elusive, staving off all of her advances with infuriatingly noble refusals.

But things change when a new terror threatens the Thirteen Kingdoms. Following prophecy, Astar and Zeph—along with a mismatched group of shapeshifter, warrior, and sorceress friends—go on a quest to stop a magic rift before it grows beyond anyone's ability to stop. Thrust together with Zephyr, Astar finds himself increasingly unable to resist her seductive invitations. And in the face of life-and-death battles with lethal monsters, he begins to lose sight of why having her, just once, is such a terrible idea...

ACKNOWLEDGMENTS

Many thanks to beta readers Reese Hogan, Emily Mah Tippetts, and Jim Sorenson. Particular—and grudging—thanks to Darynda Jones for last-minute advice that gave me a panicked meltdown (especially since she was right); to Jim, who held my hand through solving the problem; and Emily for a fast read to confirm it was all good.

As always, love to Grace (Darling) Draven for the long conversations, excellent advice, and strategy. Here's to being smart and not working for free!

Thanks and love to Carien Ubink for reading, answering questions at all hours, and "general assisting."

Appreciation to Netters, for weighing in on hunkiness and shirtlessness—and for not griping (too much) about getting sent on errands.

As ever, love and immense gratitude to David, who is there every day, and who makes everything possible.

Thank you for reading!

Credits
Proofreading: Pikko's House (www.pikkoshouse.com)
Cover: Ravven (www.ravven.com)

NORTHERN WASTES

BRANLI

CARIENNE

LAKE SULLIVAN

PHOENIX RIVER

ONYX OCEAN

MOHRAYA

ODFELL'S PASS

CASTLE ORDNUNG

WILDLANDS

LOUSON

LIANORE

CRANE ISTHMUS

WINDROVEN

CASTLE AVONLIDGH

AVONLIDGH

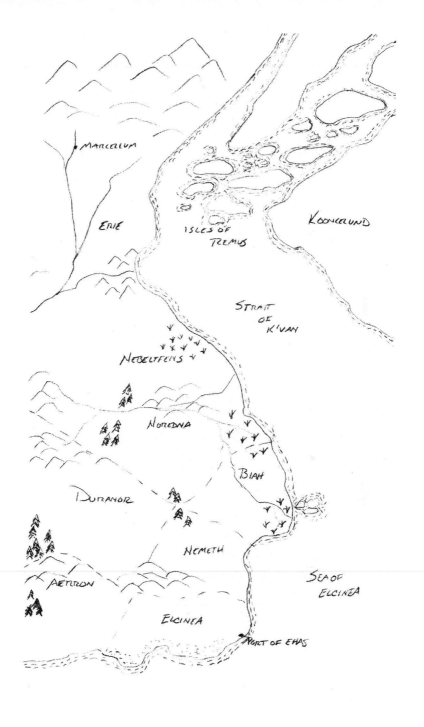

NORTHERN WASTES

BRANLI

Phoenix River

Lake Sullivan

Castle Elderhorst

Carienne

Grace River

Confluence

Gieneke

Duranor

Mohraya

Castle Ordnung

Dahl River

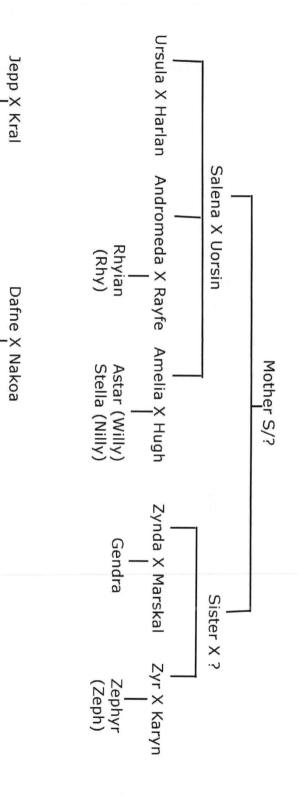

Mother S/?

Salena X Uorsin

Ursula X Harlan

Andromeda X Rayfe

Rhyian
(Rhy)

Amelia X Hugh

Astar (Willy)
Stella (Nilly)

Sister X ?

Zynda X Marskal

Gendra

Zyr X Karyn

Zephyr
(Zeph)

Dafne X Nakoa

Salena (Lena)
Bethany

Jepp X Kral

Jakral
(Jak)

~ PROLOGUE ~

"**A** STAR—WATCH THIS!" ZEPHYR'S musical shout rang out from the cliff's edge high above. Shading his eyes against the bright tropical sun, Astar picked out Zephyr's slim silhouette perched on tiptoe, precariously clinging to a rock outcropping. Her light silken shift fluttered around her as she raised her arms, the coastal breeze catching the long banner of her glossy black hair. He tried very hard not to notice how the thin material clung to her full breasts and the enticing flare of her hips. A gentleman didn't stare at women that way, especially not at his friends—and particularly not at Zephyr, who could never be his.

But Astar dutifully looked in her direction and waved, knowing perfectly well she wouldn't perform whatever trick she had planned until he was watching. Assured she had his attention, she leapt into the air in a perfect swan dive, plummeting to the glittering sea below—a drop far too great for any ordinary human to survive.

Zephyr, however, was anything but ordinary.

Still, his heart climbed into his throat as he counted the endless moments of her fall, mentally begging her to shapeshift already. An instant before she hit the water, she exploded into golden fur and feathers, her wings tightly folded against her

1

back, lion's body still sleekly aimed toward the waves—and she dove in, disappearing entirely.

Starting his count over, he waited for her to surface. Though she was still in her mid-teens, Zephyr was already talented and proficient enough to shift into any number of water-breathing forms. She could shapeshift into a fish and stay below the surface for hours—days, even, if it wasn't inadvisable for the Tala shapeshifters to remain in animal form too long—and she might do exactly that, just to tease him.

Zephyr loved to tease him, and Astar did his best to pretend he wasn't enthralled by her.

Stretching out on the white sand beach, resting his head on folded arms and enjoying Annfwn's warm sunshine and cloudless soft blue skies, Astar tried to relax. Though he was supposed to be done growing, his joints still occasionally ached, and his mother had declared he had another finger width or two of height left in him. Like he needed to get any taller. Despite the aches and the worrying about Zephyr he couldn't easily dismiss, he did his best to savor his last day in Annfwn. Tomorrow he'd be back at wintry Castle Ordnung, continuing under High Queen Ursula's relentless tutelage. As her heir, he would follow in her footsteps and ascend to the high throne of the Thirteen Kingdoms someday. A crushing thought, for so many reasons.

Unable to resist checking on Zephyr, he turned his head to study the turquoise water. What if she had misjudged? The eagle parts of her gryphon form—the gríobhth, in the Tala language—might be equipped for a dive like that, but he didn't think the lion half would be. Scowling to himself, he sat up.

Should he get someone to look for her? He didn't have an aquatic form, as he was only a partblood shapeshifter, one who only had First Form, and his was a grizzly bear. He could swim well enough as the bear, but not dive underwater for any length of time.

And Zephyr knew that, much as she liked to taunt him about trying for more forms. A frustrated growl rose in him, the bear restless and worried, pushing to be released.

Astar was just getting to his feet when a porpoise burst from the waves, becoming a songbird in mid-leap and winging to him to become Zephyr in human form—standing before him on the sand, once again in her ocean-blue silk shift, her hair tumbling in gleaming curls, sapphire eyes sparkling as she laughed at him.

Poking him in the chest with a pointed finger, she wrinkled her nose. "I gave up too soon! You were about to come rescue me, weren't you?"

"Like you needed rescuing," he growled at her.

Undaunted, she gentled her skewering finger to slide down his midline. "I always need rescuing by you, my bear," she purred. "And you were coming after me."

He brushed her finger away—letting Zephyr touch him tested his control too far—and pretended to yawn.

"Nope. I was bored while you were playing fish. I was about to head back to the cliff city."

"Liar. You could never abandon a damsel in distress. You're far too noble for that."

"You were hardly in distress," he reminded her, which wasn't a lie, even if he *had* worried.

"Come swim with me," she wheedled, taking his hand and tugging him toward the water. "Try for a fish form. Just once. For me." She batted the lush fringe of her black lashes, pushing her crimson lips into an enticing pout.

He managed to extract his hand from her grip, his fingers burning with the desire to touch her more and more and more. "You know I can't."

Punching her fists on her hips, she stood in the ankle-deep surf, eyes flashing with impatience. "You could do more forms when you were a boy. That means you still can."

"That's not true," he countered, packing up their picnic things. They'd have a bit of a walk back to the cliff city, and people would be waiting for him. Ursula had drilled into him the importance of being on time. "You know that many Tala explore forms they never take again. I'm happy with my grizzly bear. That's more than most people in the world have."

"What are you doing?" she asked, frowning at his actions. "It can't be time to go back yet."

"I have to meet with King Rayfe and Queen Andromeda," he reminded her. "Duty calls," he added with what he hoped was a charming grin—though it did nothing to alleviate her annoyance.

"Astar, this is your last day in Annfwn. You promised me a picnic."

He held up the empty basket in demonstration. "And picnic we did. You can stay and play, but I have responsibilities."

She swooped up to him, too fast for him to dodge, and set her palms flat on his bare chest, her sapphire eyes glittering with irritation. "You *always* have responsibilities."

It was true. Being heir demanded a great deal—and Astar lived in dread of not being up to the job, of disappointing all the people who believed in him. Something the enviably carefree Zephyr could never understand. Her nails scratched lightly over his skin, and her scent, like tropical flowers blooming in high mountain air, made him want to wrap his arms around her and inhale all she offered. Something else his duties kept him from indulging in.

"Stay and play with me," she purred invitingly, palms flattening to caress his chest, answering desire thrumming through him. "Just a little longer. You can have all the boring meetings you like... *later*."

With a groan, he wrenched himself from her alluring touch, covering it with a laugh. "I can't," he told her with determination, sweeping up the last of his things and turning his back firmly to her.

"You mean you *won't*," she called after him, frustration ripe in her voice.

That was also true. Zephyr could never be his, and he could never be hers. As heir to the high throne, he'd have to make a marriage of state with whoever they picked for him— and Her Majesty would never choose a half-wild Tala girl with a First Form most people thought existed only in myth. Far better never to start an affair that would only break him when it ended.

Zephyr, of course, would be fine. She always was, brighter and better than life itself.

"You can run from me, Astar, but I swear that one day I'll get you to break your stupid rules!" she yelled.

He lifted a hand in farewell, in acknowledgment. If he let Zephyr get him alone again, she'd no doubt wear him down. So he'd have to make sure she didn't get the opportunity.

"Mark my words," her taunting voice carried on the ocean breeze. "You will be mine! You already are, you just don't know it yet."

The problem was, he knew that all too well. And it didn't change anything.

~ I ~

Seven Years Later

A CHILL OF foreboding ran down Astar's spine as the footman relayed the urgent summons. Though Astar was as magical as a clod of dirt, it didn't take sorcery to know that it was bad news when the high queen commands her heir's immediate attendance. And that it would have to be especially terrible news to draw Her Majesty from the anniversary celebration of her long reign. The festival ball had been going most of the night, and no one in the vast crowd thronging Castle Ordnung was in any shape to be handling anything but another celebratory toast.

Case in point, Astar's quite drunken companions burst into laughing protests at the footman's message. Not that they ever took much seriously, much to the dismay of their parents and mentors.

"Surely we don't *all* have to go," Astar's cousin immediately argued. "His Highness Crown Prince Astar is the dutiful heir," Rhy said, giving Astar a lethally innocent grin. "Let him answer the summons, attend Her Majestyness," he added irreverently, "We'll stay here and keep the mjed warm."

"Her Majesty High Queen Ursula asked for all seven of

you, Prince Rhyian," the footman replied to Rhy's protest. "She commands that you meet her immediately in her study."

"Not really a prince," Rhy muttered darkly.

"I'll go with you, Astar," Zephyr purred, leaning her breast against his arm. She'd been seizing every opportunity that night to flirt with him. This was nothing new, as that was Zephyr's nature. She flirted with anyone and everyone, and—in typical Tala fashion—the free-spirited shapeshifter woman took as many lovers as she liked. Astar had managed to keep from being alone with her all these years, which had worked to keep her from testing his resistance beyond recovering. That night, however, she had changed tactics. She'd focused entirely on him, uncaring who noticed, intent on seduction. She'd been working on wearing him down for hours now.

She'd even given him a secret promise to honor the Feast of Moranu. The folded piece of paper in his pocket burned there like a live coal. He was afraid to read it, unsure if he could hold out against whatever temptation she'd seen fit to write down.

It had already nearly killed him to deflect her subtle—and progressively more overt—suggestions. Only the long habit of refusing her shored up his strained willpower. Zephyr had been a pretty girl, but she'd become an outrageously beautiful woman. Especially so that night, all dressed up to celebrate the Feast of Moranu. With her curling black hair tumbling nearly to the hem of her crimson ballgown, her sensual lips painted the same shade, deep blue eyes huge in her gorgeous face... well, his lifelong weakness for her had billowed into raging desire. With her natural ebullience, verve, and zest for life,

Zephyr was everything he wasn't. Even after all these years, every time he saw Zephyr, he found it harder to resist her.

And he must resist, at all costs.

"Please, Your Highnesses, lords and ladies, you must *all* go," the footman begged, practically dancing from foot to foot in impatience. "Her Majesty is waiting."

Astar didn't bother telling the footman that particular argument didn't carry much weight with this group. "Can you tell us what this is about?" he asked, hoping that might convince the crew of merrymakers to sober up—literally.

The footman gulped. "No, Your Highness. It's a matter of both utmost secrecy and urgency."

How strange. "All right, everyone," Astar said, stepping up to lead the group and extracting himself from Zephyr's intoxicating touch. They'd all been indulging in whiskey, mjed, and wine—to the point that even the shapeshifters with their high metabolisms were tipsy, which made them even more difficult to corral than usual. Astar was glad that he'd been moderate in his drinking, as always excruciatingly aware of his responsibilities as heir to the high throne. Plus, he'd figured fending off Zephyr's advances would go from next to impossible to disastrous failure if he got tipsy. "We must obey the summons of the High Queen," he reminded them. "If Her Majesty truly doesn't need some of you, you'll be back to the party soon enough."

"Fine," Rhy grumbled. "But we're bringing our plates. Salena is starving after that prodigious display of magic." He gave her a proud smile, and she blushed with pleasure.

"It really was amazing, Lena," Gen gushed. "I'm sorry I

didn't say so immediately. The way you cleared the storm and revealed the moon with your weather magic exactly at the dark of midnight, I got chills. It was an incandescent experience."

"I'll get our sorceress celebrity more wine," Zephyr declared, heading to the ice sculpture of Castle Ordnung with its cascading fountain of white-gold sparkling wine. "Anyone else—Astar, darling?"

"No, thank you," Astar called to her, giving the footman a sympathetic nod. "We'll start walking, and you catch up." Setting the example, he briskly moved the group in the direction of the queen's study. "Don't be concerned," he told the footman, who looked anxiously back at Zephyr. "She won't miss this." Zephyr might seem flighty to some—sometimes Astar suspected she deliberately cultivated that impression—but she always came through when needed.

Astar's sister, Stella, slipped a hand through the crook of his elbow, her presence a steady comfort. Sensitive to emotions and a powerful healer, his twin rarely touched anyone except for him. She'd often commented that putting a hand on his arm felt the same as putting one hand in the other, and he knew just what she meant. Without her, Astar often thought he'd drown in the turbulent sea of court intrigue.

"What do you think?" he asked under his breath, knowing she'd hear. They couldn't exactly speak mind to mind—Astar didn't have enough sorcery in him for that—but they did share a special twin language. It allowed them to have conversations too cryptic for anyone else to understand, so quietly that no one else could overhear. *"Right before the footman arrived, you*

said that challenges lie ahead and nothing will ever be the same. It sounded like prophecy."

"*Something deeply unsettling happened—and the future suddenly shifted,*" she replied. "*So fast that I haven't had time to track the possible patterns of events.*"

"What are you two whispering about?" Zephyr asked, catching up to them after passing Lena a dangerously full flute of sparkling wine and sipping her own without spilling a drop. *Conversations that almost no one else could hear,* Astar mentally corrected himself. As astute as she was gorgeous, Zephyr picked up on all sorts of things most people didn't—just as she could move with that inherent grace that let her carry brimming glasses of wine without spilling a drop.

"Speculating on Her Majesty's emergency," Astar answered with a smile.

Zephyr shrugged in the extravagant Tala style. "Who knows what mossbacks think is an emergency?"

"Hey," Jak grumbled, "enough with the mossback insults."

"Jak is right," Stella agreed gently. "It's unkind and hurtful. Shapeshifters are no better than anyone else."

"And shapeshifters can be fried with lightning just like anyone else," Lena put in with a broad smile, narrowing her eyes at Zephyr, who hmphed at her.

"Or have their throats cut," Jak added, cheerfully spinning a silver dagger between his nimble fingers.

"All right, everyone," Astar said, calling them to attention as they turned down the hall to the queen's study. "I know we've all had a substantial amount of Jak's mjed, but—"

"And your Branlian whiskey before *that*," Rhy put in.

"As if your shapeshifter metabolism is even touched by it," Lena muttered at him.

"Feeling tipsy, love? Perhaps we should go somewhere quiet to lie down," he murmured suggestively, and she giggled.

"I know we wanted them to make up and start talking to each other again," Gen said to no one in particular, "but isn't this billing and cooing a league or two beyond that?"

"What I'm saying is," Astar added authority and volume to his voice as Rhy and Lena protested and the others weighed with their opinions, "we all need to focus and take this situation seriously." They'd reached the study and its closed doors—and Astar signaled the footman to wait before announcing them. "Despite close relationships to the people who are no doubt inside this room, this is an official audience before the High Queen of the Thirteen Kingdoms."

"We're not children," Rhy grumbled.

"Then don't act like children," Astar retorted. "This is a serious situation."

They all stared at him with wide eyes. Then Jak snickered, and they all broke into laughter, even Stella.

His sister patted his arm. "Don't worry. They're just nervous. Once the doors are open, they'll behave."

He could only hope so.

~ 2 ~

THE FOOTMAN OPENED the doors and announced their arrival, Astar leading the way, as he did so well. Much as Zeph liked to tease him about being too responsible, excessively noble, and honorable to a fault, he wore the mantle of heir to the high throne well. Especially considering how much the responsibility weighed on him ever since he was a boy.

Zeph sipped her sparkling wine, using the excuse to slow her steps so she fell to the back of the group. Nobody in this room wanted to see *her*, regardless of the terms of the summons. No one expected much of her. She didn't have to be a mind reader to figure that out. Zeph was the person you called when you wanted to have fun, not to solve a secret and urgent emergency.

Her campaign to seduce Astar hadn't helped endear her to the powers-that-be either. They all thought it was important to marry Astar off to some prim mossback princess so they could make royal babies and live inside walls, upholding laws and so forth. None of them cared about Astar being happy, not like Zeph did. All she wanted was for him to live a little before they locked the door on the cage.

Well, and she wanted him in her bed for a few selfish reasons, too.

Naturally, his keepers didn't want her to succeed. Goddesses forbid their golden prince get the idea that there was more to life than following the rules. What if he got all disobedient about whatever marriage of state they settled on for him? A ridiculous thought, as Astar would never shirk his duty to the high throne—and it wasn't as if he'd ever marry *her*. Astar was far too committed to the good of the realm to do anything that reckless. He knew as well as Zeph did what a terrible queen she'd be.

Besides, Tala weren't the marrying type. She just wanted to enjoy Astar while he was still unmarried. Once he said actual marriage vows, Astar would die a painful death before breaking them. Unfortunately, he also seemed virtuously intent on not dallying before that unhappy day either. Zeph had finally concluded that she'd have to play dirty if she wanted into his pants. Which she absolutely did—especially the ones he was currently wearing. The powder-blue velvet clung to his perfect ass with delicious results, also showing off his lean hips and muscular thighs. Astar had been training with a heavier broadsword in the last year, which had broadened his shoulders and developed his chest muscles to a delectable degree. With his summer-sky-blue eyes and golden hair, Astar was a beautiful man regardless, but in that outfit, he looked downright edible.

Enough to make her mouth water.

"Stop staring at Astar's behind," Gen hissed in her ear.

"How did you know I was?" she whispered back, sliding an arm around Gen's slim waist. "Unless you were looking, too."

Gen blushed furiously, which never ceased to amaze Zeph. They were first cousins who were close as sisters. But, though Gen had inherited her Tala mother's extraordinary shapeshifting talent, Gen took after her mossback father in many ways, conservative to the point of primness at times. "I can't believe you're so irreverent," Gen chided, glaring in disapproval.

"And yet you've known me my whole life," Zeph retorted.

"Silence." High Queen Ursula's steely voice rang out, cutting through their whispered chatter. Standing from her chair at the end of the long table, Her Majesty pulled the light in the room to her, the gleaming sheath of her argent gown making her—already a lean blade of a woman—look like a lethal sword herself.

Zeph took in the three people waiting for them. Beside High Queen Ursula sat her sister, Queen Andromeda, whose sorcery made her scary imposing, her eyes silvery with shimmering magic. On the other side of the high queen sat Dafne, the high queen's spymaster, intently marking a large document with notes and calculations.

Zeph wasn't any expert on politics, but even she could recognize that a meeting with this trio—and no one else—meant something serious indeed. They were keeping the pool of people who knew about this secret and urgent happening very small—and they'd decided to more than double the number by summoning the seven of them. Ursula never did anything capriciously, but what under Moranu's shadowy gaze could possibly involve Zeph?

A chill of foreboding ran up her spine, the delightful fizz of the wine evaporating from her bloodstream.

"I apologize for pulling you away from the celebration," Ursula continued in a more even tone, "but something unprecedented has occurred, and we must take immediate steps. Andi?"

Queen Andromeda rose from her chair, layered gown rustling like the night itself and glinting with silver threads like moonlight. She'd acted as Moranu's avatar at midnight, and the goddess's hand still sat heavily upon her, numinous and full of shadows. "Just now, over the Strait of K'van, there was a full lunar eclipse."

An astonished silence fell, everyone's expressions far too serious for this to be a joke.

"But," Lena said, nearly stammering as she struggled to grasp that news, "that's... not possible. What could possibly occlude the crystalline full moon? There's nothing even close that could tonight. I know. I studied everything in preparation for the viewing tonight and—"

"Lena," Dafne, who was also Lena's mother, gently but firmly cut off Lena's perilously rising tone, "no one knows why, only that it happened. Something unknown and possibly malicious briefly obscured the full moon."

"Why do you say malicious?" Astar asked, frowning. He'd be taking responsibility for this himself, trying to fix it for them all.

"At the moment of this unnatural eclipse, a vision of the future assailed me, rather violently," Queen Andromeda said, a tremor in her voice, which she immediately suppressed. "I cannot give you all specifics without risking even worse future scenarios, but I can say that unless we act now, we face certain disaster."

Lena's brown skin had paled to a sickly amber, twin spots of color rising to her cheekbones. "A lunar eclipse. Did I... did I do something to cause this?"

"No," Queen Andromeda replied firmly, then gave Lena a rueful smile. "This doesn't have the feel of your magic or mine, I can determine that much. The timing is suspicious, however, so we cannot escape that our magic working at midnight is somehow connected. Still, you were working under my guidance, so I bear all responsibility. This is most emphatically *not* your fault."

Lena nodded, though she had tears in her eyes, and Rhy, standing beside her, looked like he wanted to kill someone to protect her. Dafne tipped down her spectacles to perch on the tip of her nose and looked over the top of them at her daughter. "Correlation is not causation, and cause and effect do not imply fault, Lena. Remember that."

"Besides which," Ursula inserted crisply, "I was the one to ask Lena to work her weather magic so that we could enjoy and celebrate the rare appearance of the crystalline moon. The ultimate responsibility rests with me."

"You give yourself far too much credit," Queen Andromeda said to her sister with some impatience. "No one could have predicted this result from the magic we worked, not even me—and I *did* look at the futures, as a basic precaution. This is something far beyond our ken, and control. Something so far beyond the normal flow of time that it wasn't there to be seen until now."

That was far from comforting news, and judging by everyone else's expressions, Zeph wasn't the only one to feel that way.

"I've sent for reports from people I have in the region, to gather data on the phenomenon—and any attendant aftereffects," Dafne said into the fraught silence.

"Until then—and likely even then—I have only Andi's vision to go on," Ursula said crisply.

"And mine," Stella offered in a soft voice.

Queen Andromeda looked to Stella, something about that startling her. "You had a vision, too?"

Stella nodded, her gaze troubled. "I saw many things I can't quite understand, but all... horrible."

"Yes." Andromeda bowed her head briefly, then lifted it, purpose in her expression. "I could use your insight. The future is shifting by the moment, and fracturing into multiple paths too rapidly for me to trace the patterns beyond a certain nexus in time in the near future. What I can tell you all is that the nexus in time seems to focus around the formation of some sort of metaphysical rift in the north, centered in the Strait of K'van, and running in either direction through the Thirteen Kingdoms and beyond."

"For those of us who don't speak sorcery," Jak said with a frown, "what is a metaphysical rift?"

Queen Andromeda held up her palms, a line between her brows. "That's the best way I can describe it. It's like a fault line—the sort that causes earthquakes and opens chasms in the ground—but on a nonphysical plane. From what I can see of the future, it causes fluctuations in magic, producing effects like I've never seen before. Allowing creatures into our realm that have existed only in mythology."

"Or allowing unexpected objects to cause a lunar eclipse," Astar murmured, and Zeph had to suppress another shiver. What could possibly block the moon?

"I've been transcribing Andi's near-future predictions onto this map," Dafne put in, practical as ever. "From what she's been able to detail so far, the rift seems to be capable of spilling magic at volatile intervals. Those levels might be increasing exponentially, though I haven't been able to complete all the calculations yet—and, of course, I have no empirical data, only anecdotes and projections. And it keeps changing."

Zeph didn't quite follow all of that, but whatever Dafne had said, it had Queen Andromeda glaring at her. "I can't control the future, only tell you what I see. Forecasting the future is more art than science."

"Besides which, it's early hours yet," Ursula interrupted. "As Andi says, there's a great deal of work to be done to sort out what may occur in the near or distant future. Still, from what she has been able to determine and relate to me, there is a single step we can take at this time that will tilt the progression of events in our favor. Which brings us to why I have summoned the seven of you—and pledge you to secrecy."

Zeph glanced at Stella, who nodded in regretful affirmation. Stella understood the intricacies of prophecy far better than anyone but Queen Andromeda herself, but Zeph knew enough to guess the implications. Andi had seen enough of the near future to know that the seven of them would be neck deep in it. Predicting the future wasn't easy; acting on it was even more difficult, full of precarious dangers.

Sure enough, Ursula continued, leveling a steely gaze on their rapidly sobering group. "The primary reason for this meeting is to put the seven of you on notice that we will be sending you north first thing tomorrow."

"Even me?" Jak asked in genuine surprise. "I'm just a sailor. No royal blood, sorcery, or shapeshifting in me. Not like the rest of this lot."

Queen Andromeda gave Jak a half-smile. "Especially you, Jak. I realize that I'm asking a great deal of all of you, to trust in something we can't—and won't—fully explain. You've read your histories, if only because Dafne forced you." She cast a grin at Dafne, who shrugged without remorse. "So, you all understand how foresight works. I can't give you information that might affect decisions you make in the moment. I can only point you in the general direction that will lead to the most positive outcome for us all."

"Which is why everyone hates prophecies," Jak muttered.

"And understandably so," Queen Andromeda replied wearily. "Suffice to say that I wouldn't have sounded this alarm if the futures currently condensing didn't spell disaster. I wouldn't have advised Her Majesty to send the seven of you on this quest if I didn't believe that you are our one chance to avert a cataclysm that will eventually tear our world stone from stone, until nothing remains."

~ 3 ~

AN EVEN HEAVIER burden than usual slammed down on Astar's shoulders. Ever since the war ended when he was but a toddler, the world had been more or less at peace. Sure, magic had been released to spill out everywhere instead of being contained in Annfwn, which had caused all kinds of ripple effects. But those ripples were mostly along the lines of the odd creature cropping up in a forgotten lake or ancestral sorcery reappearing in people who'd lived ordinary lives until then.

Nothing world ending.

Astar had done his time being schooled by Dafne, as they all had. As even Jak had, when he wasn't off sailing the seas. The former librarian had taught them as much as she could get them to sit still for, and Astar had sat still for more than most. Between Dafne and High Queen Ursula, they'd stuffed as much information into Astar's head as it could hold—which was never as much as they liked. Of course, dealing with high expectations, including and especially his own, was part of being heir to the high throne.

Not that realizing that particular truth made it any easier for him. Sometimes Astar wished he'd gotten Rhy's life, or

Jak's. They both did pretty much as they pleased—though Astar wouldn't wish his life on them, nor were either of them foolish enough to envy his. He could also wish that Ursula had decided to have children of her own, rather than depending on her nephew Astar to be her heir.

Though they'd cleaned up that history somewhat, Astar knew that the late, unlamented tyrant of a high king, Uorsin, had named his grandson Astar as heir to the high throne upon Astar's birth. And Uorsin had done so entirely to undermine his firstborn, Ursula. One would think that Ursula would've picked anyone else to be her heir once she ascended to the high throne, but no—she'd upheld her father's decision and set to molding Astar to be the kind of high king she believed her precious realm deserved.

Thus, he knew from many conversations on long-term strategy to protect and nurture the Thirteen Kingdoms, that Dafne had been concerned for years that the magic unleashed upon the world would continue to grow in unexpected ways. She'd studied every text on magic she could find, and she'd developed a theory that magic behaved more like an organic force than a physical one. She theorized that magic could feed on itself, acting as its own fuel to essentially reproduce like a living organism. He didn't think she'd predicted anything like this.

Something far beyond our ken, and control. Something so far beyond the normal flow of time that it wasn't there to be seen until now.

What could the seven of them possibly do about something like that? He and his friends had often bemoaned how their parents liked to tell stories of their heroism and the glory days of the Deyrr War—complaining, too, that their lives were so unexciting by comparison—but this news sounded more frightening than exciting. They should've appreciated boring while they had it.

Zephyr sidled over, giving him a dubious look. "I think we are not the heroes they're looking for," she whispered. A laugh snorted out of him, despite himself and the gravity of the situation. Zephyr always had a knack for making him laugh.

"Questions or discussion?" Ursula asked sharply, giving him a narrow look. "I can't promise to give clear answers, as there are few to be had, but we'll do our best."

"Your Majesty," Lena said in a clear and steady voice, though her face was tense with agitation. "I can't go on this quest. I have to return to my work in the Aerron Desert. We've made such inroads on shifting the weather patterns there, and I believe we're at a tipping point in—"

"Restoring what were once the fertile pastures and farms of Aerron has been a priority since the first days of my reign," Ursula reminded Lena pointedly. "Make no mistake but that your work there is greatly appreciated. I'm telling you now that *this* is far more important." She glanced at Andi, who nodded firmly, and with a dark look in her eyes.

Dafne gave Lena an owlish stare over her spectacles. "We need you in the north, Lena. From what Andi has told us, your gifts are going to be critical."

"And," Ursula added, "this isn't a request. I don't want to make it a royal command, but I will if I have to. This quest is that important."

Lena looked like she wanted to argue, but pressed her lips together and acquiesced, fixing her gaze on the floor. Rhy, lounging against the wall nearby, studied her with an odd expression on his face. He'd been trying to catch her eye—and she'd been diligently avoiding meeting his gaze. That didn't bode well.

"*It's one thing,*" Stella subvocalized to Astar, "*to kiss and make up with the guy who tore your heart to pieces when you only have to deal with him for a single night. It's another proposition if it looks like you'll be weeks, or even months, in each other's company.*"

Ah. That made sense.

"Can you tell us *nothing*, Mother," Rhy said with slicing irritation, "that would be useful? Everything is 'important' and 'urgent' and 'critical' and totally vague."

Astar felt sure he wasn't the only one to notice how Queen Andromeda flinched ever so slightly at Rhy's challenging tone. "I *cannot* tell you more," she said, addressing all of them. "Any hints I might give you could alter decisions you make in the moment. Trust that you're going because you are meant to be there, each of you, with your unique talents, skills, and... gifts." She finished with a different word than she'd planned to, her gaze on her son, a wealth of unspoken emotion between them.

"Clearly," Ursula said, breaking the tension, "we have information still to collect and decisions to make. That doesn't mean we can't plan your departure tomorrow. Stella and Lena, I'd like you to consult with Andi. Astar, you're with me and Dafne. I want to go over the kingdoms and political alliances you'll be navigating. Jak—have you ever sailed the Strait of

K'van?"

"No, Your Majesty," he replied, sounding startled to be called upon.

"I want you to be prepared to do so," she replied cryptically. "That means you have studying to do—and charts to acquire."

"We'll be sailing?" Zephyr asked in surprise.

"Unless you, Gen, or Rhy have mastered dragon form?" Ursula returned drily.

Rhy coughed out a harsh laugh. "That would *not* be me."

The high queen gave Rhy a bland but not unsympathetic look. "All three of you have winged forms, I know, but the rest of your cohort does not. Thus, unless you all want to swim, I suggest sailing. I want you three shapeshifters to make a plan for an overland journey to whichever port looks best for sailing into the strait. I'll also expect you to work up a schedule so you can scout ahead from the sky. You will need to keep a constant lookout for unexpected dangers."

"I hate when people tell me to expect the unexpected," Zephyr muttered.

"I have several winged forms, too," Stella volunteered. Astar said nothing, since he only had his bear form, pretty much useless for anything but brawn.

Ursula inclined her head. "We need your sorcery more. If you and Lena are to deal with this metaphysical rift—which I might logically predict will involve closing it again, but that decision lies in the future, and will be up to you—then you two must conserve your energies for that."

"Me?" Lena gasped. "I have weather sorcery. I can make it

rain and that's it. I don't know anything about metaphysical rifts."

"Not to be pedantic," Dafne said, frowning as she completed a calculation before she looked up, "but *no one* knows anything about it, since the metaphysical rift is unprecedented. From Andi's visions of the rift so far, it seems to be in part a force of nature, which makes it not unlike weather."

Astar frowned to himself. Their logic wasn't making perfect sense—which meant they were dancing around giving them too much information about what Andi had glimpsed of their future efforts.

Lena looked dubious, but Andi looked *through* her in that way that meant she saw beyond the present or the physical. "When you were first born, and Dafne told me she wanted to name you Salena, for our mother, I had a vision of you. I believe what I saw then may be coming true now." She smiled, comfort and sorrow mixed in it. "You're in the middle of this, Salena, like it or not." Scanning the group, her gaze lingered again on her son, a shadow of sorrow in it. "You all are. For better or worse."

~ 4 ~

ZEPH FELT MORE than a little useless—not for the first time in her life, but that didn't mean she liked it.

"*Unless you've mastered dragon form,*" she muttered to herself, mimicking Ursula in a snotty voice. Like it was so easy. Gen's mother, Zynda, had nearly died to discover the trick, and she'd been the first shapeshifter in centuries to do it. Even though Zynda couldn't—or wouldn't—explain the trick, everyone seemed to expect them to figure out the miracle, too.

"Guess we're just surplus shapeshifter support to the actual heroes," Rhy griped, sidling up and looking as annoyed as Zeph felt.

"That's a bit dramatic," Gen replied. "Queen Andromeda said she'd seen in her visions that we all have critical roles to play."

"Yes, well, the servants who empty the chamber pots in this mossback monstrosity of a castle play a critical role, too," Rhy pointed out with a smirk. "Doesn't mean it's not literally a shit job."

"You don't have to go," Gen replied, an unusual snap in her voice.

"Royal command, remember?" he countered. "I *do* have to

go."

"Well, there goes your busy schedule of sex, drinking, and lazing around."

Rhy eyed her. "You've been chewing my ass all night, Gen. What is your problem? I thought you *wanted* me to make up with Salena."

"I did," Gen hissed. "I said *talk* to her—not seduce her!"

"Jealous?" Zeph teased, mostly because it was the easy joke, but Gen whirled on her, real hurt in her expression. Something had indeed been bothering Gen all evening. Something more than Rhy making up with Lena or Zeph trying to seduce Astar, which Gen was plenty annoyed about, too.

"Oh, sure, remind me how I'm the odd one out in our merry crew." Gen's voice broke. "Poor Gendra, the plain one, the boring one. It's so easy for you, isn't it, Zeph? You're gorgeous and talented and sexy. Everyone who looks at you wants you. It must be nice."

Zeph gazed back at her, flabbergasted. "You are *not* plain or boring. As for shapeshifting talent, we both know you're far more likely to nail the trick of dragon form before I do."

"That is not my point," Gen gritted out. "You're so self-absorbed you can't even hear what I'm saying to your face."

"Then say it," Zeph snapped. She could sympathize with Rhy here. Gen was usually the nurturer, the friend she could count on to always be on her side. Sure, they bickered sometimes, but she'd had no idea Gen harbored so much resentment. *Maybe that's part of the problem,* a voice whispered in the back of her mind.

"Do the math," Gen replied with heat. "Seven of us are going on this quest. *You* will no doubt succeed in seducing Astar. With Rhy and Lena paired up, and Jak with Stella, where will that leave *me* on this quest? That's right: all on my lonesome, the odd duck. I guess at least you can send me to scout ahead while you all have fun."

"We won't be having fun," Zeph retorted. "We'll be saving the world from this metaphysical thingy."

Gen actually sneered. "Oh, don't pretend to care about saving the world, Zeph. We all know *you* only care about one thing."

Zeph, not at all sure how to reply, opened her mouth, hoping words would come, but Gen had already stomped off.

"Seems she doesn't want to plan our route just now," Rhy observed.

"Do you really think Jak and Stella are a thing?" Zeph wondered.

"I suspect Gen would say your question is missing the point of her little tirade." Rhy raked back his waving black hair. "Tonight has been one for painful conversations of all kinds. I blame the crystalline moon. The mossbacks have all kinds of superstitions about it. If it makes you feel better, Gen lit into Salena and me earlier for letting our relationship and breakup affect all of you."

Zeph frowned in puzzlement. "It never bothered me that you and Lena weren't speaking."

"Yes, Zephyr, darling, but nothing bothers *you*," he drawled.

"So, what, I'm a bad person now?" The unexpected hurt

drilled into her heart. She'd always thought her friends loved her, but now it seemed they all saw her as an uncaring flirt.

"Not a bad person, but Gen is right that you're self-absorbed." Rhy held up his hands in surrender at whatever he saw in her face. "No insult intended. You and I are alike that way."

"I am not self-absorbed," she protested. If anything, she'd been Astar-absorbed, and that was practically a noble cause, wanting him to live a little and enjoy life. At least this quest would be the perfect opportunity to wear him down on his ridiculous rules and finally get him between her thighs.

"Zeph, you're standing here thinking how this quest is the perfect opportunity to seduce Astar, when we're supposed to be heroically contemplating saving the world."

Zeph narrowed her eyes, wondering how much of Queen Andromeda's mind-reading skills Rhy had inherited. He always said none, but he'd come too close to her actual thoughts.

Rhy laughed at her, wagging a finger in her face. "No, I didn't read your mind. You're just transparent, especially to me, because I'm frankly thrilled that Salena won't be escaping to her desert studies. This gives me time to make things up to her. I don't really care about saving the world, either."

Hearing the words from Rhy's mouth had a chilling effect. "I *do* care about fixing this magical metaphysical rift and saving the world!" When Rhy raised a knowing eyebrow, she glared at him. "You heard the assignments same as I did. The sorceresses will do the actual saving. Astar will do the leading. Jak will do the sailing. And the shapeshifters get to be…" She trailed off in realization.

"Surplus shapeshifter support to the real heroes," Rhy finished, smugly repeating himself. "I, for one, am not embarrassed to be simply along for the ride."

She nearly retorted that he'd made that terribly clear with his approach to life, but abruptly realized those words could be turned back on her, too. "Great. We're both assholes," she said, feeling terribly glum all of a sudden. And this was supposed to have been a fun night. The party of the century. The crystalline moon was supposed to be romantic, and she'd planned to dazzle Astar.

No luck there. Even now, he'd forgotten her existence, his golden head bent close to the high queen's as they discussed some political strategy about the region. He was so noble and handsome that the sight sent a pang through her heart.

Astar would give everything of himself to this quest, just as he did with every task tossed his direction. So, if she really wanted to be a friend to him, she'd have to try to be helpful. Responsible, even—as awful as that sounded. *Just be Astar-absorbed*, she told herself, *and it will be fine.*

Are you sure about that? the back-of-her-mind voice said mockingly.

Yes, so shut up, she told it. If nothing else, she absolutely cared about saving Astar. Helpful and responsible. Caring about saving the world. The new Zeph. "I guess we should look at a map," she said, trying to sound helpful and responsible, "if we're going to pick the overland route to this Strait of K'van." Wherever that was.

"Probably a good start," Rhy agreed, looking pained. "Maybe it will soothe Gen's temper if we show we are going to do work to help."

"Though I don't know why they're asking *us* to pick the route," she had to mention, moving toward Dafne, who seemed to have all the maps. "Shouldn't someone who actually knows the Thirteen Kingdoms do it?"

"That's a good question." Rhy sounded thoughtful. "Her Majestyness doesn't make decisions based on nothing. Why did she assign *us* this job?"

"Probably to keep us occupied while the real heroes concentrate on saving the world," Zeph quipped.

"Maybe." Rhy didn't sound like he thought so—and he was even less inclined to pay attention to court wrangling and politics than she was. Before she could ask what he was thinking, though, they were at Dafne's corner of the table, where she sat with her piles of maps. She held up a finger, counting under her breath as she added a column of figures, then looked up at them, sliding her spectacles down her nose.

"Not quite the party we expected, hmm?" she asked wryly. "How are you guys holding up?"

Surprised by the question, Zeph nearly said she was fine— then decided Dafne wanted the truth. She wasn't one to ask idle questions. "I think we're all in shock," she confided. "Things are happening so fast. It's hard to grasp it all."

Rhy gave her a considering look, but Dafne nodded. "It's really happening, but I understand. You think you want adventure until one seizes you by the throat and drags you out of your nice, warm bed. Saving the world sounds good in stories. In reality, it guts you, and you end up wishing for your dull life again."

Zeph had been about to say that she'd never wanted adventure, but maybe that wasn't entirely true. They'd all grown up on the stories of the Deyrr War and the glorious heroics of their parents. Zeph's own parents had been the ones to discover the lost land of n'Andana—Zyr nearly dying to get them there and Karyn almost meeting a gruesome fate as the bride of the god Deyrr. Even when she was a girl, Zeph had noticed how they focused on the high points of that tale, avoiding the darkest moments. During Zeph's morbid phase, she'd asked her mother about the details of the ritual that would've wed her to the god, and Karyn had replied that it was private, and Zeph didn't need such things in her head.

In reality, it guts you. That was how Karyn had looked when Zeph asked about the ritual: gutted. Her own stomach turned with chill dread.

"If we're to plan this overland route," Rhy was saying, "we need maps."

"Of course." Dafne shook her head, shuffling through her stack. "I'm thinking of too many things at once. Do you two remember how to read maps? I know Gen does, but I don't see her."

"Gen had to take care of something," Rhy said, gallantly covering for her, "but we remember how. You're the one who made us learn."

"Ha. Which is why I remember perfectly well who was a diligent student and who wasn't. As I recall, you two had a propensity for slipping off to go swimming or flying."

That was accurate, sadly. Rhy had always been Zeph's partner in skipping lessons to go be porpoises or gulls. No wonder everyone had a poor opinion of them. "I remember the maps," she said staunchly, giving Rhy a warning look. They would figure it out.

Dafne wasn't fooled. "I understand how the Tala feel about written things, so let me give you a quick refresher." She laid out a set of colorful papers, reminding them how the codes on the edges showed where they matched up, and how to look up the key to see what the various lines and symbols meant. When she finished, she advised them to try the study next door and lay the maps out on the big table there.

Feeling like a naughty schoolkid—as she never had back then—Zeph went with Rhy to the study. Astar hadn't looked in her direction even once the whole time they'd been standing right on the other side of Dafne.

"Who knew learning maps would turn out to be important?" Rhy complained, bringing over several silver candelabras with white candles burning to illuminate the maps Zeph laid out.

"Maybe this whole crisis is a hoax, and they're doing this to us just to make a point," Zeph offered, wanting that to be true. "You know—to teach us responsibility or something."

Rhy cocked his head, considering, then shook it. "I don't see them concocting a lunar eclipse and a metaphysical rift just to get us to be more responsible."

She sighed. She'd meant it as a joke, but it had been a poor one. "Well, we thought maps weren't important then, and we think they're important now. Let's put our heads together and figure this out."

Then maybe she wouldn't feel like the frivolous dead

weight on this quest. Maybe she'd do something important—to save the world—and then Astar would finally take her seriously.

~ 5 ~

"THE DIPLOMACY IS going to be one of your greatest challenges, at least initially," Ursula warned Astar, not for the first time. She was more talking to herself than to him as she reviewed the list of potentially impacted kingdoms and uncharted realms.

"That's part of why you're sending us," Astar guessed, though it wasn't really a question. "We're a bunch of young people who won't be seen as any kind of threat."

She leveled her astute and steely gaze on him. "I'm sending the seven of you because the sorceress who has never failed to steer me in the right direction says that it needs to be the seven of you."

He flushed in chagrin. "Of course. Foolish of me."

Thawing a bit, her narrow mouth quirked in a wry smile. "Not entirely foolish. It also fits my strategy well to have it be a group who will be underestimated by many. Well done, figuring that out."

His flush turned to pleasure at the praise. While his auntie Essla could be a warm and even funny person in private, when she wore the crown—literally or figuratively—she rarely thought beyond making decisions and cleaving to the goddess

Danu's clear, bright lines of justice. Ursula wasn't lavish with praise, and never offered idle flattery.

"Yes," she mused, long finger trailing down the list of realms and rulers, "I'm hoping a group of young people on a pleasure excursion will seem innocuous enough. I don't want any of the thirteen kingdoms to be concerned about the stability of the realm or my rule. And I don't want any country outside the Thirteen to get the notion that I'm thinking about conquest—or that I'm vulnerable to one. And, though we have reasonably good relations with Dasnaria, Empress Inga is still barely holding the cap on those factions unhappy with the social change she's instigated. If it looks like I'm attempting to gain power, they'll use that against her."

"They haven't forgotten that they planned to conquer us and failed," Astar mused.

"Memories are long and resentments immortal," Ursula agreed in an absent voice. "In some ways, it would've been better if we'd accomplished the job through might rather than a coup from the inside."

"But you prevented countless innocent deaths that way."

Ursula looked up from her list, expression somber. "Don't get me wrong. I wouldn't go back and change it. Danu is always a champion of the innocent and the defenseless, regardless of how their leaders may behave." She blew out a breath. "But those who beat their chests for war would've been cowed by a show of power. If we'd crippled the Dasnarian Empire, I'd worry less about what kind of problems I'm leaving for you to face. Especially now."

Was that fear on her face?

"You're not going anywhere soon, Auntie Essla," he said, giving her a charming grin to cover the unsettling sense of seeing weakness in her. Of the prospect of losing her someday. Of having to be the high king and handle things all on his own.

"Unlike resentments, *I* am not immortal," she replied wryly. "At any rate, I'm not worried about the Dasnarians with this crisis. Not yet, anyway. They are fortuitously on the opposite side of the world from this rift—thank Danu—so that's not your concern. If we handle this situation deftly, they won't even know I've sent an envoy to realms beyond my own. Which I'm not doing, since you won't be on official crown business. By the time events escalate to the point where it impacts far Dasnaria, well…" She closed her mouth over the next words, saying nothing more.

"So, we're to seem like a group of friends on a pleasure jaunt," he said, filling in the hole made by unspoken terrors. "Touring through the northern kingdoms, sailing the strait in midwinter, traveling to the northeast Isles of Remus, and maybe even far Kooncelund?" Astar wasn't as delicate about the cold as his Annfwn cousin and friends—after all, he'd spent many a bitter winter snowed in at Windroven or Ordnung—but this didn't sound like anyone's idea of fun.

"That's where your creative diplomacy will come in," Ursula replied drily. "And we'll concoct a story for you to spread about the lunar eclipse, to ease people's concerns. I could wish that it had happened on a night when every blessed soul wasn't already gazing at the moon."

"Maybe that's part of why it happened," Astar tendered, and she gave him a sharp look.

"A deliberate warning?" she mused. "Could be. Could be. But that doesn't help us in the moment. This cover gives you curiosity as a reason to investigate odd occurrences, explore unusual corners of the realm. I'm sure you and your cohort of mischief makers will come up with suitable excuses for your larks."

Astar wanted to protest that assessment—because it wasn't accurate about Stella, Gen, or Lena—but it was certainly true that Rhy, Jak, and Zephyr got into plenty of trouble. Astar always felt somewhat like the middle child, though he was technically the oldest of the group, able to see both sides of situation. When he was with the more serious girls, he enjoyed their conversations about sorcery, weather magic, taking dragon form, and why shapeshifting didn't require conservation of mass. Rhy and Jak had a tendency to get Astar into mischief, it was true—but he'd had some of the most fun of his life with them.

And Zephyr... Surreptitiously, he scanned the room, catching no glimpse of her brilliant scarlet gown, no hint of her musical laugh. Zephyr would get him into the *worst* kind of trouble if he let her. He'd been so tempted, so close to capitulating any number of times. If she knew how close, which of her flirtatious techniques had widened the cracks in his determined resistance, well... he wouldn't stand a chance. And with these developments, he needed to shut her out more firmly than ever.

Astar made himself meet the queen's gaze steadily. "Should I apologize for past mischief?"

Her stern façade softened a bit. "You've done remarkably

well keeping the, shall we say, more unruly elements duly corralled. I'm not going to ask about the cask in the outer courtyard or the damage done to the well housing there only hours ago."

Astar winced. He hadn't even considered that the well housing might've cracked during the escapade with Rhy and Jak's giant cask of mjed. What was amazing was that the problem had already been noted and that the high queen knew about it, despite the ongoing celebration and ensuing crisis. "I'll see that it's fixed."

"No." Ursula tapped the list. "*You* will see to getting this quest underway. The well housing is being dealt with." She eyed him like the hawk that was her emblem. "You'll learn this: pick good people to work for you, trust in their expertise. Handle problems immediately."

"Are we still talking about the well housing or the quest?" he ventured.

"Same principles apply to both situations," she replied crisply. "Know what your people do well and let them do it. Know their cracks and weaknesses and make decisions accordingly. Librarian, what do you have for us?"

Dafne passed over a new piece of paper. "I need to confirm with the sorceresses," she said, "but this is my projected timeline from Andi's initial forecasts."

Ursula took it in with one keen glance and passed it to Astar, looking expectant. A test, then. Wonderful. He studied Dafne's neat notes, her handwriting familiar from years of being tutored by her. She'd sketched a jagged line over the map, with circles radiating outward, various inscrutable symbols at particular locations, and various time signatures noted on each. Making sure he understood, he went over it again, then looked up to find both women watching him.

"So, this line indicates the rift, the circles are ripple effects, and these symbols are some sort of catastrophic event Aunt Andi saw but can't divulge more details about?"

As Dafne nodded, Ursula tapped the paper. "So, given that—where do you go first?"

Astar rubbed his forehead, willing himself to think. It was hours past midnight, and he rarely stayed up anywhere near this late, especially recently, since Harlan had him out in the training yard sparring with broadswords at dawn. He studied the time signatures and the odd symbols. "Lake Sullivan, but I don't understand what could be happening there."

"What lives in Lake Sullivan?" Dafne prompted.

"The sea monster?" Astar frowned.

"It's likely a misnomer to call it a sea monster," Dafne replied. "According to local legend, it's been living in the lake for centuries, only recently sighted again—recently being a relative term—with the return of magic twenty-five years ago. It could be that Lake Sullivan was once an inland sea, one that covered most of the Grace River Valley. As the seas withdrew, the creature became isolated, and the lake gradually turned fresh. However, there is contradictory evidence in the geological record that implies—" Catching Ursula's expression, Dafne stopped, clearing her throat. "Regardless, the creature is elusive, and we don't know how it came to be in the lake, but we do know the people of Carienne regard it as a symbol of good luck and prosperity."

Astar nodded, making a mental note. "So, we need to travel to Castle Elderhorst to warn King Groningen in Carienne about a potential catastrophe at Lake Sullivan concerning their good-luck lake monster, and tell him the cataclysmic lunar eclipse is nothing to worry about." He studied their faces, receiving neither confirmation nor denial, and continued with a mental sigh. "After that, the other points of concern are the Isles of Remus, which are independent allies with varying levels of interaction with the high throne—mostly distant—and Kooncelund, which has been historically insular and resistant to diplomatic overtures."

Ursula nodded. "With one salient exception. King Cavan of Erie married a princess of one of the Isles of Remus and formed a covert alliance."

Astar searched his brain. Less whiskey and mjed would've been wise, though their uplifting effects had long since faded. "Did I know that?"

The high queen smiled thinly. "Uorsin didn't know. Cavan and Nix—then prince and princess of Erie—attended my coronation. Her existence as Cavan's bride came as a... surprise."

"The queen's name is Nix?"

"It's a long story and something to hear," Dafne replied with some enthusiasm. "I have it in the library at Nahanau. There may be a copy here in Ordnung."

"He can hear it from the horse's mouth, as it were," Ursula put in, an odd lilt of humor in her voice. "You'll see. So, yes, after Elderhorst, you could go to Castle Marcellum in Erie and ask for a pass to the Isles of Remus, where Nix and Cavan's son, King Isyn, now rules."

"What kind of pass?" Astar couldn't quite figure why he hadn't known any of this.

"We don't know," Dafne mused. "I'm very much hoping you'll be able to tell us if you—when you return."

Taking pity on Astar's confusion, Ursula clarified. "I realize that we can count the number of things the librarian doesn't know on one hand, but the Isles of Remus have long been shrouded in mystery.

"But some are almost certainly warded," Dafne put in, brown eyes sparkling with academic interest. "It's said they appear and disappear according to the wishes of the denizens."

"I'm calling that a bit of groundless superstition," Ursula said with asperity. "Land does not appear or disappear, but it *can* be hidden from perception." Behind her back, Dafne made a face, studiously looking at her document when Ursula glanced her way. "You, Astar, will be in a position to determine fact from fancy—and I'll rely on your levelheadedness. Follow your intuition; use your head."

"So, the Isles of Remus and King Isyn are the eventual goal," Astar tendered. When neither woman replied, he sighed, out loud this time. "I'd best go find Rhy, Zephyr, and Gen, as it sounds like our overland route is already set."

"That exercise was mostly to get our imprudent Tala to actually familiarize themselves with a map of the Thirteen and beyond." Ursula cracked a thin smile at his surprise. "I'm not above a bit of trickery."

"They won't be pleased at wasting their time," Astar said, feeling weary already.

"Well, then." Ursula pushed the timeline document toward him. "Sounds like you have your first crisis in leadership before you. Payment for the damage to the well housing."

Wonderful. Just wonderful. "All right, I'll handle it."

"Speaking of leadership," Ursula continued, "you know that some of these more distant kingdoms retain old superstitions and misbegotten beliefs about shapeshifters and the Tala."

"Yes?" He wasn't sure what the high queen was getting at now. Ursula had always encouraged him to be discreet about his bear form outside of Mohraya and Avonlidgh, where the people had known him since he was a baby. His more far-flung subjects didn't need to be reminded that their high king could become a grizzly bear at will.

"Try to keep a rein on the shapeshifters," she suggested gently. "No showing off unnecessarily. Keep the forms that might incite questions—or panic—out of sight."

She meant Zephyr, whose First Form was the gríobhth, like her father's. A creature that many considered mythical, and most thought of as a monster. He could control himself. Controlling Zephyr was another matter entirely. And not something he'd ever thought of doing. He liked Zephyr wild. "I'll do my best," he promised anyway.

"One more thing." Ursula dug through a stack of papers and withdrew a sheet, passing it to him. He stared at the list of names in dull incomprehension. "A list of your potential brides," she said, raising a brow at his confusion. "Since you'll be traveling through the realms where some of them dwell, this is a good opportunity for you to meet them, perhaps form an attachment."

Ursula met his gaze evenly, her eyes steel gray, and he swallowed the protests and questions. It was no coincidence that his loving auntie Essla had handed him a list of suitable brides and cautioned him about Zephyr's gríobhth form in nearly the same breath. The high queen had been a warrior first and foremost, and very little escaped her keen attention.

He folded the list and put it in the pocket of his trousers—as far from the paper bearing Zephyr's unknown promise as he could get it. "Understood," he replied as neutrally as he could.

"Good." She nodded in satisfaction. "Courting your potential brides adds to the cover story of your journey as well. Also, if any of the disasters Andi has foreseen manifest, the news of a royal wedding will be a welcome spot of joy to mitigate difficult days ahead. If you do find a girl—from the list, mind you—that you like enough to marry, give her this." She set a ruby ring in front of him, the cabochon shape making the color deep and dark as blood.

He stared at it, oddly unwilling to pick it up. "One of Salena's rubies."

"Appropriate for a crown princess and the next high queen," Ursula replied crisply.

Taking the ring with a sigh, he put it in his pocket with the list.

"Astar," Ursula said more gently, "no one is asking you to marry someone you don't like. There are a lot of names on that list, and all would bring beneficial alliances or relationships with the high throne. All I'm asking is that you meet these women and give them a fair chance to win your affection.

Don't be distracted by other... pretty faces."

"I know," he conceded. After all, they'd had this conversation before, more than once, and he knew where his duty lay. "I will, of course, do my best to be charming—and act as duty demands."

She cracked a wistful smile. "You're so much like your father that way. I know I can depend upon your honor and integrity."

He nodded, unable to say anything, thoughts of his long-dead father lodging in his throat. "I should go find the gang studying the maps, stop them from going in the wrong direction for too long."

Nodding, Ursula turned her attention to new information Dafne handed her, while Dafne met his gaze with warm brown eyes, a hint of sympathy in them.

~ 6 ~

ZEPH WAS GETTING a headache from trying to decipher the mossback collage of lines and color when Astar came into their study, bringing—oh, joy—more pieces of paper with him. He looked tired, and worse, apprehensive. She'd love to smooth those lines from his brow and kiss him until desire fogged his summer-blue eyes instead of trouble. The man worried way too much.

"Where's Gen?" he asked, looking around the small room as if he'd expected a lot more people than the two of them.

Zeph and Rhy exchanged glances. "She went to take care of something," Zeph said, using the excuse Rhy had given Dafne. Seemed like a good all-purpose-yet-vague reply. "But look," she told him proudly, responsibly, "we've been studying the maps."

"The Port of Ehas is a place with many ships," Rhy added, nodding wisely. They'd both been pleased to determine that much. "We can sail from there. Plus, it's a warm place, like summer all the time!"

Astar looked pained, and Zeph felt herself deflate. She hadn't expected lavish praise, exactly—though maybe she'd fantasized about Astar saying how proud he was of her—but she and Rhy had *tried*. It seemed like effort should count for something.

Tossing his papers on the table, Astar sat on the other side of Rhy, letting out a sigh. "I have additional information. Her Majesty wants us to take this route." He pulled the map more in his direction, showing them where he meant. "We'll take the big trade road along the River Danu to Castle Elderhorst in Carienne. We'll meet with King Groningen, then from there to Marcellum, where we'll meet with King Cavan and Queen Nix. At that point, they'll hopefully give us permission to visit King Isyn in the Isles of Remus. There might be a port to depart from in northern Erie." He skated his finger along the line that indicated the coast. Astar had big hands, with long, clever fingers. Zeph could just imagine how they'd feel on her skin.

"If not," Astar was saying, and Zeph had to remind herself to pay attention to his words, "we'll have to go back down to the Grace River estuary. There's a port city here that will also work." He took in their silent stares and grimaced. "It's not nearly as big, nor as warm, as Ehas—you're right that the Port of Ehas *is* the best port in the Thirteen—but Ehas is kind of in the wrong direction."

Rhy sat back in his chair, kicking out his long legs and lacing his hands behind his neck. *Uh-oh.* The more relaxed Rhy looked, the more dangerous he was. His eyes glinted with predatory light as he studied Astar. "Why," he asked softly, "were we tasked to do this work that meant nothing?"

"It meant something," Astar promised, earnest and unde-terred by the implicit threat in Rhy's posture. Of course, Astar was the definition of earnest, and Rhy would never hurt him. They *had* gone around more than a few times over the years, however. Zeph found she wasn't inclined to intervene in this case. If she and Rhy weren't useful, then they could've been dancing or moongazing—not breaking their brains on mossback maps.

As if he sensed her irritation, Astar gave her a tired smile. "I apologize, to both of you. Things are happening quickly in there. But remember: no effort is truly wasted."

"What is that—mossback wisdom?" Zeph asked. "It makes no sense to me."

"For example," Astar replied, the soul of patience, "you both know a lot more about the landscape now."

Zeph snorted, flipping a disdainful hand at the maps. "This isn't landscape. It looks nothing like landscape, and I know nothing more now than I did an hour ago. It's mossback lines and pictures. If I want to know a landscape, I'll fly over it."

Astar returned her gaze steadily. "Not all of us can fly, Zeph. Those less fortunate have to make do with lines and pictures."

She looked away, chagrined, but refusing to let him see it. Astar could fly if he wanted to badly enough. He just wanted to be a "normal" mossback more. "Then I'll fly for you and tell you what things look like. Any of us will. We're happy to— you know that."

"I know." He offered her a gentle smile. "And I know we're all feeling stressed. It's not the night we hoped it would be."

Aha! An opening. Not exactly an engraved invitation, but

an indication that Astar also regretted what hadn't happened between them that night. Yet. There was still time. She nudged Rhy's foot under the table, and he flicked a glance at her. With a knowing smirk, he stood. "I'll go find Gen," he said, "and tell Jak and the sorceresses where to find us. Eventually."

"You don't need to—" Astar began, but Rhy, Moranu bless him, was already out the door, even remembering to close it behind him.

"You look tired," Zeph said, which she didn't even have to make up because he did.

"True." Astar rubbed the back of his neck ruefully. "This is late for me. And being quizzed by Her Majesty—and Queen Dafne, both—can be draining."

"Let me do that for you," Zeph purred, going behind him and threading her fingers through his shoulder-length golden hair. So pretty, like sunshine, and soft as seawater. She loved his hair, fancying it felt as warm to the touch as rays of light. Combing through it lightly, she rubbed her fingertips over his scalp, rubbing and soothing. When he tensed, she hummed softly, "Just a massage."

With a soft sound of pleasure, Astar dropped his head, giving her access to the tight cords at the base of his neck. He had more muscles there now, his neck thicker, his shoulders sculpted beneath the blue velvet, from all that broadsword work. She'd like to watch him train sometime. That would be a sight to see. Maybe he'd be shirtless and sweating—she hadn't seen Astar bare-chested for years and years. She could be a morning songbird and he'd never know.

Working the tense muscles and ligaments, she savored the

way Astar relaxed under her touch, the occasional involuntary groan of pleasure evocative of how he might sound during sex. She loved that she was the one to coax those seductive sounds out of him. If he'd let her, she could massage him all over, turn those groans into pants, then reduce him to incoherence. He needed the release, he was so tightly wound. She could give him that. She *wanted* to give him that, if he'd only give in.

Gentling her touch, she caressed his hot skin, so sweet and smooth. Bending down, she inhaled his masculine scent, like a summer day, with a hint of forest beneath that came from his bear First Form. Moranu, how she wanted him. She brushed her lips against his temple, drawing in that scent.

He tensed. "Zephyr..."

"Astar..." she replied throatily, brushing another kiss along his cheek.

"I can't do this," he said in a strangled voice.

"*We* can," she murmured. "It's still the longest night. There's nothing more for us to do until we leave tomorrow. We can go to your rooms and—"

Shrugging her off, he burst up from the chair and backed away, holding up his hands as if fending off attack. "No, we *cannot.*"

"Why not?" She glided closer, reaching out to trail a finger down the lush velvet covering his powerful chest. The powder blue somehow only emphasized his masculine lines. He didn't stop her, his hands out to the sides, fingers twitching as if he didn't know what to do with them, his breathing uneven.

"Zephyr," he said again, even more raggedly, his gaze hot and drifting to her mouth, then lower, before he resolutely wrenched it up again. "You're a beautiful woman."

Her heart took a little tumble. Astar had never said anything like that to her before. Others teased her about knowing she was pretty, but hearing it from Astar—the only person whose opinion truly mattered—meant everything. She smiled at him. "Thank you. I think you're beautiful, too."

He didn't smile back, instead releasing a breath of exasperation. "You're so Tala to say that."

She laid both palms firmly on his chest, sliding close enough to revel in his body heat. "You are Tala, too, my bear. Don't let the walls and rules make you forget."

He shook his head slightly, finally—thankfully—settling his hands on her hips, though carefully chaste in their position. His fingers flexed, though, telling her without words how much he longed to touch her more. "I'm not really Tala. Not like you are. I belong to the world of the Thirteen much more than to Annfwn. You know that."

She slid her hands behind his neck, pressing against him and nuzzling his strong throat. He swallowed hard, and she just had to kiss that enticing laryngeal prominence, her tongue darting out to taste his skin. Making an incoherent sound deep in his chest, his hands spasmed on her hips. "Zephyr," he said, voice hoarse with the desire that vibrated through him. "We can't do this."

"But we *can*," she said again. Maybe if she said it enough, the truth would sink in. She pressed her lips to the sweet hollow at the base of his throat, savoring his rumbling response, then tipped her head back, stroking the nape of his neck with caresses both soothing and seductive. "It's not against any rules for you to have one thing that's just for yourself, to help you cope with the burden of leadership. I'd like to be that for you. Kiss me."

His simmering blue gaze focused on her mouth, and he lowered his head, as if pulled by a riptide he'd ceased fighting. "Zephyr, you have no idea how much I want to."

"I do," she murmured. "I do know, because I want it, too. Just as much, maybe even more." She parted her lips, tasting his warm breath, anticipating the sparkling moment of connection.

"No," he said, reaching up to grip her wrists and setting her away from him. He held on tightly, like he couldn't bear to let her go, despite his words.

"Why not?" she demanded, frustrated enough to want to scream. So close... "I want you and you want me. That's a natural and beautiful thing. We're adults, free to do as we please."

He gazed at her, almost pleadingly. "I'm not. It's not. I mean—" He took a breath, dropping her wrists as if she'd burned him. "I can't. I don't."

Bereft of his nearness, feeling the chill of the sudden separation, Zeph put her hands on her hips, glaring at him in confused frustration. "Don't *what*? I defy you to say that you don't want me."

"I—" He reached out as if to touch her again, then flattened his hands on the table, staring hard at the polished surface. "I *can't* want you."

Relief fluttered through her. He did want her—she hadn't been wrong—so this was about his stupid rules. "'Don't' and 'can't' are not the same thing."

"Maybe not," he said to the table, then straightened and faced her—though he focused his gaze carefully beyond her. "The result, however, is the same. *You* are free to do as you please—and I sometimes envy that—but I am not. I know you understand this."

"No." She wanted to stomp her foot in exasperation, the fierce impatience of her First Form fulminating in her heart. The gríobhth was not a patient creature. "I do *not* understand your silly and limiting mossback rules. You *are* free, Astar. You are not married, you're not engaged or even promised to be engaged. I don't understand why those things are important to mossbacks, or why there are so many levels of them. They're like rules to a game no one wants to play. Right now— *tonight*—and in the next few weeks of our journey, you *are* free to be with me, and you may not be in the future."

He focused on her, a thousand thoughts passing behind his summer-sky eyes—and a dread feeling warned her those thoughts weren't about the joys of sharing their bodies while they could. In fact, the longer he stayed silent, the more she worried she'd said exactly the wrong thing.

Finally, Astar shook his head, bearlike, which meant he was upset enough for his own First Form to be close to the surface. "I will be someday," he said, like it was an apology. "I will be promised, engaged, and married—to someone who will bring a needed alliance to the Thirteen. Those are important political interactions, not a game."

"Someday," she scoffed. "Someday is what parents tell children to stop their nagging. Someday means nothing."

"Not in this case," he replied firmly. "But all right, I'll correct myself. It will be soon. I've seen the list."

"A list?" Her heart thudded, claws wanting to extend. "Show me this *list*." She hissed that last word. Mossbacks with their maps and lines and *lists*. There would be names on it. Names of prim princesses deemed suitable for Crown Prince Astar. Women who could never understand her bear like she did.

Astar cocked his head, a smile tugging at his mouth—rueful, but also with a sparkle of admiration that warmed her. "I don't think that would be a good idea. We can't have you going about murdering my potential brides."

"Hmph. I wouldn't do that." *Just terrorize them a little.*

His smile widened. "Just the same, I think we'll play it safe and keep the list as it is: secret."

She would see about that. There were ways to uncover secrets. Still, Astar had diverted her from the immediate moment. "All of this talk is the future, not now, not tonight. The present is all that matters, not some future that may never arrive."

"We're making plans to avert disasters that haven't yet happened," he reasoned. "The future clearly does matter. You've agreed to go on this quest, so you must acknowledge that truth."

She stabbed a finger at him. "Don't play mossback logic games with me."

He sighed, then took her hand and folded it between his, deliciously big, warm, and callused from sword work. "Zephyr." Astar searched her face. "We have been friends as long as I can remember. You are precious to me. I—" He stopped himself, firming his chin and pressing his lips together. "I care about you as a friend, the same as I love Gen and Lena."

"You don't want Gen or Lena like you want me." She'd meant it as a statement, but it came out like a question, Moranu take her.

"Nevertheless, friends is all we can ever be. I refuse to lead you on, to let you believe it can ever be more."

"I can handle myself," she replied. "You don't have to worry about me."

"But I do," he argued, squeezing her hand between his. "Because I do care about you. Zephyr, it would kill me if I broke your heart."

She laughed, because her heart already felt a little broken. "I promise: my heart is my responsibility and will be just fine. It's very strong. Besides, I'm talking about sex, not love."

Sorrow deepened his eyes, like a cloud passing over the sun. "But what about *my* heart?"

Her mouth went dry. "What about it?" she whispered.

Still holding her hand with one of his, he reached up with the other to tuck a long lock of hair behind her ear. "I think you don't realize how beautiful you are. How magical and passionate. So vivid and alive. Sometimes I wish that—well, I wish I could give you my heart, promise you forever, but I can't. And because I can't, I won't."

"I never asked for forever," she argued, but her voice came out like a plea.

"No, I know that." He shook his head again ruefully. "And maybe that's part of the problem for me. I'm just... not like you. I can't separate sex and love."

Of all the... "That's just silly," she burst out, tugging her hand free. As much as she wanted to touch him, she couldn't stand still for this. "When they marry you off to some princess on this *list*," she hissed, hating the word more than ever. "When you offer yourself up on this altar of mossback adherence to duty, you'll be expected to have sex with *her*. You'll have to pop out a new heir, so your poor child can have a miserable life, too. Do you plan to love this *wife*?"

"Yes," Astar replied gravely. "I will do my best to love her and honor that love with my fidelity—emotional and physical." He dug into his breast pocket, extracting the folded promise she'd put there earlier. Her Feast of Moranu gift to him, a promise she'd written down only hours before in the fullness of hope and anticipation. He held it out to her, in the same folds she'd put there. He hadn't read it. "Because of that, I can't keep this. It would be doing a dishonor to my future wife."

She stared at him, completely aghast, taking the note with numb fingers. "I don't understand you at all."

He winced, scrubbing his hands over his scalp, looking weary and tense again. All of her good work, undone by a stupid argument. "I know you don't understand my reasons. That's part of the problem, too."

Unexpected anguish rose up in her chest, squeezing her heart as if Astar had taken it in his fist. "All I ever wanted was to pleasure you," she managed to say through the pain. "To give you happiness when you're so clearly unhappy. I just wanted to be with you for as long as you could be mine."

He nodded, face a rictus of misery as he stared at his toes. "I know. I wish I… I sometimes wish I could be the kind of man who'd let you."

"You could be, if you wanted to."

Blowing out a heavy breath, he met her gaze. "That's the thing, lovely Zephyr. I don't want to. You asked me to deny that I want you. I can't do that, because I *do* want you."

Hope inflated her crushed heart. "I want you, too! Let's—"

"No, you don't get it." He leveled a cold and determined gaze on her. "I don't want you enough. Not enough to compromise my principles. That will never change."

~ 7 ~

FOR AN ENDLESS, throbbing moment, Astar thought Zephyr might collapse. She looked so stricken, like an arrow had mortally pierced her, knocked her low in a way he'd never seen. And he'd been the one to deal the painful blow. He wanted nothing more than to take it back, to pull her close and kiss her shining hair—but he'd let this go on too long already. That's why it hurt so much now. If he'd been less of a coward, he'd have told her this long ago instead of avoiding being alone with her. He could've saved them both this pain.

She pulled herself together, visibly rebuilding her poise, swallowing back the tears that made her sapphire eyes look even brighter than jewels. Licking her lushly crimson lips, she parted them, mesmerizing him as always. "Astar, I—"

The door swung open, startling them both enough that they jumped apart, even though they hadn't even been touching. Jak strode in, rolled charts tucked under his arm. He looked back and forth between them. "Ah... I can leave."

"Please stay," Astar said, seizing the excuse to be saved from this gut-wrenching conversation like the coward he was. Zephyr gave him a long glittering look, condemning him for his spinelessness, and rightfully so.

"If you say so," Jak replied doubtfully.

"Absolutely. There's a great deal of planning to do. I see you were able to obtain charts?"

"Yep." Jak tossed them onto the table. "For the entire strait—as much as we've mapped anyway. Apparently there are parts of the Kooncelund coast and entire islands in the Isles of Remus that are uncharted. But I've got everything there is from the southern coast of Ehas all the way up."

"Revised instructions indicate we won't hit the strait south of the Grace River estuary," Astar said, keeping one eye on Zephyr, who slunk to a seat and pretended to look at a map. She put on a decent appearance of it, and would fool anyone who didn't know how much she loathed the things. He hated that he'd wounded her—especially when everything he'd said had been to prevent future hurt. *Now is all that matters, not some future that may never arrive.*

"Good to know," Jak was saying, sorting through his charts and setting some aside. "Fewer charts to drag around."

Astar sighed in relief, glad that at least Jak wouldn't be annoyed about the wasted effort like Rhy had been. As if summoned by the thought, Rhy strolled in, looking like a cat in the cream with Lena on his arm—though Lena looked less happy—and Gen and Stella following behind. "Excellent," Astar said with cheer he hoped didn't sound too forced. "Everyone is here. I have updates."

Rhy held out a chair for Lena, who gave him a suspicious glance, but sat, while Gen went to sit by Zephyr, the two exchanging quiet words he didn't try to overhear. Stella came to his side and slipped her narrow hand into his, so familiar and so unlike Zephyr's burning touch. His twin looked up at him, storm-gray gaze discerning, a sweet wash of soothing comfort radiating from her.

"I'm all right," he told her subvocally.

"You're not, but I understand," she replied the same way, and took the chair beside him.

He slid Dafne's timeline to Stella and nodded to Lena, who came over to look, too. Rhy gave him a searingly annoyed look, which Astar returned blandly. The traitor had deliberately left him alone with Zephyr when he'd expressly asked him not to. "Here's the predicted timeline of the rift and potential ripple effects," he said. "Did your glimpses into the future reveal anything different?"

"More detail," Stella said, "but not much different. Aunt Andi says that the plan to find King Isyn via Marcellum and stopping at Castle Elderhorst on the way is as good a plan as any."

Gen frowned. "When did that become the plan?"

"Sometime after you took off in a huff," Rhy replied. "Where did you go?"

"I needed a moment," she retorted crisply. "Get off my tail."

He narrowed his eyes at her. "You smell of snow and fresh air. You went flying, didn't you?"

"We were assigned scouting duty," she replied primly.

"Not at Ordnung," he countered. "Why did you shift back wearing your fancy ballgown, anyway?"

Gen smoothed the shining sapphire silk. The gown was a good choice for her, as it matched her eyes. "Because it's pretty. You're just jealous that you can't come back to human form wearing anything but what any child can do."

"No," Rhy bit out with considerable irritation. "I'm annoyed that you left me and Zeph to do all the work."

She sniffed in disdain. "Like you two *ever* have to do any work."

"What matters," Astar said forcefully, "is that we're all here now, discussing a mission of critical importance. I'm asking you to hear me out without interruptions. We all have to work together, so let's begin, as we wish to go on. No effort is truly wasted." He caught the mocking glint in Zephyr's eye and could just hear her voice asking about mossback wisdom. She had a point, in a way. He was taking refuge in these tired maxims because he had no idea how to lead, not really. Not without someone looking over his shoulder, ready to step in if things went awry. They'd be on safe territory for a while, but out in the mysterious Isles of Remus or strange Kooncelund... Well, this group—the people he loved best in the world— would be looking to him for guidance, and he didn't know if he'd be up to the job.

Zephyr was looking back at him more soberly now, as if she understood his thoughts. For all Zephyr's wild ways, and as opposite as they were, she always had understood him, sometimes even better than Stella did. No—just differently than Stella did. And now he might've ruined their friendship forever, right when they'd be thrust into close quarters together, depending on each other. No help for it, though. With a concerted effort, he looked away from her and set to outlining the plan as Ursula had given it to him.

They all listened more or less attentively, staying silent, and no one immediately began to argue, which he took as a good sign. None of them looked particularly happy, however.

"Thank you for your attention," he said, feeling stuffy and pompous as he said it. He avoided Zephyr's gaze, knowing she'd be rolling her eyes at him. "Questions? Comments? Discussion?"

"I really think we should have brought the mjed to this little meeting," Jak commented.

"Agreed," Rhy said fervently, staring across the table to where Lena had remained beside Stella.

"You won't be able to take refuge in liquor on this quest," Gen informed them primly.

Jak widened his eyes in exaggerated astonishment. "I know you've spent most of your time in Annfwn, practicing your shapeshifting and Danu knows what all, but even you have to know that courts the world over excel in wallowing in liquor and other decadence. We'll be at Castle Elderhorst in Carienne, then again at Marcellum. I know for a fact that Elderhorst is a social whirl and probably—"

"How?" Stella asked curiously. Though she always spoke softly, she also spoke so rarely that Jak immediately broke off, fixing his dark eyes on her.

"How do I know about Elderhorst, dear Nilly?" She nodded, and he grinned. "I've been there on, ah, trading runs." He slid a look to Astar and away again. "You'll love it there. Maybe we can go up to Lake Sullivan. It's so huge it looks like the sea, but dark and cold, so the water is nearly black, and usually glassy smooth. And there are colored lights that dance in the sky at night."

"A rainbow at night?" Lena asked, intrigued.

"Bigger, brighter, more colors." Jak waved his hands in the air, fluttering his fingers. "And without storm clouds."

"What causes them?" Lena reached for a piece of notepaper.

"Nobody knows," Jak replied in sepulchral tones. "It's a mystery, like the sea monster, which is enormous, bigger than a dragon!"

"I don't like the word 'monster,'" Zeph commented. "It's so judgmental."

"Apologies, charming Zeph," Jak half-bowed in her direction. "Present company excepted."

She wrinkled her nose at him. "So, have you seen this lake creature?"

Jak shook his head. "It rarely shows itself. Maybe some of you shapeshifters could go swimming to—"

"This trip is not for sightseeing," Astar cut in, feeling even more stuffy, especially when they all made faces at him. "It's not," he insisted. "This is a critical expedition to repair a rift caused by unknown forces, both of which can destroy the world."

"Willy is right," Stella put in, using Astar's childhood nickname. Back then, the exasperated adults exhausted from chasing rambunctious shapeshifting twin toddlers had dubbed him and Stella "Willy" and "Nilly." "There will be challenges for us ahead, grave ones. Lena and I have seen them." Because Stella looked to her, Lena nodded reluctantly, seeming unusually subdued.

Rhy watched her with narrowed eyes, then flicked a glance at Astar. "But we're to appear as a group of friends—and lovers—out for a fun tour through the countryside. Leaving out why we'd be crazy enough to think traveling through the mossback northlands in bitter winter is a good idea, we should engage in activities like sightseeing, indulging in local drink, dancing at balls." He cast a grin at Lena, but she didn't look up from the notes she was scribbling.

"Rhy is right," Zephyr joined in, a malicious glint in her eyes. "A group of friends—and lovers—won't attract the wrong kind of attention. Rhy and Lena are already a couple. Astar and I can... pretend to be." She fluttered her lashes at him.

Uh-oh. He should've known Zephyr wouldn't be daunted for long.

"I think that's a terrible idea," Gen said flatly. "If you haven't noticed, we're an uneven number."

"You can be my sweetheart," Jak said in a generous tone, sliding a charming smile to Stella. "You and Nilly and I can be a triad."

Astar would've sensed his twin's embarrassed flush even without seeing the flags of color on her cheeks. "Jak, that's not appropriate," he put in, feeling any control he had of this group slipping through his fingers, "and—"

"And it's not happening," Gen spat at him. "I'd rather be dead."

Jak clapped a hand to his heart. "You wound me, sweet Gen."

"Not yet, but I'm considering it," she retorted.

"Let's all take a step back and—" Astar tried, but no one listened. He was losing control of a rapidly dissolving situation, and they hadn't even left Ordnung yet. He risked a glance at Zephyr, who raised one raven-winged brow at him, glossy red lips curving in a sardonic smile.

Lena rose to her feet, everyone falling silent at her movement. Her white gown, sewn with crystals, scattered the light and set off her creamy brown skin, her hair like caramel falling down her narrow back to her slim waist. She wasn't a sorceress in the same way Stella was, but her weather magic felt similar, intensifying in the room like a gathering storm. She pinned Zephyr with a fierce look. "Why do you say Rhyian and I are a couple?"

Zephyr sat back in her chair with languid ease and a knowing smile. "Aren't you?"

"No," Lena replied.

"Yes," Rhy said at the same time.

Very slowly—excruciatingly so—Lena turned her head and fastened her intense gaze on Rhy. His smile faded, and he seemed to shrink inside his skin. "We. Agreed. Just. Until. Dawn." She spaced her words evenly, like she spoke to a person somewhat dense. Astar cringed for Rhy, giving him a warning look in place of the words he wished he could say, to urge his cousin to tread carefully.

Unfortunately, "careful" wasn't in Rhy's vocabulary. "Until dawn—*at least*," he corrected. "Doesn't it seem meant that we kissed under the crystalline moon, and now that very magic, that same moon, has changed the world so that we'll be together?"

Astar would've sworn he heard distant thunder, his skin prickling like lightning might strike.

"Only you," she said in a menacing hiss, "could manage to make this cataclysm be about you."

"Not just me. You *and* me." Rhy grinned at Lena—a fool in the face of the wrath about to descend on him—and everyone else watched with avid interest.

"Rhyian," Lena said in that same endlessly patient, nerve-scraping tone, "I'm going to say this clearly, since you seem intent on having this out in front of all of our friends. I will never, *ever* be your lover again." She flicked a glance at Gen, who smiled grimly. "I'd rather die," she echoed, looking back at Rhy. "Tell me you understand."

Rhy's face had gone cold and set, eyes glittering a predatory blue. "We talked this out."

"We talked, yes," she replied evenly. "And I'm glad we did. It doesn't change what happened."

"We can't change the past, Salena," he gritted out, "but we *can* change the future."

"That's exactly right," she retorted, planting her palms on the table. "And my future has no place for you. If I could excise you from my past, I would."

Rhy blanched, staring at her as if wounded—reminding Astar uncomfortably of the look on Zephyr's face just a while ago. Sneaking a glance at her, he found Zephyr staring right at him, blue eyes shadowed with the pain he'd been afraid to see.

"You don't mean that, Salena," Rhy said, his voice rough.

"I do mean it. And *you* mean nothing to me." She said the words with such cool disinterest that Astar felt sick for his cousin.

Rhy seemed to have no response—a telling sign for his usually glib cousin—and Astar wracked his brain for a way to end this confrontation.

It was Jak who broke the silence. "Maybe you two should just do each other and put the rest of us out of your misery," he quipped, then held up his hands when Rhy pinned him with a lethal glare. Astar rubbed a hand over his gritty eyes.

"We're all tired," he tried, "and—"

"We did do each other," Lena announced calmly. "It didn't take."

"What?" Jak, who'd had his chair tipped back on two legs, thumped it down in surprise. "When?"

Lena stared at Rhy, daring him to comment. He seemed shocked, and a little green around the gills. "It was a long time ago," she said breezily. "Rhy was my first, in fact."

"You were my first, too," he said very quietly.

That gave her pause. "You never said."

He shrugged, not meeting her gaze. "I didn't say a lot of things."

"True." She let out a long, weary sigh. "It doesn't matter that I was your first—since your second, and *third*—" Her voice shook a little, but she straightened her spine. "Those happened while my bed was still warm from your body."

Riveted by the reveal, everyone's heads swiveled to Rhy. "I apologized for that," he said tightly.

Lena shook her head, mouth pinched with pain. "Oh, Rhyian. Apologies don't necessarily change anything. *You* would have to change."

"I can change," he protested. "I made mistakes, yes, and I know I hurt you, but I was young, and I told you I don't know why I went with those girls. Besides, you know the Tala aren't monogamous. You can't put mossback expectations on us."

Gen put her face in her hands, and even Zephyr shook her head sadly. Jak clapped a hand on Rhy's shoulder. "I'd stop talking if I were you, my friend. You're not coming off very well in this story."

To be honest, Astar thought none of them were. Surely the heroes of old setting out to save the world hadn't had to deal with this kind of thing.

~ 8 ~

A STAR CLEARED HIS throat, drawing all eyes to him. He looked so pained, so supremely uncomfortable that Zeph nearly felt sorry for him. Except she wasn't feeling all that charitable toward the thick-skulled, too-noble prince at the moment. In fact, she allowed herself a bit of gleeful anticipation for how Astar would put his foot in it now.

"This meeting is about an important quest," he said, much too pompously for this group, then leveled a paternal smile on Lena. "This is not the time or place to air old romantic entanglements, and such." He waved a hand uncomfortably.

Oh, Astar. Zeph cringed as Lena turned her formidable glare on him.

"Are you saying this conversation is *my* fault?" she inquired in a lethally even voice.

"Ah…" Astar's face reddened as he scrambled for a response. "Um, no, Lena, I—"

"I would hope not," she continued in that slicing tone. "Because *I* didn't ask for this quest." She held up a hand to forestall further comment. "Don't fret. I will go. With the stakes we've glimpsed, with Her Majesty, the King and Queen of Annfwn, and my own esteemed royal parents commanding it, I can hardly refuse. Nevertheless, this venture is forcing me to give up my work in the Aerron Desert." Her fulminous glare swept all of them, except for Stella. "I know none of you care a fig for what I'm doing there, but *I* care. It's good work. Meaningful. Important. It's taken me years to develop my skills to this level, and endless hours of delicate manipulations to get to where we are. I'm proud of what I'm doing there."

"The high throne appreciates—" Astar began, ignoring Zeph's horrified head-shaking.

"*Don't.*" Lena spun on Astar. Though he topped her by a head—and Stella sat between them—he flinched. "Don't you dare pander to me, Willy," she hissed. "You might be leader of this quest, but you don't outrank me. And I am not airing 'old romantic entanglements.' This conversation is about now, and about the personnel *you* are supposed to be commanding. It's up to you to ensure that I feel safe and comfortable in this group."

Astar straightened, face set, and nodded. "You're right, Princess Salena Nakoa KauPo. I forgot myself, and I apologize."

"I've had enough apologies for one night," Lena said wearily. "I think I've made myself clear." She didn't look at Rhy, who simmered visibly with miserable fury. Zeph hadn't known before this what had happened to break them up so dramatically, but it was worse than she'd guessed. They'd been blissfully in love one day, the next, Lena had fled Annfwn for Aerron. Then Lena had stayed in Aerron, barely ever taking a day off from her work there, and Rhy had started his tumble into a seven-year feckless sulk.

Lena turned back to Astar. "I'll go. I'll help repair this problem. But I am sacrificing a great deal to do this, and I will *never* act as Rhyian's lover, in reality or in pretense. Rhyian, you *will* leave me alone. Astar, I expect you to enforce that if it becomes necessary. Is anyone at all unclear on what I'm saying?"

Everyone looked at Astar, who slowly stood, then bowed deeply to Lena. "You have indeed made yourself clear, and I regret that you felt the need." He straightened and looked around the table. "I've come to a decision. We may be dressing up this trip as a pleasure jaunt, but we must keep firmly in mind that we are embarking on a critical mission. We carry the trust of all our realms with us. To seal the gravity of this quest in our minds, I hereby decree that there will be no romantic entanglements of *any* kind from this moment until we return with our task completed."

Zeph felt her mouth sag open. Not that she wanted to give Astar another chance after the dreadful things he'd said to her, but to issue an ultimatum like this... He carefully wasn't looking at her, which made her wonder—how much of this was about Lena and Rhy, and how much about her?

"You don't command us," Rhy snarled, seething with frustration and fury.

"You're mistaken there, Rhy," Astar replied with admirable calm. He did wear leadership well, Zeph had to admit—when he wasn't being stiff about it. "If you prefer, I can ask High Queen Ursula to reinforce the command. Of course, that will entail explaining to Her Majesty why it's necessary. I don't think anybody here wants that." He swept the gathering with eyes hot as the summer sky at high noon. Not so much the charming, golden prince now, but with a hardness to him. For the first time, Zeph glimpsed the king Astar would be some-day, and—far from quelling her infatuation with him—she wanted him even more.

Of course you do, said the voice. *You're contrary that way.*

This time she didn't bother replying. Maybe if she ignored it—whatever this new voice was—it would go away.

"I don't want Astar to have to explain any of this to Her Majesty," Lena said, hard gaze on Rhy. "I prefer that no one knows my personal business. Rhyian?"

Rhy met her gaze, a wealth of unspoken words hanging between them. "You know I don't," he replied softly.

"Then are we agreed?" Astar asked. "I want a verbal reply." He caught and held the gaze of each of them until they said yes, starting with Rhy, who hissed his agreement without taking his eyes off Lena. It did nothing to mollify her resolve.

Astar came to Zeph last, clearly steeling himself to meet her gaze. She had an answer ready. And a clever plan in mind. "I don't always understand mossback rules," she said lightly, batting her lashes. "Allow me to clarify: this moratorium of yours means no romantic entanglements within the group, but that leaves us free to pursue interests outside the people in this room, correct?"

Astar paused, not expecting that. Jak and Gen turned hope-ful faces to him. "That's a good point," Jak said. "We might need to flirt and possibly seduce people as part of our cover. For the good of the cause, naturally."

Gen nodded in vigorous agreement. "We should be free to

pursue our own interests. It's not as if Willy can command us to be celibate for the next half a year, or however long this mission takes. It's not fair that it be a blanket moratorium."

Zeph just barely bit back the comment that living a celibate life on the quest wouldn't be any different for Gen, but she didn't want to ruin her gambit. Besides, maybe travel would open up some possibilities for Gen. She'd always been far too picky. Being a shy introvert amidst a boisterous extroverted people like the Tala didn't help either. Meeting new people might be good for her.

"The Dasnarians sometimes command celibacy, depending," Jak pointed out, and Zeph had to nod in agreement. She'd spent some time in Dasnaria, mostly visiting her mother's family, and she'd heard plenty of stories. Nobody beat the Dasnarians in iron control of, well, everything. "A moratorium on all sex wouldn't be unusual."

"Stop calling it a moratorium," Astar said, darting Zeph an irritated glance. She smiled at him mercilessly.

"But we are not Dasnarians," Stella spoke up. "Not even Jak and Zeph can be considered Dasnarian, because they grew up in our culture. We're friends, and we are adults. We should not be forbidding each other romantic pursuits so long as they don't interfere with the quest. I agree that Willy's Moratorium should not extend beyond this group." She looked up at Astar with a sweet smile and slipped her hand into his.

He returned her gaze with exasperation but kept her hand in his. "All right, then, we're agreed. I suggest you all get as much sleep as you can. We'll leave around noon tomorrow."

No one pointed out that tomorrow was today. And Zeph

was keeping a low profile, hiding her glee that Astar hadn't noticed that she'd dodged agreeing to his decree. Across the table, Stella met her gaze, the gray of Stella's eyes crystal bright as she smiled knowingly. Astounded, Zeph processed that Stella might actually be on her side, and had spoken as she did to help her cause.

Stella stood. "Lena, Zeph, Gen," she said, "you can sleep in my rooms if you like. There's plenty of space for all of us."

"Same with mine," Astar belatedly said. "Jak, Rhy—if you want to bunk with me."

Rhy pushed violently away from the table, glaring at Lena. "It's not dawn yet," he shot at her.

She lifted her chin, expression cold. "I rescind the offer."

"You can't do that," he growled.

"We're under royal orders now," she replied coolly, gesturing to Astar. "Those supersede any carelessly made and inadvisable personal agreements. See you all tomorrow." As they headed out of the room, Zeph heard something crash behind them, followed by Astar's soothing tones.

"No thanks," came Rhy's snarled denial. "I'd rather sleep outside."

A moment later, the distinctive whistling of black wings whooshed over their heads. Rhy, in his raven form, sailed past with furious speed and was gone. Lena watched him go with a jaundiced expression, shaking her head slightly.

"Just you and me, Willy," Jak's voice rang down the hall. "Fancy some mjed? There's plenty."

ZEPH TRAILED ALONG behind Gen and Lena, who walked arm in arm, heads bent together. Stella, looking tired, walked beside her.

"Are you holding up all right?" Zeph remembered to ask. That had been an emotional scene, and Stella didn't handle those well. She felt everything. Shielding herself from the turbulent emotions, on top of whatever sorcerous scrying she and Lena had been doing with Queen Andromeda, had to have left her wrung out.

Stella shook her head, then nodded. "I'm tired—trying to keep up with Auntie Andi while she's working at full power is *not* easy. My shielding is strong, though, so I wasn't too bothered by the emotions in that scene just now. You upset Willy a great deal."

Surprised by the stab of guilt, she slid Stella a searching look. "Just now?"

"Before we walked in. I sensed his turmoil from a distance."

His *turmoil*. Ha! What about *her* turmoil? For some reason, all of her friends, even Stella the empath, seemed to think Zeph didn't get hurt and upset like anyone else would. "I'm sorry you were disturbed," she said stiffly, then wondered if she sounded like Astar at his most awkward.

Stella cocked her head, eyes wide and concerned. "Oh, no, honey—I didn't mean that at all." She brushed her fingers over Zeph's bare arm, a rare and fleeting touch, and Stella's face crumpled. "Oh, Zeph, I'm so sorry. I feel Astar all the time from anywhere, so that can make me insensitive to others. I didn't realize how much he hurt you."

Tears stung Zeph's eyes, a rarity for her, but it had been a trying few hours. "Thank you," she replied quietly. "I don't expect you to be monitoring my emotions, though. And I appreciated your covert assistance at the end there."

Stella's face lit with mischief. "That was clever of you, ensuring that neither you nor Astar agreed to Willy's Moratorium."

Clever, yes—but to what purpose? Zeph wasn't even sure why she'd been so determined to keep that option open. Except that she'd never been one to give up easily. Some people called her competitive, but she'd never wanted to be better than anyone else. She just had high expectations for herself. If she wanted something, then she felt she should push herself to attain it. She'd wanted Astar for as long as she could remember. Now he'd finally admitted he wanted her just as much—but not enough to set aside his obstinacy about his misguided code of conduct.

"Not that my cleverness will do any good," Zeph sighed. Because Stella was a good listener, she went on in a rush, speaking quietly, trusting to Stella's sharp shapeshifter's ears to pick up her words—and that Gen would be too distracted talking with Lena to overhear. Gen had always been firmly against Zeph seducing Astar, though it had never been entirely clear to Zeph why Gen would care. "He told me that he doesn't want me enough to compromise his principles. That we can't ever be together, not even for a fling, because he 'can't separate sex and love' like I do." The last came out more bitter than she expected.

Stella groaned deep in her throat. "Oh, Willy. You idiot."

Zeph glanced at her in surprise. "I thought you'd be on his side, to be honest."

"I am," Stella replied. "I'm also on your side. Both things can be equally true."

"He's probably right," Zeph admitted. "Love and sex aren't the same thing for me."

"Have you ever been in love?" Stella asked curiously.

"No, have you?"

Stella shrugged, gray eyes staring at some distant point, then turning her pensive gaze on Zeph. "How do you know if you are?" she asked.

Zeph echoed the shrug with a far more elaborate Tala one. "You're asking me? The Tala don't really do love, not with promises, engagements, and marriages, anyway. Rhy was harsh in there, but there is truth in what he said."

"Some truth, yes, but not all of the truth," Stella argued. "Your father is Tala, and he married your mother."

"Because she's Dasnarian. She wouldn't have been happy any other way."

"And he loved her enough to go against Tala ways, so that she would be happy. Same with Gen's parents. Zynda married Marskal because it meant something to him."

Zeph didn't know what to say to that.

"Anyway," Stella said after a moment, "I don't think Willy knows either, about being in love, or about sex versus love. I think he's just afraid."

The one thing Astar never seemed to her was afraid. "Of

what?"

Stella gave her an owlish look. "Something for you to figure out, perhaps."

Zeph frowned—not at all sure why Stella thought she needed to figure things out if Astar was the one being wrongheaded—and had opened her mouth to argue when she caught sight of her father ahead. Zyr lounged against the wall, looking restless and bored but brightening when he spotted Zeph.

"Hello, ladies," he said, sweeping a bow to all of them. "I'm wondering if I can borrow my daughter."

"Of course," Stella replied, standing back as Lena and Gendra gave Zyr enthusiastic hugs. "Just come in whenever, Zeph, and pick a spot to sleep."

Zeph waved goodnight to the others, then turned to her dad. She didn't think any of the parents knew about the quest yet. Ursula planned to take care of that, telling them only the cover story. "Is something wrong?"

He shuddered. "Walls. Manners. Social things and talking talking talking. I thought I'd see if you wanted to go fly. Enjoy the moon the Tala way."

"Yes," she replied immediately. She hadn't realized until that moment just how badly she needed to stretch her wings.

He grinned at her and offered a hand. "We can take off from a balcony over here."

"Where's Mom?"

"Sleeping." He rolled his eyes. "She says she's too old to dance all night anymore. Why aren't you dancing?"

She shrugged, adding an insouciant smile. "Too many walls, manners, and social things."

Smiling back, Zyr opened the doors to a windswept ter-
race, snow blowing thickly and whipping through her clothes.
Once Lena had released the magic that had created clear skies
and a bubble of warmth for the midnight viewing of the
crystalline moon, the storm had returned with a vengeance.
Brr. She quickly shifted into owl form, grateful for the downy
feathers. Zyr shifted into gríobhth form, surprising her. He
didn't typically take that form around mossbacks, since the
sight of the supposedly mythical creature—a monster to some
eyes—tended to upset them. But then, who would see them in
this weather? He dove off the balcony, snapping out his black
wings to catch the wind, long black tail lashing, and releasing a
triumphant caw from his lethally curved eagle's beak.

Changing her mind, Zeph shifted straight from owl to
gríobhth, too. Might as well take advantage of the high
balcony, as the heavy lion body of the form made lifting off
from the ground nigh impossible. Zyr could do it with a
running start, but Zeph had yet to master the technique. She
would, though, someday. Just like she'd get the trick of dragon
form, too.

Zeph leapt into the sky, fighting the drop and working her
wings to find the pattern in the winds that would assist her
flight instead of buffeting her. The pumping work warmed her,
and she followed the black gríobhth up and up, through the
tumultuous clouds—then popped free into the clear cold
moonlit night above the storm.

The crystalline moon had begun to set, but still dominated
the sky with extraordinary clarity, silver light illuminating the
roiling sea of clouds below. She searched for any sign of the

shadow that had obscured the moon but saw nothing. Only the bright face, clear and pure, as if all was well with the world.

Zeph never thought of herself as all that spiritual, but it seemed Moranu's regard followed their flight with approval. The goddess of the moon, the night, the shifting shadows and many faces smiled upon Her shapeshifter children. The black gríobhth and the golden soared through the moonlit sea of stars like creatures from another time.

Only Zeph and her father could take the form of the gríobhth, also known as a gryphon in the Common Tongue. The Tala knew, however, that if a shapeshifter could take the form, then the creature must have existed at some point in time—or some place. Shapeshifters couldn't just pile pieces of animals together. The form had to come from somewhere. But no one had ever seen a real-life gríobhth, though it showed up in illustrations and tapestries, especially in the once-lost land of n'Andana. Then Zyr had been born with the gríobhth astonishingly as his First Form, the form that shapeshifter children instinctively took on their first shift, sometimes while still in the cradle.

And Zeph had been the same, except where Zyr was obsidian black in gríobhth form, from the tip of his lethally curved beak to the tip of his whiplike lion's tail, Zeph was all in shades of gold. It was as if her mother's golden Dasnarian coloring showed up in Zeph's First Form, even though she looked like her father in human form.

As the gryphon, she liked to think of herself as the best of both of her parents. And she sent thanks to Moranu for Her many blessings, but especially this one.

Flying like this, more than anything else that night, felt like an appropriate honoring of the goddess's feast. The moonlight silvered the glossy black fur and feathers of her father's gríobhth form flying beside her, and he seemed more relaxed, too, a sense of peace about him. It seemed the moonlight fell palpably over her own golden fur and feathers, a benediction, the loving caress she'd hoped for from Astar and had been so coldly denied.

Zeph had hoped to kiss Astar beneath the crystalline moon at midnight, and she had to squelch her bitter jealousy that Lena had apparently enjoyed a magical moment like that with Rhy. At least she'd had that moment, no matter how brief or how it had fallen out later. Zeph had even spun some fantasies about how it would be, finally kissing Astar. And she was not the spin-romantic-fantasies type, usually. Still, she'd thought the festival night, the special moon, the beautiful dress she'd labored to create and faithfully reproduce after shifting—she'd thought maybe Astar would finally notice her. That he'd finally admit to wanting her.

She hadn't imagined the longed-for admission would be followed by such a cruel rejection.

I don't want you enough to compromise my principles.

Like she was something dirty, only a potential stain upon his shining honor.

Up here, in the clear moonlight, with the gríobhth's wild distance from the tumult of human-shaped hearts, the words didn't quite slice at her as they had in the moment, when she was in her sadly vulnerable human body. With distance, she could even consider that it could be wiser to simply let Astar go. He didn't want her enough to change. Maybe that was Stella's point, that someone has to want it enough, and Astar had been very clear that he didn't.

I don't want you enough to compromise my principles. That will never change.

Maybe *she* didn't want him enough to keep smashing her skull bloody on the wall of his obstinacy. She'd thought that if she could just show him the fun side of life, how to enjoy his body instead of being so conflicted about his shapeshifter nature and mossback duties, that he would break out of his invisible chains. But no—he'd embraced those chains instead of her, adamantly pushing her away.

Given how she felt like she was bleeding inside, she must have invested more in the fantasy than she'd realized. Astar had certainly hurt her more deeply than she'd thought possible. He didn't want her enough to compromise his principles. It didn't get clearer than that.

Enough then. Like Lena, Zeph would go on this quest and do her utmost to be responsible and useful—and she would let Astar go.

He didn't want her enough. Full stop.

Time to let him go.

Under the full moon, Zyr roared with leonine pride—and Zeph added her own wild call of golden harmony. This could be enough.

This *would* be enough. She'd make sure of it.

~ 9 ~

A STAR NODDED ABSENTLY along with Ursula's last-minute suggestions on navigating the political waters in the various courts. Truly, he was listening, but Ursula had a tendency to repeat herself out of understandable frustration at having to stay behind and leave the heroics to others. She preferred to be able to control things directly, so in lieu of that, she gave detailed instructions. And Astar did her the courtesy of listening. He could do that and keep an eye on his friends. Five of them milled around the two carriages that would take them north into Carienne, Lena and Rhy studiously ignoring each other while talking animatedly to others.

Everyone was there but Zephyr. He hadn't seen any sign of her. Where could she be? She couldn't possibly have gotten hurt, not in the safety of Ordnung.

A messenger ran up to Ursula with some urgent matter, so Astar seized the opportunity to ease over to Stella. She was standing a bit apart from the others, with her face turned up to the sky. Her red-black hair spilled over her silvery cloak, the smoky fur framing her delicate profile. Eyes closed and lips curved in a smile of quiet delight, she allowed the fat snow-flakes to fall on her upturned face, where they clung for a crystalline moment before melting. She looked so serene that Astar hated to interrupt her moment of peace. Stella had so little of that at Castle Ordnung, with its constant hubbub and daily crises. She'd be much happier at Windroven, or in Annfwn—but she stayed in Ordnung for him, because that was where he had to be. Such were the depths of her loyalty to him.

He'd hitched his step and started to reverse so as not to disturb her, but too late. Stella opened her eyes and smiled at him, holding out her gloved hands, her gray eyes clear and sparkling. "What's wrong, Willy?"

Taking her hands, he brushed a kiss on her cheek. "Nothing's wrong. Maybe I just wanted to say good morning to my lovely sister."

She made a face at him. "It's past noon, so too late for that greeting, and you didn't escape Ursula's clutches just for that."

"True," he admitted. "Have you seen Zephyr?"

"Not yet. She didn't come back last night."

"What?" He nearly barked the question in his shock. Where could she have gone? Maybe she'd returned to the party after all, and found someone else to take to her bed. Someone who'd been more than happy to peel her out of that crimson gown, to bury his face in her veil of black hair and stroke her creamy skin... He clenched his fists, wanting nothing more than to crush the skull of whoever it was.

Stella raised a brow at him. "What has upset you, Willy?"

He eyed her. His twin knew very well how he felt—usually before he did. She had no reason to play coy now. "I thought the girls were all staying in your rooms."

She shook her head. "Not Zeph. She took off."

Took off. A growl rose in his chest, and Stella's serene façade cracked. She snickered, her eyes glinting mischievously. He narrowed his own at her. "Nilly, I am not in the mood to be teased."

"You never are, you grump. I swear you were born a grandpa in a baby's body. Zeph *literally* took off. Zyr asked her to go flying, and she jumped at the chance." Stella dipped her chin, giving him a knowing look. "She seemed happy to get outside the walls for a bit, burn off some energy. I think she was upset, too."

"She was," he admitted. "I finally made it clear to her that we could never be together. In any way. Even before I set the morator—" No, he refused to call it that. It was a good rule, to protect them all from trouble. The word "moratorium" made it sound so dire. "Before we had the conversation about limiting romantic entanglements within the group."

"Ah." Stella closed her lips and said nothing more. Her eyes held compassion for him, but also something else.

"Did she talk to you?" he asked, suddenly suspicious.

"I talk to all of my friends," she replied coolly, "and I don't gossip about them to others."

That was a turnabout. Very nearly a betrayal, since he and Stella had never had secrets from each other. "We tell each other everything," he complained.

"Don't go feeling all betrayed like that. This is between you and Zeph. I'm happy to lend an ear to each of you, to offer what comfort and advice I can, but I won't take sides."

"I'm your brother. Your twin." He wanted to tell her she

had to be on his side, had to put him first, but the deepening gray in her stormy eyes warned him against it.

"Yes, and Zeph is my friend. You are my family by birth. She is my family by choice. It would be dishonorable of you to ask me to choose between you."

"I'm not—" He broke off, unwilling to lie, to be even more dishonorable than she accused. Honor was all he had. An accident of birth had made him heir to the high throne of the Thirteen Kingdoms. His own father, Prince Hugh, had died before he and Stella were born. Hugh had died young, his honor forever unstained. Astar didn't know how he could ever live up to either his father's noble legacy, or Ursula's, but he was determined to try. Stella knew that about him. Implying that he would be dishonorable... Well, it was a low blow. "I see," he finished stiffly.

"You can stop worrying," Stella said gently, not quite an apology. "Zeph is here."

He turned in the direction she was looking to see Zephyr entering the outer courtyard where they assembled. Not that anyone could miss her in that cape of golden fur. It swathed her from the deeply cowled hood to the ground, where her booted toes kicked out just below the hem as she walked, a longer section trailing over the snow behind her. Her sapphire eyes shone brightly against her pale face, crimson lips startlingly full beneath.

More than anything in that moment, he wanted to pull her into his arms and kiss those lips. During the few hours he'd slept, he kept dreaming about her mouth on his throat, the way her clever fingers had found the sensitive place at the nape of his neck, the sensation going straight to his groin where he'd hardened embarrassingly.

He should've kissed her.

No, he shouldn't have.

It was right that he hadn't, since he'd be seeing a potential bride at Castle Elderhorst in Carienne.

But it had been his one chance, now forever lost because of his own moratorium. And it had been such a near thing, her mouth barely a breath away, her scent going to his head, reminding him of the crisp, pristine air of high mountains entwined with tropical flowers—an odd juxtaposition that was quintessentially Zephyr. Then, in his dream, he *had* kissed her, hot and passionate and wrenchingly sweet all at once. Quenching and scorching. Like coming home and taking flight. Utter bliss.

Then he'd jolted awake, horrified at himself that he'd compromised his honor—only to realize it had been a dream, which sent him crashing immediately into disappointment that it hadn't been real. When he fell back asleep, the dream claimed him again. Reliving the might-have-been, he kissed lovely, wild Zephyr—to awake and repeat the gut-wrenching cycle of bliss to horror to relief to crushing regret.

With the snowflakes falling like lace around Zephyr, swirling in the mist of her passage, she might've stepped out of those dreams—and for a confused, roiling moment, he wasn't sure if he was awake or asleep. Had he kissed her? Or… not.

Those perfectly crimson lips quirked with amusement as she raised raven-winged brows at him. "Good morning, Willy and Nilly. Are you ready for our adventure?"

"It's past noon," Astar corrected foolishly, his brain feeling too numb to come up with anything else. He felt like an idiot, however, so he must be awake.

"Is it?" She peered at the cloud cover, snowflakes clinging to her thick black lashes. "I don't see how you can tell. Morning, noon, evening—all winter light looks the same."

"You sound like Rhy," Astar muttered under his breath.

Her eyes glinted with wry acknowledgment. "There's a reason for that."

He opened his mouth to say something—he didn't know what, as the usually lighthearted Zephyr seemed to be in a dangerous mood—but she plowed on. "Speaking of shapeshifters being all alike, Gen, Rhy, and I have set up a scouting rotation, trading off every two hours. Does that meet with your approval, Your Highness?"

Astar set his teeth, certain he heard Stella muffle a giggle. "Yes, thank you."

Zephyr smiled, a lethal curve that reminded him of her gríobhth form. He'd only seen her in that form a few times, and always in Annfwn, but something about her attitude, her *feel*, or the hard glint in her sapphire-sharp eyes, made him think of the gríobhth. Maybe it was the golden-furred cloak, so like her extraordinary coloring in that form.

Maybe something else.

"I don't want to tell you your business, Your Highness," she continued, "but when Rhy isn't on scout duty, I recommend that you do *not* put him in the same carriage as Lena."

Astar glanced over her head where Rhy and Lena were still ostentatiously ignoring each other, and sighed internally. This was ridiculous. He could talk normally to Zephyr. Those two could be civil to each other also. "The whole point of the morator—the no entanglements rule," he corrected grimly, "is to prevent exactly this sort of ridiculous maneuvering. We're all friends. We have to work together. I expect anyone to ride with whoever, with no complaints."

Zephyr exchanged speaking glances with Stella, then shrugged in her elaborate Tala style—the gesture clear even in her enveloping cloak. "Have it your way, Your Highness. Just don't say I didn't warn you."

Setting his teeth, he managed not to growl at her. "Stop calling me that."

"Your Highness?" She widened her eyes in mock surprise. "Isn't that the correct address for the crown prince, heir to the high throne of the Thirteen Kingdoms? You know I get so confused by mossback ranks and traditions."

"Nilly, would you give us a moment?" Astar ground out.

"Of course." Stella simpered, far too amused with his suffering. "I see Mother and Ash anyway. They'll no doubt have last words of advice and so forth. I suggest you join us after you've, ah, finished your conversation. You know Mother. She won't wait long."

Astar took Zeph by the arm—the golden fur cloak even softer than it looked—and steered her farther away from any eavesdroppers. "What is *wrong* with you?" Frustration made his lowered voice sound harsh.

Zeph jerked herself from his grip. "I'm practicing following orders and being a good soldier. Am I doing it wrong?"

"I never said you had to—"

"No, but you *have* been issuing plenty of commands, Your Highness," she snapped back. "You made the difference in our goals and *desires* very clear last night. I'm abiding by your edict."

He swallowed back his anger, because he could see he deserved some of that. Raking a hand through his hair, he snagged on the icy wet snarls where snow had accumulated. Somehow that just figured, too. "It wasn't an edict," he said, searching for the words to soothe her ire. And hurt. It was there in her eyes, a shadow behind the sapphire hardness. "I just wanted you to understand why I—"

"Oh, I understand, Your Highness." She smiled sweetly, showing a hint of fang. Zephyr was a talented enough shapeshifter to do a bit of selective alteration—so he knew she'd done that on purpose. "You made yourself crystal clear. May I be excused?"

"Willy!" Astar's mother waved, jumping up and down a little, as if she might not be noticed otherwise. "Willy, darling! We're here to say goodbye. You and Zeph can talk anytime, as you'll be together nonstop for the next half a year. Come kiss your mother goodbye!"

"She's right," Zephyr taunted in a velvet-smooth voice. "We'll be together nonstop. We can have this exact conversation over and over and ov—"

"I get it," he bit out, cutting her off with a sharp gesture.

"Oh, good." She batted her lashes. "I just want you to understand."

"I understand, all right. You plan to punish me for what I said, when I was only trying to save us both pain and heartache, and you—"

"No, Astar," she hissed, dropping her façade and letting her fury shine bright, all gríobhth now. "You want to save yourself pain, because you're afraid. You're terrified of who you might be if you let go even a smidge. You call it honor, but that's a shield you're hiding behind. Your First Form is a grizzly bear for Moranu's sake, not a mouse. But you're so locked down, so determined to be a mossback prince in every way, that you stop yourself from embracing the ferocity of your nature—or of taking on any other form."

"That's not fair," he replied weakly, stunned by her vitriol. Zeph had always flirted with and teased him, never giving him a cross word before this.

"Fair?" She snorted, focusing her gaze on him, the predator ready to deliver the killing blow. "Kids worry about what's fair. You just don't want to face the truth about yourself."

"And what's that?"

"Your hero is a man who died because he couldn't see the truth. Mull that one over."

"Willy darling!" his mother called insistently.

Zeph gave him a cool look. "Mommy's calling."

Oh, she did *not*. A growl rose from him, the bear waking from sleep. He stuck a finger in her face. "You and I are going to talk," he threatened.

She cocked her head, looking at his finger from the side, and burst out laughing. "Anytime, Your Highness. But if you point that finger at me again..." She abruptly sobered, smile going deadly in a blink. "I'll bite it off," she hissed, then strode away, her cloak flaring out like golden wings.

Gutted by the exchange, Astar dutifully went to join his mother and stepfather. Before he made it all the way, Ami flung herself at him, embracing him in a bright tumble of silken curls, fur-trimmed velvet, and a cloud of rose perfume. He still hadn't accustomed himself to being so much bigger than she was. In his sense memory, his mother was a bulwark of love and fervent hugs. Some people underestimated Ami, with her dazzling, goddess-bestowed beauty and festive nature. But Astar and Stella knew the fierce side of her maternal love. Their mother might not be a shapeshifter, but she was a lioness in every other sense.

Holding on, he hugged her back, closing his eyes and allowing himself to wallow—just for a moment—in her unconditional love. Her affection salved the stinging cuts of Zephyr's slicing verbal claws. When Ami let him go, she framed his face with her velvet-gloved hands, violet eyes shimmering with tears. "You are the very image of your father, you know," she whispered, then smiled tremulously. "But bigger."

Your hero is a man who died because he couldn't see the truth. "Mom..." He didn't know how to ask this. Behind her, Ash was showing Stella a dagger, both of them absorbed in their own conversation. "Was Hugh—my father... a fool?" He settled on the word uneasily, and Ami sobered, dropping her hands to take his cold ones in hers.

"Why are you asking me this now?" Her twilight eyes studied him with keen intelligence. That was something else many people failed to notice about her, her lavish beauty distracting them from her canny mind. "Is there some other reason for this sudden trip that no one is telling me? Because I swear to Glorianna, if Her Fucking Majesty is lying to me, I'll—"

"No, no," he said, hastening to stop her rising voice. "I've just been thinking about it. It's just that everyone always speaks well of Hugh," he explained. "How noble he was, honorable and good. How he died believing he was rescuing Aunt Andi from the Tala. But he was wrong. We know that now. So... did he die a fool?"

Ami sighed, a heartfelt and wistful sound. "It's hard for you and Nilly, that you never knew the real man he was. When someone dies, people tend to focus only on the good, they idealize the memory and forget the bad. To hear the stories, Hugh was Glorianna's gift to the world, perfect in every way."

Astar nodded, a lump catching in his throat.

"But he was only a man," Ami continued, squeezing his hands. "A good man, yes, but one with flaws like any of us. Both of those things can be true. I loved him with all my heart, but I was only a girl, and he was no older than you are now. It's not easy to explain how the world seemed to us then, compared to how it is now, but he believed—and I did, too— that the Tala were demons and monsters." She grimaced ruefully. "Neither of us could see past our fears to the truth. In a way, I suppose you could call him a fool for not seeing the truth—that Andi was happily married and in love with Rayfe, who is also a man like any other, and a good one in his own right—but then you'd have to call me a fool, too. We were blinded by unreasoning hatred. If Hugh had lived..." She smiled ruefully. "Well, I'm sure he would've grown wiser with time, as we all do." Her smile quirked with wry humor. "Hopefully, anyway."

"You are wise, indeed," he said, pulling her into another hug. "I'll miss you."

"Yes, you will," she informed him sassily, giving him one more squeeze and letting him go. "But this trip will be good for you. Go have fun with your friends. It's past time for you to escape Essla's talons for a while. Go sow some wild oats, live a little."

"*Mother!*" he said, shocked.

She laughed gaily and punched his arm with her delicate fist. "Hey, I was a virgin when I married Hugh—so was he— and I can vouch that it was not a brilliant start." She glanced back at Ash, a light flush gracing her cheekbones as she turned back to Astar and leaned in confidingly. "I recommend finding someone totally unsuitable to teach you the really filthy—"

"Please stop," he begged her.

Her eyes danced with mischief. "Fine. But only because you're bright red." She patted his cheek. "Keep it in mind, however. I know Essla has given you the list of potential brides—and yes, I looked it over—and that you're to scope some out on this journey. Just..." She stopped herself, pressing her lips together and holding up her palms in surrender.

Ash clapped him on the shoulder, his scarred face twisting with his lopsided smile. "Has your darling mother embarrassed you enough?" he inquired in his ruined voice, sliding Ami a look when she beamed innocently. "You looked like you needed saving."

"Yes," Astar replied fervently. "Thank you." He looked

into the corrugated face of the man who'd been his father in every way but biology, and seized him in a bear hug. "Thank you," he repeated roughly.

Ash tensed, startled by the unusual show of affection, then chuckled and squeezed Astar in return. For a lean man, the older warrior could produce a considerable amount of strength, and Astar felt a couple of joints pop in his spine. "It's a good time to tell you, Willy boy," Ash said. "I'm proud of the man you've become."

Astar manfully swallowed back the tears that pricked his eyes. This was apparently a day for him to be tossed from one emotion to the next, drowning and tumbling in them like the time Lena tried to teach him to surf in Nahanau. He even felt like he'd drunk a bellyful of seawater, the way it ached.

"I have a gift for you," Ash said, letting go. He held out a sheathed sword, the hilt and sheath echoes of the dagger he'd been showing Stella. His sister held up her dagger to show him, smiling happily, while their mother fussed with Stella's hair, talking to her rapidly—no doubt issuing more inappropriate advice.

Astar slid the sword from its tooled sheath and whistled in appreciation. "Is this the White Monks' make?"

"Good eye." Ash took the sword by the hilt, tilting it in the winter light so the chased design showed on the blade's folded metal edge. "Silversteel."

Astar raised a brow. The White Monks kept to themselves—and kept their own counsel. Though they served Glorianna, they had nothing to do with the common observances of the goddess. With the return of magic to the greater world, the monks had grown even more secretive, though rumors of arcane rituals had been making their way to Ursula's ear of late. Did the high queen realize Ash still kept in contact with his former brothers? Judging by the wary expression in Ash's bright green eyes, probably not. As Ursula's heir, Astar was duty-bound to report this. His stepfather, however, was the man who'd carved Astar's first sword out of wood—a Feast of Moranu gift, in fact, which included sword lessons—and Ash had risked this secret to give them these extraordinary blades.

"An odd gift to give for a pleasure trip," Astar said quietly.

Ash met his gaze soberly. "I think we all know there's more to this sudden jaunt than whim, even if we can't know what exactly. Ursula knows what she's doing, so I trust in that. And I trust in the blades I'm giving you and Nilly. The edges will never dull, and Silversteel can be used in magic rituals."

"But I have no magic," Astar pointed out, taking the sword, sheathing it discreetly, and holding it inside his cloak.

Ash nodded, an acknowledgment of Astar's discretion. "You might surprise yourself," he commented, sounding as if he speculated on whether the snowstorm might clear off. "Free of Ordnung and your duties to the high throne, you'll have a chance to spread your wings some."

"The way you and Mother talk, you make it sound like I've been chained up here."

Ash regarded him seriously. "Not all chains are made of metal."

Astar flushed, realizing his clumsy words might've seemed to hint at Ash's past, when he'd lived in an actual prison. "I didn't mean to—"

"You didn't," Ash interrupted kindly. "It's not the life we would've picked for you is all. You were named heir to this throne before you were days old—a heavy burden for anyone, let alone a little kid. I always kind of hoped that would change."

"Fortunately, you and Mom have seven more bratlings back at Windroven to train up for the throne of Avonlidgh," Astar replied with a fond smile for his many half-siblings. Ami had more than lived up to the mother aspect of being Glorianna's avatar.

"Aye, and your mother would love it to be you or Nilly to succeed her in Avonlidgh, but you're for the high throne, and Nilly bears the mark of the Tala, wherever that will take her. Still, that's not what I'm trying to say." Ash paused, squinting at the sky. A man of few words, he still sometimes struggled to express himself. "Zephyr is a beautiful woman," he said—and very little could've shocked Astar more. "A talented shapeshifter, too."

Now Astar was the one to struggle for words. "Ah... You don't need to be concerned. I know my duty to the high throne."

Ash winced. "That's what I'm afraid of." He glanced at Ami, love and desire naked in his green eyes. "I'm going to give you the best piece of advice I know—a lesson it took me way too long to learn."

"All right," Astar replied cautiously.

Ash leaned in close, dropping his hoarse voice to a confiding whisper. "Fuck the rules."

~ 10 ~

THE TRIUMPHANT THRILL of her parting shot at Astar lasted about ten steps—before Zeph crashed into misery and remorse. She'd been so determined to be cool and poised with Astar, but one look at him had sent those noble ambitions scattering to the winds. He'd had the utter gall to stare at her like he wanted to kiss her—and more. If anyone else had looked at her with such naked desire, Zeph would have taken them by the hand and led them straight to bed.

But not Astar, nooo... He'd just torment them both with his stupid rules and ridiculous honor. So she'd gone and said those unforgivable things. She hadn't planned to, but her temper had flown away from her. Probably it hadn't been wise to spend so long in gríobhth form, flying instead of sleeping. The gríobhth had little patience for human vicissitudes, and some sleep might've been helpful to bring her down to earth again. Though she'd felt good until she saw *him*. Especially when he'd run so very hot on her when she'd been reconciled to cold indifference.

"Infuriating bear," she snarled under her breath.

"I advised you to stop chasing Astar," her mother said, putting an arm around her in an affectionate hug. "I believe

I've predicted more than once that it would only bring you grief."

"Yes, but I don't listen to your advice, remember?" Zeph teased her mom, turning to give her a full hug, just to make sure Karyn knew it was a joke. The way Zeph's day was going, she'd offend everyone before it was done. "It's a Tala tradition to ignore our mothers to our peril."

Karyn sighed, squeezing her, then letting her go so she could scrutinize her daughter's appearance. "True, but that's because so many Tala don't grow up with mothers," she replied sternly. "In Dasnarian tradition, you would've grown up surrounded by women giving you advice. Sisters, aunts, your father's other wives, who would also want to mother you."

"No wonder you escaped," Zeph replied with a mock shudder. "Sounds horrifying."

Her mother shook her head. "*You* are entirely too much like your father."

"You love my father," Zeph had to point out.

Karyn sighed, a dreamy sound to it. "I do love him." She fixed that stern look on her daughter again. "But he is still irreverent, irresponsible, and prone to chasing after whatever shiny object—"

"Talking about me, gréine?" Zyr put his arms around Karyn's waist from behind, pulling her against him and fastening his teeth on her ear, making nibbling sounds as he did.

"Oh, you," she exclaimed, wriggling but not trying to escape. "The pair of you spent all night in gríobhth form, didn't you?"

Zyr caught Zeph's eye with a rueful smile. "It was a pretty moon. And technically the mossbacks kept us up most of the night with their rituals. In the end, it was only a few hours until dawn." He winked at Zeph, since they'd kept flying well past dawn, enjoying the brilliant sunrise high above the winter weather.

"No one saw us," Zeph assured her mother.

"I'm sure you were careful," Karyn replied, putting her hands over Zyr's and leaning her head back on his shoulder, craning her neck so she could see his face. "Weren't you?"

"With our precious daughter, always," he replied gravely.

She let out a breath and nodded, still looking unhappy as she fastened her intent gaze once again on Zeph. "I worry about you, being out there on your own. And for such a frivolous reason. Why this sudden trip?"

"Mother," Zeph said in exasperation. "This is just for fun. I won't get into any trouble. Besides, I'm an adult woman and—"

"Adult women can get into plenty of trouble," Karyn argued.

"And *besides*," Zeph repeated over her, "I won't be on my own. I'll be with six other people, including other shapeshifters capable of fighting forms, a couple of warriors, and two scary sorceresses. And I'm a gríobhth—no one messes with us."

Zyr grinned at her, but Karyn's expression hardened. "Don't be overconfident. The high priestess of Deyrr took your father captive in gríobhth form, and he was—"

"I know, I know," Zeph interrupted as her father looked pained. "I've heard the story countless times. But that priestess is dead, and the god laid to rest. We are going to be sightseeing and visiting fancy courts. You worry too much."

Karyn drew herself up, managing to look down her nose at her taller daughter, fully the former imperial princess of Dasnaria now. "You be careful of that impertinent tongue you inherited from your father, too, young lady. You don't know everything about the world. If you did, you'd know that gods are eternal. Deyrr may yet return. Even if He doesn't, there are other dangers in the world, even greater ones than we know."

Behind her, Zyr was silently flapping his lips, sobering instantly when Karyn pinned him with a glare. "You are *not* helping," she hissed.

"Gréine," he said on a sigh, turning her to face him—and not incidentally removing Karyn's escalating worry-focus from her daughter, "Zephyr is capable of taking care of herself, and so are her friends. They're going on a little jaunt is all."

"Am I stopping her?" Karyn demanded.

Zyr lifted a brow at her in reply.

"Oh, stop that," she told him irritably, pulling out of his hands and frowning at Astar a distance off, deep in conversation with Queen Amelia. "I know you're not a virgin, Zeph, and—"

"*Mother*," Zeph said warningly as Zyr clapped a hand over his mouth, eyes dancing with laughter.

Karyn put her hands on her hips. "*And* I don't expect you to be. Times have changed, and I never tried to impose Dasnarian customs on you. But that boy is—"

"Which boy?" Zeph interrupted. "His Highness Crown Prince Astar, heir to the high throne?"

"Remarkable," her mother said drily. "You do remember

to use rank and titles when you want to. I certainly hope you'll exercise that skill when you are in foreign courts representing Her Majesty High Queen Ursula." Karyn slid a reproving look at Zyr, who beamed innocently, then turned her expectant glare on Zeph.

"Yes, ma'am," Zeph replied, trying to sound meek.

Karyn huffed in exasperation and took Zeph's hands in hers. "Astar will have to marry a highborn princess for the good of the Thirteen Kingdoms."

"Why does everyone keep mentioning this to me?" Zeph wondered aloud.

"Because you're throwing yourself at a man you can never have," her mother replied crisply.

"I am not *throwing* myself—"

"He will never marry you, Zephyr," Karyn continued in an urgent tone.

Zeph yanked her hands away, throwing them in the air. "Why does everyone think I even want to marry Astar? I don't! I would make a terrible high queen."

"That's right," Karyn agreed triumphantly, "because you are far too much like your father." She smiled sweetly at Zyr, who clutched his heart and fell into the snow as if dead.

Karyn nudged him with the toe of her boot. "Oh, get up."

Zyr toyed with the hem of her skirt. "I don't know… the view is lovely from down here."

She groaned in exasperation and stepped away, Zyr uncoiling to his feet with a grin. He tapped her on the nose. "Zephyr understands the challenges of our unusual First Form." He slid Zeph a sly smile.

"Exactly," Karyn said, pouncing on that point. "The gríobhth nature is possessive, passionate, and hot-headed."

"Ah, gréine," he murmured, tugging a strand of her long golden hair, "you say the sweetest things."

"'Not easily controlled' were your exact words, as I recall," she replied, unmoved.

"Gorgeous *and* with a memory like an elephant." He grinned as she rolled her eyes.

"My point," she said to Zeph, "is that you need to be aware of these tendencies in yourself. This isn't a game. And if you get yourself into trouble, we won't be there to save you."

"Have I ever asked to be saved?" Zeph demanded pointedly.

"No," her mother fired back, "which is part of the problem. I'd feel better if I thought you'd ask for help when you needed it." Her face crumpled. "I know you two think I'm silly, but you are my only child, and..." Her mouth wobbled, and she didn't finish.

"Mom." Zeph embraced her mother, who sniffled in her distress. "Here: I promise I'll ask for help if I need it. All right?"

"Even if you think you don't need it," Karyn corrected, hugging her back.

Zeph laughed. "I'll work on that."

"And stop chasing Astar. He's not for you."

"I know, I know, I know." Still laughing, Zeph let her mother go, then hugged her father. "Don't worry. We're not going all that far. It's not like we're going to the other side of the world." As she said the words, she wondered if that was even true.

"All right, everyone!" Astar called. "Finish the goodbyes and let's load up!"

ZEPH SAT IN the carriage beside Stella, with Gen and Lena across from them. From her position riding backward, she could watch Ordnung receding in the distance as they headed north on the great trade road. Though the road was smooth enough, they bounced along at a painfully slow pace. Traveling like a mossback left a great deal to be desired, and she greatly missed the stretch of wings and crisp, fresh air. Plus, even annoyed as she was with Astar, it was galling that he was avoiding her to the extent of riding in the other carriage.

"Really?" she said. "Willy's Moratorium dictates that boys ride with boys and girls with girls?" All she'd suggested was they keep Rhy and Lena apart for a bit, not... *this.*

Gen gave her a narrow look. "It's your own fault. If you hadn't been relentlessly *hunting* Willy, then—"

Zeph rolled her eyes. "I was not *hunting* him." Was there anyone who didn't have an opinion about this? Jak, maybe. But he was riding with Astar in the other carriage, while Rhy took first shift scouting.

"It's *my* fault," Lena said firmly. "I caused all of this by losing sight of the excruciatingly obvious truth that Rhyian and I can never, ever, ever be together. I shouldn't have let things go so far last night." She rubbed her forehead, wincing as if in pain. "Also, *why* did I drink so much?"

"You were keeping company with shapeshifters," Zeph

reminded her. "Your metabolism just isn't the same."

"Shapeshifters and Jak," Stella put in, nodding wisely. "Though he isn't a shapeshifter, he seems to be able to drink anyone under the table. He was downing mjed like water."

Lena groaned, looking green. "Don't say 'mjed.'"

"Also you performed a major magic working, Lena," Stella said, "and followed it up with contorting your usual magic to keep up with Aunt Andi and me. That alone will give anyone a headache. Let me..." Stella leaned across the space and brushed her fingers over Lena's hand.

"You don't have to—*ohh*." Lena let out a long sigh of pure relief and dropped her head back against the padded seat.

One good aspect of pretending to be spoiled nobles on a pleasure jaunt—they were at least traveling in style. Ursula had provided her fanciest carriages along with excellent horses and servants to drive them. It would be wonderful—if Zeph liked being driven around like a helpless lump. Maybe she could take a turn as a horse sometime... Though, *ugh*, harnesses.

She'd just have to savor her shifts on scout duty.

"So," Gen said, eyeing Lena speculatively, "there was more than the kiss we saw in the feast hall. Which looked nice, don't get me wrong, but on the sweet side. What else happened?"

Lena cracked one eye open at Gen. "I told you, I don't want to rehash the gory details."

"You mean, I didn't miss the rehash?" Zeph asked, pouncing with glee. "I figured you all discussed the Rhyian Situation while I was out flying."

"Lena begged off," Gen explained with an annoyed huff.

Stella smiled ruefully. "Lena was tired."

"Lena was drunk, angry, and full of regret," Lena correct-ed. "And she still doesn't want to talk about it."

"Oh, come on," Gen begged. "Please? For those of us who enjoyed zero romance last night and need to live vicariously through our more beautiful and glamorous friends."

"I'm hardly glamorous," Lena countered. "I don't under-stand why you're always putting yourself down. I'm basically a boring weather scientist, not a multitalented shapeshifter like you are."

"Shapeshifting isn't all that spectacular," Gen grumbled. "And I know that, while I'm not ugly, I am the least pretty of the four of us. I don't kid myself otherwise."

Zeph studied Gen, assessing the truth of that. Gen had always been more concerned with relative beauty, which wasn't something Zeph thought about a lot. Of course, Gen would argue that was because Zeph didn't have to. With her father's dusty brown hair, along with his strong nose and stern jaw, Gen definitely looked more mossback than Tala. But that wasn't a bad thing. To look at her, though, no one would guess her First Form was a hummingbird, like her mother, and Zeph privately thought Gen should worry less about looks and just enjoy life more. Her blue eyes were certainly striking, a depthless indigo unusual even among the Tala, where the shade of blue or gray indicated their shapeshifting and sorcerous abilities.

Rhy was a rare exception there. His eyes were all Tala blue, and yet he had only a few forms, mainly sticking to his raven First Form. But Zyr had told Zeph—and Rhy to his face—that it wasn't lack of ability holding Rhy back. And Zyr would know, having taught generations of Tala shapeshifters.

Stella and Lena were busily pointing out Gen's positive physical attributes, trying to cheer her up—but Gen cut them off and pinned Zeph with a pointed look. "Zeph won't blow sunshine up my tail. What do you say?"

"I think to the right person we are all the most beautiful in the world," Zeph replied honestly.

Stella gave her a radiant smile, Lena nodded, and Gen burst into tears. "Oh, Gen, don't," Lena said, putting her arm around their friend and giving Zeph an exasperated glare. "Couldn't you just tell her she's pretty?"

"Gen is pretty," Zeph protested.

"Don't... lie..." Gen sobbed.

"I am not lying," Zeph retorted and kicked Gen lightly on the shin.

"Ow!" Gen stopped her weeping and glared.

"Baby," Zeph taunted. "That didn't hurt."

"Then why did you kick me?" Gen demanded, proving Zeph's point.

"Because you're being a goofball. You're the most talented living shapeshifter, besides your mother, and including me and my dad. You'll probably get dragon form before I do, if I get it at all. Why are you spending a moment's thought ranking who's prettiest among the three women who are your best friends in all the world? Be who you are."

Gen's face went through a series of emotional transformations worthy of the many-faced goddess. Finally, she settled on resignation. "I just really hoped last night would be different. I felt pretty in that gown—and I thought someone would notice me."

"Who were you hoping for—anyone I know?" Lena asked.

Gen threw up her hands. "No, because *I* don't know him. Astar, Jak, and Rhy all treat me as just a friend."

"We *are* all friends," Zeph pointed out.

"If not siblings and cousins," Stella added.

"Yes, but Jak watches Stella when she's not looking. Astar is ripping himself up wanting Zeph. And Rhy has only ever wanted Lena, hard as he's tried all these years to change that."

Zeph worked really hard not to look pleased about Gen's assessment of Astar. Good. Let him rip himself up wanting her, because that gríobhth had well and truly flown.

"Rhy told me last night that he was in love with me, back then," Lena admitted softly.

Stella clasped her hands together, eyes sparkling silver with delight. "Lena, that's the best news! All this time we thought you'd imagined he felt more than he did."

Lena shook her head, her generous lips in a tight line. "It's not good news. I mean—yes, it's good to know I didn't completely delude myself, but he did what he did *even though* he loved me."

"Maybe he did it *because* he loved you," Zeph mused.

Lena pinned her with a sharp look. "Why do you say that?"

Zeph snorted. "We're talking about Rhy here. Broody and takes everything way too seriously."

"Most people complain Rhy doesn't take things seriously enough," Lena corrected, but with a curious note in her voice.

Rolling her eyes at that, Zeph shook her head. "Who—the adults? The heroes of the golden age of the Deyrr War? We grew up with Rhy and we all know how much it gnaws at him, being Moranu's chosen. He's lived his whole life in sheer terror of when the goddess will pluck him up and make him do Her bidding like a puppet."

"Is that how you think it will work?" Gen asked, fascinated.

"*I* don't think so," Stella put in.

Zeph waved that off. "The point is that Rhy thinks that's how it will be. He loves his mother, but he's also furious with Queen Andromeda for bargaining him away to Moranu. And she feels so guilty about it that she hasn't ever slapped him upside the head and told him he's got nothing on her, with the onus *she* was born under. So, for Rhy, love is this fraught thing that's about guilt and anger, on top of him feeling like he's got no real control over his life. Thus, when Lena—not incidentally the namesake of the sorceress who kicked of all these generations of obligation to fate to begin with—told him she loved him, then of course he charged off to do the first thing he could think of to destroy it."

Lena stared at her, lips parted in astonishment. "I never thought of it that way—and I had no idea you have so much insight into people, Zeph."

Zeph shrugged, making it extra elaborate. "I'm not just another pretty face." She wrinkled her nose at Gen, who sighed.

"I know I shouldn't worry about it," Gen admitted. "And if I had to pick between being as gorgeous as Zeph or dragon form, I'd absolutely pick dragon. I'm just tired of feeling invisible. And with the crystalline moon and the ball last night... I just thought—hoped—that I would meet someone special. It was silly, but I had this romantic idea that my true love would suddenly appear and sweep me off my feet."

All four of them, even Stella, who usually seemed oblivious to such longings, sighed with sympathetic yearning.

"I know you all don't approve of me chasing Astar," Zeph admitted ruefully. "Moranu knows, *everyone* disapproves. But I'd had a similar, foolish romantic fantasy—that Astar would finally kiss me under that beautiful moon and it would be... something special."

Stella watched her with keen gray eyes. "*I* don't disapprove," she said gravely.

Gen actually jolted in surprise. "You don't? But Astar has responsibilities to the throne."

"Willy knows the demands of those responsibilities better than anyone," Stella reasoned. "He doesn't need us to tell him how to handle them. That's something he has to figure out on his own."

Gen narrowed her eyes. "Do you *know* something?"

Stella smiled enigmatically. "That's all I'm going to say about it. But none of you were foolish to hope. Longing for romance is natural and human." Her smile widened. "Even for Tala."

"So," Gen said, turning to Lena, "you're the only one who got the fantasy last night. You're duty-bound to tell us everything."

Lena's eyes misted and everything about her softened, like a fog rolling in off the ocean. "It was magical. Rhyian and I had it out, and I got caught up in the emotions of it all. The nostalgia, maybe. He went up with me to the battlements and kept me company while I cleared a space in the storm for the moon viewing. And, yes, we kissed under that amazing moon. It was shortsighted of me, but also—in the moment—it was everything." She heaved a sigh and gave Gen a rueful look. "Being swept off your feet sounds romantic, but it also means you're ungrounded. I lost sight of some essential truths."

Gen took her hand. "But you said he admitted that he was in love with you."

"*Was*," Lena emphasized, "in the past tense."

"I'm not sure that's changed," Gen insisted.

"It doesn't matter." Lena patted her hand and pulled hers away, lacing her fingers deliberately together. "Think about it. Even if Zeph's theory is true—and I think you're probably right on the nose there—then Rhyian still deliberately broke my heart because he couldn't handle being in love with me, or with me loving him. He hasn't changed, not in any way that matters, so he'll just do it again. He might promise he won't, but he will. He can't help himself."

None of them had an argument for that.

Lena raised a bronze brow, vindicated and sorrowful at once. "He can't help himself," she repeated, "and I can't go through that kind of heartbreak again. The only answer is to refuse to engage with him."

"Thus Willy's Moratorium," Gen said glumly. "And we've come full circle. Girls in one carriage. Boys in the other."

Zeph grimaced in agreement, looking out the carriage window. Castle Ordnung looked barely any farther away. This trip was going to take forever. Hopefully something interesting would happen soon.

~ II ~

THIS JOURNEY SEEMED to be taking forever and they'd only been on the road for two days. For all that they were going on an epic quest to save the world, Astar had expected things to be a lot more... shiny.

Splitting up the boys and girls into two carriages had been a terrible idea. He missed Stella's steadying presence, Lena's intelligent conversation, Gen's sweet nature—and Zephyr's vivid one. Jak was frankly bored and Rhy alternated between broody silence and caustic remarks. Fortunately, they'd soon reach the city of Gieneke, which sat at the crossroads of several major trade routes and at the confluence of the Phoenix and Grace Rivers, the massive juncture where the two became the River Danu, apparently a grand sight.

It would be their first opportunity to play the part of noble tourists, and that—along with the delights of the bustling city—should at least give everyone a task to focus their energies upon. He knew better than to wish for something to happen—Ursula had impressed that warrior's superstition on him enough times, that wanting something exciting to happen usually meant people got hurt or killed. *Never invite excitement,* Ursula's voice said in his head. *It's never the kind you want.*

Still, everyone was so restless, it would be good if…

He narrowed his eyes at the fawn-colored peregrine falcon plummeting toward the carriage at top speed. Calling the driver to a halt, Astar jumped out before the vehicle stopped moving. He'd recognize Zephyr's peregrine form anywhere, even if he hadn't known she was the one on scout duty. And she always took her time returning, tracing lazy circles in the sky long after Rhy or Gen went ahead to take over scouting, reluctant to return to human form.

He could understand that. If he had a form capable of flight, he'd probably want to stay in the air as long as possible, too. As it was, while he didn't relish being in bear form the way Zephyr loved all of her forms, he'd still been tempted more than once on this journey to shift and toss some trees around in the nearby woods.

Zephyr shifted as she landed, her boots hitting the snow with a puff of impact, golden-furred cloak and glossy black hair falling into place after the rest of her had stopped.

"What's wrong?" he demanded, forgetting himself and grasping her arms. She looked unhurt—but she was also talented enough to heal herself as she shifted.

Though she'd been giving him the cold shoulder the last couple of days, Zephyr grasped his forearms, her sapphire eyes wild as she panted, out of breath from her frantic flight. She opened her mouth, but nothing came out. Instead she shuddered violently.

"Take it slow," he said soothingly, pulling her into his arms, settling her with his strength. It was his job to calm her down enough to report, to remind her of her human side, the thinking and speaking aspect. He'd never seen Zephyr this rattled, which was enough to put him on full alert.

When she relaxed fractionally, he took her by the shoulders and held her gaze. "Focus on me. I'm right here and you're safe. Just tell me what you saw, beginning to end."

She nodded, clinging to him, still breathing too fast. Her eyes held too much of the falcon, her human mind clearly consumed by the animal's atavistic reaction. Astar slowed his own breathing to calm her. "In and out," he encouraged. "From the beginning. You were flying..."

"I was flying..." she echoed, and he breathed a sigh of relief that she'd found her words again. Sometimes shapeshifters who were badly frightened in animal form didn't shift back to human with their full capacities. He should've known Zephyr was far too talented and practiced for that. Still, she'd given him a scare. "I was flying up the River Danu, to the confluence." Her human sense returned enough for her to look chagrined. "I wanted to see it first."

"That's all right," he replied with an encouraging smile, aware that the others had gathered around them. He concentrated on Zephyr, on calming her, keeping her focused. "Did you see the confluence?"

She shook her head, then nodded. "It's beautiful from the air. Just like Lena told us it would be—the red clay of the Phoenix doesn't mix with the Grace's brown for leagues downstream. Two currents, side by side."

"Sounds amazing," he agreed. Someone inhaled with an impatient breath and he subtly shook his head. Zephyr's eyes were looking more human now as she thought about the mechanics of the dual currents. "Did you make it all the way to the confluence?" he coaxed, when it seemed she'd say nothing more. "Is something happening at Gieneke?"

"No," she breathed. "I didn't see the city. I didn't go all the way to the confluence, but there's something wrong. Very wrong. I've never seen anything like it."

A chill of dread weighted his limbs. Gieneke was home to thousands of people and would be hosting hundreds more, trade busy even in winter. This might be the first disaster. Sooner and closer than anyone had predicted.

"Can you describe the wrongness?" As he asked, Stella slipped up beside him, putting a hand on Zephyr's arm, unobtrusively adding her healing calm.

"It was... They were..." She let out a long, trembling breath. "You know I don't like this word, but I can't think of another: monsters."

"What did they look like?" he asked matter-of-factly. Zephyr, whose gríobhth form seemed monstrous to the ignorant, wasn't inclined to use that word lightly.

"Like humans, plants, and animals had been somehow mashed together. Some were alive, but clearly in pain, filling the air with screams like wounded prey. And others were too wrong to ever have lived. And they *smelled* wrong." She'd calmed as she got the words out, cognizant now of the others gathered around them. "They didn't smell edible, you know?"

Everyone but Jak and Lena nodded, knowing what she meant.

"Did they smell poisonous?" Gen asked.

Zephyr frowned in concentration. "Not exactly. But

wrong. We have to help them, Astar." She clutched his arms, fully human gaze pleading with him. "No one should have to…" She broke off, unable to say it, and he tucked her under his arm, holding her against his side. Wrapping her arms around his waist, she buried her face against him. A small, dishonorable piece of himself savored that she could take comfort from him, despite how badly he'd handled things between them.

"Thoughts?" he asked the rest. "Nilly?"

Stella shook her head, gaze opaque. "I didn't see this coming—and Aunt Andi didn't mention anything like it—but we all know from history and the way the Deyrr high priestess manipulated events that sudden changes can fool those with foresight."

"Do you think this could be Deyrr?" Astar asked her. He nearly subvocalized out of reflexive horror, but he figured everyone deserved to know what they were up against.

"I don't know." Stella held up her palms. "I don't know what Deyrr magic feels like. They've been gone from the world for twenty-five years now."

"Not entirely," Zephyr said, recovered enough to straighten and step out from under his sheltering arm—leaving a cold and lonely spot where she'd been. "Deyrr came from Dasnaria, and I've been to the former Temple of Deyrr in Jofarstyrr when I was over visiting my mother's family there."

"The temple still exists?" Gen asked in horror.

"Not as a temple, per se," Jak put in, nodding at Zeph. "We went for the tour, too, one time when we were visiting Dad's family. Her Imperial Majesty Empress Inga officially outlawed the worship of the god Deyrr—punishable by immediate execution—and the temple is maintained as a museum. It's educational to see just how warped that kind of religion can be."

Zephyr pulled her fur cloak tighter around her, still looking far too pale. "No one but me noticed the smell—but the scent of Deyrr is all over that place. I'll never forget it. Whatever is at the confluence, it isn't Deyrr."

"Hmm." That was a relief on one hand. On the other, it would've been helpful to know what they were dealing with. "If it isn't Deyrr, is it the rift? I thought that hadn't actually occurred yet."

Lena had her head tipped back, apparently studying the gray skies, but likely stretching out with her weather magic. "There *is* something odd in the energy overlays of the region. It's kind of like an intense storm, except it's not in the atmosphere so much, not like real weather would be." She frowned, putting a finger to her temple. "It's like it's a storm but made of magic."

"Maybe that's what it is," Stella offered. "The histories are full of anecdotes and documented examples of the impacts from the magic barrier moving back in the day. Some from magic bursting over a region that had been bereft of it, some from the movement of the barrier itself. This could be something like that. I can't guess more than that, though."

Lena nodded. "People in Nahanau still talk about the storm that resulted when the barrier expanded over the archipelago. It was a disaster. But why would that happen here and now? The barrier is long gone. Even if the rift is opening early, it's not the same as before. Magic isn't suddenly flooding into a previously parched region—which we could compare to a destructive flash flood when it suddenly rains in the desert—this area has been drenched in magic for a quarter century."

They all looked at Astar, as if he'd have the answer. "These are good questions," he said judiciously, "and ones we can only address if we go investigate."

Rhy, leaning against one of the carriages, pretending like he wasn't staring at Lena, raised a black-winged brow at him. "Is that wise? We could be rabbits bouncing into the mouth of the tiger."

"Wise or not, it's what we were tasked to do," Astar replied patiently. "We cannot fail in our duty to the high throne. And I cannot turn my back on all the people in Gieneke looking to me for help."

"Is it what Ursula sent us to do, though?" Gen asked. "No one mentioned battling monsters."

"What *did* you think we'd be doing?" Lena asked with a hint of impatience. "Or did you only listen to the bits about dressing up and visiting other royal courts?"

Gen made a face at her. "I distinctly recall that no one thought we'd run into trouble before the one at Lake Sullivan—and that's probably just the tame, good-luck lake creature."

"I'm all for battling monsters," Jak put in cheerfully, idly flipping a throwing dagger. "This quest has been deadly dull so far. I'm not afraid—and it's about time we had some excitement."

Astar groaned internally at the bad luck there. *Never invite excitement. It's never the kind you want.* And now look what had happened.

"I'm not afraid either," Rhy snapped. "Not wanting to be mashed into a dying half-human monster is exercising a healthy sense of caution. I'm not interested in being honorable—or in being a dead hero."

"Of course you aren't," Lena remarked sardonically. "You'd have to actually care about other people."

His head whipped around to her in shock. "That is dramatically unfair, Salena. I—"

"We're getting off target," Astar said forcefully. Clearly keeping Rhy and Lena apart for a few days hadn't done anything to defuse the tension between them. "Stella, do you see anything either way?"

His twin shook her head. "Nothing useful. My foresight is all over the place—too many possibilities to sort even a few. Aunt Andi could possibly do better."

"We could go back to Ordnung," Gen suggested. "Let the experts decide. There's no shame in knowing your limitations."

"No," Rhy said with a clenched jaw. "Even I don't want to run home to mommy and daddy at the first sign of trouble. Her Majestyness assigned this mission to us for a reason."

"That's my man," Jak crowed, slapping Rhy on the shoulder.

"Besides," Stella put in, "I said that Aunt Andi could *maybe* do better. That's by no means certain—and she also warned me to expect the unexpected, as this rift has everything jumbled."

"I really hate when people say to expect the unexpected," Gen complained. "What does that even mean?"

Jak grinned at her. "It means to embrace chaos. I'd think a shapeshifter and child of the trickster goddess would be all over that."

"That's Zeph, not me," Gen snapped, then narrowed her eyes at Zephyr in concern. Astar felt the same—the naturally ebullient Zephyr had yet to fully rebound from her harrowing experience. That, more than anything, gave Astar pause.

"What do you say, Zephyr?" he asked, waiting for her to meet his eyes. Hers were a deep and troubled blue, lacking their usual sparkle. "You're the one who saw. Should we go around or not?"

"You said it already. We have to help them," she replied simply. "It's not even a question. And there's no time to lose."

"All right," Astar said, giving her a grave nod of thanks. "I'm decided. Here are your assignments."

THEY LEFT THE carriages—and drivers—safely outside the boundary Zephyr designated. With the others well out of earshot, Astar instructed the drivers to return to Ordnung if the group didn't return within a day, or at any sign of trouble. They'd traveled close enough to the confluence that the waters here were divided into their headwaters striping—the effect as remarkable as Zephyr had described, though no one was in the mood to sightsee now.

Zephyr and Lena had headed out already—Lena riding

Zephyr, who was in horse form—to find a high point for Zephyr to take off in gríobhth form. Zephyr had been confident that she could carry Lena, the smallest member of the group, though they'd never tested it before. Astar kicked himself for that oversight. The days of boring travel on the road could've been put to better purpose, working out fighting teams and logistics like this.

He simply hadn't been thinking they'd encounter trouble this soon either, something Ursula would chide him for. Too complacent with growing up in a time of peace and plenty— they'd all heard that complaint from their parents. Lowering to find out they were right all along.

Lesson learned.

Rhy had offered to scout ahead in raven form. If he'd hoped to redeem himself in Lena's eyes, the verdict there was inconclusive. She'd barely seemed to notice, instead consumed with discussing logistics with Zephyr. Gen had also taken horse form, with Jak astride. She didn't have an aerial form big enough to carry another person, not until she nailed dragon form. As Jak would be on the ground, as it were, and capable of speech, Astar handed over command to him before he shifted to bear form. Stella shifted to a black jaguar, the two of them able to pace Gen's lope as they cut through the forest lining the banks of the river.

Astar kept one eye on the sky, hoping Zephyr would demonstrate good sense and abort takeoff as the gríobhth if Lena's weight proved too much for her. The image of her broken-winged at the bottom of a cliff plagued him until he caught sight of her golden form in the sky. Even in the low light of the persistent winter overcast, she shone like a ray of sunlight. Astar breathed an internal sigh of relief—then switched to worrying that she'd be careless about being observed, though they'd all agreed having her get Lena close to the weather anomaly took precedence over discretion—and picked up his pace.

Zephyr had said they'd know it when they were getting close—and Astar didn't need Rhy's raven call to confirm it. Everything felt *wrong*, and in a way that particularly unsettled his bear senses. Gen snorted, her steady hoofbeats on the loam breaking into a scattered rhythm as she pranced nervously. Jak patted her neck soothingly. "Steady on, Gen," he said, then glanced at Astar. "Problem?"

Astar shook his great head, the best he could do in that form. Not a problem they'd be running away from, that was. Stella snarled quietly, but otherwise leapt on undaunted.

At Rhy's croaking signal, they diverged. Astar plunged into the River Danu, swimming swiftly to reach the distant bank. Gen kicked up her speed, galloping away to cross the Phoenix above the confluence, and Stella disappeared into the woods, where she'd be pacing him on that side of the river. Zephyr had said most of the disruption was in the triangle of land upstream of the confluence, so hopefully by coming in at it from all sides, they'd get a better sense of what was going on—and possibly be able to outflank it.

Or he'd divided his forces so they'd be picked off by whatever was out there. Astar had studied plenty of strategy, but making decisions in the moment was totally different—especially when he was sweating over losing the people he loved, not just a valued game piece to the ruthless Ursula or canny Dafne. He could never beat either of them—and hadn't even come close the few times Dafne had pressed him to play the convoluted Nahanaun strategy game of *kiauo*. Lena insisted that the only person who could beat Dafne was Nakoa, but Lena at least challenged her mother. Whereas Astar was always left trying to figure out how he'd lost so fast.

That always gave him a feeling of futility, of being supremely not up to the challenge, uncomfortably close to how he felt right then. Surely commanders in battles didn't feel this way—simultaneously shocked that everyone just ran off to do their bidding, and a guilty desperation to call them back.

Too late now.

He plunged forward into the wrongness, skin shivering with it so his ruff stood on end. No wonder Zephyr had come back in such a panic. If he hadn't been braced for it and firmly decided in his human brain to keep going forward, he no doubt would have gone scampering back to safety.

As it was, he drew on the grizzly's inherent confidence that came from being at the top of the food chain, something he wished he had more of in human form. Through the trees, he glimpsed the confluence ahead and slowed his pace, keeping to the shadows. He sensed Stella doing the same across the river, though he couldn't see her and the wind was wrong for him to catch her scent.

Rhy landed nearby, transforming into human shape in his standard attire of black pants and loose shirt. Quickly crouching behind some brush, he kept his eyes on the triangle of land across the confluence and spoke quietly. "Everyone is in position but Jak and Gen—she had to go a bit farther upstream to find a good ford. Zeph and Lena are circling just above the cloud ceiling where she's out of sight and it's sunny enough to keep Lena warm while she concentrates on mapping out the magic disturbance."

Astar grunted in acknowledgment. Shifting consumed energy, especially for a single-form shifter like him, so he'd stay in bear form unless he needed thumbs or speech.

Jak's shout echoed down the river. "That's our signal," Rhy said. "They're across, so I'm taking bear form too for fighting, unless you still want me aloft."

Astar shook his head and pointed his snout at the tumult on the opposite shore. Rhy grinned, tossing him a little salute. "I hope this isn't the stupidest thing I've ever done," Rhy remarked. "Although I wouldn't mind seeing some of my past mistakes knocked off the top ten list." With that, he shivered with enviable ease into black bear form, and the two of them plunged into the river, making for the troubled shore.

~ 12 ~

I T WAS ALMOST peaceful, circling above the clouds in the golden sunshine, Lena a soft and quiet weight on her back. Yes, her wings were getting a little tired—she wasn't accustomed to carrying any weight at all, and now regretted ignoring her father's advice to train more—but even with the strain of staying aloft at that height, being up there in the clean air was so much better than that... *turmoil* below.

She'd been glad enough of Astar's assignment that she carry Lena, because it spared her the continuing embarrassment of how she'd acted like a frightened gruntling, scurrying to safety with her metaphorical tail between her legs. Good thing the peregrine form couldn't contort that way, or she might've done it literally. Even more humiliating, she'd flung herself into Astar's arms, clinging to him like a limpet—and it hadn't been sexually motivated at all.

After what she'd seen and felt, sex was the last thing on her mind, and all she'd wanted from Astar's gorgeously muscled body was comfort. Which he'd offered and she'd sucked up like a babe with a bottle of warm milk.

What was *wrong* with her?

"All right, Zeph," Lena said. "I think I've got an idea what's going on here, but I need to convene with Nilly. Can you take us down?"

Zeph clacked her beak in agreement, steeling herself not to be such a coward, folded her wings, and dove into the clouds. She hadn't changed her mind that they needed to help those people down there—but conviction didn't make one brave, it turned out.

Lena whooped with excitement as they dropped, which bolstered Zeph's spirits. Taking someone flying for the first time brought a special pleasure Zeph hadn't expected. Of course, flying was among her earliest memories, since her First Form was winged—and somehow she'd never thought about how Lena had never experienced it. From the first moments of their takeoff—Zeph not at all sure she'd be able to keep from crashing—Lena had sung out with joy that flying was even better than surfing. A strong statement from Lena, and one that heartened Zeph enough to find the power in her body to pump her wings and compensate for the ungainly weight.

They burst through the clouds into a dismal scene. The malevolent fog swirled over the entire city of Gieneke, which filled the triangle of land formed by the joining of the Grace and Phoenix Rivers. The ferry boats that plied the two rivers above the confluence were all docked on the far banks, people thronging the shores, pointing at the bizarre sight in the town. Some people were trying to swim to the other shore, but struggled as if against a mighty current that had nothing to do with the flow of the rivers. Some even moved backward, flailing against the invisible pull to no avail. Hopefully no one would be paying attention to the sight of a gríobhth in the sky—or would assume she was just another mishmash monster, galling as that was.

"There's Stella!" Lena shouted, pointing alongside Zeph's neck to the black jaguar climbing onto a deserted pier and vigorously shaking herself dry. "Can you put us down there?"

Not sure if that was the best idea, Zeph dove for the spot. So far everyone seemed to be unharmed. Was the malicious force attacking only the townsfolk? Astar and Rhy, both in bear form, were still swimming toward a set of piers on the opposite side of town. With her sharp gríobhth eyes, Zeph picked out Gen galloping at full speed down the deserted trade road that led to the town from the north, Jak low on her back. Only Stella so far had physically entered the town itself, where the wrongness was most intense. She and Lena would be next.

I'm not interested in being a dead hero, she thought to herself, echoing Rhy's sentiment. It wasn't a noble one, not like pretty much everything that came out of Astar's mouth, but she sympathized with Rhy's cynical take.

She hit the planks of the wooden pier harder than she meant to, not quite compensating for the extra weight, and galloped a distance to scrub off speed and impact, Stella loping into a sprint alongside them. When Zeph pulled to a halt, panting with the effort, Lena immediately jumped off. "Can you stay in this form to defend us?" she asked. "I don't think anyone's around to see you. But you could switch to another fighting form, especially if you need to shift to recover."

Zeph shook her head and stationed herself between Lena and Stella—who'd shifted to human form at Lena's signal—and the boiling fog consuming the town. She positioned herself so she could see both her friends and the town, keeping her keen ears sharp for sounds coming from the water behind them, just in case. It would be good to shift and restore herself, but she also wanted to be ready for anything—and the advantage of the gríobhth form was she had multiple methods of defense: beak, talons, and the whiplike tail. Even her powerful wings worked to thrust attackers away.

She might be a monster to some, but she was a monster very good at killing.

Lena and Stella were holding hands and saying a chant together—something Zeph had never seen them do before. Could be they were revealing arcane sorceress secrets under pressure, or they'd recently learned the method, maybe from Andi at Ordnung that night. Or they were making something up on the fly. Whichever it was, Zeph prayed to Moranu to clear their path—because trouble was coming their way. She clacked her beak in warning, but the sorceresses didn't respond.

An immense form began to take shape as it emerged from the amorphous cloud. A grinning head sat atop a spindly neck that shouldn't be able to support the weight of that misshapen globe. Mostly featureless, the face consisted mainly of two enormous dark eyes and a gaping mouth. Glowing chalk white, the hugely tall figure was roughly human shaped, but there its connection to humanity ended. The gangly body moved with disjointed and eerie grace, the long limbs clearly made of something other than flesh. Stone, perhaps.

And, as Zeph watched, it cocked its head almost curiously at a group of actual humans fleeing before it. With ease, it plucked up two of the people, unperturbed by their struggles and wildly stabbing weapons. One fired an arrow at the thing's face, and it bounced off harmlessly. The monster held the two flailing humans up, examined them, then casually bit the heads off of both.

Then it mashed the mangled bodies together, a putrid green glow of magic shining briefly. The monster smiled in pleasure and set its creation down, clapping merrily as the floundering amalgam ran in panicked circles, four arms waving helplessly.

Though the gríobhth tended to be fierce and less subject to sentiment in general, Zeph's gorge rose—and her heart hurt for the people who screamed and wailed, running after their erstwhile loved ones. Still alive for the moment, but beyond recovery. The giant, apparently bored, looked around for new prey and took a step toward their pier. Zeph clacked another warning, the sorceresses oblivious, no longer chanting, but with magic swirling densely in the air around them.

Either Zeph herself or the building magic caught the giant's attention. It stared across the distance at her, then pointed like a little kid and giggled. The sound scratched over Zeph's keen ears—and she had to fight not to panic again and flee. She leaned into the gríobhth's natural ferocity, the hot-blooded territoriality that had made Zyr so unsuitable for kingship. In this case, that worked in her favor, and she was far more capable of holding her ground than the skittish peregrine had been.

The giant was definitely focused on them, gliding in their direction with that uncanny light grace—and with no regard for a row of pretty cottages arranged on the bank, directly in its path. One bonelike foot kicked a cottage and it burst like a balloon, spilling screaming children like ants. Their scurrying caught the giant's attention and it crouched to watch with gleeful fascination.

A lone woman ran up, a bow in hand, placing herself between the monster and the fleeing children as she took the stance of an experienced archer. Though her hair was dark and curly, she could otherwise be Zeph's mother, Karyn. She might come close to Karyn's skill, too, the way she began smoothly firing arrows at the monster's eyes, so rapidly there was no discernible pause between release and nocking a new arrow.

She hit her mark every time, too, the arrows flying cleanly into the open orbits of the eye cavities—and seeming to disappear into the void within. Though the giant seemed to be using those "eyes" to see—judging by its behavior—they clearly were no more made of living flesh than the rest of it. The giant rubbed the hole where its nose would be, snorting as if something tickled. Then it lowered its spindly hand, cocked its spidery fingers like a kid shooting marbles, and flicked the archer into the river.

The woman sailed limply, falling like a rock and sinking— and everything in Zeph wanted to fly to her assistance, to drag her out of the water—but she couldn't leave Lena and Stella unprotected. The archer's bow popped up, floating lazily in the red clay current, and Zeph began praying to Moranu for assistance. If they had a chance to stop this thing, it had to be sorcery.

The archer had at least bought time for the escaping children, because they'd all disappeared from sight. The giant looked around, picked up a couple of cottages off their foundations, and shook them, looking disappointed when no more scurrying distractions emerged.

Zeph saw the moment the monster remembered her, and the sorceresses broiling their attractive magic—who were no more cognizant of the danger than before. Maybe less so, with the zing of magic in the air like lightning poised to strike. What would she do if the giant reached them—push the pair of them into the water? She couldn't lift them onto her back, and even if she could, she could only carry one at a time.

If she could only take dragon form, it would solve all her problems. She could incinerate that giant to ash, pluck up her friends in her front talons, and fly them back to the safety of Ordnung's walls in no time.

But she didn't have dragon form—and likely never would.

She did have the power of the gríobhth, however, and she would have to use every bit of that form's ability to fight the giant. And hope. But that would mean leaving the oblivious sorceresses completely undefended. Astar had ordered her to defend Lena at all costs—but didn't that mean figuring out the best way to protect her? This being-a-soldier thing was terrible. She was no good at it. The giant was sniffing the air, then zeroed in on her and smiled. *Moranu, I know I'm not a devoted acolyte or your chosen, but now would be an excellent time to convince me.*

Instead of standing again, the giant dropped onto hands and knees, crawling forward as it advanced on her. And it morphed as it moved, limbs becoming leonine tipped with talons, a long whiplike tail growing into the sky, wings spreading, face contorting into a rough approximation of her own eagle's head and curved beak.

Charming.

It wasn't a shapeshifter—not like the Tala who instantly took on a new shape, as if swapping it out from another, intangible realm—but more like a chameleon, taking on the image of something that intrigued it.

By the time it stepped onto the pier, the monster looked like a child's modeling clay version of a gryphon—and easily five times her height. The sorceresses still hadn't moved. And Zeph couldn't risk the giant coming close to Lena and Stella.

Zeph charged.

With a sharp-edged lion's roar, she galloped at full speed down the pier. More cottages, shops, and vendor's stalls filled the middle section of the pier, so Zeph picked the side away from where Lena and Stella stood at the end, keeping the giant's gaze on her, with the buildings between its line of sight and her friends. Hopefully it couldn't just look over the top at them from its soaring height.

Moranu, she really hoped she wasn't sacrificing herself for them. Especially so early in the quest—and without realizing her goal of bedding Astar. *I'm not interested in being a dead hero.* Well, she wouldn't be. She could do this.

Racing at her top speed, she also hoped the giant wouldn't realize she could fly. It crouched down like a playful cat, rump in the air and tail lashing as if it would pounce. Closer. Just a little closer. This was like the Tala children's game of I Eat

You, where the one able to take the form that did the most damage won—and she had no intention of losing.

Closer. Closer...

The giant leapt, front talons outstretched to pin her like an unlucky mouse. She jagged to the side—and poured speed into a powerful leap. Her wings screamed, not built to take her heavy lion's body straight up into the air like that.

But she pulled out enough lift to evade those descending talons—and with perfect timing so the monster plowed beak first into the pier. Splintering wooden planks, shredded awnings, and countless colorful mossback things flew through the air. The pier creaked, groaned mightily, and the pylons beneath the giant snapped under the stress. The whole length tilted, debris pounding the monster's beaked face.

A small black body zipped around her head, cawing furiously. Rhy, back in raven form. He flew away, zooming toward Lena and Stella. Relief washed through Zeph like cool water. Rhy would protect them.

The giant screamed—not a sound of pain, but of profound frustration—and threw back its head, massive pale wings crashing all around, tail clearing swaths of buildings.

Seeing her opportunity, Zeph didn't hesitate. Folding her wings, she dove into the monster's gaping black eye.

~ 13 ~

A STAR ROARED WITH furious denial as Zephyr's golden form folded its wings—and plummeted into the giant faux-gryphon's black eye.

What in Danu was she thinking? She couldn't possibly survive that. He could only hope that Rhy had managed to find Lena and Stella. He knew beyond the shadow of a doubt that Nilly was alive, so he could only hope she and Lena could work some magic to destroy the monster—and that they all could somehow retrieve Zephyr.

He scrambled over wreckage of houses, doing his best to ignore the dead bodies—or, worse, the mashed-together leavings of still-twitching people and animals—grateful for his powerful grizzly body and claws that made short work of barriers. The town was a complete wreck. It would take massive efforts to rebuild the town and restore trade to the upper parts of the Thirteen Kingdoms. If the townsfolk were even willing to return to a place of such horror.

He'd have to be the one to tell Ursula and King Groningen—not a pleasant duty, but at least the burden of dealing with the aftermath would be theirs.

He only wanted to get to Zephyr.

Able-bodied people gaped at the sight of the massive grizzly bear rampaging down the street, but they were stunned from the giant's attack and did little more than clear the way for him. What would they think if they knew the bear was their future high king?

He thrust that worry aside, taking sharp-angled turns to follow narrow lanes that frustratingly didn't run straight toward anything. What you got for building a town on a triangle of land. The giant misshapen gryphon loomed in the sky above, guiding him to Zephyr.

Galloping hooves on cobblestones alerted him along with Jak's shout. "Astar!"

Gen, foam dripping from her muzzle, galloped toward him from an intersecting alley. Jak had his sword out. He pointed it at the giant gryphon that looked unsettlingly like Zephyr, and also horribly distorted. "Is that?" Jak yelled, and Astar roared without slowing, figuring they'd follow.

They rounded a sharp corner and burst into scene of decimation. The monster's tail cleaved great swaths of wreckage, clearing piles of detritus into huge mounds on either side of it. Its wings battered everything into crumbles and dust, but it didn't seem to know how to use them to fly. A bit of luck there, as the last thing they needed was for it to fly off to destroy another town and people—and take Zephyr with it.

With one taloned paw, it raked at the eye Zephyr had flown into. Maybe she was alive in there, wreaking havoc on the inside of the creature's skull. They needed to get to her and help. More than ever, Astar cursed himself for having only First Form, and a grounded one. What wouldn't he give to be able to fly right then?

You're so locked down, so determined to be a mossback prince in every way, that you stop yourself from embracing the ferocity of your nature—or of taking on any other form. Zephyr's voice and accusing eyes flared in his memory. She was right. And he was failing her.

Should he try for a winged form? Desperation might lend him impetus. Zynda was forever preaching that emotional drive affected shapeshifting—and that if he wanted it badly enough, he'd find other forms as he had when he was too young to worry about it.

But no—it would be irresponsible to experiment right then. He had a duty to the others, and trying for other forms wouldn't serve anyone.

They all skidded to a halt outside the flailing of the giant gryphon's wings and tail. Needing speech, Astar shifted to human form, the cold air hitting his sadly unfurred skin with a vicious bite. "Gen—take wing. Your choice of form. Zephyr went into its eye."

Jak nodded. "Smart. Looks like she's driving it crazy."

"Let's drive it more crazy, then. I need to get up there. Jak, you're with me."

Blessedly, neither argued. Gen burst into the form of a large eagle—good choice—and took off with a scream of fury that belied her previous exhaustion. Probably she'd been able to restore her energy by shifting, something else Astar would love to be able to do. "Ever ridden a bear?" he asked Jak, who grinned jauntily at him and sheathed his sword.

"An excellent chapter for my memoirs," he declared. "This

will be amazing."

"Just watch the giant's wings and tail for me," Astar replied with a huff—surprised he could feel amusement at this grim moment—then shifted back to bear form. It wasn't easy, as he'd shifted so many times in a row, and tiredness swamped him. He tried following Zynda's advice, leaning into the heart of the grizzly, the hot-blooded need to defend his mate. Jak clambered aboard, knees squeezing into Astar's ribs, arms coming around his thick neck.

"No good handholds," Jak said. "Don't shake me off."

Astar started at a walk, growling at having to restrain himself as Jak found his balance. Above, Gen harried the giant gryphon, flying at its other eye so it stopped digging at the one to swat at her. With a screech, she ducked, and the giant echoed the sound with warped harmonies.

"I'm good, I'm good," Jak yelled. "Go!"

Needing no further prompting, Astar picked up speed, building into a lope, then putting on a burst of speed. Keeping his eyes on the uneven and precarious path, he trusted Jak to warn him of the crashing wings and lashing tail.

"Wing. Tail. Wing. Wing. Tail." Jak called the warnings a second or two before the impact of said body part, Astar taking evasive action each time. "Wing. Wing. Wing. Oh, shit—fast tail!"

Astar dodged, but the impact of the huge whip of a tail shattered stone beside him, making Jak yelp. "A scratch," he yelled. "Go go go. Wing. Anndd… talons!"

The taloned paw crashed down beside them. Good to be inside the wing reach. Now they had to evade the paws as the monster danced about, trying to swat Gen out of the air like an annoying fly.

"Calling right paw," Jak shouted, vaulting from Astar's back and rolling in a bare patch of what had been someone's garden. He bounced to his feet with native agility, drew a set of twin daggers, and launched himself at the nearby paw, leaping atop it and plunging one dagger in. "Like chalk," he called, stabbing in the other dagger as the giant lifted its foot and hanging on as he swung through the air.

Astar followed Jak's example, galloping to a back paw—the other front paw still high in the air, alternately batting at Gen and clawing at the eye socket Zephyr had disappeared into— and launching himself to climb the hind leg like a tree.

His claws slipped and scrabbled, but Astar refused to be shaken. Rounding the haunch, he ducked the whipping tip of the tail and ran for the head. The creature had imitated the look of Zephyr's feathered neck, but not the texture of the feathers. The serrated stony ridges of its neck worked in Astar's favor, and he climbed with renewed strength and speed— though he occasionally had to pause to hang on as the monster tried to shake them off.

He'd nearly made it to the creature's eye—truly a gaping hole like a cave—when the texture of the stony body under his claws began to soften, the ridges shifting and sliding. Shape-changing. He didn't have time to contemplate what that meant, or to wonder if the appearance of Rhy in raven form, joining Gen in harrying the monster, was a good sign or a bad one. Nilly burned bright in his mind still, so he fervently hoped it was a good sign.

Clawing his way over the lip of the eye cavity, which was like rapidly shifting sand as the whole head rose higher into the sky, he leapt into the abyss.

It wasn't bottomless, but the drop steepened, sliding him precariously along a skidding slope. Scrabbling for purchase, he roared. Not her name, but he knew Zephyr would recognize his voice anyway.

She roared back, leonine and powerful. With a gust of wings, she landed beside him, digging her talons into the shifting surface and pumping her wings for balance. Then she hammered her beak into a bony protrusion, ripping out a chunk and spitting it out again. Outside, the monster howled and they both had to cling to the inside of its skull as it hit itself hard enough to rattle them.

Following her example, he used his claws to rip out a piece. A drop in the bucket of its great mass, but satisfying to hear it react in apparent distress. They couldn't take it apart this way, he realized. All they could do was delay for the sorceresses to do... *something*.

At least Zephyr was alive—though bleeding and bedraggled, one hind leg drawn up in injury. It infuriated him to see beautiful, carefree Zephyr wounded, and he poured that rage into wounding the grotesque monster, little as that might be. Shouts echoed from outside and Rhy zipped in, circling their heads and shooting out again.

The message to get out was clear. The method less so. Even if they scaled up to the eye socket, they had a huge drop to deal with. Zephyr could fly out, though. He shifted to human form—shit, it was cold without fur—his clawless fingers sadly inadequate for holding onto much of anything. But he did have words. "Go!" he shouted at Zephyr. "Get out of here."

Perched on the lip of the eye socket above, Rhy cawed at them urgently.

"You can fly," he told Zephyr. "I can't. Go."

She shook her head, clacking her beak rapidly and pointing it at her back.

"I'm too heavy for you," he argued. "We'll both go down. Save yourself."

She clacked angrily, shoving her lethally curved beak into his face. He batted it away. As if Zephyr would ever hurt him. "Go! That's an order."

She raised her golden crest in obvious and arrogant refusal.

"Hey!" Rhy, now in human form, sitting on the eye-socket ridge, bare feet dangling, waved furiously at them. "Salena and Nilly are about to hit this thing hard. Get out now or I'll have to tell them to hold off."

That wasn't going to happen. No way would he jeopardize destroying this thing just to save himself. "We'll be right behind you. Go!"

Rhy didn't waste time, the raven shooting into the sky before Astar fully realized Rhy had shifted. Zephyr poked him hard in the chest with the sharp point of her beak, one front paw on his belly, her talons extended as she glared at him meaningfully. Around them, the skull shuddered, bouncing as the giant apparently broke into a run. Good thing Zephyr had him pinned, or he might've brained himself on a stony protrusion. She pricked him with her talons and snapped her beak at him.

"You don't scare me," he ground out. "I gave you an order."

She shifted to human form, fully splayed against him with one hand on his belly and most of her draped between his thighs. She was naked. "I am not a soldier in your army," she snapped, the words carrying the echo of her biting beak, her sapphire eyes scorching. "And I'm not interested in your noble self-sacrifice. You have three choices: shift to a bird form, get on my gríobhth back so I can fly us out of here, or fuck me now because I'm not leaving you. If we're both going to die in human form, let's do it happy."

He gaped at her, overcome by her blazing nudity against him, the absurdity of even considering having her here and now as they faced probable death—and how urgently he wanted her. "Zephyr..." he choked out.

"Save it," she bit out. "No arguing. Put your mouth on me or take option one or two." She gripped his jaw. "Decide."

"You can't carry me," he argued anyway.

"We don't know that. And I don't have to lift, only glide us to the ground."

"And what if you get killed trying to save me?"

"Better than getting killed inside this stinking stone creature." She grinned salaciously, nimble fingers undoing his pants. "Think of the ballads, how they found our broken bodies naked and joined, in the midst of—"

He cut her off with an incoherent growl of hunger and horror. The image she painted had him instantly hard, desperate for her—and horrified at what everyone would say.

"Fine, I'll ride."

She smiled, not pleased so much as sadly vindicated, withdrawing her hand. "At least I know how to get to you. If you don't get on my back immediately, I'm shifting back to human with my mouth on that hard cock."

She became the gríobhth before he could react—and by the gleam in her eye, he knew she meant every word. Climbing onto her lion's back, he nearly muttered that her threat was hardly a disincentive, but he wasn't going to tempt her mercurial nature. As much as he thought he might be willing to face death right then to have her luscious mouth on him, that would be a bad idea.

Right?

He had no time to think because he had to concentrate on hanging on as she scaled the nearly vertical slope to the eye socket, digging in her talons for purchase. It would've been smart for him to climb up as the bear and meet her there, save her the effort, but too late now. Her lower body was strong anyway. It was her wings he worried about. Unbidden, a memory came back to him of that last picnic in Annfwn, when Zephyr dove from the cliff in human form and pierced the water as the gríobhth. Maybe this could work.

She reached the lip of the eye orbit right as the giant shrieked, a ghastly sound that pierced his ears. The world outside bounced and spun—the ground unbelievably far below. Before he could think to fret, Zephyr leapt into the air, wings spread.

~ 14 ~

HE WAS TOO heavy. Zeph's wings trembled with strain as she fought not to drop like a rock. Her shoulder muscles burned with agony, the muscle fibers tearing as they tried to sustain the glide. She aimed for the river, figuring an icy, slightly softer landing was better than the debris-strewn ground. Get them down alive and she could shift to heal.

Then she'd tear Astar up one side and down the other for being such a stubborn, stupidly noble idiot. At least the fear that she'd taint his shining honor had impelled him to act to save himself. If she lived, she'd have to sort out how messed up she could be in the head that she so desperately wanted a man who reacted with such visceral horror to the thought of bedding her.

She banked, trying to catch a current, but the icy air— nicely thick, at least—had no handy thermals to provide lift. They were going down and going down fast.

Behind them, magic exploded, a wave of it rippling through the air, followed by shards of stone from the giant. Fine shards pierced her hide, but worse—the impact of the wave unbalanced her, nearly sending her into an uncontrolled and tumbling fall that would certainly kill Astar. She threw everything into regaining her glide, a howl of agony ripping from her throat as her left wing ripped out of its socket.

"Zephyr!" Astar screamed her name, clutching her shoulders as if he could hold her aloft. He began to swing a leg over, clearly intending to jump, but she snaked her tail to whip him across the cheek. "Ow! What the—"

But it was enough to distract him. Letting the dislocated wing drag—agonizing, but the pain kept her alert—she focused on the water. They would hit harder than she'd like, but so it went. Rhy flew wide circles around them, croaking encouragement, and Gen in eagle form winged ahead like a guiding star. Astar held on, chanting words of encouragement. At least he wasn't fighting her anymore.

They hit with a violent splash of bone-chilling water and chunks of ice. Zeph went under, sucking in too much water, but kicked for the surface with all four still-strong legs. Gen was already there in manatee form—which had to be miserable in those temperatures—shouldering under her wrenched wing, Moranu bless her.

Astar had fallen away and she cast about wildly, searching for him—then spotted the grizzly bear swimming toward her with powerful strokes, ice forming on the long guard hairs mantling his powerful neck and shoulders. He wedged under her other side, pushing up beneath her to hold her afloat. Gratefully, she clung to him as he struck out for shore, the ice at least numbing the agony in her wing, and all over her body where they'd hit, but exhaustion sweeping through her.

"Shift, Zeph," Gen urged, back in human form and wearing an enviably warm-looking fur cloak, helping Astar deposit her as gently as possible on the bank. It still hurt, her body on fire with pain—though she felt oddly detached from it. She had no energy to lift her head, despite the chill of the snowy bank against her drenched fur and feathers. Her wings hung heavily, dragging with the weight of water. A harsh panting sound disturbed her, until she realized it was her.

"Zephyr," Astar said, wearing only the shirt and pants he shifted back to human in. She really needed to teach him to come back wearing something moderately warmer. Trying to scold him, only a hiss emerged from her beak. Oh, right. She was the gríobhth still. But why did she hurt so much? "Zephyr, listen to me." Astar grasped her head on either side of her beak, panicked summer-sky blue eyes staring into hers. He was so pretty, even with his golden hair soaking wet and freezing into snarls, and that bleeding cut on his cheek. "You have to shift, to heal yourself. Pick any form. Just do it. That's an order."

She snorted at him, wanting to tell him where to shove his orders, but she choked, bloody water coughing out of her beak and nares. That couldn't be good. "She has to shift or she won't make it," Astar said to someone else.

"She might not have the energy." Gen. Gen was her friend. "Can Stella heal her?"

"Stella and Salena are both out cold," another voice said. Rhy crouched down, gently stroking her head. "Good news is they destroyed the giant. Jak is standing watch over them, but we'd have to either take Zeph to them and wait for Stella to wake up, or bring them here."

"I don't think we should move her with that bad wing,"

Gen said. Her gentle fingers patted Zeph's side, and she whimpered like a broken kitten.

"I don't think I can carry her gríobhth weight, even as the bear," Astar said, still holding her head. Blood dripped down his face, and not just from the cut on his cheek. "I guess that means bringing Lena and Nilly here. How long will it take?"

"Too long," Gen cut in before Rhy could speak. "She has broken ribs and they must've pierced her lungs. That explains why her breathing is so labored, and the blood bubbling out of her nares."

Rhy cursed softly. Astar frowned, but wiped the blood clear of her nares, getting that determined look in his eye. "That settles it. Zephyr, you will shift and shift now. Don't try to heal. Just shift to something smaller so I can carry you. Do it now."

She whimpered, unable to imagine the effort involved. The possibility of being anything but what she was, wracked with pain and gulping for air, seemed as far away as the moon. She would just lie where she was and have a lovely nap. The cold had let up, leaving her nicely warm and comfortable. Letting her eyes drift close, she relaxed against the ground.

"We're losing her," Rhy warned. Gen stifled a sob.

"Zephyr, open your eyes and pay attention." Astar's crisp order penetrated her fuzzy brain. She forced her eyes open—not because he'd told her to, but to tell him off. His Highness the Crown Prince could suck it. "Shift," he told her. "Unless you're too lazy and talentless," he added with a sneer. "What's the easiest shift? She's already in First Form. Human?"

"Yes," Gen said. "That's also First Form, in a way."

"Human body, Zephyr. Right now."

She couldn't. Just… couldn't. Vaguely she considered that she had promised to ask for help, even if she thought she didn't need it, but that had never seemed like an option.

Astar leaned in close and dropped his voice. "Shift to human—and if you do, I'll have sex with you. You can do whatever you want to me. Or you die here in a pitiful broken heap, never knowing what could have been. Your choice."

He did not say that. Throwing her own ultimatum back at her. Offering the one temptation he knew she couldn't resist.

"You need a human body if you want to have me," he coaxed, taunting and seductive. "I've never broken a vow in my whole life, so you know I mean it. I promise you an entire night with me. I'll give you anything you ask for, let you do anything you want to me—if you'll take human form right now."

He thought she wouldn't take him up on it. That she'd forget and let him off the hook later, but he was wrong. Never make promises to a gríobhth. They never forget—and their victims always pay up. With that last bit of fire, she reached for human form, hitting a blazing wall of agony.

She plunged on, fighting for the shift, knowing if she lost it partway, her death would be even more swift and terrible. Few fates frightened shapeshifters more than bungling a shift and ending up as something in between.

It hurt, like knives slicing her very cells apart. And she remembered Aunt Zynda's tales of how she'd been unable to shift for so long after the dragon Kiraka immolated her. *Fear is a wall*, Zynda had often reflected. *Fear of pain is more powerful than we realize.* Well, Zeph refused to let a little pain stop her—especially with the promised reward on the other side. Astar. An entire night with Astar, and she could do whatever she wanted to him.

With a final, desperate push, she found human form and transitioned—a howl of agony shrieking from her throat before blackness claimed her.

ASTAR CARRIED ZEPHYR'S limp and broken body—wrapped in Gen's fur cloak—as carefully as he could. They'd crash-landed farther upstream than he'd realized and the walk back to Gieneke and the confluence was taking forever. Rhy had flown ahead, scouting in raven form, periodically circling back to check on them.

"We could try horseback again," Gen said, trudging beside him. They'd tried at first to have Gen take horse form with Astar riding, Zephyr cradled in his arms. But even with Gen picking her way as smoothly as she could, the bouncing had pained Zephyr, making her whimper and pale even more. Blood still occasionally dripped from her nose or leaked from the corner of her mouth, and her breathing remained shaky, and far too shallow. He'd love to get her to Stella faster, but speed would kill her before they got there.

He shook his head, remembering to reply to Gen. "We'll have to hope that slow and steady really does win the race. We got her this far."

"True." Gen sighed, exasperation and worry in it. "I can't

believe you promised her sex to get her to shift."

"It worked."

"It just figures that Zeph would be motivated by the chance to finally debauch you."

He slanted her a look. "She saved my life."

Gen held up gloved hands. She'd come back from horse form wearing a different cloak, while Astar was still freezing in his shirt and pants. He'd be so much warmer in his grizzly body, but he couldn't walk *that* far on his hind legs carrying Zeph. Besides, the exercise was keeping him reasonably warm.

"I'm not saying anything against Zeph," Gen protested. "She's my friend, too, and I'm just as afraid for her as you are." She was silent a moment. "Maybe more, because either way I worry there's pain ahead for her."

"Nilly is waking up and can heal her." He'd been feeling his twin's gradual return to consciousness for the last little while, and with profound gratitude.

"That's not what I mean," Gen pressed. "What happens if, once Zeph has you, she doesn't want to let you go? You know how possessive that gríobhth nature is."

I never asked for forever, Zephyr had said. She hadn't and she never would. It was his heart that would be broken by giving her up. A small price to pay, given the alternative. "Gendra," he said, making sure not to sound unkind. "I get that you're concerned, and that you love both of us and want the best for us, but I'm going to ask this of you once and once only. Stay out of our relationship."

She flashed him a wry—and fortunately unoffended—look. "When your *relationship* goes up in flames, I can only hope we can all stay out of it. It didn't work that way with Rhy and Lena."

"At this point, I'll take any pain, as long as Zephyr lives," he retorted gruffly.

"You're right." Gen was quiet a few steps. "I apologize. I just feel so helpless."

He understood that perfectly. Rhy arrived just then, landing on the road ahead of them and shifting into human form. "Stella is awake and will fly here after she recovers just a bit more," he informed them. "She'll be here soon. I scouted a sheltered spot up ahead. We figure we need to stay put overnight. Gen, if you'll come with me, we can be horses to carry Jak, Salena, and supplies back here."

Astar's arms burned with exhaustion, as if his muscles had heard he could set Zephyr down and already wanted to let go. "Or you could fly to the carriages and have them drive up to meet us," he said, scanning for the spot Rhy had mentioned and hoping it was close.

Rhy shook his head, falling in beside him. "They're on the wrong side of the river, and the ferries aren't operating yet. Probably won't be until tomorrow at the soonest. There's a lot of damage."

Astar nodded wearily, thinking longingly of his trunks of clothing back at the carriages. And his Silversteel sword. He'd left it behind since he'd planned to shift to grizzly form and he was no good at keeping things in a metaphysical cache, not like Zephyr and the others were. It would make him feel better to have a weapon in human form. "Find me a sword or dagger, and some warmer clothes, would you?"

Rhy shivered in sympathy. "You and me both, buddy. Want me to carry Zeph for a bit? You look wiped out."

"I've got her," he replied, knowing he was being unreasonably stubborn, but also feeling physically incapable of handing her over to anyone else.

Rhy nodded, not arguing at all, which said something right there. "It's not far now. Good thing, as it will be night soon."

They walked on just a bit farther, the light definitely failing, he realized. From pale gray to dark gray. He focused on putting one foot in front of the other, while Gen and Rhy consulted quietly on supplies they'd need to pass a comfortable night. Their discussion of food had him salivating.

"Right here," Rhy said, putting hands on his shoulders to physically turn him toward a path leading off the road. "Surprise."

Astar took in the little cottage with considerable surprise and relief. "Unoccupied?"

"Apparently. I checked it every time I flew past," Rhy said. "If the occupants show up, we'll pay them or something. It's small, but I figured having a fireplace and a roof would make up for the size. And some of us can always sleep out in some cold-weather tolerant form if quarters are too tight."

Astar followed him up the narrow walk and in through the door. It was warm inside, blessedly so, with a fire burning hot in the fireplace and a teakettle whistling on a hook nearby.

"There's a bed through there," Rhy said, "but it's also cold, so I put these blankets by the fire. Thought you could put Zeph there."

"Good idea," Astar grunted, sinking to his knees—more of

a controlled fall—and laying Zephyr gently on the blankets. Gen took the whistling kettle and set to concocting something on the nearby table. "You said nobody was here all afternoon—did you light the fire and put the kettle on?"

Rhy jerked his chin in self-conscious acknowledgment. "Yeah. I figured you both needed to warm up. And I went back and forth a *lot* of times. I kept an eye on the place."

"That's a lot of shifting in a short span of time," Astar noted, eyeing Rhy and seeing how drawn he looked. "How tired are you?"

"Not enough to be on the edge of death," Rhy shot back. "Let me do what I can. I know my limits—and I could stand to push them, according to everyone."

"All right then," Astar acknowledged. He'd never thought it was fair, the way everyone rode Rhy about working harder, practicing more, acquiring more forms, doing better. Better than anyone, Astar understood what it was like to grow up under the weight of enormous expectations. He and Rhy had a lot in common that way—and very different styles of dealing with the pressure. Astar had chosen a crippling sense of responsibility and obligation to duty, while Rhy had chosen the polar opposite.

"Stella is here," Astar announced, the arrival of his twin feeling like hot broth on an empty stomach. "You two go ahead. Be careful, though. We're all exhausted and coming down from a battle like that leads to a crash eventually. That's when people make mistakes and we don't want that."

Gen and Rhy exchanged a look. "You sound just like Ursula," Gen commented, pushing the hot mug into his hands.

"Drink this. We'll be back soon."

The door opened and Stella came in, expression composed and eyes storm dark. "How bad is she?" she asked, coming straight to Zeph's side as Gen and Rhy slipped out.

"Bad," he replied, hating to admit it. He studied his twin, assessing her physically and the feel of her magic. "But are you up to this?"

She flicked an opaque glance at him. "I have to be because we're not going to let Zeph die. Help me peel this cloak off her. It's sticking."

"Blood. Frozen and dried." He reached to help, wondered why a mug was in his hands. Shaking his increasingly muzzy head, he went to set it aside, but Stella stopped him with a hand over his.

"Drink it," she told him gravely, her gray eyes dark as the underbelly of a storm. "You're not in great shape either, and that will help. You know Gen's tonics are always good."

Unable to muster the will to argue, he took the easiest path and drank. Whatever Gen had whipped up, it was creamy and sweet—almost enough to disguise the bitter herbal flavor. Gen had spent time with her father's family outside Ordnung, learning mossback herbs from her grandmother, aunts, and older cousins. Distantly, he wondered what she'd dosed him with, blinking when Stella slipped the cup from his hands.

"Lie down and rest, Willy," she told him gently.

"I need to help you." His tongue felt thick and he couldn't keep his eyes open.

"I can handle this on my own. You did your part. I'll do mine. Lie down before you fall down."

He was already leaning, so it was easy enough to let himself crumple the rest of the way to horizontal. He turned to his side, though, to keep an eye on them both. That was something he could do lying down. "Love you, Nilly," he said thickly, tears pricking his eyes for no reason.

"I love you, Willy," she answered, giving him a warm smile as she laid her hands on Zeph's bared collarbones, green healing light flowing out. "I'll take care of your Zephyr. Trust me. You can sleep now."

Because he trusted his sister with not only his life, but with Zeph's, he let his eyes close and sleep drag him under.

~ 15 ~

Astar only slept a few hours, waking to the welcome commotion of too many people in too small a space attempting to be quiet cooking food when most of them had no idea what they were doing. With a rush of love for all of his great-hearted and cantankerous friends, he lay there a moment just listening to their whispered bickering.

Jak archly informed the group that, as he'd never been able to hunt for food in animal form, he was vastly more qualified on the topic of mossback cooking. Lena took exception to that, pointing out that she wasn't a shapeshifter either. Then Rhy chimed in, teasing her about how she was a princess and everyone knew princesses never lifted their dainty fingers on household tasks. Lena launched into a blistering breakdown of life in the Aerron Desert and all the tasks she'd bloodied her fingers on. Rhy made a salacious suggestion about her talented fingers, resulting in a wordless screech from Lena—and Astar decided maybe he should lever himself fully awake and enforce peace before they woke Zephyr.

Zephyr.

His eyes popped open with a spurt of pure panic, the tight anxiety in his chest relaxing as he took in Zephyr lying on her back in front of him. Her delicate profile looked too sharp, her complexion pale beyond even her usually fair skin, but the blood and terrible bruising was gone. Someone had laid a blanket over her, and the faint blush on her cheeks indicated she should be warm. Someone had put a blanket on him, too, though his body felt stiff and heavy as a rock from lying on his side, apparently unmoving all that time.

On the other side of Zephyr, Stella lay on her side, too, head pillowed on the crook of her arm, and she smiled at him. She looked so at peace that he knew Zephyr would be all right.

"Our friends do not excel at being quiet," she subvocalized to him, eyes a lighter, silvery gray now and sparkling with amusement.

"Fortunately they have other redeeming qualities," he replied, immensely grateful for her in his life. *"Zephyr?"* he asked.

"Healed," she answered. *"She's sleeping it off is all—and will likely sleep all night as her body finds its equilibrium again. Anything I wasn't able to repair, she should be able to fix the next time she shifts."*

Though he'd been nearly sure of that answer, he sighed in relief, restraining the urge to reach out and touch Zephyr, just to reassure himself. Stella watched him with a sad and wise smile, making him wonder what she saw for his future. No happy ending for him and Zephyr, that much was certain. *"What about you—shouldn't you be sleeping off the healing, too? Along with whatever magic-working you did."*

"I'm all right," she replied, *"and we have problems. Word of your promise to Zeph got around and Rhy apparently decided Willy's Moratorium is off. He made a move on Lena and she is not happy."*

A crash sounded from the cooking area and she winced. *"Perhaps you should…"*

"Perhaps I should," he agreed, and sat up with a bearish roar to stifle the argument. "Everyone knows," he said, getting to his feet, "that I am the best at cooking meat. Give me those steaks."

A WHILE LATER, the six of them sat crowded around the one small table, everyone stuffed with only partially burnt steaks, thankfully supplemented by fluffy rolls baked by Gen—who'd apparently been studying more than herb lore—and root vegetables Lena had discovered in the cellar and roasted over the fire. They'd moved Zephyr to the lone bedroom, covering her with blankets and keeping the door open a crack in case she woke. The others had argued that their noise would wake Zephyr and they should shut the door, but Stella backed him up, saying that nothing would wake Zephyr before her body was ready.

He was grateful to seize on that rationale. He mostly didn't want Zephyr to wake up alone in a strange place and be frightened, even for a moment. Not that anything seemed to scare the bold and courageous shapeshifter, but he still worried. Mostly he wanted to crawl under those blankets with her and be there when she woke. He couldn't allow himself that—regardless of the bargain they'd made—but he could sit where he could see her sleeping, a slant of warm light falling over her gently rising and falling breast.

"We should debrief," he said into the lull created by tired bodies finally warm and sated enough to sleep. "While our memories are fresh."

Rhy groaned and dropped his forehead onto folded hands. "Do we have to?" he mumbled.

"And shouldn't we wait for Zeph?" Lena asked, glancing at the darkened bedroom with a concerned frown. None of them would be completely reassured until they saw Zephyr up and about again.

"We can fill her in tomorrow," Astar said, doing his best to assume an air of command. The nap had helped, but not enough. "It's my responsibility to debrief you all—and send a report back to Ordnung. Her Majesty will need to know what happened here, because Gieneke will need help reconstructing."

"If they even can rebuild," Jak noted.

"If they even *want* to." Stella shuddered. "Some of the things we saw... I wish I could erase them from my mind."

Beside her, Jak stroked Stella's hair, careful not to touch her otherwise, and she leaned into the comfort. Astar found himself frowning, which Jak caught and grinned at him jauntily—before swiftly removing his hand.

"Rebuilding will be critical," Astar said forbiddingly. "This is a major intersection of road and river trade. We can't afford to have it disrupted, not with a significant amount of winter still ahead." He let them absorb the implications. "Let's start with Lena," he said. "Tell us what you found out aloft, and then you and Nilly can explain what you did."

"And try to use small words," Rhy put in, "for those of us

who don't speak bookworm."

Lena narrowed her eyes at him, but didn't dignify that sally with a reply. "It was some kind of magic storm in the upper atmosphere, but at a much higher altitude than affects normal weather. Above the mesosphere, which is where the—" She glared at Rhy's snort, but dropped the explanation. "At any rate, I recognized hints of my own magic, and Andi's, but changed. It was as if something had taken our combined magic from the night of the crystalline moon and—this is not a perfect analogy, but—digested it and spit it out again."

"Something alive?" Astar asked, trying to get his head around what kind of being that could be.

"Maybe?" Lena answered dubiously. "There's an intelligence, but what kind and how much I can't say at this point. Still, something was directing the regurgitated magic, if you will, in order to cause mischief."

"Mischief?" Rhy echoed in astonishment. "You're calling the devastation we witnessed 'mischief'?"

"Stop picking on me, Rhyian," she responded in a too-calm tone. "Or you will make me angry."

"Ooh," he mocked, fluttering his hands in the air. "I'm so scared of—"

"Rhyian," Astar cut in forbiddingly. "Knock it off. Continue, Lena."

She flashed him a grateful smile, then poked at a bit of discarded gristle with a rudimentary fork they'd dug out of the cabinets. "That's the best word I have for what I sensed. Not malice so much as... a desire to cause trouble."

"I can confirm Lena's impression," Stella put in somberly.

"I sensed an intelligence—though not like anything I've encountered before—and what I'd also call mischief. There wasn't any remorse or malevolence. It was almost as if something got a taste of that magic and wanted to do something with it."

"So it created that stone monster," Astar mused.

"Not created," Lena corrected. "More like, animated it."

"Or resurrected," Stella said, nodding. "Depending on what it was before."

"Possibly," Lena agreed. "The hills around here have images embedded in them, left there by people so ancient we don't have any information about them, not even in the library in Nahanau."

"And here I thought—" Rhy started.

"Don't think," Astar cut him off with a stabbing finger. "Don't speak."

"One of those figures," Lena continued as if the interruption hadn't occurred, "was of a giant carrying a club. It was delineated by an outline of white stone."

Jak whistled low and long, and Gen hummed with interest. "So this magical mischief-maker somehow brought the stone giant to life and unleashed it on the town?"

"Seems like a logical explanation," Lena returned.

"How did it become a gríobhth then?" Gen asked. "We saw the giant from a distance, but it looked kind of human shaped at that point."

"It morphed when it saw Zeph," Stella explained. "Lena and I were working together to create a single astral projection to battle the intelligence fueling the giant."

"Smart, to go to the source," Astar said, nodding.

"Lena's idea," Stella said.

"You provided the power, though. I couldn't have done it on my own," Lena replied. "We did something similar with Andi, back at Ordnung, but we clearly need to practice more because it took us way too long to mesh our magics."

"Zeph was guarding us—I could see that much—and when the giant spotted her, it acted fascinated and changed shape to look like her."

"Very roughly, though," Astar mused. "Not shapeshifting."

"No," Gen agreed. "It sounds like some other kind of magic entirely. One we haven't encountered before."

"May I say something?" Rhy asked.

"Does it involve needling Lena?" Astar asked.

Rhy slammed a fist on the table, making the wooden plates jump. "I have not been—"

"No," Astar said, cutting him off. He was heartily tired of this and just wanted to lie down again. "You may not speak."

Rhy clenched his jaw, a muscle bulging there. "It's relevant to the stone giant."

"Oh," Astar said, sitting back and smiling affably, "then, by all means, proceed."

Glaring, Rhy visibly calmed himself. "When we arrived, the giant was messing around, taking people apart and mashing them together to make new... things."

"We saw that, too," Jak said. "Mostly the results of it. Which corresponds to what Zeph saw initially."

"Exactly." Rhy nodded. "So what if this intelligence Salena sensed was more like... animating the stone giant, and infusing it with its own interest in making new creatures. The intelligence might've reshaped the stone giant into something more exciting once it got a look at Zeph."

They all contemplated that. "Good thought, Rhy, thank you," Astar said with a nod of respect. When Rhy gave up being difficult, he could be the sharpest one in the group, besides Lena, of course. "It makes sense," he continued, "since the giant didn't seem to be a living creature. The inside of its head was hollow. No eyes, no brain."

"Because the senses and thoughts came from whatever was using it, more like a puppet than anything," Gen said.

Astar nodded thoughtfully, then looked to Lena and Stella. "So, how did you destroy it?"

"We basically cut the connection between the intelligence and the giant," Lena said.

"And scared the intelligence," Stella added, looking troubled. Here was whatever was bothering her.

"How did you do that?" he asked.

She met his gaze, a rueful half-smile flattening her mouth. "I gathered up all the fear and grief from the townsfolk and..." She gestured with both hands, as if shaping an invisible ball between them. "I kind of compressed it and hurled those emotions at it."

"It vanished," Lena said softly, "like it ran away screaming and crying."

Stella focused on her plate, deeply unhappy, swirling a withered carrot in some gravy.

"I didn't know you could do that, Nilly," Astar said, reaching over to take her hand.

She clutched it gratefully. "I didn't either."

They all sat in silence for a moment, broken only by the crackle of the fire. Astar glanced at Zeph's sleeping form in the other room. Still unmoving. Still breathing. "So, we have to expect that it might come back," he said, "when it recovers."

"Yes," Lena agreed, "though not necessarily to here. I got the feeling that it showing up here, at the confluence, was happenstance."

"All right." Astar squeezed Stella's hand and let it go. "I'll write up a report for Her Majesty, and Rhy can carry it back to Ordnung. I'll report to King Groningen personally. We should be able to get to Castle Elderhorst by the night after tomorrow, if we leave in the morning."

"No carriages," Jak pointed out.

"We'll go on our own," Astar replied, "shapeshifters carrying non-shifters. The carriages can catch up with us when the ferries are repaired. We'll be at Elderhorst for a few days anyway. Everyone get some sleep." He levered himself to his feet, glancing in at Zephyr's sleeping form. Would anyone argue if he slept beside her?

"A word with you, if you please," Rhy said through his teeth, though quietly, standing beside him.

Well, at least Rhy was attempting to follow rules of politeness. Astar nodded, gesturing to the bedroom. Nothing would wake Zephyr at this point if the ruckus up till now hadn't. "Step into my study," he said wryly.

Rhy nodded stiffly, then waited for Astar to shut the door. "Why are you sending me back?"

Astar raked a hand through his hair. "I need to send a message to Ordnung. You have a winged form that can carry it unobtrusively."

"Are you getting rid of me?" Rhy demanded, tense enough to break.

"Wouldn't it be easier?" Astar asked, not unkindly. "I know it's rough for you, being around Lena. I'm offering you an out. If you go to Ordnung and don't come back, no one will think less of you for it." Lena would likely be grateful, in fact.

Rhy stared at him in consternation. "I know everyone else thinks I'm feckless, lazy, and always looking for the way out, but I thought you knew me better than that, Willy."

He was too tired for this conversation. Scrubbing his hands over his face, he willed himself to think clearly. "I do know better," he replied. "I know you would never back down from this challenge, so that's why I'm offering you this opportunity. You don't have to torture yourself anymore. You certainly don't have to torture Lena by hounding her relentlessly."

Rhy sagged, going from bristling for a fight to lost and wounded. "Is that what you all think I'm doing?"

"What *is* your plan, cousin?" Astar asked. Really, Stella should be having this conversation with him.

"I want to win her back," Rhy said, bracing himself for a scathing reply—and even glancing at the sleeping Zephyr as if she might sit up and laugh at him.

In truth, Astar had to school his expression not to look incredulous. The room was shadowed, but Rhy's shapeshifter vision was keen enough to see clearly. "Why?" he asked simply.

"What do you mean?" Rhy snarled. "I think that's pretty

obvious."

"It's not," Astar replied crisply. "I find it interesting that you used the word 'win.' Is that what this is about—you simply can't resist the challenge?"

Rhy's face hardened with temper. "That's a foul thing to suggest."

"You asked what everyone thinks you're doing," Astar replied evenly, giving in to the weariness to sit at the end of the bed. "That's what it looks like. You had Lena before—and you deliberately extricated yourself from the relationship with the cruelest betrayal you could think up on short notice."

"I was an idiot," Rhy bit out.

"Can't argue with that, cousin. But you still haven't told me what your long-term plan is. Do you want to marry her?"

Rhy scoffed reflexively, a very Tala sound. "You've been around mossbacks too long, Willy. You know Tala don't think that way."

"Lena isn't Tala, and she *does* think that way. She wants what her parents have—a lifelong commitment founded on deep love and respect. She wants a partnership like they have, and children. Even I know that about Lena, and I'm hardly in her confidence. How can you *not* know that about her?"

"I know it," Rhy insisted, sounding sullen. "I also know she loves her work in that desert more than she loves any person."

"I imagine there's a reason for that," Astar commented wryly. Apparently keen shapeshifter vision didn't make for keen shapeshifter insight. The man was blind to so much.

"Explain."

"She can give her love to the work and it will never throw

it back in her face."

Rhy raked a hand through his hair. "That's what I'm trying to prove to her. I loved her then. I love her still. But she won't listen to me, and your fucking moratorium is—"

Astar chopped a hand in the air to cut off Rhy's rising volume, pointing at Zephyr. He didn't think anything would wake her at this point, but he also didn't want to listen to Rhyian's complaints. "I put the moratorium in place partially to protect Lena from you," he said bluntly.

Rhy clenched his fists. "I knew it. Salena doesn't need protecting from me. I'd do anything for her."

"Good." Astar said. "There's plenty for you to do—starting with the task I assigned you."

"I can't prove myself to Salena if I'm not here," Rhy growled in frustration.

"Then go and come back. Prove that you can do something against your self-interest," Astar growled back, then relented, softening his tone. "You broke more than Lena's heart all those years ago, Rhy. You broke her trust. That's what you should be trying to fix."

Rhy threw up his hands. "And how in Moranu am I supposed to do that?"

"By demonstrating your trustworthiness."

"Not all of us are infatuated with honor, Willy," Rhy sneered. "You're so bound by inflexible rules that you might as well be walking around in a cage. Tell me, oh noble crown prince, how are you going to reconcile your two vows? You can't keep your promise to Zeph and abide by your moratorium. Unless you're hoping she won't remember. She was pretty far out of her head at the time."

Astar slowly rubbed his hands together, not letting himself look at Zephyr. A part of him—a reckless, wild, and dangerous part—was secretly thrilled at the bind he'd gotten himself into. At last he had a reasonably honorable excuse to give into his longing for her. But he wouldn't confess that to Rhy. He and his cousin both had enough trouble governing their wilder natures as it was.

"Even if she doesn't remember, I'd abide by my vow to her," he explained slowly. "You might have contempt for the rigidity of the rules of honor, but this is how being trustworthy works. Being worthy of someone's trust means that you abide by your promises to them—stated and implied—whether they are aware of it or not."

"I don't need lessons from you," Rhy ground out.

"You certainly don't have to listen to them," Astar agreed. "Which is why I'm giving you an out. Take the message to Ordnung. If you don't rejoin us, no harm, no foul. But if you do come back, no more teasing Lena. No more needling her for a reaction."

"I'm just trying to get through to her. She's giving me the cold shoulder and—"

"And that's her choice," Astar cut in. "She told you, in front of everyone, that she does not want to get back together with you."

"Yeah, but—"

"No. There is nothing after 'but' in that sentence. She said no. So there will be no more flirting or attempts at seduction. You will be a friend to Lena and nothing more."

"I am not your subject," Rhy spat out, pacing away from him.

"If you're here, you are. You want to be free? Don't come back. It's that simple, Rhy."

Rhy spun back. "Go write your report. I'll take your message. Now. Tonight."

Astar inclined his head, opening the bedroom door and gesturing for Rhy to precede him. He'd far rather sleep now and write it in the morning, but no sense stalling Rhy's departure, especially with him in such a foul mood.

In the outer room, Stella lay on the rug by the fire, curled up in cat form and sound asleep. Jak sprawled snoring on the hard floor nearby, twin daggers close to each hand, guarding her even in his sleep. No sign of Gen—she'd probably elected to sleep in owl form in the nearby woods. Lena, who'd been sitting at the now-cleared and scrubbed wooden table, dozing with her head on her folded hands, woke with a start. She flinched at the sight of Rhyian, averting her sleepy gaze immediately, and he growled under his breath—both of which reactions only confirmed Astar's decisions.

"Why don't you take the bed with Zephyr, Lena?" he suggested gently. "I need to write up this report."

She nodded, looking grateful, and headed for the darkened bedroom, giving Rhy a wide berth. He started to reach for her, dropping his hand at Astar's quelling look. "I'm leaving for Ordnung tonight," Rhy told her, his tone fraught with enough meaning that Astar wanted to slap him upside the head. The guy simply wouldn't learn.

"Oh," Lena said, rubbing one sleepy eye. "Fair travels,

then."

"I might not be back," he warned her, flicking his gaze at Astar, the defiant glint in his eye making it clear he knew he was skirting Astar's instructions—and that he didn't care.

Astar was opening his mouth to intervene when Lena straightened her spine, looking far more alert as she sparkled with irritation. "No surprise there, Rhyian. We've all learned better than to count on you to commit to anything." With that, she slipped into the bedroom, closing the door behind her.

Rhy looked like he'd been gutted where he stood, and Astar figured that would suffice for the last word. "Give me a few minutes to write this up."

"I'm not an idiot," Rhy hissed. "I can give a complete report. Or am I not even that trustworthy?"

Astar hesitated, preferring to relate the story in his own words—and also aware that was him wanting to retain control. And him not trusting Rhy. "All right," he agreed, sending a mental plea to Moranu that Rhy would come through. Rhy belonged to Her, whether he liked it or not, so it would be helpful if the goddess gave him some guidance.

A bit surprised at Astar's ready capitulation, Rhy paused a moment before heading for the door. "Rhy?" Astar called to him, waiting until Rhy looked over his shoulder warily. "I really hope you come back."

Rhy's lip curled, and he left without another word.

~ 16 ~

A VERY ODD experience, to go from crushing agony and struggling against impending death to feeling singingly alive and better than she had in years. Zeph had never had to be healed by someone else—that truly spectacular wreck had been the first time in her life that she hadn't been able to heal herself—and Zeph figured she owed Stella a huge favor.

Stella, however, had brushed off that suggestion with a gentle smile and seemed none the worse for wear. By the time Zeph woke, the others had cleaned up the cottage where they'd spent the night, pressed some breakfast on her, then herded her onto the road north, away from Gieneke and the area's lingering air of disaster. Astar was all business, in crown prince mode, spurring them all to move on. He wanted to reach Castle Elderhorst as quickly as possible, so he could discuss the disaster with King Groningen in detail, conveying the reassurances of the high throne and whatever else mossback manners demanded.

Though Astar greeted her with a broad smile and inquiries after her health, he treated Zeph with his previous formal distance. Back to cold Willy. So much so, that Zeph wondered if his impassioned promise to let her do anything she wanted to his mouthwatering body for an entire night was something she'd dreamed up in the delirium of near-death. Stories had it that some people saw a bright light when they nearly died. It would just figure that she would hear promises of longed-for sexual favors.

At any rate, after leaving their extra supplies and a bag of coin as a gesture of appreciation for the cottage's occupants—who were hopefully not casualties of the stone giant—the six of them were soon on their way. When she asked where Rhy had gone, everyone exchanged looks from amused to annoyed—and Astar had tersely replied that Rhy went to report to Ordnung.

Clearly there was more to know, but she'd find out.

Though Zeph felt fine, she'd been instructed not to shapeshift yet, and instead conserve her energy by riding double with Lena on Gen, who'd showed off by taking the form of a massive white draft horse, easily strong enough to carry both of them all day. Most shapeshifters were happy to acquire one kind of a particular animal, but not Gen. No, she probably had tried every breed of horse possible. Jak rode Stella, a much more delicate bay mare, while Astar ambled along at point in grizzly-bear form.

Zeph had defied Astar's order just long enough to momentarily shift away and back, so she could be wearing her fighting leathers and her golden-furred cloak. He gave her a narrow look, but didn't comment. Lena made a good riding companion. As a librarian's daughter, and a serious student herself, Lena had a rare gift for accurate storytelling. She related everything that had happened the day before, and Zeph repaid the favor by filling in her own details.

Checking that Astar was far enough ahead not to hear, Zeph moved Lena's long hair to the side and propped her chin on her friend's shoulder, mouth close to her ear. Gen would hear, but maybe not Jak or Stella. He seemed to be relating a long story to Stella anyway, and she listened, one ear swiveled back in interest. "So," Zeph said quietly, "was I delirious, or did Astar promise me a night of wild debauchery?"

Gen snorted and stomped a hoof, while Lena shook with silent laughter. "I'm only amazed that this isn't the first thing you asked me."

"I have a modicum of self-control," Zeph replied, casting a glance to be sure Jak was keeping Stella occupied. Stella might not be against Zeph's interest in her twin, but she also might not enjoy picturing him doing the nasty things with Zeph that she had fantasized. "And discretion—though I'm guessing it actually *was* real and everyone knows?"

"True and true," Lena replied cheerfully. Gen's hide twitched, and she flicked her tail in irritation. "Gen will want me to tell you that the promise was made under duress—out of fear for your life—and though we all know Willy will honor his vow, that you should do the gracious thing and release him from it."

Gen snorted and bobbed her head vigorously.

"What do you think?" Zeph asked.

"I think I am the *last* person to give anyone romantic advice," Lena replied bitterly. "I'm abiding by Willy's Moratorium and considering a full-out vow of celibacy. Some priestesses of Danu take them."

"Are you going to become an acolyte?" Zeph couldn't quite see it.

"I've made worse decisions."

"If you take Astar up on the Night of Debauchery," Jak said, breaking in with a knowing grin, revealing that he had his spy mother's skill of talking and eavesdropping simultaneously, "it is technically a violation of Willy's Moratorium. You jeopardize the harmony of the group at your peril."

Except neither she nor Astar was bound by that vow. Had he realized that—or was he even now struggling with his conscience? Strike that—of course he was struggling with his conscience, as that was practically Astar's favorite hobby.

The real question was, would she release him from the vow? On the one hand, he had made it under duress, out of fear for her life, and it didn't get more honorable than that. On the other, she had zero qualms about taking him up on the offer. And not just for herself either, though getting her hands—along with the rest of her body—on him would be the culmination of everything she'd wanted for years. She also firmly believed it would be good for him. He wanted her as badly as she wanted him. That had been abundantly clear in that interaction in the giant's skull. Astar did want her enough and, arguably, he was looking for a reason to compromise his principles.

Who was she kidding? There wasn't even a decision. She was going to ravish him to unconsciousness.

"I never agreed to Willy's Moratorium," she announced. "For that matter, neither did Astar, if you think back."

Lena stiffened, making a small noise in her throat. "You're

right. You asked about romantic entanglements outside the group and everyone got distracted." She glanced over her shoulder. "I have newfound respect for your wily gríobhth mind."

Zeph preened, feathers glossily shining in her wily mind.

"If Rhy returns," Lena continued, "it will be interesting to hear how he takes that news."

"If?" This was the gossip Zeph wanted, the other reason she hadn't minded riding with Lena. "So he didn't just take the report to Ordnung?"

"He did," Lena allowed. "But Astar also told him that he was sending Rhy away to give him an out, that if he couldn't control himself and stop trying to seduce me—or tease me to death—then he could just not come back."

Wow. Good for Astar. "He said that in front of everyone?"

"No," Jak put in. "We eavesdropped at the door while they had it out. You were in the room for the whole thing, but asleep."

Dang. That was another downside of nearly killing yourself—you missed all the titillating stuff while you were passed out in healing sleep. Surely that conversation was buried in her subconscious somewhere. She'd love to dig that out—though she also felt bad for Rhy. He had superbly terrible judgment at times. "What did Rhy do to set this off?" she asked on a sigh.

Gen pricked her ears, and even Stella sidled closer, Jak looking interested. Aha, so this story wasn't known yet. Zeph hadn't missed *everything*.

"You can all stuff your curiosity," Lena said tightly, "because I am not discussing it."

Zeph squeezed Lena's waist. "All right. Don't get mad. Please don't go become a celibate Priestess of Danu. You hate sparring."

Lena choked out a laugh and sagged back against Zeph. "True. I just..." She sighed heavily. "It's so much easier now that he's gone, and I hate that it's true."

Zeph agreed. She also figured Rhy wouldn't be able to stay away for long.

THEY SPENT THAT night at an inn perched on the banks of the Grace River, which was fully frozen in that region. Astar arranged for rooms and set it up so that he and Jak shared and the four girls a much larger one. All too worn out for much, they ate and crashed, rising groggily in the gloom of another late sunrise and a snowy final leg to Castle Elderhorst.

They arrived at the castle a couple of hours after full dark, which fell early that time of year and even just that little bit farther north, so it was only late afternoon. By Zeph's count, it had been daylight for barely six hours, something even Lena griped about. So it was good to see the end of traveling in the nonstop blizzard.

An ancient edifice, Castle Elderhorst looked like it had grown out of the granite hills surrounding it, rambling with additional wings, courts, and the occasional tower. Snow covered the gray stones, and warm lights glowed from the walls and battlements. It should've looked haphazard and graceless, but Zeph found herself liking it far better than

Ordnung.

Of course, Ordnung was barely more than fifty years old, and had been built as a monument to a tyrant's ego. Ordnung's white towers were striking, and perfectly aesthetic, but always somehow cold and arrogant to Zeph's mind. One of the many reasons she didn't much like being in Ordnung.

In contrast, Elderhorst reminded her of a kindly grandmother, skin no longer pure and smooth, some ungainly folds and more than a few wrinkles, but someone who'd weathered all kinds of trials and could still win a game of I Eat You handily. It also looked warm, and she was more than eager to get out of the wind, even if it meant walls. Humans weren't naturally equipped for winter weather. She would have switched to a furred form for the day's journey, if not for solidarity with Lena and Jak.

They stopped short of the actual approach, so the shapeshifters could return to human form and change clothes, in Astar's case, then continued on foot, ready to take up their cover story. Upon hearing who they were—who Astar was, really—the gate guards almost immediately produced King Groningen's seneschal, who greeted them with lavish manners. He said that court had adjourned for the day, but that the king would receive His Highness Crown Prince Astar immediately in his private study.

Though they all teased Willy about being Ursula's heir, times like this reminded Zeph of the rank—and respect—that he truly held among the mossbacks. Karyn was right that the Tala tended toward irreverence, truly honoring only King Rayfe and Queen Andromeda, and then not with much pomp or circumstance. So, Zeph tended to forget the burden of Astar's role in life. But seeing him gravely receive the bows and honorifics, standing so tall and handsome, Zeph was sharply reminded that Astar lived in a very different world. One she truly didn't belong to.

Gen, who spent far more time in the mossback world, visiting with her father's family in the house Zynda and Marskal kept on a lake on their land, never forgot the role Astar played in the Thirteen Kingdoms. And sure enough, Gen was sliding Zeph a look to see if she was paying attention to how the seneschal conferred with Astar. Gen's determination to protect Astar from Zeph would be more irritating if Zeph didn't understand her reasons.

"I know you all are tired," Astar said, returning to the group, "so I'll meet with the king alone. I've asked the seneschal to take you all to your rooms, where you'll get hot baths and a warm supper."

"Thank you, thank you, thank you," Lena said fervently. "Those of us who can't shapeshift clean are forever in your debt."

"Also, I bet the steaks won't be burnt," Jak quipped, and Gen elbowed him.

"Wait," Lena said, halting the incipient charge for baths and food. "Willy shouldn't have to deliver the bad news to Groningen alone. I'll go with you." She looked down at her bedraggled self. "Though I'm not exactly presentation-ready."

"Neither am I," Astar told her with a smile. "Nothing wrong with being a little travel-worn." He didn't look mussed to Zeph's eye—of course, he always looked good to her—but he could at least shapeshift back as a clean human with orderly hair. His clothes were wrinkled from being crammed in the saddlebags, though. "That said, it's kind of you to offer, but this is my responsibility."

"I can go with Willy," Stella said. "I'm not that tired."

"You're gray with exhaustion," Jak corrected, nothing playful in him now. "You aren't recovered yet from all the sorcery and healing, plus carting my heavy ass all day."

"You're not that heavy," she countered, "and—"

"Nilly," Astar broke in, "Jak is right. You need rest."

"So do you," she shot back with a concerned frown.

"I'm fine," he soothed her, standing straight and smiling broadly. The shadows of weariness clung to him, though. "This shouldn't take long, then I won't be far behind you all."

"You forget that we've met Groningen," Lena inserted. "He may be ancient, but he can still drink anyone under the table. He'll expect you to keep up with him, go over the report at least three times, and strategize a response, rebuild, and how to prevent recurrences."

Stella nodded. "Lena is right. He'll keep you up all night if you let him, and we know you—you won't extract yourself. You need at least one of us to help wrangle the king."

"I'll go with Astar," Zeph said impulsively, not at all flattered when they gaped at her in very real surprise.

"You do realize it's not *that* kind of up-all-night with Astar, don't you?" Gen asked.

Zeph ignored that snide remark, though it was fair enough. The last time she'd volunteered to go to a meeting with Astar, when the high queen had first summoned them for this quest, her intentions had been far from pure. "I had a long, healing sleep thanks to Nilly, and have been lazily riding for two days thanks to Gen." She quickly shapeshifted away and back again, wearing a formal gown, her hair up in mossback-lady coils. "I can do this."

"I so wish I could do *that*," Lena murmured enviously.

"It's not the same as having an actual bath," Zeph reassured her, then turned to Astar. "I can help."

"But can you be diplomatic?" Gen muttered.

"I can keep my mouth shut," Zeph replied sweetly, "which is more than I can say for some people."

"All right," Jak said, taking Gen by the shoulders and steering her toward Stella and Lena. "All cranky people are going to their rooms."

"I'm not cranky," Gen complained in a decidedly cranky tone as they followed the patient seneschal. "I'm just concerned that—" Her voice cut off abruptly, either by a door closing or some other means.

Zeph turned back to Astar with a bright smile. "I think Gen is concerned that I'll seduce you and the king into a kinky three-way, but Groningen's probably too old to take on more than one at a time, hmm?"

Astar laughed and offered his arm, patting her hand when she slipped it through the crook of his elbow. "If anyone could seduce him into it, it's you." He gave her hand one more squeeze before letting it go, as they followed another page through the long and rambling hallways. "I know you hate walls and talking, so thank you for coming with me."

"Thank you for saving my life," she replied with a saucy

flutter of her lashes.

He didn't respond in kind. "You saved mine first."

"Are we keeping score?"

Shaking his head, he slanted her a warm smile. "I can't help it. It's an honor thing—and you know I would've died up there in that giant's skull if you hadn't insisted on carrying me out."

"Yes, well, you shouldn't have come in there after me." Remembering the chill of horror at seeing him, along with the thrill that he'd come to save her... She still wasn't sure which was stronger. Maybe both could be equally true at the same time. "You really need a form with wings."

He sighed. "I've thought about what you said, but I think I have to reconcile myself to the reality that I'm going to be one of those shapeshifters who only ever has First Form."

"Not true," she countered. "You had more forms as a small child. That means the ability is in you."

"Your dad, of course, says the same thing—but Zyr has also officially given up on trying to teach me."

"Again, not true. What were his exact words to you?" She knew already, but she wanted Astar to say them. Zyr had trained thousands of shapeshifters—including Zynda when she thought she'd lost the ability forever—and he had a favorite maxim for the one group that always fell into this category.

"That he can't teach what I don't want to learn," Astar answered, his smile weary. "I know, I know."

The page stopped at a small salon with a lovely fireplace blazing with heat. "Your Highness Crown Prince Astar, Lady Zephyr—His Highness King Groningen will be with you momentarily. Please make yourselves comfortable."

Zeph beelined to the fire, standing as close as she could without igniting her fancy skirts. "I like Castle Elderhorst. Suddenly I'm a lady!"

Astar laughed, bringing her a copper goblet of hearty red wine. It was warm and redolent of spices like those that scented the air at Ordnung for the Feast of Moranu. Tasting it gingerly—*should* wine smell like pinecones and bark?—she moaned at the delicious flavor and drained the goblet. It hit her empty stomach like sunshine, and she immediately went to find the source for a refill.

"More?" she asked Astar.

He shook his head. "I'll sip this one, so I can keep my wits sharp. Wine on an empty stomach is a recipe for trouble with me."

"Yes," she said, rejoining him by the fire. "I'm so hungry I could eat a bear."

Choking a little, Astar actually blushed. She couldn't wait to show him things far more blushworthy than that mild comment. "We, ah, haven't talked," he said, staring intently into the fire, "about the promise I made you."

Was he going to ask to be released from the vow? And, if he did, would she grant the request? *Probably.* Though the prospect filled her with bitter disappointment—an abrupt wave of it that nearly crushed the breath from her—she didn't want him unwilling. She'd had enough of Astar's noble sacrifices. Especially if bedding her became one of them. "It doesn't violate Willy's Moratorium," she said in a sadly desperate bid to take at least *that* ethical quandary off his mind.

"I know." He raised a brow at her consternation. "I could

hear everything you all were saying. Grizzlies aren't deaf." He tapped her on the nose, a gesture that made her want to smile and weep simultaneously at the simple, sincere affection. "Clever girl," he added, his gaze admiring. "I never had a chance of eluding you, did I?"

Her heart, which seemed to be behaving in an absurdly silly manner, leapt with hope. "You're not going to ask me to release you from the promise?"

He frowned. "Never. Asking to be released from a vow is nearly as bad as breaking one."

She would never be able to keep track of all these rules. Something occurred to her, maybe Gen's unwelcome voice in the back of her mind. "Would it be honorable thing for me to do if I released you from the promise without you requesting it?" she asked hesitantly, while part of herself jumped up and down, screaming with rage, wanting to know what in Moranu she was doing. "Because of duress," she added, when he gave her a quizzical look.

Something about that made his summer-sky eyes dance with amusement, but he otherwise regarded her seriously. "Have *you* changed your mind?"

"Never," she replied, exactly the way he'd said it to her— except her reasons were entirely about going after what she wanted, while his were about putting honor ahead of his own desires. "But I don't want to force you into anything."

He smiled then, though it had a wistful slant, and he trailed a finger over the curve of her cheek. "I made the offer of my own free will."

"Because you were afraid for me."

"Because you matter to me."

Tracing the edge of her jaw, he seemed fascinated, desire heating in his eyes. Hot Astar now. His thumb brushed over her lower lip, and only severe self-restraint—well, and not wanting to scare him off—kept her from sucking it into her mouth. "I should be honest with you, Zephyr," he said, very quietly, and her silly, jumping heart clenched with trepidation. He leaned in closer, his thumb tugging on her lip gently, his gaze focused there as if he meant to kiss her. "I'm relieved to have an excuse to discard my better judgment."

He lowered his mouth. His breath, warm and wine-scented, wafted over her skin…

A door flew open, sending the pair of them flying apart. She nearly shifted into a bird, she was so startled.

"Prince Willy, my boy!" King Groningen boomed out. "Up to your usual shenanigans, I see. *And* you brought me a beautiful Tala woman." Though he carried a cane, the broad-chested man with a massively bushy white beard strode toward her with no apparent impairment. Picking up her hand, he bowed over it, then peered at her cannily. "You're not Nilly."

"No, indeed," she replied, immediately charmed. "I'm Zephyr."

He narrowed his eyes, studying her face. "Daughter of Zyr and Karyn, if I don't miss my mark." He grinned at her surprise. "You have your father's eyes and blue-black hair, and your lovely mother's complexion and bone structure." Then he winked. "And your wily father's tricksy nature, no doubt."

Absurdly, she flushed with pleasure. "I'm surprised you

know my parents."

"Oh, we've encountered one another a few times over the years."

"My sympathies," she offered very seriously.

He boomed out a laugh. "Gorgeous *and* clever. I approve, Willy boy. Excellent choice, for a *mistress*." He added that last with a peculiar emphasis.

Astar opened his mouth, and Zeph anticipated with some mischievous amusement what excuse he might offer for their near-kiss, which Groningen had clearly witnessed. But Astar only inclined his head and put his hand on the small of Zeph's back. "Zephyr is an amazing woman," he said.

Zeph couldn't have been more surprised. In fact, she lost track of the conversation until she was being gently but firmly ushered into Groningen's inner study. Astar pressed her still-full wine goblet into her hand. "You look like you need this," he whispered, lips brushing her ear with a tantalizing caress.

As she certainly did, she drained the cup—and wondered when Astar had taken the reins.

~ 17 ~

T RUE TO LENA'S prediction, King Groningen kept them there until well into the night—and asked to hear the particulars of what happened several times, including from Zeph's perspective. She hadn't expected he'd grill her so thoroughly, nor that he'd ask such penetrating questions. Groningen extracted salient details from her that she hadn't realized she'd noticed at the time. He also didn't buy into Astar's glib explanation about the freak lunar eclipse being caused by an unusually dense storm cloud, but he noted it down and didn't press further.

Fortunately—after he'd discovered they hadn't eaten since morning—he also sent for food for all of them. Eating gave Astar a second wind, but after several more hours of discussion, he was flagging. So much so that Zeph was thinking up excuses to end the meeting, or at least postpone until morning, when the sharp-eyed king noticed and relented. "Bah! I'm four times your age and outlasting you, Willy boy. What is the world coming to?"

"I don't think it's quite four times," Astar replied wryly, spoiling it by having to stifle a yawn.

"He also battled a stone giant and saved my life, twice,"

Zeph added, then cocked her head, tapping her chin in thought. "Or three times, depending on how you divide it up. Anyway, Astar is a hero and has probably earned his bed for the night."

Groningen glared at her fiercely, bushy brows lowered. Then he abruptly slapped the table, laughing in that booming way of his. "I like her," he informed Astar. "I bet she has some sharp claws, too. If I were a younger man... Ah, well." He heaved his considerable bulk up from the chair, reaching to tug on a braided silk rope. "I'll have someone show you to your rooms. We can go over this in the morning. I'll want to hear the tale again from everyone, along with their perspectives on what Queen Andromeda saw with this rift." When the same page returned to guide them, Groningen issued a set of rapid-fire orders, including summoning half a dozen people to attend him.

Astar and Zeph followed the page out and were handed off to another, who led them back through hallways as twisty within as Elderhorst looked from without. "Apparently King Groningen isn't done discussing the problem," Zeph observed to Astar.

He smiled wearily. "I'm just relieved he let us go for now. I don't know where the man gets his energy."

"How old is he anyway?"

"I don't think anyone knows exactly. He was already king of Carienne when late High King Uorsin was an upstart troublemaking sailor from Elcinea."

Zeph did the mental math, figuring Ursula's age against her father's likely age when she was born—and came up with a figure that *could* put Groningen at close to four times Astar's age. Tala tended to be long-lived—shapeshifting made for an excellent rejuvenator of aging flesh—but Groningen seemed impressively vital for a mossback. Maybe he had some Tala blood in him from way back. Many mossback families did, from the days before Annfwn sealed itself off.

"You did well in there," Astar offered with a smile. "I was glad to have you with me—you remembered things I forgot or didn't notice."

She preened under the praise, though the prickly side of her nature registered the hint of surprise in his voice. "I'm not that flighty," she replied, remembering Gen's jibe about keeping her mouth shut. "And I can be discreet if I choose—I just don't see the point most of the time."

"I know," Astar said soothingly, taking her hand. "Don't get your feathers ruffled."

If she'd been in gríobhth form, she would've clacked her beak at him. As it was, she settled for sniffing haughtily.

"Your Highness Crown Prince Astar, Lady Zephyr," the page said, giving no sign that she'd heard any of the conversation, "your rooms. There are hot baths waiting, wine, and cold snacks to hold you until morning. However, if you need anything else, I can arrange for that."

Astar lifted a brow at Zeph as he gestured for her to precede him through the double doors the page opened, and she shook her head. "No, thank you," Astar told the page. "We'll be fine till then."

"Will you be needing a lady's maid, Lady Zephyr?" the page inquired.

"Moranu, no!" Zeph replied, a bit too forcefully—partly because she'd just registered that she and Astar would apparently be sharing a room. And the one bed. Praise the goddess. She hoped, anyway, as she and Astar hadn't quite finished the conversation by the fire. A sneaky and most unfamiliar feeling kept prodding at her that she should release Astar from that vow. While another and far more familiar voice tried to shout it down. Why shouldn't they enjoy each other?

Because it will tear him apart and you know it, the annoying voice replied.

Shush, she told it. *He'll enjoy being with me and I know* that. *He'll be better for sowing some oats before they lock him up to play stud for the high throne.*

Astar isn't the kind to bed a woman lightly. If you do this, it will change everything for him. Are you willing to take responsibility for that?

Look, voice, she replied, *I don't know where you came from, but you are not welcome in my head.*

I've always been here. You just don't ever listen.

"Zephyr?" Astar said her name in a tone that indicated it wasn't the first time.

She realized she'd been staring at the one—albeit quite large and enticing—bed while she argued with the annoying voice in her head. Wonderful. Now she was losing her mind. She pasted on a bright smile. "So," she said as neutrally as possible, "they put us in the same room?"

Astar nodded slowly, watching her with a hooded expression. "You heard Groningen—he assumes we're a couple, given that scene he witnessed," he added, flushing lightly. "I am sorry he called you my mistress, and that I didn't say anything. I didn't want to correct him."

Ah, dear Moranu, how this man delighted her. She prowled up to him, sliding her hands over the velvety material of his jacket, and began unbuttoning it. "Is being a mistress a bad thing?"

"No," he answered uneasily, "but I don't want to shame you in any way."

"I can't be shamed," she reminded him, opening his jacket to splay her hands over his shirt-clad chest, his heart pounding beneath as he gazed down at her, cold and hot at once, wariness and anticipation crowding each other in his pretty eyes. "I have no obligation to live up to any sort of prudish mossback standards."

He winced, but settled his hands on her hips. "Allow me to rephrase. I wouldn't want anyone to think I hold you in anything less than the highest esteem. Groningen thinks you're mine, so I'll treat you as I would if you truly were."

There went her heart, leaping about in a giddy dance. "So, are we doing this?" she asked, feeling unduly cautious. The conscience-voice wrested control of her mouth right then. "I will release you from your vow, if you wish." *Stupid voice.*

"Don't," he replied, voice rough, hands tightening on her waist. "Please don't."

Her lips curved in sensual triumph. As she'd thought— Astar wanted an excuse to break his own rules, an out that would let them have each other, if only for a little while. She would be forever his first lover, and the possessive gríobhth in her took fierce delight in that. No matter who Astar eventually chained himself to, he would never forget her. She dug her nails into his chest, growing them just a little longer so he'd feel the light prick of them.

"I have a complaint to register, however," she purred.

"I may not be experienced in this," he offered with a half-smile, "but even I know I can't have failed to please you at this stage."

She laughed, utterly enchanted by his artless honesty and sincerity. "The night is half gone," she pointed out. "If I only get one night, then I want my full allotment."

"We'll be here several nights at least," he said, one hand sliding up to pluck a pin from her elaborately styled hair, dropping it on the floor where it made no sound on the plush rug. Nevertheless, it sent an arousing *ping* through her blood. "Unless you ask to be moved, we'll be sharing this room—and bed—all that time. What if," he asked in a measured tone, "we agree to extend the bargain to the entire time we're here at Elderhorst?"

"I would be amenable to an extension," she breathed, hardly able to believe her luck.

It's because he's lost his moral compass, the voice suggested. *He was determined to save himself for marriage, and that was a clear line he knew not to cross. Now that he's crossing it, where is the next line? Maybe there isn't one…*

"Excellent news," Astar said, his smile warm. He reached to pluck out another pin, hesitated. "May I take your hair down?"

"Of course—though it would be faster for me to shift."

"I'd like to do it the slow way, if it's all right."

"I said yes already," she replied.

"Just being sure." His fingers deftly searched for the pins in her hair, meticulously extracting them one by one. "These look just like the pins the Ordnung ladies use," he commented. "It's amazing to me that you can just... conjure them."

"I don't. Not really. These pins *are* from Ordnung. I gathered various supplies I thought I'd need to play noble mossback lady on this trip. My mother found several gowns for me, and I had a maid put up my hair in a few different styles, then I shapeshifted and cached them all for future use."

"You're amazing. I can't do anything like that."

"You could. It just takes practice."

His gaze focused on her hair, he caressed each long coil as he freed it. "That's why you were late meeting us. I'm sorry I assumed you were being irresponsible."

"To be fair, I did stay up all night flying, which also made me late meeting my mother. If it makes you feel better, she explained my irresponsibility at great length."

"It doesn't make me feel better, and I know Karyn holds you to high standards. I think I haven't always been fair to you," he replied cryptically, kissed her forehead, then frowned. "Is this all right?"

"Astar, darling," she said on a sigh, "you have blanket permission to do anything you like to me. That means you may simply take instead of asking."

He nodded—but still with that vague frown. "I don't know if I know how to do that. It's not how I operate normally."

His famous self-restraint. No, Astar would never take anything for himself. The quality would make him a good king, and they all loved him for it. She supposed changing his normal rules of behavior was all part of debauching him. Still, she didn't want him fretting. Nimbly undoing the laces of his quite-wrinkled shirt, she glanced up at his intent expression. "If you do anything I don't like, I'll tell you. And you do the same," she offered.

It was the right thing to say, because he relaxed under her hands, glancing down at her as he combed his fingers into her hair, the mass of it falling heavy down her back. "I've wanted to do this," he murmured, "for as long as I can remember. You're so beautiful, Zephyr. Sometimes I thought my hands would burst into flame from wanting to touch you."

Parting the cloth of his shirt, she spread her hands over his broad chest, savoring the crisp hairs gilding his impressive musculature. Pressing a kiss over his heart, she smiled against his skin, inhaling him. *Mine*, the gríobhth in her hissed. *Only for now*, she reminded herself, though she wasn't sure if anyone was listening. Tipping her head back, she gazed up at Astar's beautiful face. "I've wanted this for as long as I can remember, too."

"I know you don't want me to ask," he replied in a hushed voice, summer-sky eyes lingering on her lips, "but you'll have to guide me. I've never kissed a woman before."

"Lips to lips," she breathed, holding perfectly still, as if any careless movement on her part might shatter the moment. She'd wanted this for so long that it seemed nearly impossible that it would actually happen. Surely something would intervene, cruelly extending her longing into something eternally unrequited.

Astar's gorgeously formed lips curved in a slight smile. "Lips to lips," he echoed. Cupping her head in his hands, he lowered his mouth to hers. She held her breath. His breath wafted warm and fragrant over her parted lips.

And he kissed her.

That first contact, his mouth to hers, felt like lightning forking through the sky as she flew through a thunderstorm, an exhilarating reminder of her own mortality. It shot through her with all the potency of an enchantment released, tearing a moan from her. One Astar echoed, the sound thrumming through her as he gathered her close against him. He tasted her mouth again, a brush of his lips, as if testing their texture. She tilted her head slightly to improve the fit, showing him wordlessly how to move their lips together, an enticing caress that spoke of more intimate caresses to come.

He proved an eager student, deepening the kiss on his own with increasing fervor. With the first touch of their tongues, he growled, the rumbling thunder thrilling her, and she found herself clinging to him. Sliding her hands up to his muscled shoulders, she dug her nails into him as he slid one hand to the small of her back, arching her against him and cupping her head as if her mouth were a goblet of wine he drank from. For the first time in her fierce life, she felt fragile, vulnerable even. And paradoxically safe and protected. Some small part of her was frightened by the rush of such foreign feelings, but that edge of uncertainty only added to the excitement of the moment. Astar supported her entire weight, as if he'd never let her fall, and she reveled in being held by him.

He drew away reluctantly, showering her lips with small

kisses, both of them breathing heavily as he searched her face. "Lips to lips," he whispered. "So simple and yet..."

"And yet," she agreed with a smile. Her entire body pulsed with need, throbbing for more. "What next?" she asked, feeling oddly tender toward him. In her fantasies, she'd imagined herself in control, ravishing him and taking him by storm. In the moment, however, she only wanted to coax him along, let him dissolve the walls he'd placed between them at his own pace.

His mouth quirked in a puzzled smile. "Don't *you* know?"

She had to laugh, framing his beloved face in her hands and pressing a lingering kiss to his mouth. "Yes, I know. I'm asking what *you* want."

"I... I want everything at once, and I also want to draw this out, savor crossing each threshold." He frowned self-consciously. "Does that sound ridiculous?"

"Not at all." She kissed him again, gliding her fingers through his silky hair. "I feel the same. And we have the time to go slowly."

"I also need a bath," he admitted.

"I can help with that," she purred, lightly scratching the back of his neck, so he shivered, hands vising on her.

"An offer I can't refuse," he replied, then swept her up into his arms, carrying her into the next room where a large tub sat before another cheerful fire.

"I hope the water is still hot for you," she noted ruefully.

"There's more. Elderhorst is built over a hot spring, keeps the place warm, and there's enough pressure that it rises up and fills the pipes." He grinned at her consternation. "You really weren't listening when the page explained everything."

"I was thinking," she retorted loftily.

"Yes, I know you well enough to have guessed what you were thinking about." He set her on her feet, letting her body slide against his. "You don't have to worry about corrupting me, Zephyr. I want this, too." Then he hesitated, his hands stilling. "I want to apologize, for my words back at Ordnung. I know I hurt you and—"

She laid a finger over his lips. "It's in the past. This is now and it's good. You can make it up to me by getting naked."

Smiling, he shrugged out of his jacket and shirt at once, shaking his golden hair back, and she nearly salivated at the sight. Noticing her stare, he smiled shyly, then gestured at her. "I'd like to undress you. The slow way."

In mute reply, she scooped her long fall of hair to the side and turned her back, where the elaborate mossback gown had many fastenings. When she'd refused the page's offer of a lady's maid, she'd intended to simply shapeshift the dress into storage again. Once she'd been dressed in it, she could simply return to human form wearing it. That was about the only way she'd have patience with the ridiculous and infuriating styles women of court favored.

But, as Astar started at the nape of the gown, slowly parting the velvet and caressing her skin as he bared it, her whole body sighed with sensual delight at the deliciously slow build of anticipation. Especially when he followed the light caresses of his callused fingertips with the hot brush of his mouth. He slid kisses down her spine, the gown loosening and sagging away from her. Reaching her hips, he paused, tracing the dimples at the top of her buttocks, pressing a long, lingering kiss exactly at the sensitive small of her back.

~ 18 ~

Skin hot as sunshine under his lips, Zephyr trembled as if the breeze she was named for had shivered through the room, though the bathing chamber was tightly built, none of the winter winds making it into the sweetly humid warmth. Moving under his hands, she slid the rest of the exquisite gown off her arms, letting it fall to the floor—and baring her long, lovely body to his gaze.

The sight about knocked his heart out of his chest. He'd heard other men talk about women's asses, their various shapes and which they favored, but his own experience had been limited to accidental glimpses he'd done his best to forget, as he wasn't supposed to have seen them in the first place.

Zephyr's body, of course, was as breathtakingly gorgeous as her face—and all his, at least for now—and he could fill his memory with every aspect of her. He'd been an idiot to resist her offers for so long when he could've been storing up images and sensations to last him the rest of his life.

He framed her bottom in his hands, shaping the fullness, beguiled by the dimples on either side, the sweetly enticing curves. He'd never felt much inclination to worship any of the goddesses—beyond Danu's governance of the high throne—but kneeling there on the floor, he wanted to offer a prayer of gratitude to Zephyr, his personal goddess. Trickster and siren, friend and lover. The innocent boy in him wanted to shower her pristine skin with kisses, the bear wanting to bite. Clearing his throat, he wrestled back that voracious—and surely inappropriate—desire.

Zephyr moved a little, and he realized she was looking over her shoulder at him, eyes sapphire dark, expression gravely musing until she smiled slightly—and he realized Zephyr would never judge him for any of his darker impulses. Not only had she offered herself freely, she'd given him the freedom to do as he liked. She must be the only person in his life who didn't expect him to conform to some standard of behavior. Even Nilly expected him to be good and kind and honorable.

With Zephyr, he could be and do anything—and she would still feel the same about him. Holding her gaze, he licked the taut globe of her ass, watching her eyes darken further, savoring the tremor of her flesh—then sank his teeth in.

She gasped, arching in his grip, but didn't pull away. The scent of her arousal flooded his senses, and he knew she not only allowed it, she loved it. "My, my," she murmured hoarsely, "look who's awaking from hibernation."

He felt like it, too, like he'd been asleep for years, decades or longer, and at last he'd woken from the drugging, chilly depths. His blood ran hot and vital, his hunger fierce.

"Turn around," he told her, not caring that he growled the

order.

Her eyes widened, flushed and plump lips parting. Turning in his grip, she kicked away the puddle of the gown, standing before him naked except for knitted wool stockings tied over her knees and the little pointed ankle boots currently in fashion at court. His mouth went dry, his tongue thick as he slowly raised his gaze from there.

Her hair fell like a black cloak framing her deliciously delicate figure. Glossy black curls nestled at the juncture of her long, slim thighs, hips curving to nip in at her slender waist. Her full breasts as round as her ass, tipped with tightly pointed nipples the same shade as her deep-red lips. A seductive smile played on her lips, her eyes a new shade of sapphire. Before this, he'd have said he'd seen Zephyr in all her moods, that he knew them as well as his own.

But this Zephyr was a woman he'd never glimpsed before—and he'd been poorer for it.

"You are indescribably beautiful," he told her. "I wish I could tell you what I see."

"Sometimes words are unnecessary, my bear," she murmured, threading her fingers into his hair, her touch cool and arousing. "Your eyes tell me everything."

Turning his face into her palm, he kissed it, momentarily overcome by an avalanche of emotions he couldn't name. "What next?" he asked with a smile, deliberately echoing her words.

She arched a brow. "You seem to have plenty of ideas so far."

"I want to touch you, to taste you, but I'm afraid I'll spend in my pants," he admitted. Frankly, he was surprised he hadn't already, the way his swollen cock throbbed in the tight confines. Probably if he'd done this years ago when the other boys were experimenting—and relating their hilarious failures—he wouldn't feel so awkward now.

"That's easily taken care of," Zephyr answered, tugging him to his feet, nimble fingers going to his belt.

He grabbed her hands, stopping her. "What are you doing?"

She looked up through her lush, curling lashes, a sardonic lift to her mouth. "Astar, love, I know you can't be *that* innocent."

He flushed, though out of embarrassment or sheer need, he couldn't say. "I just... I, ah, haven't bathed yet."

"You smell like yourself. I don't care about such things."

"Yes, but..." He gripped her hands in place, not sure what to say.

"Do you not want this?" she asked, hands still under his.

He'd never wanted anything more in his entire life. In fact, that was what scared him, how badly he wanted this, her, what she would do to him... And he was terrified of making a mistake, of losing her good opinion.

Somehow, she read it in him. "There's no wrong way to do this, as long as we're both willing. Forget your rules and however you think you might be judged or found wanting. I want to please you. That's all this is."

"Zephyr..." he said, her name a prayer and a promise, all the things he didn't dare tell her.

She smiled, affection and understanding in it. "I know."

He released her hands, and she made quick work of his pants, pulling the tight material down his thighs. The sensation of his cock springing out—and engorging even more with the freedom—made him momentarily dizzy, and he groped for the high side of the tub. Revealing weakness was better than actually falling over. A moment later, he forgot even that chagrin, only grateful for the support as Zephyr's long and clever fingers wrapped around his shaft. It took all the control he had not to spend right then. As it was, every muscle in his body clenched, and his eyes rolled back in his head with the sheer intensity.

"I've wanted to get my hands on this for a long time," Zephyr purred, "and you exceed even my high expectations." She glanced up at him, one hand circling the base of his cock in a firm grip, the other stroking up in a long, slow caress.

He choked out some inarticulate, completely unsexy garble, his body shaking as he gripped the edge of the tub. "Please..." he managed to get out.

"Yes, love. Let go. I've got you."

She stroked once more and released her lower grip—and he came like a wave breaking. His whole body convulsed, contracting in an arc as his seed shot from him and into Zephyr's hands and, oh sweet Moranu, onto her full breasts. With a darkly delighted smile, she milked him with her hands, prolonging the climax until nearly the point of pain—and right when he thought he wouldn't be able to withstand any more, her touch gentled, going soothing, hands sliding away from his cock to run over his bare chest.

Slithering up against him, despite the sticky mess—or

maybe because of it—she nestled into him, lifting her mouth for a kiss. He obliged—no, he took what she offered like a taste of food offered a starving man—his arms coming around her as he kissed her deeply, drinking her in and needing more. In the back of his mind, he thought he must be crushing her, perhaps bruising her mouth in his desperation to inhale her very essence. High mountain air and tropical flowers, ferocity and delicacy, hot flesh and sweet salvation.

At last he was able to make himself let her go, but she didn't tear away. Instead she smiled and reached up to trail her fingers over his cheek. "Better now?" she asked softly.

"Sorry," he said, heaving out a breath and forcing himself to gentle his grip.

She looked surprised. "For what part?" She wriggled against him. His cock, which hadn't entirely softened, at more than half-mast and stirring again. "The first one is to take the edge off, and you, my darling bear, have a *lot* of edge to take off at this point."

Was he blushing? Fuck it, he didn't care if he was. "I meant, I'm sorry if I hurt you." He pressed a thumb to her lower lip, swollen from his kisses. "You're so... soft and slender."

"Silly bear," she replied, laughter in her voice. "Shapeshifter, remember? You'd have to do a lot more than that to actually hurt me—at least in a way I don't enjoy," she added in a darkly sensual murmur.

"You mean, like plummet out of the sky and hit ground with a massive weight on your back?" he asked pointedly.

She made a face, releasing him and ticking off the points

her fingers. "It was a *controlled glide*, thank you very much, I hit water not ground, and you're a deliciously big man, but I wouldn't call you massive. Where is this hot water I didn't hear about because I was too busy thinking about tying you to that big four-poster bed?"

"I'll get it," he said, face hot, cock stiffening further—and resigning himself to being in that state pretty much perpetually if he was going to be keeping company with the luscious and mischievous Zephyr. Realizing that his pants were still around his ankles and he'd look like an idiot shuffling to the hot-water tap the page had shown him, he perched his butt against the tub rim, toeing off his boots and finally shedding the rest of his pants. She did likewise, lifting one foot to set the tight little boot with its pointed heel on a table holding a stack of towels, and bending over it to unlace the boot. Her outrageously long hair sifted around her gloriously naked body, veiling and revealing her in a perfect tease.

She undid the ribbons on her stocking and slid it off—then glanced at him. "How's that hot water coming along?" she asked silkily, clearly aware of how she affected him.

"Maybe you should put on a robe," he muttered, "if you want me to concentrate."

A delighted smile lit her face, and she lifted the other foot to the table. "Where's the fun in that?"

Amused by her, he crossed to her and cupped her darling bottom in one hand. Without setting her foot down, she straightened enough to kiss him. Her mouth unlike anything he could've imagined, velvet sweet with tensile heat. "You have no idea what you do to me," he said against her mouth, like a secret confessed.

She took his hand in hers and slid it up her thigh to cup her mound. Hot and slick, plump and enticing, her sex slid against his fingers with buttery welcome. "This is what you do to me," she replied, lips moving against his with seductive trembles. "So I do have some idea."

He moved his fingers and she sighed with pleasure, undulating against him. "What do I do?" he asked.

She nipped his bottom lip, a light sting. "Get the hot water. Time enough to teach you mine, which is a bit less straightforward than yours, in more ways than one. I don't mind a bit of anticipation."

"You have a *lot* less edge," he agreed and, with reluctance, made himself turn away from her to find that spigot. There it was. He gave it a few turns with the tool hanging on the wall nearby, grunting in satisfaction when the steaming water gushed out.

"Do you mind that?" she asked, her voice lightly neutral. She'd dispensed with her other boot and stocking and stood fully naked, winding up her long hair to fasten it with some pins.

"Are you joining me in the tub?" he asked with some surprise.

"It's big enough," she pointed out. "And I did promise to help. Unless you don't want me to?"

"No, I was just surprised. I figured you'd shapeshift clean." He tested the water, decided it was hot enough, and turned off the spigot. "Though it might be overfull now, for both of us. We might spill water on the floor," he added, eyeing the pretty tiles.

"*What?!*" she gasped in such dismay that he spun to look at her. She had her hands clasped to her heart, face a rictus of horror. "Not. Water. On. The. Floor."

"Ha ha," he replied, relaxing. She might kill him before their affair was done. "Get in already."

"Nooo…" Now she flung the back of her hand against her forehead, the other braced on the table as she swooned as dramatically as any court lady. "What about the water? What if it *splashes*? Whatever shall become of us?"

Yes, she thought she was pretty funny. With a bearish growl, he strode to her, swept her up in his arms, and carried her—shrieking with laughter—and deposited her in the tub, though he was careful not to dunk her head, since she'd gone to pains to keep her hair dry. Ignoring the wave that spilled over the edge, he joined her more gingerly. Substantially more water slopped onto the floor, and he did his best not to wince.

She moved her legs out of the way, giving him room and relaxing against the sloping back of the tub. "I meant what I told Lena," she said. "A real hot bath is still a treat in a way that shapeshifting clean will never be. Especially with a gorgeous man."

He grunted at that, displeased to find a tickle of jealousy at the image of his beautiful Zephyr bathing like this with anyone else. With her uncanny knack of seeming to read his mind, she eyed him. "You didn't answer my question before."

When he raised a brow, taking up the soap to wash himself, her face smoothed, and she gave him a carefree smile. Ah, that expression was one he knew. The question mattered to her, more than she wanted him to know. He thought back, glad for once that Ursula had so ruthlessly tested him on keeping track of what people had said in a conversation. "No," he replied, tugging on one slim ankle. "I don't mind that you have had sex with other people before me."

"A *lot* of people," she emphasized.

He bit down internally on that odd, unwelcome flicker of jealousy. The bear in him, no doubt, and something needing exacting control. "I don't care how many," he told her honestly. Then thought he'd better be fully honest. "Though I *would* mind if you were with anyone else while we're... seeing each other."

Amusement blossomed over her face. "Is that what we're doing?" She extended the leg he held and nudged his chest with her dainty toe. "*Seeing* each other?"

He knew she found his values hopelessly quaint and mossback, but he didn't know any other way to be. So, he lifted her foot and sucked her toe into his mouth, nibbling the meaty pad lightly. "And tasting and touching," he added, enjoying the way her eyes darkened and her posture went supple. "Hearing, smelling." He tugged her toward him, gratified at how willingly she came, unfolding herself to drape over him. "Devouring," he whispered before taking her mouth in a deep and drugging kiss.

She moved against him, a sensual writhing that had his blood steaming. He ran his hands over her, relishing the velvet glide of her skin, the endlessly fascinating curves that captivated him. Her hand found his rigid length, and she purred in pleasure, a true rumbling sound emanating from deep within.

Her gríobhth nature peeking through. She dragged her hand up his shaft, and his hips surged helplessly after.

"Wait," he said into her mouth, and she stilled, pulling back to see his face.

"Problem?"

"It's your turn," he explained, shaking his head when laughter lit her eyes. "I know you think I'm inflexible about fairness, but I want to give you pleasure too."

Her hand stroked him. "Sometimes rigidity is a good thing," she murmured, kissing him lingeringly. "And touching you is a great pleasure for me."

"Still," he replied stubbornly, moving her hand off of him. "Indulge me."

"Why don't we indulge each other?" she suggested with a gamine smile. Kneeling up, she straddled him. "I'd like to have you inside me, Astar. Unless you'd rather wait."

"No," he replied, hoarse at the tantalizing sight of her sleekly wet and naked breasts at nearly eye level. "I'm done with waiting."

"You can touch them," she said, taking his hands and guiding them to caress her breasts. "Kiss and lick. Careful with the biting, as I have tender nipples."

In awe, he held her gorgeous breasts, marveling at their supple texture, trying to be gentle with the fragile-seeming globes even as Zephyr closed her eyes in pleasure, rocking her hips so the folds of her sex glided along the length of his cock. Even through the hot water, her slick heat pounded through him. Drawing one deep-red nipple into his mouth, he groaned with her at the delicious texture, the flavor of her heady and sending him out of his mind.

She rocked against him more urgently, and he had to drop one hand to her waist to stop her. "I won't last to get inside you if you keep doing that."

"Then you better get inside me," she replied, fierce demand in her eyes.

"Show me," he demanded in return.

With a sharp and hungry smile, she reached down, touching him just enough to lift him into position, nestling the sensitive head against her sweet sex. Holding his gaze, she slowly slid down, sheathing him in her slick and welcoming heat.

The shock of intense pleasure rolled through him, unlike anything he'd ever experienced, and he shouted her name, hands vising on her hips as he panted for control. She didn't move, though she gripped him from inside, a steel fist within a velvet glove. When he managed to open his eyes, she was watching him, sapphire eyes dark and predatory.

"Yesss," she hissed. "Oh, my bear, you are all I hoped for." Holding his gaze still, she undulated, slowly riding him, the pleasure climbing rapidly to an excruciating peak.

"I can't last long," he panted. "I'm sorry."

"Still a lot of edge," she replied, unbothered, her breasts rising and falling with her own rapid breathing. "And I'm right with you."

He couldn't look away, rapt at the sight of the ecstasy suffusing her face. She rose up and plunged down, throwing her head back as she released a cry of erotic rapture, her whole body trembling under his grip, arcing with the force of her climax. She wrenched his own climax from him, her internal muscles squeezing him as firmly as her hands had done, extracting every drop from them both, until she collapsed boneless over him.

Suffused with pleasure, he let himself fall into the depths of replete relaxation. Holding Zephyr close against his heart, he fell asleep, knowing perfect peace for the first time in a very long time, maybe ever.

~ 19 ~

ZEPH AWOKE SLOWLY, stretching as she did, and releasing a happily sated sigh. Her body ached in the best possible way, throbbing here and there from the bruises and bites of her—best surprise ever—fierce lover. She even ached between her thighs from his considerable girth, and before this, she'd have said that wasn't possible. Sighing again at the visceral memory of him deep inside her, she snuggled into the cozy bed. Her gríobhth senses reported it was well past dawn. But, reluctant to leave her warm nest of covers and face the bright light of the cold winter day, she kept her eyes closed, replaying her favorite bits of the night before.

Since she'd loved every moment, there were a lot of bits to replay.

"I know you're awake," Astar said, a callused hand sliding down her ribs to her waist. Something he'd been doing for a while, she realized. "Faker," he teased.

Grudgingly—and because the only thing better than Dream Astar was Real Life Astar—she opened one eye to find him propped up on his elbow, golden hair tumbling wildly around his handsome face as he smiled sweetly down at her. Lifting a hand, she brushed the hair out of his eyes, summer-sky blue even in the dimness of the bedchamber. "You're so pretty," she murmured. "Let's stay in bed all day."

"Tempting," he agreed, lowering his head to kiss her. Already it felt so normal and right to kiss him, as natural as breathing, as if they'd been lovers all their lives. She rolled into him, tangling her legs with his hairy ones, delighting in the contrast. "But," he said, breaking the kiss and crushing her hopes, "I have responsibilities."

She narrowed her eyes at him. "I'm going to hear that a lot from you, aren't I?"

He grinned, kissing her on the nose. "It's like you know me." Lightly smacking her bottom—though she didn't miss how his hand lingered a moment longer there, fingers curling lovingly over the curve he could hold in one hand—he threw back the covers and strode away.

She levered up to watch him go, his tautly muscled ass a mouthwatering sight. Perfectly shaped, it flexed with a mesmerizing rhythm over the golden-haired backs of his thighs, his hips narrow and shoulders broad. What a gorgeous man. He glanced over his shoulder, catching her looking. She crooked a finger to beckon him back, but he shook his head. "We have a breakfast meeting," he informed her and disappeared into the bathing chamber.

"Who is 'we'?" she said suspiciously.

"Groningen asked for you, too, or I wouldn't have wakened you," he called from the bathing chamber, splashing water vigorously. "A messenger has already been and gone. The king is waiting."

Groaning, she flopped onto her back, cocooning the covers

around her and gripping them under her chin. "Does he never sleep? The man is a monster," she complained. "Hey, don't you technically outrank him?"

"I'm only an heir. Until and unless I'm crowned high king, I'm basically a nobody."

"That's obviously not true," she muttered.

Astar came back into the room, still naked and briskly toweling dry his wet hair. Zeph debated with herself over which view was better. While his back would be enough to satisfy her eye for masculine beauty, the front had the added features of the golden treasure trail arrowing down to his truly impressive cock, which she'd barely gotten to play with at all. After that truly spectacular, if abbreviated consummation of her long-held desires—and she wasn't complaining, but she also wanted much, much more—they'd fallen asleep in the tub. She might've stayed that way, solidly unconscious in the rapidly cooling water, if Astar hadn't dragged her out and carried her to bed, where they'd both passed out again. She was developing a fondness for him carrying her around in those big, strong arms.

"Zephyr," Astar said, snapping the towel playfully at her. "You have to get up."

"Make me," she invited, letting the covers fall away from her bare breasts and stretching her arms languidly over her head.

He eyed her and came to the bed, edging one knee onto it and bending to kiss her. That was more like it. She received the kiss with enthusiasm, tangling her fingers in his damp curls while he ran a hand down her side, brushing the covers away to bare her body. She moved under his touch, humming in encouragement.

In the next moment, he'd scooped her up and tossed her over his shoulder, her naked bottom high in the air as she draped over his back, her hair falling all around her face. Shrieking in surprise, she hammered on his back with the meat of her fists, kicking, too—but he grasped her firmly and smacked her on her bottom as he carried her into the bathing chamber.

He seemed to like doing that—which she could work with. However, her delight in being carried by him didn't extend to this upside-down thing. So, she shifted into a small cat, giving him a good scratch as she leapt away. Shifting back to human form wearing a simple burgundy velvet dress adequate for court breakfast—or it should be, according to her mother's complex and detailed instructions—and with her hair clean and neatly falling free, she smirked at Astar. "I'm ready to go. Why are you still undressed?"

He grinned at her, apparently unbothered by the scratches. "Got you up, didn't I? Dressing won't take long."

THE WHOLE GROUP—SAVE Rhy, of course—was at breakfast, along with assorted other advisers and some of Groningen's multitudes of heirs. She and Astar were among the last to arrive, giving everyone ample opportunity to observe that they arrived together. Whatever resolution Astar had come to about their liaison, he was sticking to it. Not that Astar would ever deviate from the course he'd decided was the honorable one. He escorted her into the hall with her hand tucked into the crook of his elbow, and he seated her beside him with gallant concern.

Gen had clearly been watching the doorway, because she spotted them immediately, paling in shock before her face solidified into outrage, twin flags of color on her cheeks as she followed them with a hard gaze. Zeph was more than a little tired of Gen's attitude, but the deed was done now, so hopefully Gen would let it go. Zeph couldn't unfuck Astar even if she wanted to. Gen would have to live with that reality.

Fortunately for the privacy of Zeph's sex life, the conversation about the stone giant and odd magical occurrences around Lake Sullivan dominated all conversation. They ate breakfast, yes, but Groningen also required each member of the group to relate their version of events, and his advisers subjected them to more questions. Groningen was seemingly inexhaustible, keeping them there for several hours before releasing most of them to enjoy the charms of Elderhorst, in keeping with their cover story.

Astar, however, had to stay behind for yet more talking, kissing Zeph's hand and giving her an intimate smile full of promise for later. No sooner had she strolled out of the hall than Gen and Lena both pounced on her, Jak and Stella trailing behind.

Lena gave her an arch look. "Well??"

Zeph only gave a close-lipped catlike smile.

"I cannot believe you," Gen hissed. "After everything we discussed!"

"You lectured," Zeph corrected. "Now your worst fears have been realized, so you can move on with your life."

"Oh, no," Gen replied darkly, "my worst fears just became more likely."

"What's going on?" Jak wanted to know.

"Astar and Zeph are sharing a *room*," Gen answered, making it sound like they'd spent the night roasting small children over a fire.

"Oh yeah?" Jak grinned at Zeph. "He's a lucky guy and you look happy, so well done."

"It is *not* well done," Gen gritted out.

Stella came to Zeph, giving her a somber smile, her eyes a quiet dove gray. Breaking her habitual distance, she embraced Zeph and kissed her on the cheek, a buzz of green healing magic in it. "He's so happy," Stella whispered in her ear. "Thank you."

Zeph gazed back in surprise, not sure why Nilly was *thanking* her for ravishing her brother. Except that Astar did seem relaxed and happy in a different way this morning. See? It had been good for him to shed some of those confining rules.

"I want to hear everything," Lena announced.

Stella put her hands over her ears. "Oh, I don't!"

"I think I'll skip that, too," Jak said, turning to Stella. "Shall we go find something more interesting to do?"

"Yes. I'd love to see that museum about the lake creature," she replied with enthusiasm. "Sorry, Zeph."

"Oh, wait for me," Lena said. "I want to see that, too."

Jak rolled his eyes, but Stella nodded. "All right. We could go see the geothermal pools beneath the castle instead."

"But I want to see those, too," Lena protested.

Jak narrowed his eyes at her. "Look, Lena—"

"Why don't you all go," Zeph interrupted. "Gen and I need to have a private conversation anyway."

"I really don't want to hear the details," Gen snarled.

"I don't plan to tell you," Zeph replied sweetly, taking her by the arm and all but dragging her away. "But we *are* going to talk. It's either that or a few rounds of I Eat You, and you know I'll win."

"You don't *always* win," Gen retorted, yanking her arm from Zeph's grip but still stalking along beside her. "And we're not supposed to put on shapeshifter displays," she added primly.

Zeph turned down the hall to the room she and Astar were sharing, opening the door and waving Gen in. The maids had been there, so the room had been neatened and cleaned—but Zeph had no doubt that Gen's keen shapeshifter nose would pick up the lingering scents of sex. A concept that Zeph fully intended to drive home. Judging by the scowl on Gen's face, Zeph's point had been made.

"Sit." Zeph pointed at a chair by the fire and took the other, pouring them both wine.

"Isn't it a bit early in the day?" Gen inquired silkily, and Zeph congratulated herself on not throwing the wine in Gen's face. But the two of them had known each other all their lives. With their parents being twins, she and Gen were more like sisters than cousins. Which probably explained some of their sometimes thorny relationship.

"It goes with our cover," she pointed out instead, pushing

the full goblet into Gen's hands. "We're supposed to be carefree and having fun. And *you* need whatever it takes for you to relax."

"I'm relaxed," Gen snapped, hands clenched on the goblet.

"Are you in love with Astar?" Zeph asked bluntly.

Gen blinked at her, then took a long swallow of wine.

"Is that a yes?" Zeph asked as gently as she knew how.

"No. I didn't dignify that question with any answer at all."

"Definitely a yes," Zeph decided, then held up her hands in a peacemaking gesture when Gen looked like she might chuck the wine in Zeph's face. "It's all right. Astar is easy to love. We all do. It's like loving warm sunshine and blue summer skies. You'd be crazy *not* to love him."

"Are you claiming that you're in love with Astar?" Gen asked cagily.

A question that absolutely took Zeph by surprise. She blinked at Gen, then took a long swallow of wine.

"That's a no," Gen said smugly. "And *that* is my problem."

Zeph wasn't sure how she'd lost control of this confrontation. "My feelings for Astar are my own business," she decided. That answer would do, especially since she suddenly had no idea what those feelings were. She lusted after him, yes. She also loved him the way she loved warm sunshine and blue summer skies, and she loved how he clung to his ideas of honor, forever trying to do the right thing instead of serving himself first. And the sex had been amazing—but also surprisingly tender, even playful. She'd had so many lovers, but now when she thought about sex, all she could think of was Astar, how he tasted, smelled, and felt. *Hearing. Devouring.*

The way he looked at and touched her. The artless honesty in how he gazed at her, even in the most intense throes of climax, as if only she existed for him.

"It's *not* just your business, Zeph. Please listen to me," Gen was saying, and Zeph jerked herself from her musings to pay attention. "You're not in love with Astar. You've said it yourself that you have no intention of marrying him, of being his queen. You're in this for the fun, for the thrill of the chase, the hunt, and he is the most elusive prey out there. Astar is the trophy, and you could never resist the challenge of going for the unattainable."

"I certainly attained him last night," Zeph retorted, more baldly that she would've otherwise, as Gen's harsh assessment of her character stung.

"Yes." Gen turned the wine goblet thoughtfully in her hands. "Have you thought about what happens now that you have?"

"We're staying at Elderhorst at least a couple more nights, so Astar and I will continue to share a room. We discussed it." There. They had discussed their arrangements and made an adult decision. That should stick in Gen's craw.

But Gen shook her head in exasperation. "And after *that*?"

"It depends, I guess." Though maybe they could share rooms at other inns and castles, or perhaps sneak off into the woods...

"Zeph!" Gen snapped her fingers in Zeph's face. "This is what I'm trying to tell you. You're not capable of thinking past the moment, or past the next few weeks. It's not your fault, your gríobhth First Form drives that kind of spontaneousness and irresponsibility, but—"

"Oh, like a hummingbird is the epitome of groundedness?" Zeph shot back.

Gen glared. "No, but I'm half mossback."

"So am I," Zeph pointed out.

"You might be half Dasnarian by blood, but you are *all* Tala by nature. You'll enjoy Astar until you get bored, and then you'll move on."

Zeph nearly ground her teeth, mentally clacking her beak. "If so, that fits perfectly with the plan. As you may recall, since you pummel me with this fact at every opportunity, Astar has to marry for the high throne. So, we will enjoy each other until it's time for me to move on and him to marry his paid-for princess." The thought made her stomach turn, an unfamiliar pang of sickness and banked rage to destroy this faceless woman, the gríobhth fierce in her blood. "Maybe she'll thank me," Zeph added flippantly, mostly to make herself feel better. "He'll come to her well-taught in pleasing a woman in bed."

"Fine," Gen hissed, throwing up her hands. "I can't talk to you. I don't know why I'm even trying."

Because Zeph had wanted to have this out, and some-how—as always seemed to happen when she argued with Gen—she ended up on the losing side of the battle. Zeph might be able to consistently beat Gen in I Eat You, but Gen could win I Argue You to Death every time. Well, no one could say Zeph lacked persistence. Gen could make fun of her for following the scent of prey until she got it, but that could be a virtue. Zeph wasn't one to give up. If that made her a bad person, then so be it. She couldn't help who she was.

"Sit down," she said to Gen, who'd risen to leave. "We're not done here."

Gen narrowed her indigo eyes, unusual fire in them. "You don't get to tell me."

"Please," Zeph added pointedly. "I need to know the truth. Are you in love with Astar? Is that why you're so pissed at me? It's like we're enemies these days, and I—I hate that. I wish you would talk to me, like we used to."

Gen stood there, vibrating with tension, then threw herself back down in the chair, releasing a huff of air. With her head tipped back, she stared at the ceiling, the anger seeping out of her. "I'm sorry, Zeph."

"Surely that's my line," Zeph replied lightly, taken aback by the sudden change—and the sense of profound despair coming off her cousin.

Gen shook her head, rolling it against the chair, eyes closed as if in pain. "No, I apologize. I know I've been awful—and I know everybody is sick of me."

"That's not true," Zeph lied, then searched for a better lie. "Everyone is much more annoyed with Rhy than with you."

Gen rolled her head in Zeph's direction and opened one eye. "Somehow that does not make me feel better."

Yeah. For all her flaws, Zeph was honest to a fault. Even when she should find softer words, she seemed to miss the mark. "So what's the problem?" she asked. "If you're in love with Astar, you can tell me. It might help me to know."

"It might help *me* to know," Gen said, returning her baleful gaze to the ceiling. "For a while I thought I was," she admitted. "I've also thought I was in love Rhy, and with Jak."

"All excellent choices," Zeph ventured, trying to think of what someone more sensitive than she was—like Nilly or Lena—might say. "They're all the best of men, and they care for you."

"As a *friend*," Gen spat, as if that were the worst thing in the world.

"Astar and I were friends before we became lovers," Zeph pointed out, not understanding. Wasn't it always better to like the people you took to bed? She realized her misstep when Gen emitted an incoherent sound reminiscent of a screech owl.

"It's not the same," Gen wailed, clutching the arms of the chair and banging her head against the high back. "You can't possibly understand."

"I'm trying to understand," Zeph ground out in pure frustration. "*You* aren't explaining."

Gen lifted her head and glared. "You're really terrible at this."

"I know. You should absolutely talk to Nilly or Lena instead."

"I have," Gen admitted. "And they don't understand either. Lena has been in love with Rhy for so much of her life that she has no idea what it's like not to have someone like that. Nilly sympathizes, but she's so above stuff like this that she doesn't get it. And you—"

She broke off so abruptly that Zeph braced herself. "Just say it," she said.

Gen sighed. "You are so beautiful, sexy, wild, and free. You can have anyone you want—and pretty much have."

"I haven't had *everyone* I ever wanted," Zeph protested.

"You have now," Gen said soberly. "Astar was the only holdout, and now he's yours, just like all the rest."

That might be true—and she'd have to think about that later. "So, who *do* you want?"

"That's the problem," Gen replied, sounding hopeless. "I don't know."

"I'm really confused," Zeph confessed. "You're all upset because you want a lover that you don't know who it is?"

"Yes!" Gen pounced on that, eyes brightening. "That's exactly it."

"But how can you want someone you haven't met?"

"It's impossible," Gen agreed. "You *do* understand."

Zeph really didn't think so—but her head was starting to swim from the circular conversation, so she hesitated to say as much. She settled for nodding sagely, which seemed to soothe Gen.

"What if I go my whole life never meeting my true love?" Gen asked, stricken. "I'll die a miserable virgin. Dead without having lived."

A melodramatic, miserable virgin, Zeph thought to herself, but wisely didn't say aloud. Who said she didn't know how to keep her mouth shut? "It's entirely possible to lose your virginity without meeting your true love," she said instead. "In fact, I think it's preferable. Healthy and natural."

Gen shook her head. "No, it should be magical. Look at Lena and Rhy, losing their virginity to each other. First love. *True* love." She sighed dreamily.

"And Rhy immediately screwed someone else, making the whole thing a lie."

Gen shot her a reproving look. "That's another story and

not relevant."

Seemed *particularly* relevant to Zeph. Maybe if Lena hadn't been so quick to confess undying love for Rhy, he wouldn't have reacted so badly. Another opinion she kept to herself. "I didn't lose my virginity to any true love."

"Yes, but you're you. I doubt you even remember who it was."

That would sting, except it was kind of true. It really depended on what you considered to be actual virginity and what exact act constituted losing it. For Zeph, it had been a more gradual process. Not like with Astar, who'd done almost nothing before her. "And I might be Astar's first sex," she continued that line of thought, "but he's not in love with me."

Gen gave her a canny stare. "Isn't he?"

"No." Zeph laughed, but Gen didn't. "I don't believe people fall in love overnight."

"Maybe they do; maybe they don't. That's another debate entirely. *I* think Astar has been in love with you for years."

Zeph huffed in exasperation. "Then he had a funny way of showing it, because until this, he's rejected my advances. Sometimes harshly." *I don't want you enough to compromise my principles. That will never change.* But it did change. Did he decide he wanted her enough?

"Yes, until you wore him down and he gave in," Gen insisted. "He resisted because he loves you and knew it would only lead to heartbreak and ruin."

Heartbreak and Ruin—sounded like twin cities one would never want to visit. "He hasn't said anything like that."

"He won't because he knows that you won't return the feeling. Astar doesn't want to play Salena to your Rhyian."

Ouch. "I would not do to Astar what Rhy did to Lena. I would never hurt him that way."

"So you'll be faithful to him for the rest of your life?"

"What? No, that's not the same thing."

"For me, it is."

"Not everything has to be in terms of forever!"

Gen stood, smoothing her skirts as Zeph sat, stunned into silence. "For Astar, it does—but I won't say anything more. Thank you for listening to what I had to say, though I know it won't change anything. Nothing has ever stopped you from seizing what you want." She smile ruefully. "I actually envy that about you. Maybe I wouldn't be so unhappy if I were more like you."

Zeph caught her hand. "Consider playing around some. There's a ball tonight, yes? Lots of new faces, new bodies to dance with."

"Yes. I'm hoping—though not counting on—maybe meeting someone special."

Zeph shook her head vigorously. "No. Ditch that idea. Stop evaluating every person you meet for true-love potential and just find one thing to enjoy about them. Think about it like shapeshifting. You try out a lot of forms that you never go back to, right? But you learn from them what you *do* like."

"Interesting analogy. I'll give it some thought." Gen squeezed her hand, swinging it lightly. "I do wish you happy, Zephyr. You know that, right?"

She hadn't been sure at all, so that was good to hear. "I'll be careful with Astar's heart," she said impulsively.

Gen smiled, relief in it. "That's all I ask."

~ 20 ~

THE BALL WAS in full swing by the time Astar made it there. Between short sleep the night before and an excruciatingly long day of meetings with Groningen—plus his multitudes of heirs, advisers, and minor nobles, who'd been arriving in an unending stream—Astar was tempted to simply head to his room and bed.

If he thought Zephyr would be there, he'd do exactly that. As it was, he knew he'd find all of his friends at the ball, if only because they'd be dedicated to preserving the cover story. He'd give a bit of service to the role-playing himself, dance a time or two with his gorgeous lover, then tempt her back to their room. He'd been building several detailed fantasies over the course of the day—only during the boring and repetitive bits, otherwise he observed his duty and paid close attention— of things he'd like to do with her.

Feeling like a lad again, he craned his neck, trying to see over the crowd—anticipating the first glimpse of her. He should've found out what color she'd be wearing. In that crush of people, it would take forever to find her.

"Astar, my boy," Groningen boomed out—and Astar had to exert a lifetime's worth of disciplining himself not to flinch at the call of a demanding monarch—the king striding up to him. He couldn't let his amusement show, but maybe Zephyr was right that the man was some kind of mythical beast who didn't need rest. Groningen certainly looked no worse for wear. He'd changed into more elaborate robes for the ball, and escorted a pretty young woman on his arm. She wore a rich gown that practically screamed royalty and a glittering tiara.

She gave Astar a blinding smile. He got a very bad feeling.

"Astar, my boy," Groningen repeated, patting the young woman's hand, "may I present my granddaughter Princess Berendina." He winked broadly. "I think you will have seen her name before."

Yes, on the list Ursula had pressed onto him. Except she wasn't supposed to be here. Astar had thought her safely distant from Zephyr, in some small realm even farther north and east. "It's a pleasure to meet you, Princess Berendina," he said, taking the hand she offered and bowing over it. Not touching her otherwise. At least his ingrained manners allowed him to appear gallant, despite the sick feeling in his stomach. Good thing he hadn't found Zephyr yet, after all.

"Dina, please," she corrected with a gracious smile. "And likewise, Your Highness Crown Prince Astar."

"Dina just arrived from her home in Jorrit, one my northern principalities, and I thought, what luck!" Groningen said, as if he hadn't been the one to summon his very eligible granddaughter to meet Astar. He disconnected himself from his granddaughter and stepped away. "This is an excellent opportunity for you to get to know each other. A party." He waved expansively. "Dancing," he added, giving Astar a meaningful stare.

Jorrit. That was the place, right on the border with Branli, and a potentially critical gateway to the mineral riches of the Northern Wastes. Consigning his hopes to the fire that he might find Zephyr quickly and drown in her affection while he could, Astar nodded pleasantly. "I'd be delighted if you'd favor me with a dance?"

She twinkled at him, a convincing show of pleasure, with no clue as to her genuine feelings. After Zephyr's blunt honesty, he was hard-pressed not to think poorly of Dina for her pretty, political façade. It wasn't at all fair to her, as none of this was any more her fault than his own. She'd been raised as a princess and probably relentlessly groomed her entire life with the ultimate goal of winning the position of high queen. Astar doubted anything could budge her from her training or the script she'd memorized for playing out this particular encounter.

Soonest done, soonest over with. He led Dina onto the dance floor, grateful for the crowd that now shielded him from Zephyr spotting him in turn. Given her reaction to the mere existence of the list, he didn't want to rely on her good behavior at seeing him dance with a princess whose name was on it. Zephyr was no fool—even if she hadn't seen the actual list, she'd put things together. At least Salena's ruby ring was back with his clothes in the carriage and not here where her sharp eyes might pick it out among his things.

If he'd had time to plan for this moment, he would've had Nilly intervene and distract Zephyr. But no luck there. Maybe Zephyr's flirtatious ways would work in his favor this time.

She could hardly fault him for dancing with someone else. The Tala weren't jealous like that, no matter how possessive the gríobhth nature might be. In truth, it would be more likely that Zephyr had found someone new to titillate her ever-roving eye. Now that she'd finally achieved her goal of bedding him, she'd be losing interest. He didn't harbor any illusions about Zephyr. He'd known from the beginning that she would never be exclusively his, or even his for very long. And he could hardly blame her, as he could never be hers, either.

He had hoped, however, that their affair would last just a little longer. Still, he'd be gracious and let her go, if she truly was ready to move on already. At least, he'd make a convincing show of it.

"Is dancing with me *that* much of a trial, Your Highness?" Dina inquired, a teasing smile on her lips. "With such a frown, you're making me worry I'm crushing your toes."

Danu take him—he'd been so caught up in dark thoughts that he'd let his own polite façade lapse. He knew better. Zephyr just had a way of tangling him up so he lost his bearings. Thinking about her was not unlike plummeting through the sky on her back, exhilarating, terrifying, and leaving him unable to think about anything else.

"Forgive me," he said, adding his most charming smile. Dina relaxed immediately, beaming back at him with every appearance of sincerity. "It's been a difficult journey and a long day of meetings. And please, call me Astar."

"I've been hearing the rumors," she breathed. "People can't stop talking about that lunar eclipse over the Strait of K'van on the night of the crystalline moon. Do you believe it's a terrible omen?"

"Not at all," he replied smoothly, the lie coming easily to the tongue now. "There was simply an unusually dense storm that formed suddenly, temporarily obscuring the moon before it moved on again."

"How fascinating. But then what did anyone expect? Nothing is so large as to obscure the moon!" She laughed gaily, and Astar did his best to smile along. Nothing they knew of... *yet.*

"I also heard how you single-handedly defeated that stone monster," she added with widened eyes.

"You flatter me." Irked but determined to do a better job of being entertaining, he tried to gently correct her misunderstanding. "I was but part of a group, and probably the least heroic of the lot."

"I heard you fell from the sky." She added a delicate shudder, all big, wide eyes and slightly parted lips. "How strong you must be to survive such a trauma!"

Only because Zephyr had taken the brunt of the fall. He didn't like to question Her Majesty's wisdom—and would certainly never countermand her orders—but it felt wrong to deny Zephyr's extraordinary gríobhth form, and her role in saving them all. "Rumors exaggerate," he said, adding a warm smile to mitigate the somewhat harsh words.

"Oh, you're so humble," she returned with a similarly practiced smile. "I hadn't expected such a virtue in our next high king. But I should have. All anyone says about you is how noble, honorable, and charming you are." Her pink lips curved in a coy smile. "The stories did not do justice to how handsome you are as well. You exceed my expectations in every way."

She trailed off hopefully, leaving him the perfect opening to return the compliment—which he might be able to do if he wasn't remembering Zephyr's hands on his cock as she purred nearly those very words. Scrambling to banish that titillating image from his mind, he searched for a suitable compliment to give Dina. No doubt he'd been told lovely things about her. Even before the final list had been presented to him, Ursula and her advisers had provided him with detailed information about each potential candidate. Yes, the descriptions tended to focus on the political advantages of each match, but they had included bits they thought might tempt Astar.

He'd committed the list to memory, as was his duty to do, but for the life of him, he couldn't recall any of it now. When he asked his usually reliable brain for information on his potential brides, all it delivered were images of a naked Zephyr rising above him as he sheathed himself in her, glossy black hair escaping in wild coils around her full breasts, her eyes flashing sapphires and lush lips parted as she—

"Astar," Dina asked, a slight frown marring her brow, "are you well? You're quite flushed."

He didn't doubt it. What he did question was how he'd allowed himself to fantasize about another woman while dancing with a potential fiancée. Wonderful. Now he was losing his mind. "I must apologize again. I'm afraid I am a bit out of sorts this evening, and I'm being unforgivably rude."

Her frown vanished, her expression entirely sympathetic. "Not at all. I'm the one who's put you in a difficult position, keeping you on the dance floor when you told me how exhausted you are. Perhaps we should find a quiet alcove where we can talk, get to know one—"

"Your Highness Crown Prince Astar," Zephyr said from right behind him, sounding polite for her, but he didn't miss the sardonic lilt in her use of his title. "I'm sorry to interrupt your *dance*, but there's a message from Ordnung. Urgent."

He and Dina had already halted, both turning to face Zephyr as the ballroom full of dancers whirled around them. She wore the scarlet gown she'd had on at the Feast of Moranu ball—no doubt had cached it to shift into for occasions like this—and it displayed her full bosom and lithe figure to distracting advantage. With her dramatic coloring, she made a distinct contrast to Dina, whose demurely elegant gown and blonde prettiness dimmed in comparison. The three of them formed a tense triangle, a still point in a spinning universe of music and color.

"Zephyr." He cleared his throat. "This is Princess Berendina of Jorrit, one of King Groningen's granddaughters."

"Delighted to meet any friend of Astar's," Dina said, offering a hand.

Zephyr smiled thinly, eyes glittering, not taking Dina's hand. If she'd been in gríobhth form, she might've bitten the hand off. As it was, she looked dangerously lethal. "I look forward to learning everything about you," she purred, nearly a growl, then transferred her sapphire gaze to Astar. "The urgent message?"

"Yes. Of course." He gave Dina a quarter bow. "I apologize yet again, but I must—"

She waved that off, serene and unbothered. "I understand

very well the demands of the throne." Her gaze slid to Zephyr, who stared at her with loathing, invisible tail whipping palpably. "I've been raised to be aware of political responsibilities. Duty must come first, yes?"

"Indeed." He almost promised to find Dina later, but he didn't care to test Zephyr's temper any further. Taking Zephyr's arm in a firm grip, he steered her away before she decided to grow actual claws. "What is the message from Ordnung?" he asked in a low voice.

She snarled, curling her lip. "There isn't one."

"You lied?" He shouldn't be surprised. Zephyr—and the Tala in general—didn't place much value on truth. Not because they were inherently dishonest—in their candor, they could be honest to a fault—but because they saw a spectrum of truths rather than an absolute. Not surprising for a people who exchanged bodies as easily as breathing, but occasionally frustrating nonetheless.

"It was that or shift into gríobhth form and frighten the mossbacks by gutting Princess Berendina on the ballroom floor," Zephyr hissed.

"Not to mention causing a diplomatic incident with Groningen," he murmured, trying very hard not to be amused by her—but he was also intensely flattered by her possessiveness. And here he'd been worrying that she'd found someone else.

"As if I care." She tugged on her arm, but he firmed his grip, not letting her go.

"Please, don't run." He found a space for them to stand. "All I've thought about all day was getting to see you. What have you been doing?"

She rolled her eyes, but relaxed under his hand enough that he dared to let her go. "I had a big fight with Gen, saw more of this sprawl of stone than any person should want to, and then I've been at this dance. For *hours*."

"What did you and Gen fight about?" He had a feeling he knew—verified when she folded her arms and looked away, eyes glittering as she eyed the crowd, the gríobhth studying potential prey.

"We've come to an understanding," she said, firming her lips over any more words on the subject. Restlessness shimmered off of her, tangible as heat from a flame.

"I'm surprised you didn't go on a ramble, or flying." Zephyr rarely went a full day without shifting. If she hadn't, no wonder she seemed about to burst out of her skin.

She slid him an opaque look. "I'm trying to be a good citizen. Just a normal mossback, like you pretend to be. I don't know how you do it."

"I'm used to it. You aren't."

Snorting in patent disbelief, she didn't reply otherwise. The crowd swirled past them, Lena dancing by with one of Groningen's heirs. She had a faraway look in her eyes, her mind clearly elsewhere, though the blithely chatting young man didn't seem to notice. "There's Lena," he noted. "Where are the others?"

"Gen is also dancing—and searching for true love. Jak went off to some game of chance, and Stella turned in for the night. She'd had enough of people for one day. I can't say I blame her."

"But you stayed."

"Waiting for you," she replied pointedly. "I didn't realize you were here but occupied with *Princess Berendina*." She hissed the name, ire heating again.

"I was on my way to find you when I was waylaid by Groningen," he said. "His granddaughter had just arrived and he made a point of introducing us."

"Is Princess Berendina on the *list*?"

Lying at this point would be the easiest course—and likely safer for Dina. He, however, *did* place a high value on honesty. Besides, Zephyr would find out the truth easily enough. "She is indeed on the list. And I promised Auntie Essla that I would meet and be polite to the young women on the list. One dance was the courteous thing to do."

"Oh, as long as you're *courteous*," she replied scathingly.

He set his teeth against replying in kind. He'd known this would be a peril of dallying with Zephyr. Her gríobhth nature didn't fit well into ballrooms and polite political maneuvering. He wouldn't try to soothe her ire, either, as it would likely only seem condescending. He didn't blame her for getting her hackles up—he'd feel the same if he saw her dancing with another—but this was also the reality they had to deal with. "Courtesy and attendance to duty is all it was, because all day long I've been looking forward to dancing with *you*. Lovely Zephyr, would you favor me with a dance?"

She slid him an unamused look, eyes full of blue fire as she scanned the crowded ballroom, her face pinched with what he'd call anxiety on someone else. "This really isn't my sort of dancing."

He snorted a laugh. He'd been to enough parties in

Annfwn to know exactly what she meant. The Tala loved to dance—but without structure, often shapeshifting through various forms, as many-faced and defiant of boundaries as the goddess of shadows. "Would you rather withdraw for the evening?"

"Can we?" She looked so pleasantly startled, so grateful, that his heart twisted for her. He needed to keep in mind that being enclosed in a castle with so many people would grate on her, especially if she felt she couldn't go on her usual rambles.

"We can and will." Offering her his arm, he set them on a course to take them out of the ballroom as quickly as possible. "The advantage of being courteous and attending promptly to duty is that once one's responsibilities are discharged, one may discreetly withdraw."

"So many rules in your life," she muttered.

He couldn't argue with that. They passed Gen dancing with a handsome young man he didn't recognize, but who had the look of Groningen's family. "Who is Gen dancing with?"

Zephyr barely glanced. "Henk, a local princeling. Apparently Carienne is riddled with available royals on the prowl."

Not taking the bait on that one, he only commented that Gen looked delighted with her partner. "True, and it's about time," Zephyr replied cryptically. They made it out the doors and into the much quieter, far cooler, and nearly deserted hallway. "I think Princess Berendina suspects I'm your lover."

Astar thought so, too. Dina would be sensitive to social cues and personal undercurrents—and Zephyr was about as subtle as, well, a glittering mythological creature in a gathering of mossbacks. "You don't need to be concerned about that," he assured her, setting a hand on the small of her waist as they climbed the narrow, twisting stairs to the wing they were staying in. "Dina knows that ours would be a political match. If she does suspect, she wouldn't cause trouble over it."

"Oh, we're calling her *Dina*?" The hiss was back in Zephyr's voice. "Sounds like what you'd call a pesky songbird, those kinds that come in flocks and hop about, chirping endlessly. Dina dina dina."

Astar manfully withheld a laugh, determined not to have it on his conscience that he'd mocked his bride, should he end up marrying Berendina. He also would never be able to call her "Dina" with a straight face again.

"Astar." Zephyr abruptly halted in the narrow stairwell, the wall sconce behind her silhouetting her glossy hair with fire. "Can I ask you a question?"

"Of course." Concerned—as Zephyr never hesitated to ask whatever she wanted to know—he caressed her cheek, sliding his arm more firmly around her waist. "What's bothering you?" *Besides the obvious,* he mentally amended.

"I thought Groningen liked me. He said he approved of me." A question haunted her voice, her expression uncharacteristically uncertain. "Was I wrong?"

"No. He wouldn't have said so if he didn't."

"He put us in a room together, but then introduces you to his granddaughter as a potential bride," she said.

Ah. "Politics," he explained, tracing the delicate line of her jaw. "He can approve of you as my mistress and still know that I have to marry for the throne. And he's savvy and ambitious enough to want a member of his family to be my bride."

She searched his face, a frown forking her brows. No carefully schooled expressions for her. "I don't understand you people."

That stung more than it should have. He'd made a deliberate effort to distance himself from Tala ways—all to be a better high king for a people who were mostly *not* Tala—but he was still a shapeshifter too. Pressing her against the wall, he slid a possessive hand over her perfect ass, pulling her against the erection he'd sported since the moment he touched her. With his hand on the back of her neck, he slanted a kiss over her lush mouth, finding it hot and welcoming as she opened to drink him in. "*I* am your people," he growled into her mouth.

She purred, a true gríobhth rumble rising through her to thrum into his chest as she wound one leg around his waist, her hands busy with the buttons of his fitted jacket. "Mine," she agreed, tearing her mouth from his and fastening it on the cord of his neck. A sharp flash of pain as she bit down made him choke out a gasp, and his cock harden impossibly more. She ground her hips against him, leg vising around his hips to hold him in place. "Say you're mine," she insisted.

His head swam, making him dizzy, the searing heat of her sex pressing through his pants. Her skirts had somehow ended up around her waist, and she was naked beneath. Even in the heat of passion, he had to smile that she hadn't bothered with traditional mossback underthings—only the ones she liked, clearly, since she wore those ribbon-tied stockings. He followed the silken texture of one to the blatant heat of her bare skin above the ribbon, and found the scorching slick folds of her sex. Crying out at his touch, she flung her head back, exposing the swanlike length of her throat.

Greedily, he licked the slender column, feasting on her skin and savoring the frantic beat of her pulse that echoed his own. He still didn't know exactly how to please her—and she'd said it was complicated, so he didn't want to do it wrong—so he cupped her sex in his palm, giving her the pressure she seemed to crave, and she rode his hand, setting her own rhythm. She came, fast and furious, her cry carrying a raptor's edge and echoing up and down the stairwell.

A public stairwell at Castle Elderhorst—a small and tremendously relevant fact he'd forgotten in his craving for her. "Not here," he muttered, batting away her hands, her fingers nimbly attempting to unlace his pants. Sweeping her into his arms, he carried her up the last distance, taking the steps several at a time, slowing only to navigate the narrow turn without scraping either of them against the occasionally rough jags of stone. Striding down the hall, just short of a run, he only hoped his pants were still laced enough not to fall around his ankles.

"I like it when you carry me," Zephyr said dreamily, arms draped languidly around his neck.

"Do you?" He risked a glance at her—a mistake, as her full mouth tempted him to kiss her again, and yet again. Now that he'd sampled the pleasure of her embrace, each taste only whetted his hunger. Instead of sating him, each time with her made him want her even more. At some point in the near future, he'd exceed some ultimate state of need and simply... explode? Go up in a burst of flame?

He didn't know and didn't particularly care. He only cared about this moment, when it seemed nothing else mattered, or could matter, ever again.

~ 21 ~

ZEPH HAD NEVER seen Astar so close to being completely out of control—and she liked it. His impassioned response to her soothed the raging gríobhth inside. *Mine.* She hadn't been joking when she'd mentioned the possibility of shifting and rending *Dina* limb from pretty limb. Then she'd find this pernicious list and take wing, finding every princess on it and disposing of them as well.

She wouldn't be sorry either.

Except that Astar would never forgive her. And it wouldn't make him truly hers. This, however, this inferno between them would seal their bonds in blood and sex, tying them inextricably together until he finally admitted that he was hers. Politics and courtesy wouldn't matter. This was real. This mattered.

Astar kicked their chamber door closed behind them, setting her on her feet, then spinning her around to tug at the laces of her gown. "I can vanish it," she protested.

"Not if you want to wear it again," he said firmly. "It will need to be cleaned and mended, or you'll run out of gowns. Besides, I like this one."

"Oh?" She'd thought she looked good in it, but he'd never

said so before.

"Yes." He got it loose enough that it fell to the floor. "I wanted to tear it off of you with my teeth that night at Ordnung."

As if in demonstration, his teeth closed over the join of her neck and shoulder, the jolt going straight to her throbbing sex, and she moaned, trying to turn.

"No," he said, pressing her down over the arm of a chair, following her so his body lay over her, hard and heavy. His hand rounded over her bottom, sliding into the cleft and finding her sex ready for him. More than ready. Needy and wanting. She spread her legs helpfully, and he groaned. "I want you like this," he growled. "Is that all right?"

"Anything you want is all right," she panted, spreading her legs even wider. "Stop asking and take."

He made a sound, more like a bear than ever, shooting a heightened thrill through her. With one hand on the back of her neck, he pressed her down, freeing himself with the other, then thrusting at her invitingly open passage. He was clumsy—no surprise there, and finesse would come with practice—but she raised herself on her tiptoes, wriggling to give him the right angle. Finding it, he plunged into her to the hilt, both of them momentarily stilling at the sweet sense of connection.

All day, she'd craved having him inside her again, filling her, completing her in a way she'd never known she needed.

"Zephyr," he whispered, her name like a prayer and a vow, then began stroking in and out of her. He was trying to be gentle, she could tell, but his control was fraying. She encouraged it, pretending to struggle against his grip on her neck, turning her head to snap at his fingers. "Oh no, you don't," he snarled, gripping her hip with his other hand and pounding into her, hard, almost painful, driving her relentlessly into a climax that punched her through the sky and into the stars where the air was too thin to breathe and she could only fold her wings.

And fall.

"ZEPHYR." A GENTLE hand stroked her hair back from her brow. "Zephyr, darling, come back to me."

"Mmm." She stretched, deliciously sated, the silk of bed-covers beneath her skin. Barely cracking her eyelids, she studied Astar and his worried expression. "Don't want to."

"I'm sure." He rubbed his forehead. "But I have to make sure you're not hurt. I'm so sorry. So very sorry."

"What for?" Suspicious, she levered herself up onto her elbows to scan the room. They were alone, the fire prepared by the solicitous servants crackling merrily. A carafe of wine and a platter of food set out for them. "Don't tell me you have to go be courteous some more," she warned. She wouldn't be responsible for her behavior if he tried to go back to dancing with *Dina*.

"What? No." He ran a hand down her body—not a sensual caress, but as if checking for injury. "I was rough with you. Unforgivably so. I was—"

"You were rough," she agreed, cutting off the rush of guilt. "And I loved every moment of it." She lay back and sprawled in invitation. "Be rough with me again."

He stared at her, clearly astonished, more than a little bewildered. "You're serious."

"Yes." Tempted to tease him, she instead decided she'd do better to take her role as teacher and debaucher seriously. "Sometimes sex is rough. There are emotions involved, and all that *edge* you have." She trailed a finger down the center of his chest, revealed in the part of the shirt he still wore. He'd probably dutifully laced up his pants again, too.

"I held you down," he argued. "I bit your neck." He feathered his fingers over the spot, which stung delightfully.

"Believe me, I know," she purred, undulating, heat and need building rapidly. "I remember every delicious moment."

"You passed out," he added, almost accusingly.

"The highest of compliments," she replied with a satisfied smile. But he looked so distraught—and seemed to be trying so hard not to look at her nakedness—that she sat up, framing his face in her hands and kissing him gently. "The only surprise was that you were the one to lose your head instead of me."

"I don't know what came over me," he admitted, though he looked less worried.

She lifted a shoulder and let it fall. "Does it matter?"

"Yes," he answered earnestly.

"No." Shaking her head, she set to work divesting him of his clothing. "And here I was holding back out of concern that I might shock you. The gríobhth in me was so angry, so determined to fight off any competitors for your attention, that I thought I'd be the one ravishing you. I'd planned to strip you naked and have my way with you until you could only think of me. I still plan to do that," she added. "Just so we're clear."

"Zephyr." He grasped her wrists, stopping her from unlacing his pants, which he had indeed knotted tightly, probably with some misguided notion of imprisoning his cock for bad behavior. It clearly wasn't listening to his big head, as it was erect and thrusting against its velvet cage. She intended to reward it lavishly. That might be the best route to getting Astar to stop overthinking and start enjoying again. "We need to discuss this," he said, so very seriously that she nearly laughed in his face.

"All right," she said, far more agreeably than she felt. "But if you're going to make me sit through a boring conversation about what should be fun, then I'm getting wine." As soon as he released his grip on her wrists, she gave his cock a firm stroke and squeeze, to keep him simmering and less inclined to talk them to death. Then she slipped off the bed and did a quick shift, coming back clean, naked, and with her hair hanging loose. Much better, as those mossback hairpins gave her a headache. Continuing her campaign to scramble Astar's overactive brain, she strolled slowly and seductively to the table with the wine carafe, posing on the far side of it and facing Astar, so he'd have a good view of her body.

Shaking back her cloak of hair, she picked up the carafe and a goblet, holding them at nipple level and subtly thrusting out her breasts. "Wine?" she inquired in a throaty voice.

He yanked his gaze up to hers, his face flushed. "Ah, what did you say?"

Putty in her hands. She smiled sensually. "I asked if you'd like wine also."

"Oh." He stared uncomprehending at the items in her hands, obviously distracted by everything else she had on display. So much edge on this man. It might take weeks, even months to bleed off all that sexuality he'd bottled up. The thought made her purr. "I better not," he finally said, a vagueness to it that hinted he'd forgotten what he was talking about.

I better not might as well be Astar's personal motto. One she intended to change before she was done with him. Or he was done with her, which was more likely at this point, sadly enough, with the *Dinas* of the world on the hunt for tender crown prince prey.

Still, he was hers for the moment and she planned to savor him while she could, rather than worrying about some terrible future when she'd be forced to turn him over to one of those *Dinas*. Pouring two goblets of wine, she brought them back to the bed, handing them to him to hold while she walked around to the other side, all strategically planned so she could crawl across the bed toward him.

Well rewarded by his rapt expression, she curled up against some pillows, took one goblet from him, and sipped from it. Waited.

It took a moment, but a wry expression replaced the dazed look on Astar's face. He drained the wine in one gulp, set it aside, and raked his hands through his hair. "I know what you're doing."

She raised a brow. "I would hope so. We've only just started being lovers, but you seem like a fast learner."

Breathing a laugh, he shook his head, ponderous bear in

the motion. "It's not fair to use how incredibly beautiful you are to distract me from important matters."

On the contrary, Zeph rather thought that distracting Astar from worrying and overthinking might be her primary calling. She would do very well in that role—but she didn't say so. Besides, it made her unreasonably happy that he called her beautiful, the gríobhth inside preening its glossy feathers. "So," she prompted. "What did you want to discuss? Or perhaps we can skip the guilt after all and go right back to using this precious time wisely."

"I notice you didn't heal the marks I put on you when you shifted."

Not entirely distracted after all. Something to keep in mind for the future. "I did not," she agreed, pulling her hair aside to expose the bite mark on her neck, tracing a nail over it to feel the shiver. "I like knowing you feel as possessive of me as I do of you. Careful, controlled Astar: a ravening beast under that handsome exterior."

He spread his hands, looking at them. "I've spent my life trying to control that beast. I don't understand why it's escaping me now."

She polished off her own wine, tossed the goblet to land with a soft *thunk* on the rug, then crawled to sit sideways on Astar's lap. "The more we tighten our grip on something, the more likely it is to slip through our fingers. How much time do you spend in bear form?"

"More this week than for months before this," he admitted.

Winding her arms around his neck, idly toying with the soft hairs at his nape, she settled her naked hip against his crotch, delighted to find him as hard as ever, and sweetly pleased when he set a big hand on her thigh. "Try as you might to be all mossback," she said, "you *are* a shapeshifter. Our First Forms inform who we are, and the grizzly bear is as much a part of you as your kind heart and dutiful nature."

Giving her a bemused look, he smoothed his hand along her thigh, following it with his gaze and seeming entranced by the dimpling of her flesh. "I was under the impression that you didn't have a high regard for my adherence to honor and duty."

"I don't understand it," she replied, "but I do admire that in you."

He glanced up, clearly startled, searching her face. "Are you just saying that?"

"To get into your pants?" she replied teasingly, wriggling suggestively so his hands tightened on her. "I seem to have done that without flattery."

"Good point," he answered with some chagrin.

"I wouldn't lie about that, though," she continued, honestly enough, as this seemed the time for it. "I think you let your rules choke and cage you, but I also know they're qualities that will make you a good king."

He smiled uncertainly. "I hope so."

"But," she added, tapping him over his heart, "the bear has qualities that will make you a good king, too. *Use* that in yourself. Don't try to strangle the life from it."

He picked up her hand and turned it over to kiss her palm, giving her a lovely shiver. "When did my free-spirited Zephyr become so wise?"

"Lots of time flying and mulling the mysteries of the universe," she replied loftily. "Spend more time in animal form and you will learn new ways of seeing things, too."

Grimacing, he toyed with her fingers. "Ursula thinks it's better if the people aren't reminded that I'm a shapeshifter."

"I know. But she is also not a shapeshifter. She can't understand how she's stifling you."

"Is that what you think, that I'm stifled?"

"*So* much edge," she replied, placing kisses along the underside of his jaw, to make him shiver in need and to make her point. "With me, you don't have to be in control. Let your bear loose. Set free all those other animals within you, too."

"I really don't think I'll ever have more than First Form."

"And I really think you will. We'll see who turns out to be correct." She tugged her hand free to lightly scratch his nipple with a nail she made longer and sharper. He hissed, stiffening, jaw tightening as he fought for that control he loved so well. "I'll tell you a secret," she continued, turning to straddle his lap, pressing her open sex against the hard and needy ridge of him, titillating them both by brushing her taut nipples against his bare chest. "When I seduced you in that stairwell, I wanted you to lose control. I'll do it again, because I love it when you snap and stop thinking."

He put his hands on her hips, under the fall of her hair, smoothing over the curves to cup her bottom. "You are a dangerous woman, Zephyr. Maybe more than I can handle."

Shimmying her bottom against his big, rough hands, she smiled. "Seems like you're handling me perfectly. No complaints here."

Laughing a little, his gaze settled on her mouth, then drifted over her face, his eyes melting summer-sky blue, filled with longing and an emotion she didn't care to name. "What next?" he asked with a teasing, heated grin. "I believe you indicated an involved plan to strip me naked and have your way with me until I can only think of you."

"It's not all that involved," she replied, giving him a lingering kiss that grew quickly hot and hungry, both of them panting when they eased apart.

"It doesn't need to be," he admitted. "Zephyr, you should know—you're all I ever think about anyway."

She smiled, well pleased to hear that. "Then we only have the stripping and having left." Reaching between them, she found the laces of his pants.

"That might not be easy," he said. "I think I made a mess of knotting them."

She could just picture him, distraught over her faint, aghast at his loss of control, frantically fastening his laces, knotting them to last forever. "I don't know," she purred, growing a single sharp claw and slicing it clean through the knots, then placing it delicately on his lower lip. She'd like to pierce that full lip with the point of her claw, draw a single bead of blood, but that might be too much for her relatively innocent prince yet. He watched her with glassy-eyed need, chest rising and falling as if he'd been running. "Take those off," she suggested, showing him the claw, "unless you don't care if I shred them."

"I don't care," he said, voice hoarse, then caught her wrist before she could move. Shapeshifter speed. Already he was loosing the stranglehold on his deeper nature. "But pants shredded by lion claws might lead to questions."

She shrugged off those silly mossback mores, but helped him shimmy out of his boots and pants. When she had him deliciously naked, she positioned herself at his feet and began kissing her way up his gorgeously muscled legs. He reached for her, urging her up toward him, but she shook him off. "No hands," she told him. "That's the rule for now."

"But I want to—"

"You have and you will." She nipped the inside of his thigh. "But it's my turn to have you." Easing her way upward, she admired his tempting cock, long and thick, perfectly formed. It twitched as she pressed a kiss to his flat stomach, only a breath away. She glanced up to make sure he was watching, which he was, his face a rictus of agony and delight. Oh yes, this teasing would be most satisfying. "By the time I'm done with you, you'll understand why passing out from sex is a good thing." Drawing her hair to the side so he could see, and licking her lips for his benefit, she lowered her head and set to proving her point.

A DEMANDING KNOCK on their locked chamber doors had her groaning in sleepy protest and pulling the covers over her head. Astar, curled around her, brushed a soothing hand down her side. "Go back to sleep," he murmured. "I'll get it."

"Ignore it," she grumbled, groping to stop him, but he'd already slid out of bed and was pulling on those powder-blue velvet pants—she *should* have shredded them—and which looked considerably rumpled. Without laces, they barely clung to his lean hips, sagging just enough to give a glimpse of the upper curves of his perfect ass, and he had to hold them up with one hand, scraping back his tangled golden hair so it hung over his broad shoulders. Livid scratches showed all down his back from her nails where she'd left her marks on him.

Mmm. Mine.

"It might be my things finally," he told her, unbolting the door and allowing a short parade of servants carrying his trunks into the dim room. Fortunately for her fraying patience, he refused their offer to unpack for him, accepted a set of scrolls with a grimace, and sent them on their way. He started reading one scroll, forgetting about his pants, which slipped enough to reveal his hip bones and the golden curls at his groin.

Mmm. "Come back to bed," she told him.

He gave her a rueful glance, shaking his head. "I have to attend more meetings, I'm afraid. My clothes are the good news—the carriages finally caught up with us in the middle of the night, so at least the servants waited until dawn to bring the trunks up—but the restored ferry service at Gieneke means a great deal more bad news arrived also."

Tossing the scroll aside with the others, he searched for clothes out of one trunk and carried them into the bathing room, emerging fully dressed soon after. "Coming to breakfast?" he asked, kneeling on the bed with one knee and kissing her softly.

"I'll catch up with you. I might take an actual bath," she replied. She frankly wasn't in any hurry to be surrounded by people again, though she was ravenously hungry.

"Good idea." He smiled, brushing a strand of hair from her face. "You can sleep longer, relax here. I can have food sent up."

It sounded good. Too good. "How are you not exhausted?" she complained. Neither of them had slept much. He'd insisted on learning how to employ the same tricks on her that she'd used on him—after he woke up from a dead faint—and they'd mainly taken brief cat naps before devouring each other anew. He was an apt, and voracious, student of the sensual delights, and she felt pleasantly battered.

"Duty calls," he replied, smiling widely when she made a rude noise. "And it seems having a beautiful woman ravish me all night is greatly restorative in other ways."

"Flatterer."

"Shall I have food sent up?"

"No." Tempting as it was, she felt an unaccustomed twinge of something like guilt at the prospect of lolling the morning away while he worked. Also, *Dina* might be there. "I'll be down soon."

"You know, it truly would be all right if you wanted to go fly or ramble," he suggested. "I know you can be discreet, and it's beautiful countryside."

That was tempting also—though she wondered if he was trying to keep her away from *Dina*. On second thought, staying away from *Dina* probably wasn't a terrible idea. She'd have to release her Astar to *a* Dina, if not *the* Dina, someday. She had no business feeling so possessive of him. *Mine*, the gríobhth snarled.

"Maybe I will go flying," she said, trying to convince her seething gríobhth with the treat.

"Zephyr," Astar said, then hesitated, looking troubled. *Uh-oh.* Was this it, the end already? She'd gotten more than the one night he'd promised, but she'd truly hoped for more.

"What?" she asked, sounding brittle to her own ears.

"Would you heal the bite mark I left on your neck, along with at least the visible bruises?" he asked tentatively. "I know you don't mind them, but I worry about the impression it will make on the others."

It was on the tip of her tongue to ask if he was ashamed—but then realized that he probably was. Astar wasn't a brutal man in any way, and it would be hard on him for anyone to think so. "All right," she agreed. When he smiled in relief, she added, "But only the visible ones. Just as you'll have to wear the scratches I put on you under your shirt."

He cupped the back of her neck and kissed her thoroughly. "I'm kind of glad I can't heal like you can. Every time I move, the sting will make me think of you and how you marked me as yours. I'll spend the day longing for the moment we're together again."

Perhaps it didn't reflect well on her, but that admission made her happy, soothing her savage thoughts about *Dina.* Then it occurred to her that Astar looked far too smug at her easy capitulation. "Are you managing me?" she asked, realizing that she'd heard Ursula accuse Harlan of that more than once.

Astar had the grace to look vaguely sheepish, despite the enduring smug. "How am I doing?"

"Hmm. Not badly," she admitted, well aware her gríobhth

nature wasn't being reasonable—and oddly warmed that Astar clearly knew this. Still… "Astar—I *do* understand that you're not really mine."

He sobered, searching her face. "In a way, I am, and forever will be. You will always be my first, no matter what happens after this."

That didn't help. Maybe that odd pricking feeling—the one that insisted it would be somehow wrong to play and relax while he faced a long day—was some stupid sense of responsibility. Or worse, *duty*. Ugh, foul word. "Should I let you go?" she asked, and knew by the look on his face that he understood she didn't mean to breakfast, though he had to go do that, too. "After all, you have fulfilled the vow you made under duress."

An uncertain and sad expression crossed his face. "Are you done with me already?"

"No." As she said it, she knew the brutal truth of that. She wasn't even close to done with him. And—far more startling— she couldn't envision the day she would be. Unsettled by the realization, she pushed up and embraced him, holding on tightly. "I'm not even close to done," she said, and her voice came out a little choked. What would she do when she had to be done, to let him go to someone else?

"Shh." He stroked her back. "Are you crying?"

She sniffled. "Maybe."

"Why?" He pulled back, thumbs brushing the tears from her cheeks. "I'm not going anywhere."

"Yet," she corrected.

"Yet," he echoed bleakly.

How had they ended up in such a dismal conversation?

Her fault—and how strange was that? "But not today," she offered, and he smiled in relief.

"Not today and not tonight," he agreed, kissing her lingeringly. "Have your bath. Go flying. You'll feel better for it."

"All right." That probably would help to settle her. So interesting that he knew that. "If you like, tonight I'll dance with you," she offered.

He smiled in real delight. "I would love that."

See? She knew how to settle him, too.

~ 22 ~

"GOOD MORNING, YOUR Highness." Berendina, who'd been lurking just inside the doorway of the breakfast hall, practically pounced on him as he walked in.

"Good morning, Princess," he said, taking her proffered hand and kissing the air over it. He immediately missed Zephyr, but at least he had habits of politeness to fall back on. "You look lovely this morning."

"Thank you. *You* don't look like you slept at all. Was the news from Castle Ordnung dire enough to keep you awake all night?"

News from Ordnung? How did she—oh. He'd forgotten Zephyr's excuse for stealing him away, and what her "message" had actually consisted of. Feeling the blush heat his face—and the sting of scratches from her claws on his back—he did his best to dissemble. "The ferries are indeed operating at the confluence again, and there's all sort of news, dire and otherwise." He brandished the scrolls he carried, suddenly aware that he'd never finished reading the missive from Ursula, because he'd gotten distracted talking to Zephyr.

Berendina gave him a knowing look, not fooled in the least. "Your friend last night—the attractive brunette—I don't think I caught her name."

Attractive brunette. A deliberately milquetoast description for Zephyr's vivid beauty. "Zephyr," he said, well aware that he had given the name when he introduced them.

The princess frowned in puzzlement. "Say it again?"

"Zephyr," he repeated. "Like the wind."

"How unusual," she said, making her disapproval clear, following him to the table where platters of food were laid out. "She's Tala, is she not?"

"Indeed she is." He piled food on his plate at random, not really caring what he ate.

"We don't see many Tala in Jorrit, though there are always tales from over the border. The northern enclaves of Tala always seem to be doing something *wild*."

Enclaves of people of all kinds always seemed to be producing trouble of one sort or another—but he refrained from pointing that out and simply declined to comment.

"Does she become..." The princess glanced around as if checking for eavesdroppers, and lowered her voice. "An *animal*?"

Yes, and so do I. Astar refrained from saying that also, Ursula's cautions echoing in his head. Princess Berendina wouldn't embrace the bear in him the way Zephyr did. Though, to be fair, it wasn't likely that any of the mossback women on the list would be expecting to marry a prince who turned into a grizzly bear on occasion. The late, unlamented High King Uorsin had been named for a bear, and Ursula named for him in turn—but not many people realized how literally true that would be of their next high king. "Not all Tala are shapeshifters," he said, keeping it light, politely ducking the question in a way that someone of Berendina's training would recognize as the mild reproof it was.

"I meant no insult." With a graceful gesture, she dismissed that lie as a polite fiction, just between them.

"Are you eating?" he asked, noting that she hadn't filled a plate.

"I already ate. I'm an early riser." She beamed, as if expecting praise—and having no way of knowing she only evoked the image of Zephyr in his mind, naked and snuggling sensually in bed, inviting him to return and... "Anyway," she said as he scanned the busy room for a seat, "I'm fully aware that not all Tala are able to shapeshift. I've studied the peoples and cultures of all the Thirteen Kingdoms, its protectorates, and allies." She delivered that information candidly, as part of her credentials to be his bride. "But your friend..."

"Zephyr," he supplied wryly, already tiring of this game. Tempted to seat himself between two people so Berendina couldn't follow, he instead did the gracious thing and chose an unoccupied round table.

"Zephyr, right," she repeated with a conspiratorial smile, inviting him to join in on the joke. "Like the wind. She must become a bird."

He shrugged noncommittally, filling his mouth with food to further excuse his lack of reply.

"I met some of your other friends last night. All so charming. Gendra is lovely, and also Tala, I believe. I've yet to meet your twin sister, Princess Stella, however—though I understand you two look nothing alike."

"As dark as I am fair," he agreed.

"Yes, I understand she has the black hair and blue eyes of the Tala. You both have some Tala blood, don't you?" she continued in an idle tone, as if making conversation.

Astar didn't need shapeshifter hearing to detect that his potential bride had reached the goal of her inquisition. Years at the court at Ordnung had attuned him to the seemingly innocuous prattle that led the unwary to blurt out expensive truths. Ursula had agreed that it would be best for him to be honest with his bride about his dual nature, but she'd also left it up to him on when and how to have that conversation. Privately, he'd decided that would happen right before he offered his grandmother Salena's ruby ring. His potential bride's reaction to the news would be the final test.

That person would not be Berendina. He'd been trying to reserve judgment, to be open to meeting her, as he'd promised—these weren't the best of circumstances to discover someone's true personality—but he didn't think the princess would improve upon better acquaintance. She possessed many fine qualities, and also plenty of prejudice against the Tala. That was a dealbreaker for him. Unfortunately, he still had to pretend to be considering her, for form's sake and for good relations with Groningen.

"Stella and I both have Tala blood, on our mother's side," he agreed. "As does Her Majesty High Queen Ursula," he added pointedly.

"Oh, to be sure. It's just so interesting that Princess Stella has such dark coloring, when your mother is as fair as the dawn, like your handsome self."

He managed not to snort at that heavy-handed bit of flattery. "I understand I look very much like my father, in truth."

"Ah, the noble Hugh, Prince of Avonlidgh. His loss was a great one for us all, but particularly so for you. My sympathies."

"Thank you, but he died before I was born, so I think Stella and I feel his loss less than the people who actually knew him."

"Still, to grow up without a father is difficult for a young man."

"Perhaps you're not aware that my mother remarried," he offered blandly. "Her husband, Ash, has been my father all my life, and is the best of men."

She winced, ever so slightly, a reproof for him mentioning the unmentionable. Royals from small and remote principalities tended to be the most conscious of status and bloodlines. An irony there, as they put so much weight on being the biggest fish in their very small ponds. Whereas the truly big fish, royal-status wise, in the biggest ponds—such as the queen of Avonlidgh and High Queen Ursula—had both chosen to marry men of questionable bloodlines. Harlan because he was an exiled Dasnarian prince, and Ash was scandalously an ex-convict, entirely due to his halfblood Tala status, which used to be a criminal offense on its own.

Some, like Princess Berendina's family, apparently, considered Ash to be an unsavory topic of conversation, preferring to pretend he didn't exist. Annoyed enough to continue, Astar said, "And my uncles, King Rayfe of Annfwn and Her Majesty's consort, Prince Harlan, have always been a presence in my life. Truly I'm privileged to have been raised by so many accomplished men of sterling character." That was very true, he realized. All this time, he'd been worrying about living up to his dead father's image, when all these living fathers had been right there, showing him the many and varied ways to be a good man, a good husband, and a good ruler.

And they'd all chosen to marry the women they loved, regardless of social consequences. *Fuck the rules,* Ash's parting advice echoed in his mind.

"I suppose that could be true," Berendina said with a frown. "Still, Prince Hugh was known throughout the lands as the most noble and honorable of royals. A trueborn son of the kingdom of Avonlidgh. I mean, Harlan is *Dasnarian,* not from here at all."

"Talking about me?" Jak plopped himself on the other side of Berendina, his overfull mug sloshing as he set it down none too gently. A genial grin creased his face, but the look in his sharp dark eyes made it clear he'd heard everything the princess had said.

"Princess Berendina of Jorrit," Astar said with neutral politeness, "my friend Jakral of the *Hákyrling.*"

"Call me Jak." He seized her hand and pumped it, being rather deliberately uncouth. "No honorifics for me. I'm a simple sailor, fighter... and lover." He added a leer, and Astar winced internally. Jak wouldn't be this rude unless his friends had compared notes on Berendina—and had decided against her. This would not go well.

"I see." The princess withdrew her hand pointedly. "I'm not familiar with Hákyrling—where is it?"

"The *Hákyrling,*" Jak corrected, emphasizing the "the" and

still smiling—but with a dangerous glint in his eye. "A sailing ship. I grew up on the high seas. My father is Kral, a former imperial prince of Dasnaria, Harlan's brother," he added offhandedly. "Say, Astar, since you and I share an uncle, when you're high king, does that mean I get some sort of royal sinecure?"

Enjoying himself far more now, Astar played along. Not only because Berendina looked appalled, though that appealed to his annoyance with her. "I don't see why not," he mused. "What do you have in mind?"

"Something that pays well and gives me an unreasonable amount of power, but requires no effort on my part."

"That should be easy—you just described half the courtiers at Ordnung."

"Oh, really, that's not—" Berendina began, but Jak talked over her.

"Excellent news," he declared, toasting with his mug—and not incidentally splashing more, which smelled strongly of alcohol—then quaffing a healthy swallow.

"Are you drinking your breakfast?" Astar inquired mildly.

"Hair of the dog. I had a very long night," Jak replied, winking broadly at Berendina.

"Gambling," Stella said from behind Astar, bending to kiss him on the cheek before she slipped into the chair beside him. "Not womanizing, so don't let him bend your ear with tales."

"How could I womanize when you are my own true love, Nilly?" Jak protested, clapping a hand to his heart.

"Nilly?" Berendina asked, turning her shoulder to Jak.

"My twin sister, Stella," Astar replied, making the introductions.

"It's an old nickname," Stella explained. "When we were little, they called us Willy and Nilly, because Astar and I were always getting into things and causing trouble."

Berendina laughed, gaily, and hugged Astar's arm. "I love that. I shall call you Willy from now on."

"If I get a vote," Stella subvocalized to him, *"it's no."*

"Of course you get a vote—and it counts second only to mine," he replied. *"But that was fast. Foresight or intuition?"*

"Neither. I can feel you don't like her."

Too true. Gen and Lena arrived right then, accompanied by the young man Gen had been dancing with the night before. Gen set a full plate before Stella. "Here you go, sweets."

"Thank you," Stella replied fervently. Catching Astar's inquiring look, she grimaced ruefully. "I didn't want to brave the crush around the food table. I'm trying to ration my resources so I can last through to the ball tonight."

Astar patted her knee under the table. This kind of a crowd was harder on Nilly than anyone. "You don't have to attend."

"I want to," she corrected.

"Are you of fragile constitution?" Berendina asked, looking from Stella to Astar as if attempting to discern a previously invisible weakness.

"Not at all," Stella replied tightly.

Jak barked out a laugh, startling Berendina so she flinched. "Nilly is the opposite of fragile." Jak caught Astar's warning look and said no more on that subject. "Sorry, though, I should've thought to grab you a plate."

"It's fine," Stella replied with a gentle smile. "I don't expect you all to cater to me." She elbowed Astar. "Introductions."

"I was getting there," he retorted, pulling her hair. "I had to wait for an opening with you lot jabbering away. Princess Salena Nakoa KauPo of Nahanau, Princess Berendina of Jorrit. I believe you already met Gendra of Annfwn."

"And this is Prince Henk of Ernst," Gen said with a pleased and proud expression, setting a hand on the man seated next to her. "His Highness Crown Prince Astar."

"Though we call him Willy," Berendina put in, with her own squeeze of Astar's arm.

Lena widened her eyes at him, crossing them ever so slightly, and he had to cover his laugh with a cough.

"I'm honored to meet you, Your Highness," Henk said. "And, may I say, utterly delighted to be invited into your close circle of friends."

"Of course," Astar replied blandly—after catching Gen's pleading expression and hopeful puppy-dog eyes.

"Such a *large* close circle of friends," Berendina noted. "But is this everyone?"

"Not quite," Jak said, pretending to scan the room. "Where *is* Zeph?" He tapped his chin in faux concern, leaning around Berendina with his elbows on the table. "Astar, have *you* seen Zeph this morning?"

Lena snorted quietly, while Stella intently focused on her plate. Gen was giggling at something Henk whispered in her ear, paying no attention to them. Astar narrowed his eyes at Jak, who grinned back, eyes dancing with mischief. "I believe Zephyr planned to sleep in a bit, then do some exploring,"

Astar said nonchalantly. "She's still recovering her health after nearly dying while saving my life."

He wasn't sure why he'd added that last. Maybe to make it clear to Berendina that he held Zephyr in high regard and that no amount of petty aspersions would change that.

"I'll bet she's recovering from *something*," Jak said, snickering. "Is that a scratch on your neck, Astar, or—"

"Let me see," Stella demanded, acting concerned. He turned to face her, using the excuse to remove his arm from Berendina's leechlike grasp. Stella stroked the scratch with a light finger, healing it instantly and giving him a smile that said everything. "You're wrong, Jak—it was a smudge, and I've wiped it clean."

"I clearly saw—" Jak continued, undaunted, but Lena cut him off.

"So, Princess Berendina," she said loudly, "tell us about Jorrit. I understand your weather patterns keep it quite cold for most of the year. Is it true your growing season is only ten weeks long?"

Berendina gamely replied, Lena keeping her going on a detailed conversation of crops, precipitation, and frost cycles— blessedly allowing the rest of them to eat in peace. Astar would have to do Lena a favor in return. As if she heard the thought, Lena met his gaze and smiled warmly—and he realized she appreciated his interference with Rhyian, and that she was paying him back.

Rhy, who could've easily returned from Ordnung by now, if he was going to. With disappointment, Astar considered that his cousin might have taken the opportunity to bail on the quest. Likely he was back in Annfwn even now, drowning his sorrows and burying memories of Lena by layering other bodies on top of his own. Though Astar had suggested this option, part of him had hoped Rhy would see his way to trying to be a better man, to return to the group and stick it out, no matter what happened.

Apparently not.

"Zeph is here," Stella subvocalized.

Astar jerked his head up, and there she was, gliding up to their table with a plate in one hand and a flute of sparkling wine in the other. As if determined to draw a contrast between herself and Berendina—as if she needed to—she had on simple silk shift of the sort the Tala generally wore in Annfwn. In chilly Elderhorst, it looked like what ladies wore under their clothes, not in place of them. The intense sapphire blue of the silk emphasized her startling eyes, and her hair hung loose nearly to the hem, glossy as a tumbling waterfall of ink. She was also barefoot.

She gave him an easy smile, daring him to comment, and Astar was hard-pressed not to laugh at her gambit. "Good morning, all," she purred. "I see I'm late to the party, but I'm afraid I had a *bear* of a night."

Good thing Astar had nothing in his mouth, or he'd have choked on it. Zephyr settled into the chair a sharp-eyed footman brought over—giving the poor young man such a dazzling smile that he tripped over his own feet as he backed away—and she gracefully slipped into the space Jak and Lena made for her.

"Sorry to hear about your *rough* night," Jak said, leaning his chin in his hand. "Was it *long* and *hard?*"

Lena pressed her napkin to her mouth, face pinking from suppressed laughter, and Astar considered his options. Kill them all? Temporary imprisonment? He didn't dare look at Berendina.

"You have *no* idea, Jak," Zephyr was saying, fluttering a hand as if to cool herself. "It was *so* hot. And I tried every position imaginable, but I—"

"Perhaps you should request a different room," Astar interrupted meaningfully, catching her gaze and sliding his own at Berendina beside him. "If you're so uncomfortable."

"Oh, I wouldn't want to impose on our hosts. Besides, my room has one salient perk I wouldn't give up without a fight." Zephyr fluttered her lashes extravagantly. "Oh, hello, *Dina*—I didn't notice you there."

"The perils of drinking before breakfast, perhaps," Berendina replied smoothly.

Zephyr smiled, drained her wine, and raised the empty flute into the air. The blushing young footman instantly brought another. "I just love Castle Elderhorst," Zephyr cooed, giving the young man a blatant once-over. "So civilized. Besides, what's a pleasure jaunt through the northern kingdoms without a few indulgences? You should try it, *Dina*. Let me request a glass for you, too."

"No, thank you," Berendina replied loftily, slipping her arm through Astar's again. "My visit here is not nearly so frivolous. I need to keep a clear head to attend to my duties."

"Is that what they call it in Jorrit?" Zephyr smiled thinly, eyes glittering, her gríobhth possessiveness rising sharp in her demeanor.

"I thought King Groningen had announcements to make," Astar cut in loudly, giving Zephyr a look of warning and pleading. Her gaze was fixed on Berendina's arm hooked through his, a hint of fang behind her parted lips. "I wonder where he could be?" he asked the table in general.

"Difficult to say," Zephyr returned. "What do you think, *Dina*? What do you imagine might make a man as virile as your grandfather late to breakfast?"

"*Save me,*" Astar subvocalized to Stella.

He caught a whiff of humor from her before a set of bugles trumpeted the arrival of Groningen. The room fell silent in expectation. Nothing happened. People began murmuring to one another. Zephyr raised a single eyebrow at him, then transferred her gimlet gaze to Berendina.

"*Nice trick, and thank you,*" Astar told Stella hastily, "*but that won't last long.*"

"*Shh. He's almost here.*"

Sure enough, the bugles blasted again—a distinctly different note—and Groningen strode into the room, followed by a train of heirs and advisers. Astar never thought he'd be relieved to see his taskmaster, but he leapt to his feet at Groningen's nod to join them. Then he hesitated. Leaving Berendina alone with Zephyr in a lethally playful mood was not a good idea.

"Shall I accompany you, Willy?" Berendina said as she stood, not waiting for an answer, and immediately reclaiming his arm. "Let's leave these happy travelers to their frivolities and pleasures while we devote ourselves to the service of Her Majesty and the people who look to us for succor."

A pained look crossed Lena's face, though she tried to suppress it. A low snarl rolled out of an unsmiling Zephyr— which Berendina fortunately lacked the sensitive ears to hear— and Jak seized Zephyr's hand, pretending to woo her with extravagantly loud compliments.

Seizing the opportunity, Astar strode after Groningen, Berendina stubbornly clinging to his arm.

~ 23 ~

"**Y**OUR LIPS ARE red as fresh heart's blood, your eyes a brighter sapphire than Zynda's dragon scales, your skin as white as—"

"What in Moranu are you going on about, Jak?" Zeph snapped, yanking her hand from his.

"She's back," Lena said in a relieved tone, releasing her grip from Zeph's knee under the table.

"What do you mean?" Zeph demanded, then caught a glimpse of Astar's tall form striding away from her with *Dina* attached to his arm like a life-sucking barnacle. She growled, rising to go after them. Lena and Jak grabbed her again.

"Down, girl," Jak warned, for once not joking.

"No killing Astar's potential brides," Lena hissed in her ear. "Get the gríobhth under control."

Oh. True. She was close to shifting, talons aching to escape her fingers, beak ready to slash and kill a little blondie birdie named *Dina*. "Let me go," she murmured, her vision sharpening to track the pair of them.

"Astar will never forgive you if you cause an incident. You don't want that," Lena insisted. "Stella, some help here?"

Stella shrugged in extravagant Tala fashion and didn't

budge.

"Help with what?" Prince Henk asked, surfacing from his whispered conversation with Gen. Poor guy didn't realize that most of the table had heard every word he'd said to Gen, most of it bragging about his wealth and rank. Gen had been doing a convincing job of looking dazzled. At least, Zeph hoped she was faking that. Henk followed Zeph's gaze. "Does Prince Willy need convincing that our Dina is the ideal choice for high queen? I feel confident this is a sure thing."

"There are many names on the list of Astar's potential brides," Zeph informed him. This moment shouldn't have come so soon. She'd only just tasted Astar—and there was no reason for him to choose the first princess to fasten her parasitic scolex into his handsome flesh.

"None so accomplished as Dina," Henk declared, starting to tick points off on his fingers. "Obviously, she's beautiful, of the purest northern bloodlines, never a scandal in *her* family. Clever. Talented—paints and plays several instruments—and is extraordinarily well educated. She's spent her entire life studying everything she needs to know to be the perfect bride for our Willy."

Zeph gave Henk a long stare. "Clearly there's not much to do in Jorrit."

Behind him, Gen widened her eyes in a look of warning. Oblivious to Zeph's sarcasm, Henk smiled condescendingly. "Ah, you are clearly not familiar with Jorrit."

"No," Zeph purred. "I simply drink wine and look pretty while others devote themselves to the service of Her Majesty and the people who look to them for succor."

"Just so," Henk said, nodding. "There are any number of amusements in Jorrit, including several winter sports. Those might be too demanding and scary for a delicate female like yourself, however. The ice-fishing tournaments are more low-key, though still intensely competitive, for example."

"Why would anyone fish for ice?" Zeph asked, baiting him now. If she couldn't eat *Dina*, this Henk would do for a snack.

He chortled. "Oh, dear girl. You misunderstand. A lovely lady like yourself probably doesn't know where fish come from, but—"

"Aren't there fish in Lake Sullivan?" Gen interrupted. "Big ones that the sea—ah, lake creature lives off of?"

Henk looked annoyed to be interrupted, but turned to Gen with an incredulous laugh. "Surely you don't believe everything you hear."

Zeph missed the rest because Jak and Lena leapt to their feet, dragging her with them, Stella drifting along behind. "I don't want to leave," Zeph hissed.

"Too bad," Jak replied, steering them to the door. For a wiry guy, he had a good grip.

"We're saving you from yourself," Lena added. "Stella is taking you flying."

"I am?" Stella sounded surprised.

"I don't need a babysitter," Zeph snarled.

"You are," Lena told Stella, "because you need to get away from the press of people for a while. And you do, Zeph. You need to bleed energy off your gríobhth now, Zeph, before you really do kill someone. Stella will keep an eye on you." Lena caught Zeph by the shoulders. "Believe me, I understand how you feel, but you need to cool down and think like a rational person, not like the gríobhth."

Zeph lost some of her fury at the sympathy in Lena's eyes. "I always forget how well you understand shapeshifters."

Lena smiled without humor. "Way too much time and effort trying to make a relationship work with one. Go on and fly. If I could, I'd go with you. Jak and I will keep an eye on Astar."

"Thank you." Abruptly overcome, she hugged Lena hard, then did the same with Jak.

He stroked her hair, holding her with surprising care. "We've got your back, Zeph."

HOURS LATER, WHEN Zeph and Stella returned to Castle Elderhorst, night had fallen, and the sprawling structure blazed with torchlight. She and Stella had both taken owl forms to discreetly return to the land of observant mossbacks, but she'd spent most of the day in gríobhth form—and both Lena and Astar had been correct. She felt much better for it.

Carienne was a spectacularly beautiful kingdom, even in winter. Well, for all she knew, it was ugly without the blanket of snow and ice. But it had been a clear day, her gríobhth form impervious to the cold, and the time aloft had given her space to think. Maybe it had partly been the grandeur of the landscape, the snowy hills and the fog rolling in the valleys like a misty sea, but she'd gained a bit of perspective.

Much as she hated to admit it, Gen was right. Zeph had

bitten off far more than even the sharpest beak could slice into ribbons. Even if Astar didn't choose Dina, then—as Zeph herself had pointed out to the odious Henk—there were more names on that list. And Astar had been tasked to meet them as they traveled, to pick one to marry. Which meant that Zeph would face this blood-boiling drive to disembowel each and every one. Over and over.

Even if the woman was someone Zeph would otherwise like, the gríobhth in her would want to rend her limb from limb the moment she laid hands on Astar.

There was only one solution: to inure herself to the truth that Astar *wasn't* hers, and never would be. Another thing that Gen had been right about, and Astar too, though Zeph would never admit it to either of them—it might've been easier to convince herself if she and Astar hadn't started. Though the thought of not having the last few nights with him made her want to cry.

She and Stella landed on the balcony outside Stella's room, the one they'd taken off from, shifted into forms like the smaller domestic cats of the castle—just in case any servants lingered inside—and scooted through the door Stella opened with her sorcery. Once they verified the room was empty, they shifted to human form. Like Zeph, Stella had already dressed for a ball, with her hair up and her grandmother Salena's rubies dangling from her ears.

Zeph had yet to have her other two gowns fixed up to cache again, so she was down to one: a silver-trimmed black velvet. At least it suited her mood. Stella looked her over, absorbing her outfit and, no doubt, assessing her emotional state.

Calm, resigned, already grieving the loss to come. Noble, even.

"You're going to tell him that it's time to end your affair," Stella said, not a question, her gray eyes full of sorrow.

"I have to," Zeph replied. "I can't keep doing this to both of us."

Stella nodded somberly.

"Look at Rhy," Zeph said, as if Stella had argued. "I thought he wouldn't be able to stay away from Lena, but he has. If he can exercise restraint, so can I."

Stella cocked her head, considering that. "Rhy stayed away from Lena for seven years—and it wasn't out of self-restraint, but cowardice."

That brought up Zeph short. "Are you saying I'm being a coward?"

"I was talking about Rhy," Stella replied with a shrug. "Only you can know what's in your heart."

Yeah, only her and the sorceress empath standing in front of her. "I'm trying to do the honorable thing here," Zeph protested. "I'll admit that's a new thing for me, but I'm going to let Astar go for... for the good of the realm." She flung her hands up in the air as she said it. It wasn't easy sounding sincere when you didn't believe in the rules in the first place.

"What about Astar's good?" Stella asked somberly.

"That too," Zeph replied immediately. "Everyone agrees I'm not good for him."

"Do they?" Stella could be so very mild and neutral, her gray eyes shimmering the same opaque silver as her gown.

"The exact opinion varies," Zeph conceded, "but the inarguable element here is that there is a list of women that Astar can marry and I'm not on it."

Stella gave her a look of wide-eyed—and deliberate—surprise. "I thought you didn't want forever from Astar."

"It just figures he tells you everything," Zeph grumbled.

"I know Astar's heart like my own," Stella replied, confessing nothing. "Are you saying you would marry Astar if you were an approved name on the list?"

"No!" Though, if he weren't going to be high king... "It's not worth puzzling over, since my name isn't on the list."

"How do you know—have you seen the list?"

"I don't need to see it. I'm not someone Ursula and her advisers would consider an appropriate high queen. I'm not *accomplished*." Or one to devote herself to the service of anything.

"Oh, fuck *that*," Stella said, eyes flashing and magic gathering with her anger. "For someone who's otherwise gloriously, and deservedly self-confident, you really don't give yourself credit."

It took Zeph a moment to get over her shock and gather her thoughts. "I... don't?"

"To begin with, you are one of the most talented shapeshifters in the world."

"So are you and Gen. And you're a sorceress and healer, and she has more forms than I do. Besides, I was born this way."

"Neither Gen nor I, nor any living shapeshifter I know of has your skill with taking objects with you when you shift and retrieving them at will from your cache."

Zeph shrugged. "That just takes practice—and a fondness for pretty dresses and hairstyles."

Stella laughed and pointed at her. "You just simultaneously refused to take credit for your accomplishments on the grounds that they're inborn and also just a matter of practice."

"So what?" Zeph snapped, her peaceful feelings from flying fading quickly.

"You just proved my point that you don't give yourself credit. You excuse it all away. My point is also this: You are sensual, vivacious, and free-spirited in all the ways that Astar isn't. You are also courageous, loyal, inventive, and focused when you want to be. We couldn't have defeated the stone giant without you—and not only because of your ferocious bravery, but because of your cleverness. How are these not excellent qualities in a high queen? Far more important than painting and music."

Zeph gaped at this unusual speech from Stella. "But I'm Tala." *But I'm a monster.*

"And Tala are citizens of the Thirteen Kingdoms."

Now, anyway.

"None of this includes the most important thing, the one that eclipses all else. Has it ever occurred to you that maybe what Astar needs is someone to be a real partner to him? Being high king will be difficult. He needs someone who wants him for himself, not for his crown. Someone who doesn't take him too seriously. A woman who will love him enough to want to kill to keep him and who's willing to give him up to save him."

Zeph had no response to that. Nothing sprang to mind,

except... "But I *don't* love him."

Stella gave her a long look, one that went *through* her in that sorcerous way. Then she nodded once, crisply. "We should get down to the ball."

ASTAR WAS WAITING for her. Oh, he of course was also fulfilling his duties, participating in yet another of the endless conversations that seemed to form the bulk of his life. See? That was another *accomplishment* she lacked. She knew she'd never be able to stand around and talk talk talk.

She also knew that, though Astar was paying attention to some diatribe that had Groningen gesturing wildly, he'd also positioned himself to be able to see the entrance to the ballroom. No *Dina* in sight. As soon as Astar spotted her and Stella's arrival, he caught her eye and precipitously excused himself from the conversation. The instant attention had her preening a little inside.

"I wondered if you two were coming back," he teased as he reached them, though his voice held a hint of relief. "Zephyr, you look gorgeous. Like the goddess of night made flesh." He bent over her hand, kissing the back of it, then—with his hair falling in a discreet golden veil—turned her hand over and placed a sensual kiss in her palm. A hot shiver went through her. Maybe she wouldn't end things tonight. Tomorrow would be soon enough. *One more night.*

"What about me?" Stella demanded. "Am I a dusty gruntling beneath notice?"

"You're my sister," he said with a fond grin. "You are beautiful like a painting. I don't see anything else." He tucked Zeph's hand in the crook of his elbow. "You promised me a dance."

"Fine." She sighed, pretending to being long-suffering, but after being away from Astar all day, the opportunity to be in his arms—for any reason—made her nearly giddy. She'd been about to ask where *Dina* was, but she didn't want to poke the bear for no reason. Or, at least, not for that reason. "But you'll have to teach me this mossback prancing and mincing."

"I can do that," he said, summer-sky eyes filled with anticipation as he led her onto a clear space on the dance floor and guided her hands into position. "It's gratifying to be able to teach *you* something for a change," he murmured sensually.

She flushed—surely with the heat of desire, not some sort of girlish fluster—and studied the position of her hands, one folded into his, the other on his delightfully bulging biceps. "What next?" she asked, deliberately using the phrase from their sexual interludes.

His face hardened with answering desire. "Follow my lead." Slowly, at half the time of the music, he eased her into the small steps, counting the beats quietly for her, eyes holding hers. She'd grown familiar enough with his body that following along felt as natural as breathing. The dance required space between them, but that structure somehow made the few points of contact between them burn even hotter. His hand at the small of her back felt like it might scorch through even the heavy silver brocade.

She hadn't expected this kind of connection in such a formal-looking dance. Only his handsome face, those beautiful eyes, seemed to be in focus, while the rest of the world blurred away. It might be only the two of them, inside a bubble of intimacy, the intensity of his regard almost more than she could bear.

Astar's gaze fell to her mouth, searingly hot, and for a moment she thought he might kiss her right there, in front of everyone. But he jerked his gaze away, clearing his throat and giving her a wry smile. "You do look lovely tonight," he said in his most elegant tones, then added, "particularly the shoes." His eyes sparkled with teasing light.

"I'm back to trying to behave," she acknowledged ruefully. "My resolutions in that direction never seem to last long. I apologize for this morning."

"There's nothing to apologize for," he assured her, gaze roving over her face. "You were simply being you."

She managed not to wince, not at all sure what had possessed her to be so capricious as to defy the mossback dress norms. She'd been all ready to wear a proper gown and shoes, but had felt defiant and rebellious at the last moment. As her mother was fond of saying, her lack of impulse control came from her father, and that wasn't a virtue. She'd always scoffed at her mother's scolding, but—for the first time—she felt vaguely ashamed of herself. Would it be so hard to be someone Astar could be proud of? "Being me isn't ideal, I know," she admitted. "I'm going to change, I promise."

"What do you mean—change what?" He looked genuinely perplexed—and her heart burst with warm affection, rather like an overripe grape in the sun.

"We both know I'm supposed to be doing better at this, blending in and such," she replied.

A faint frown formed between his golden brows. "Who said so?"

"For starters, it's our cover story, isn't it? A group of pleasure-seeking nobles on a jaunt. No scary shapeshifters here. No monsters in sheep's clothing. Nothing to be alarmed about."

With the hand pressed to the small of her back, he eased her closer, his body heat suffusing her across the stiff distance of the dance. "Who better to epitomize a pleasure-seeking noble than a beautiful Tala woman who comes to breakfast barefoot and drinking sparkling wine?"

She had to laugh. He did have a point. Still. Focusing on the hollow at the base of his throat, where his skin would taste of sweet and salt if only she could lick him there, she wrestled the turbulent emotions leaking from her heart, now that it had unexpectedly burst. "I don't want to embarrass you is all," she said, the admission painful.

"Oh, Zephyr." He abandoned the formal structure of their arms and folded their hands in, drawing her against him so her head lay in the fold of his shoulder, as she slept sometimes with him—when they did sleep. "You could never embarrass me," he said into her ear, his chest rumbling with the words. "And you being you *is* ideal. You are like the wind, like the mountain peaks, and like the lush tropical flowers of Annfwn. You are a force of nature, maybe the one person I know who is fully herself. You are the fresh air that blows into my life and makes me realize how stuffy I've let it become. Please don't change because you think it's something I want. I don't. You are perfect exactly the way you are."

Zeph almost couldn't catch her breath with so many emotions wringing her heart. What was happening to her? This wasn't the gríobhth's possessiveness, as there was none of that hot-blooded ferocity to it. No, this was a softer, though no less keen, longing for the man holding her. What if she couldn't bring herself to give him up? She would *have* to, but... What if she couldn't?

"Zephyr?" His lips kissed her ear. "Are you all right?"

She nodded, then forced herself upright, meeting his summer-sky gaze—rain-muddled with concern—and forced a smile onto her face. "Yes, I'm fine."

He didn't smile back. "You're not. Something is upsetting you. Did I say something wrong?"

"No." She spoke the word through the tightness in her chest. Too full of all those heart-juices swelling up inside and making her ribs creak. She shook her head to emphasize that. "Can we—would it be appropriate for us to withdraw yet?" She tried to sound arch and teasing, but the words came out breathless, very nearly a whimper.

"Of course." Keeping her hand in his, he threaded his way through the dancing crowd, greeting people here and there—never less than charming and never pausing. Another of his skills in literally navigating court that she lacked. Except he didn't think she lacked anything. *You are perfect exactly the way you are.*

He's also not thinking about you as a future queen, the voice just had to say. *You're perfect as a lover. Here today, gone tomorrow.*

Which is all I ever wanted, she argued with herself.

Is it? The voice had a mocking tone now. *Maybe you pretended to yourself that all you wanted was a night or two, but I know better. And you're beginning to see the truth, too.*

You are *me,* she snarled.

Exactly, the voice replied smugly.

"Are you not feeling well?" Astar asked once they reached the cool, quiet air of the deserted hall. He shifted his grip to feel the pulse at her wrist. "You're pale."

"I'm always pale," she shot back. "I got the Dasnarian winter-white skin."

Astar tilted her a look. "At least that put some color back into your cheeks. When did you last eat?"

Good question. "At breakfast, I suppose."

"Which you mostly drank, as I recall," he replied grimly. "Which is not a problem, let me hasten to add, but you barely touched the food on your plate, so unless you ate more after I left, then you've been flying all day on a couple glasses of wine." He snagged a passing page and asked that food be sent up.

"I'm not really hungry," she protested, though not strongly because his concern touched her. Her raw heart couldn't possibly take much more, but she had to pinch the bridge of her nose to keep from getting weepy. What in Moranu was *wrong* with her?

"You're going to eat," he informed her in that authoritative tone that went straight to her groin. He stopped at their chamber door and opened it, gesturing her within. Closing the door, he turned to her. "After you eat, we're going to talk more about—"

She stopped his words with her mouth, fastening her lips to his with avid hunger, climbing him like a tree until her arms were wrapped around his neck and her legs around his narrow hips, clinging to him like a cat who might know the way down but couldn't extract her claws. Astar made a sound—surprise, need, longing—and hugged her tight to him as he staggered toward the bed, collapsing back on it when his knees hit the edge.

Perfectly happy to have him under her, she feasted on his mouth, pinning him to the bed and sinuously rubbing against his big, hard body. She was starving, yes, but not for food. She only wanted him, inside, outside, around and over.

"Zephyr," he said, tearing his mouth away, his head falling back with a gasp as she only occupied her voracious mouth elsewhere. His smooth jaw, the pulse point under his ear, the corded muscle of his neck that begged to be bitten. "Wait. The servants are bringing food and—"

"Please, Astar," she begged. "Let me have you. I need... Please let me."

"Yes," he groaned back. "Always yes, but—" He took her in a firm grip and levered her off of him with the easy shapeshifter strength he so rarely used, the bearish dominance making her shiver. No matter how wild she got, Astar could handle her. She'd never thought she needed that. But then, she hadn't realized how much she needed him. "They're at the door," he said to her, slowly and firmly. He was holding her wrists, keeping her from tearing off his clothes. "Once the servants bring in the food, I'll lock the door, and you can have as much of me as you can take."

She licked her lips at that enticing promise. "I can take a lot."

"Believe me, I know that full well now," he replied with a salacious grin. Tugging out his shirt to cover the erection straining at his pants, he went to the door and let the servants in. As soon as they left, he barred the door as promised and came back to her. "Are you sure you don't want to eat first?"

In lieu of an answer, she shapeshifted herself naked, her hair unbound. There—at least that was one fancy gown and hairdo safely stored away. Reclining on her elbows, she spread her legs, one knee drawn up, and slid her fingers through the curls at her mons, slipping them into her sex to stroke herself, purring in pleasure. "I need to sate this hunger first," she told him as he watched, rapt, his jaw tight and fingers twitching. "Will you help?"

His gaze flew up to hers, and he began ripping off his clothes. "I keep thinking one of these nights we'll do this slowly. I have fantasies, of kissing you all over, of—"

One of these nights... as if they had so many to squander. "Less talk," she suggested. "Hurry."

"Now who has so much edge?" he taunted, fully naked now and crawling up her body to straddle her on all fours. Taking her wrists in each hand, he pressed them to the bed beside her head and bent to kiss her, ignoring her straining attempts to reach him. He kissed her slowly, lingeringly, with excruciating thoroughness. "I'm going to make this slow," he informed her, lifting his head so he could gaze down at her.

"Astar," she groaned. "Please..."

"Please go so slowly? Good idea." He smiled, smugly

pleased with himself, then kissed the soft point just under her jaw. With agonizing and meticulous care, he kissed his way down her throat, lavishing her skin with licks and nibbles, holding her still despite her frantic, needy thrashing beneath him.

With exquisite patience, he slowly devastated her, taking her apart until she lived only for the next brush of his lips, the nip of his teeth, the lavish stroke of his tongue. She became a quivering mass of need, obedient to his least caress, adoring and adored.

When he at last slid inside her, transferring his grip on her wrists to interlace his fingers with hers, her body took him in with ease, sweet and hot and hard, filling all of her. He paused there, fully inside of her, their bodies slicked together, skin to skin, and he gazed down at her, his face showing everything she felt. The summer sky in his eyes, the golden sun radiant as his heart, and she realized—with a sense of joy so acute it nearly rent her apart—that she loved him.

She loved him as the only sun in her world. There might be countless stars, but Astar made them all dim with his brightness. Biting down on her lip so she wouldn't blurt out the words, she moved under him, wrapping her legs around him and urging him deeper.

"Let me do that," he murmured, lowering his head to gently nibble the fullness of her lower lip, moving inside her to stoke the fire ever higher. "Let me have you, lovely Zephyr," he murmured against her lips.

"Always," she breathed, and gave herself over to be immolated in his fire.

~ 24 ~

ZEPHYR HAD CLEARLY worn herself out with flying. After that intensely intimate lovemaking session, she'd fallen asleep and hadn't stirred since—not even when he turned down the covers and gently picked her up to tuck her beneath. He'd even spread out her hair across the pillow the way she liked it, so she wasn't lying on it, and she'd only sighed and burrowed deeper in. He lingered a moment longer, caressing her glossy hair, wishing he'd gotten food into her, but glad she was getting rest.

Though she slept as deeply as a child with the purity of a clear conscience and a day spent fully exerting herself without reservation, he made himself move away from her lest he be tempted to touch her more. Pouring himself a glass of wine, he picked at the food, taking the rare moment alone to gather his thoughts.

She'd been upset, clearly agitated in a way lighthearted, carefree Zephyr never was. Maybe he'd made a mistake, saying those things to her on the dance floor. But he'd been so stricken that she would see herself as lacking in any way. And maybe her uncertainty had hit him harder after a day in Berendina's company, with her countless sly jabs at the Tala in general—and Zephyr in particular. Astar had been around court politics long enough—and had been relentlessly tutored by Ursula in strategies of all types—that he recognized a carefully waged campaign. Berendina had lost no opportunity to point out Zephyr's inappropriateness as a candidate for high queen, while simultaneously offering her own qualifications. He felt like he'd spent the day interviewing a candidate for a position in his household.

Astar had tolerated the game, mentally toting up the points for each as Berendina saw them, then adjusting them according to his own heart. Zephyr outshone Berendina—and, to be fair, all other women—in every way that mattered to him. Beauty, cleverness, sensuality, humor, a genuine love for the people who mattered to her. She was good for him, counterbalancing his tendency to be too serious, to worry over his responsibilities, to bind himself with duty. Plus, she understood the bear within. No—she embraced that side of himself, as the Berendinas of the world never could.

Then, of course, there was the bald truth that he'd fallen in love with Zephyr, just as he'd feared. Or rather, he'd finally acknowledged how much he loved her and perhaps always had. Opening his body to her had removed any hope he'd had of withholding his heart. Zephyr would have his heart as long as he lived, no matter who he married. A dismal picture formed in his head, of himself married to one woman and longing for another, seeing Zephyr at festivals and having to pretend he felt nothing.

Counting up his own private total of Zephyr's virtues had been enough to distract him from blurting out that Berendina could save her concerted attempts to oust her rival since Zephyr didn't want the job.

Not that he blamed Zephyr for it. The tales made marrying the crown prince and becoming queen sound terribly romantic, but Zephyr was no fool. Another of her many fine qualities—she saw through the pretty jewels and fancy castles and recognized the hard duty and strain of the throne. She valued the truly good things in life—the freedom of the skies, the warmth of friendship, the uninhibited tumult of sexual passion.

What if he couldn't bring himself to give her up? He would *have* to, but... What if he couldn't? Contemplating his wine, he confronted the dark possibility of abdicating as Ursula's heir. But then who would hold the high throne in his stead? He couldn't shirk his duty. He also couldn't let go of Zephyr, now that he had her.

The framework of his honor shook at the thought, his very foundations shuddering between the two impossibilities.

"Astar?" Zephyr called his name, throatily inviting. The temptation he couldn't resist. She sat up in bed, bare breasted, hair tumbling wildly around her. "Come to bed."

Because he wanted nothing more than to be with her, he did.

"I MEANT TO tell you last night," Astar said, waving a cup of hot tea under Zephyr's nose as she blinked sleepily at him, "I have to travel to Lake Sullivan today. Groningen wants me to see for myself."

"The lake creature?" she asked, her eyes sparkling with alert interest. She generally woke very slowly, stretching like an indolent cat in the big bed. People might think that the gríobhth was mostly raptor—because the head and wings drew so much attention—but Astar privately thought she was mostly cat. And Zephyr's playful, mercurial nature bore that out. Also, her love of napping curled up, on, and around him. Now he might as well have waved catnip under her nose as tea, because she practically bounced out of bed. "Can I come along?"

"I was hoping you would, since it's far enough north that we'll have to stay overnight. Everyone else is going. They seem to be excited for the excursion. I don't know about Nilly," he amended, "as I haven't talked to her about it yet, but I'm assuming she'll want to go."

"Well, yes! Everyone wants a chance at sighting the famous lake creature that's bigger than a dragon. And Jak's dancing colors in the night sky." Zephyr shook back her hair, blinked into the form of a small cat, then back to human—fully dressed in fighting leathers and with her hair in a long, single braid down her back. "When do we leave?"

He had to laugh at her enthusiasm. Going to her, he skimmed his hands over her form-fitting outfit, which revealed every enticing curve and hollow of her gorgeous body. "When did you acquire this outfit?" he asked as she curled into his caress. All cat, complete with purr.

"A while back, before this adventure," she replied, languidly twining her hands behind his neck. "I figured I should have something for combat, should I ever need to fight in human form. I was wearing this for a little while when we fought the stone giant, but you weren't there."

"Probably a good thing, as I'd have been struck dead because I couldn't take my eyes off of you."

She frowned a little. "But that was before your promise, before I seduced you. When you were still determined that you would never want me enough to compromise your principles."

He groaned internally at his own pompousness. Had he really phrased it that way? Probably. That self seemed like someone who'd lived in another lifetime—and like the boy he'd been, terrified of giving in to the one thing, the one person he did want enough to pitch every last principle out the window. "I have a confession to make," he said slowly, gazing into her clear sapphire eyes. There lay his moral compass, the most profound truth of his life. "I always wanted you, more than enough to abandon every last principle—and that terrified me."

She gazed back, not scornful as he'd feared, but perfectly serious. "What scared you about me?"

"This," he admitted. "That if I opened the door to the possibility of having you in my life, then I'd care about you more than anything else. And if I didn't have the framework of honor and duty, I'd have nothing when you inevitably left me."

She nodded solemnly. "I wanted to free you of that cage. I understand now that you don't see your responsibilities as chains, but rather as support."

"I did before. Maybe I clung to the cage because I thought it was safe, but not anymore."

"What changed?"

He smiled at her artless question, the innocent curiosity in it. Kissing her softly, sweetly, lingering over the moment to drink her in while he could, he wondered if what he was about to say would make this their last kiss. Finally, he made himself stop and tell her the truth. "Nothing changed—I can just admit now that I care about you more than anything else. I'm head over heels in love with you, Zephyr, and I find that nothing else matters as much as that anymore." He held his breath, waiting for her reaction, feeling as if his very heart had stopped beating.

She'd gone still, too. Her face like a carved marble angel, no longer warm and pliant under his hands. "I was going to end things between us this morning," she finally said, a chiming hammer of words that chipped pieces off his heart.

He nodded slowly. "I understand."

"You understand because you're convinced I'll inevitably leave you?" She smiled a little, wryly enigmatic.

"I don't want to cage you, either," he explained, running his hands over the enchanting curve of her narrow waist and flaring hips. "You were clear with me that you didn't want forever, and—as aggravated as I get with Rhyian—I do understand that the Tala are different, that monogamy simply isn't part of your culture or mindset."

"You're Tala, too, Astar," she said with quiet insistence. "You keep ignoring that fact."

He shook his head. "I'm a son of Avonlidgh and Mohraya.

291

More, I'm the son of a family committed to rule. I don't think like you do. Sometimes I wish I could. Regardless, I understand why you feel the need to end things between us." He made himself take his hands off her, the woman he loved with all his being, but who he no longer had the right to touch. The grizzly bear within howled in possessive fury. "I'm grateful I got as much time with you as I did," he made himself say, willing the bear to pay attention.

Zephyr's eyes flashed with irritation, her lush crimson lips firming and high cheekbones standing out sharply. As much as he loved her gloriously long hair loose, the sleek tightness of the braid set off the sculpted beauty of her face so that he wanted to run his fingers over the elegant, delicate lines, worshipping her like a work of art.

"Don't be *grateful*," she spat, poking him sharply in the chest with a long, pointed nail—just shy of being an actual claw—and he nearly laughed at himself for his romantic imaginings. Though he loved the ferocious aspect of her equally well. "The last thing you should feel for me is gratitude. And you'd better start listening. I said I *was* going to end things between us this morning. Actually, I was going to end things between us last night, but I couldn't bear to. I hadn't had enough of you. The truth is I don't think I'll ever have enough of you. And now you go and tell me you're in love with me??" She threw her hands up in the air. She was incandescent with fury, shadows of wings and whipping tail around her.

"I thought you should know the truth," he said between gritted teeth. "You deserve honesty from me."

"Oh," she hissed. "Let's not get into what I do and don't deserve, because I don't care. You've screwed yourself over, Your Highness Crown Prince Astar."

"How so?" he asked very carefully, unsure of what her mood indicated. *Was* it fury… or something else?

"I was going to end things because I was trying to be good and honorable and responsible. You are not for me, yes? My name is not on this *list* of approved brides."

"It's not." He met her fulminous gaze. "I'd apologize, but I didn't create the list."

She shrugged elaborately, prowling over to him, a predatory glint in her eyes. "I don't care about that fucking list. You're in love with me. Say it again."

Suspicious, overwhelmed, unable to deny her even this, he did. "I'm in love with you, Zephyr. I'll never love anyone else in my life like I love you."

She half-closed her eyes in pleasure, shivering as if he'd stroked her sex, the gríobhth sharp in her visage. "You're mine, then," she declared. "I'm never giving you up."

His heart, brain, and voice stuttered. "Ah… Erm. What?"

Her eyes flew open and she glared at him. "I'm in love with you, Astar. We are in love with each other, which means you belong to me. I don't care about your stupid throne and ridiculous rules. You had your chance to escape me, but that moment has blown away with last autumn's winds. You are *mine* now and I'll kill anyone who tries to take you from me." She bared her teeth, her smile as lethal as her black gríobhth beak. "Starting with *Dina*," she hissed.

He caught her wrist as she wheeled about. In her present

dangerous mood, he wouldn't put it past her to do as she'd threatened. "That's a waste of time."

"She can't marry you if she's dead," Zephyr pointed out with sweet reason and murder in her eye.

"She won't marry me regardless," he insisted.

She tried to tug away. "She will. I know a predator when I see one, and she's aiming to pounce on and eviscerate you."

"No, Zephyr." He released her wrist and took her by the shoulders. "Now I'm asking you to chill down and listen to *me*." When her gaze lost some of the bloodlust and focused on him, he continued. "I told Berendina yesterday that I won't be offering for her hand."

She narrowed her eyes. "You didn't tell me that."

"No, I didn't." He drew himself up. "For one reason, because it had nothing to do with you. *Listen to me*," he cut in forcefully when she opened her mouth. "I told her I thought we weren't compatible, which is my polite way of saying I don't like her. I wouldn't marry her even if I'd never met you or if we'd stayed only friends."

Cocking her head, more raptor than cat now, she gave him a long look. "I don't think we were ever only friends."

No, the heat, the fascination between them had always burned too hot and fiercely. The profound attraction had complicated their relationship far beyond the bounds of friendship. "The other reason I didn't tell you is I thought you wouldn't welcome my declaration, that I can't possibly marry someone else when I'm so thoroughly in love with you."

She considered that, a long, slow blink. "But you have to marry one of the women on the list."

He blew out a breath. "Do I?"

"You're the one who knows about rules," she pointed out. "Your honor and duty and so forth." She made them sound like dirty words.

"Why are you so angry with me?" he asked.

"Is that what I am?" she mused. "I feel like I want to take a bite out of you, so maybe so. Mostly I'm confused." She lifted clear blue eyes to his in rare uncertainty, looking to him for guidance. "I don't know what comes next."

"Me neither." He slid his hands down her arms to interlace his fingers with hers. "Though you said I'm yours now and you're never letting me go."

"There is that. And we're in love with each other. I didn't expect that."

She sounded so mystified that he laughed. "I somehow imagined our exchange of declarations of love would be more romantic."

"Yes, well." She darted in and nipped at his bottom lip, then grinned. "Saying so in the midst of an argument is much more us."

Not letting her get away, he pulled her back for a real kiss, consuming and full of desperate hunger. She melted against him, giving herself without reservation, the both of them absolutely united in their hearts, regardless of how the world would view their love affair. Finally, reluctantly, he backed out of the kiss, their lips still lingering in a mutual caress, exchanging wordless promises full of sweetness and longing. "I have to go," he told her between kisses.

She growled quietly, very close to a purr, but her displeasure clear in it. "It seems you're always saying that to me."

He grimaced ruefully, but met her gaze without flinching.

"I don't think that will ever change. Not as long as I have responsibilities to the high throne."

"And will *that* ever change?" she asked meaningfully.

"I don't know. I would like it if... Could I ask that we simply go on without hard and fast decisions from here? There's no need to decide anything, and—" What he'd like most would be to persuade Zephyr to marry him and be his queen. Convincing Ursula of that would likely be far easier than talking Zephyr into it, which was saying something. "I'd like to just be in the moment, with you."

"Living in the moment is one of my *particular accomplishments*," she informed him in a lofty tone that sounded uncannily like Berendina. "But what about when we encounter these other princesses on your *list?*"

"Then I will be polite to them, as will you."

Her winged black brows flew up in patent astonishment. "I will?"

"Yes," he replied firmly. "We have alliances to maintain, and that requires surface politeness. You'll teach me the art of living in the moment, and I will teach you how to speak the empty words of courtly manners."

"Why, Astar, my love," she murmured huskily, "that sounds very much like lying."

"Shades of truth," he corrected. "You'll find that courtiers are much like the Tala in embracing shades of gray." And this would be his first step to maneuvering her into being his queen. She wasn't the only predator in the room. Now that he'd fixed on having her—and could exult in that she'd laid claim to him—nothing would get in his way.

~ 25 ~

E VERYONE HAD GATHERED in the outer courtyard of Castle Elderhorst—around a pair of carriages. Zeph groaned to herself at the sight. "More bone-bouncing carriages," she muttered viciously.

Astar patted her gloved hand on his arm. "How did you think we'd be traveling?"

"Flying is ever so much faster," she replied sweetly.

"I'm sure it is, to the envy of all of us non-fliers."

"You could have a flight-capable form, if you'd—"

"Quit bugging me about that," he growled.

"Not likely." She grinned up at him, then narrowed her eyes at two unexpected figures in the group waiting for them. Henk, with Gen on his arm as he explained something about the castle to her, judging by his gestures and her patiently bored expression.

And *Dina*.

"You didn't mention *Dina* would be joining us," she noted, proud of herself for sounding neutral.

"I didn't know," Astar replied. "And don't snarl."

"I didn't!" she protested.

"I can feel the wind from your tail snapping in the air."

That gave her pause. "You can't possibly. I'm in human form."

He shrugged slightly. "Your gríobhth is always part of your presence, regardless of what physical form you're currently wearing. Now, be nice and remember: you won. I'm yours, not hers."

I won. Astar is mine. Zeph preened internally at the thought, then realized Astar had tossed her that tasty bit to chew on as a way to keep her happy. Oh, well—it worked. She even summoned a smile for *Dina*, who stepped forward to greet them, Zeph's supposed friends ceasing their own conversations to watch with avid interest. Even Gen turned Henk slightly so she could have a better view, though she nodded at him, obviously only pretending to listen.

"Good morning, Willy." Dina's smile twinkled as she curt-seyed. "Lady Zephyr. Don't you two look bright-eyed and pink-cheeked this morning."

"Princess Berendina," Astar replied, dipping his chin. "Traveling with us to Lake Sullivan?"

"Yes, Grandpapa asked it of me personally." She leaned in confidingly. "I'm something of an expert on the region, and the lake monster, in particular."

"Though, really," Zeph cooed, "you have such far-reaching expertise, so many accomplishments. This would be but a small example."

Dina paused, giving Zeph a cool look. "Indeed. I don't believe we've gotten to discuss *your* areas of expertise. Do you have any—besides the obvious?" Her gaze flicked over Zeph's body, though she was swathed in the golden fur cloak, then meaningfully to Astar.

"Not at all," Zeph replied with a knowing smile. "I've found that being good in bed is plenty to get me through life."

Astar coughed, then pretended to be clearing his throat. "Shall we be on our way?"

IT TOOK THE better part of the day to reach Lake Sullivan. *Dina* had been assigned to their carriage, which meant she and Zeph ignored each other, while Henk narrated the sights of the entire journey to Gen. At least Zeph didn't have to worry about *Dina* working her wiles on Astar. He might believe that politely telling *Dina* he wasn't interested would put a stop to her hunt, but Zeph knew better. She caught the calculating glint in the princess's eye and was prepared for trickery. In the meanwhile, Zeph pretended Henk's nonstop monologue was an endlessly babbling brook, and she caught up on her sleep.

When they paused for everyone to stretch their legs and answer the call of nature, Lena grabbed Zeph. "So, Henk," she said. "I'm concerned."

"Why?" Zeph glanced around and spotted Henk kissing Gen's hand while she blushed at something he said.

"Gen is smitten, and I don't think he's trustworthy."

Zeph gave Lena the side-eye. "Are you sure you're not just feeling bitter about men in general?"

"Don't go there," Lena bit out, a hint of ozone singeing the crisp winter air. She heaved out a sigh. "All right, you have a point. That's why I'm asking you. What's your take on

Princeling Henk?"

Zeph shrugged, Gen's delighted giggle ringing out. "He's an empty-headed, pompous, and pampered boy who's been told all his life that he's special, so he's never exerted himself in the slightest to be or do anything worthwhile."

Lena snorted. "But what's your real opinion?"

"He makes Gen happy. Isn't that enough?"

"It is until he makes her miserable," Lena replied, very seriously. "Gen isn't like you or me, or even Nilly. She's got an innocence to her that makes her think everyone is wonderful. Henk could damage her."

"Then let's ask her," Zeph said. "Gen, over here!"

Lena groaned. "This was not what I had in mind."

"Direct approach is always best," Zeph told her cheerfully as Gen came toward them. "So, Gen, tell us about Henk."

She pressed her lips together mulishly. "You don't like him."

"I don't have an opinion about him," Zeph corrected, then threw Lena to the wolves. "It's Lena who doesn't like him."

"Really?" Gen demanded. "Are you sure you're not just bitter about men in general?"

Zeph choked on a laugh when Lena muttered an oath of disgust. "I'm not denying the possibility," Lena admitted tersely, "and you're dodging."

Gen sighed. "I know he talks a lot, but—"

"There is no but," Lena inserted.

"*But* he likes me," Gen insisted with a glare. She twisted a long lock of chestnut hair around her finger and sighed again, this time wistfully. "He thinks I'm beautiful and exotic."

"Of course you're beautiful." Zeph rolled her eyes, though Lena gave her a warning frown for it. "What? Last time I got in trouble for *not* telling her that."

"It's not the same coming from you." Gen flicked her hair away again. "Henk has been around court ladies all his life and has very refined taste. He says I have a unique beauty and that I *fascinate* him, that I'm like no other woman he's ever known. He's never met a shapeshifter before. He thinks my abilities are miraculous. That's the word he used."

"Have you demonstrated your shapeshifting for him?" Zeph asked, knowing the answer already, but beyond surprised.

Gen brushed that off. "It's not against the law."

"Her Majesty asked us to be discreet," Lena pointed out.

"Henk is discreet," Gen insisted. "Besides, what harm is there in it? He says he's dazzled by me."

Zeph and Lena exchanged uneasy glances. "Honey," Lena said, "you have so much more going for you than any of that. You're smart, talented, and fundamentally good-hearted. You don't need some minor mossback prince to fetishize your exotic nature."

"That's not what's going on here." Gen punched her fists to her hips. "Besides, my *mossback* father fell in love with my exotic shapeshifter mother because she fascinated him. There's nothing wrong with that."

"Marskal knew Zynda for a long time," Lena countered. "They served the high queen together and were friends first. It was more than a surface attraction."

"I love that you assume Henk is so shallow," Gen fired

back. "What does it matter, anyway? I'm just doing what Zeph advised me—and it's good advice."

Lena gave Zeph such a sharp look that Zeph held up her hands in surrender. "I only said to stop evaluating each potential partner for true-love potential, to play the field a bit."

"See?" Gen smiled triumphantly. "That's all I'm doing. You two worry too much."

Never in her life had Zeph been accused of worrying too much—which made her worry that Lena was onto something.

THEY REACHED LAKE Sullivan by midafternoon, which meant the sun was sinking low in these northern climes in midwinter, the slanting light streaking across the lake like a volley of fiery arrows. The carriages queued up at a pull-out area with a view of the lake, and they all piled out to look. *Dina* and Henk immediately flanked Astar, giving him the official rundown of the region, Gen trailing a step behind Henk like a neglected puppy.

So, Zeph decided to practice being all polite and circum-spect—and not puppyish—and went to join Jak where he'd scrambled onto a spur of rocks, braced with one knee high as he leaned on it to peer into the sheer drop below. "Amazing, huh?" he said to Zeph, his dark eyes sparkling with excitement. "Makes me wish I could leap off this ledge and fly."

"Me too," Zeph admitted with a sigh. The sight was truly spectacular. Surrounded by startlingly high cliffs all around, the lake sat still and glossy black with chilly depths below. The steep grade of the hills made the drop all that much more dramatic, their pristine whiteness a stark contrast to the dark water.

"The bottom is all the way at sea level," Jak informed her. "That's why these cliffs look so unusually high. A bit of an illusion, but it's also a Danu-cursed significant change in altitude from here to there."

"Have you been talking to Henk?" she said wryly.

"That guy," Jak replied with considerable disgust. "What does our Gen see in him?"

"He thinks she's exotic."

Jak snorted. "Sounds to me like an asshole thing to say."

Zeph had to agree. "So, what happenings are we here to observe?" Everything looked perfectly quiet, the snow smoothly undisturbed, the water glass still without the slightest ripple. She frowned at that. Where was the native wildlife? Even in winter there should be fish surfacing to make ripples, birds circling in the sky or diving for those surfacing fish, trails in the snow where land mammals traveled to the lake to drink. Using selective shapeshifting, she increased the long vision of her eyes, searching for signs of life.

"I'm surprised Astar didn't give you the details during your intimate briefing." Jak snickered and waggled his eyebrows.

"Clearly you haven't had an 'intimate briefing' of your own in far too long if you think that's what happens," she replied archly.

Jak grunted, shaking his head and staring at the distant water. "You would be exactly right there, my friend. It *has* been too long."

"None of the court beauties of Elderhorst to your taste?"

He glanced over his shoulder, gaze going unerringly to Stella, who stood at the cliff's edge, by herself as usual, the wind off the higher peaks whipping her hair into a banner dark as days-old blood. Zeph frowned at that. Why was there wind up here and none below to ripple the lake surface?

"My taste seems to be off these days," Jak admitted. "I seem to have acquired a yen for the unattainable." He transferred his gaze to Zeph and grinned, cocky and self-deprecating at once. "I could star in my own tragic Dasnarian ballad of unrequited love. The beggared sailor boy pining after the princess in the tower."

"Nilly is standing right there, hardly in a tower," Zeph pointed out pragmatically. "And you're hardly poor."

He lifted a shoulder and let it fall in the fatalistic Dasnarian style. "I own nothing. I have no prospects, no particular skills or talents. She's a powerful sorceress who will be queen of Avonlidgh or Annfwn. And she might as well be in a tower, because the only person who can touch her is her twin." He assumed a tragic posture, clutching his heart. "I'm doomed to long for the one woman who is literally untouchable." He dropped the pose and put his hands on hips, staring down at the distant water. "Even if she would have me, which—let's face it—why would she?"

An odd scent teased Zeph's nostrils, her gríobhth's hackles rising, and she sharpened that sense, too. "If you're done being melodramatic," she said, "will you tell me what we're supposed to be seeing up here? It looks completely quiet."

"Too quiet," Jak intoned darkly. Then he reconsidered.

"Actually, it really is too quiet. I know the sea mon—lake creature is supposed to be elusive, but where's the rest of the wildlife?"

"Exactly," Zeph agreed. "Why is there wind up here, but not below?"

Jak frowned at the lake. "Air is different at various heights. Maybe Lena can explain the phenomenon."

"Maybe," Zeph replied doubtfully, looking farther down to where Henk and *Dina* were still expounding to Astar, Gen standing a glum short distance away. "Where *is* Lena?"

"She said she sensed something odd in the weather and needed to be alone to listen or some such. She walked off that way. As to your original question, the locals apparently regard the lake creature as a source of bounty and good luck. When Her Majesty originally busted the barrier around Annfwn lo these many years ago, one of the first signs that magic had returned to the then twelve kingdoms was the reappearance of the creature in Lake Sullivan."

Now that Zeph was hearing this, it occurred to her that the tale had been included in Henk's monologue. Maybe she should have been listening. That would've been the responsible thing to do. "But sightings are rare."

"Right—rare, but consistent. There's a bunch of mystic woo-woo theories that only the chosen blah blah blah, pure of heart and so forth see the lake creature, and they're blessed or they bless it. The stories conflict."

"And recently…" she prompted.

"Yes, recently—notably since the Feast of Moranu and the full crystalline moon—the lake creature has been seen frequently, and is acting agitated, according to witnesses."

"What witnesses?" She extended her long vision to search the distant reaches of the lake. "There's no one here. Not even a fish or bird."

"That is odd," Jak agreed. "But apparently there are villages? In the nooks and crannies." He waved vaguely. "And the manse of Groningen's we're staying at tonight is staffed, very likely with people who have eyes and ears—though I'm just guessing there."

Zeph wanted nothing more than to investigate—by wing or fin, possibly a combination of both. She seethed to go, prodded by an urge she didn't quite comprehend, mentally clacking her beak at the restraining presence of Henk and *Dina*. If not for them, she'd already be on the wing. Why did those two have to come along? Surely their presence did more to hamper the group's true quest. She was no expert on mossback travel, but if this manse of Groningen's sat at lake level, in one of Jak's nooks or crannies, it would surely take hours to get there, wending their way down in the carriages on the switchbacking road. She'd have to sit idly in the carriage all that while, pretending to be something she wasn't, waiting for an opportunity to slip away to shift. Nightfall didn't bother her, but the keen sense of urgency, as if a window had opened that would soon close, had her close to breaking her promises of discretion.

If she asked Astar's permission to shift, would he give it? More important, if she shifted without asking, would he forgive her? Once, she wouldn't have cared. Once, she wouldn't even have considered the concept of permission and forgiveness. Now, all she could imagine was his summer-sky eyes clouded with disappointment in her—and she couldn't bear it.

A faint cry touched her sensitive ears, strangely garbled, as if it came from *elsewhere*. A place on the other side of something, like where all the wind below had gone. Zeph's skin prickled with unease, a wrongness filling the air. The same wrongness she'd first sensed below the confluence, before she'd seen what was indeed so very wrong.

It turned her stomach. She growled, nothing human in it.

Stella, Gen, and Astar, sensitive to her reaction, looked too, heads swiveling to search for what bothered her. Jak leapt from his rocky perch, sword appearing in one hand like magic, a dagger in the other, keen dark eyes surveying the silent landscape. "What?" he demanded tersely. "What do you hear?"

"Lena," Zeph breathed. "She's in trouble."

Jak took off running in the direction they all were looking. "Wait!" Zeph shouted, to no avail.

Stella dashed over to her, magic thick around her, eyes dark and wild as a building storm. "Where does he think he's going?" she gasped.

"To save Lena," Zeph replied grimly.

"But she isn't—"

"I know." Lena wasn't *here* to be found. She looked desperately to Astar, who was running toward them at top speed, Gen going after Jak. All of them still stupid slow on two legs. Jak had finally stopped—in the middle of the road on the windswept hilltop—spinning wildly in a circle.

"What happened to Lena?" Astar demanded of them both.

Surely he meant to ask Stella, who actually understood this stuff, but she turned her turbulent gaze on Zeph. "I don't know. Zeph does."

"No, no, I don't know." Zeph shook her head, the buzzing wrongness getting stronger. It tasted like the wrongness at Gieneke. "Something is very wrong."

"Can you find her?" Astar asked, insistent but not terse. A good leader.

"Not in human form," she told him. "I need to be the gríobhth."

He glanced over his shoulder at Henk and Dina, strolling their way, arm in arm. "How about a regular bird?" Astar asked hopefully.

"There's nothing regular about this. Lena is not in our same realm anymore." Even as Zeph spoke the words, she knew they made no sense. "I can't reach her as a regular anything," she added with an edge of desperation.

"Zeph is right," Stella put in. "The gríobhth is a chimera, a creature of earth and air, both of this realm and the realm of the gods. Only as the gríobhth can she move beyond the boundaries of our world, which is where she must go to retrieve Lena."

Astar stared at her in some astonishment. "How do you know all that?"

"It's a sorceress thing," she answered tersely. "It comes to me unexpectedly."

With a frown, Astar turned back to Zeph, calculations passing behind his fierce stare. "Does it have to be now?" He tipped his head in Henk and Dina's direction. "Consider the implications," he warned.

Right. Don't be impulsive. There would be consequences here beyond the moment. She tried to feel for Lena, the frantic, silent call tugging at her. "I'm afraid that if I wait it will be too late to get to her. I can't explain why. I just... *feel* it."

"Do it, then." Astar stepped back with a decisive nod, giving her room to shift. "And Zephyr—come back to me. Promise."

She held his gaze, memorizing how he looked, eyes warmer and bluer than the cold winter sky framing him, his golden hair like sunlight. "I love you," she told him. "I promise to come back to you."

With a fierce rush of relief and power, she became the gríobhth.

~ 26 ~

BERENDINA'S SCREAM OF terror shrilled across Astar's nerves as Zephyr unfurled her magnificent wings. She shone like gold in the pale winter light, her fur and feathers gleaming, claws flexing. Henk charged at Zephyr, sword drawn, and Astar dealt with him by the simple expedient of thrusting a meaty arm in his path. The princeling ran smack into Astar's hard forearm and dropped like a rock.

Berendina kept screaming.

Zephyr's head turned around nearly backward at the sound, her tail snapping with a whiplash crack, her sapphire eyes full of predatory ferocity. That's all they needed—for Zephyr to be distracted by her rival. Zephyr the woman might understand that Berendina posed no threat, no competition for Astar's heart, but the gríobhth wasn't nearly so reasonable. It was another reason he'd hesitated on the wisdom of Zephyr taking gríobhth form. But she'd been sure of the necessity, and he trusted her with his life. More, with Lena's. *"Nilly, would you—"*

"On it," Stella crisply subvocalized in return, and the screaming stopped.

He didn't look to see how she'd accomplished that. Instead

he strode to Zephyr and took her lethally curved beak in his hands—well aware that the least movement on her part could slice off his finger—and making her focus on him. Her eyes were even more extraordinary in her First Form, blazing like living sapphires, fierce and otherworldly. "Lena," he said to her. "Save Lena."

Rational intelligence returned to her eyes, and she dipped her beak in acknowledgment. He lowered his voice so no one else could hear, trusting to her keen hearing. "But not at the expense of your own life. Don't make me go on without you."

She rubbed the side of her beak against his hand, the glossy surface cool and sleek, then she head-butted him away. Reaching under a wing, she plucked out a secondary feather and gave it to him. He took it, the barbs glinting like spun gold, and held it tightly. "I love you, too."

Rearing onto her powerful leonine hind legs, she spun in place and ran full speed for the cliff's edge—and leapt off into the abyss below. Though she of course knew what she was doing, his heart stopped beating until she rose again, golden wings shining in the light of the setting sun.

Jak and Gen were jogging back, Stella kneeling beside an unconscious Berendina. Henk had sat up, staring at Zephyr in the sky with open-mouthed astonishment—face a rictus of horror. "That... thing." he stammered. "She's a *monster*, and I rode in a carriage with her. What were you thinking, Willy, putting us in that kind of danger?" he demanded.

Astar clenched his fist, wishing he'd actually cold-cocked the asshole.

"She's still the woman you rode in a carriage with, Henk,"

Gen said, her arms folded as she stared at him as if seeing him for the first time. Maybe she was.

"I thought maybe you girls turned into something cute and fluffy, like a bunny rabbit, or a... a kitten! Something ladylike, and pretty." He stared at Gen suspiciously, as if seeing *her* for the first time. "*You* don't turn into a... a *monster* like that, do you?"

Gen's deep indigo eyes glinted with unusual fire. Steady and even-tempered like her father, Gen was typically slow to anger. But she was her mother's daughter, too—even her name meant "born of the dragon"—and Gendra possessed plenty of fire when pushed. Suddenly a tiger stood where Gen had been. With white fur dappled with gray spots and stripes, and long front fangs, she was no tiger that had been seen by anyone outside of Annfwn. The white saber cat prowled toward Henk, snarling a question as if to ask "like this?"

Henk emitted a thin scream, scrabbling backward on hands, feet, and butt like a panicked crab.

"Gendra!" Astar called, loudly and sharply to catch her attention. She glanced his way, the arched stripes over her intensely blue eyes giving her an inquisitive look—her jaw hanging open to reveal rows of serrated teeth besides the intimidating saber-like fangs, looking lethal enough to make even Astar want to step back. But he was the leader, and so he held his ground. "Don't eat our allies," he told her calmly and clearly.

She glanced back at Henk, seemed to shrug, then was back in human form. Turning her back on her erstwhile love interest, she prowled over to Astar, her gait revealing that a good deal of the saber cat's murderous rage lingered inside. "What can I do to help Lena?"

He nearly asked how he was supposed to know, but Stella, crouched beside an unconscious Berendina, and Jak, with a weapon in each hand, also stared at him expectantly. Tipping his head back, he searched the sky. No sign of the gríobhth. Astar had been distracted by Gen's display and had lost track of Zephyr's position. Wrestling back the panicked bear within—charging off in a fury wouldn't help Zephyr—he asked, "Did anyone see where Zephyr went?"

"She was circling," Stella said, "then vanished. There one moment, gone the next." She stood and dusted off her hands, leaving Berendina apparently asleep on the frozen ground. Behind her, Henk crawled over to pat the princess's cheeks, urging her to wake so they could escape the monsters. Likely he assumed that none of them could overhear his whispered words. He was wrong—and a slow learner. Dismembering Henk wouldn't solve anything either, so Astar ruthlessly contained that urge as well.

Astar studied the clear sky, pale winter blue and cloudless—and without any indicator of where two people could've disappeared to. *Think. Calm and rational. Be a leader.* He caressed the hilt of the Silversteel sword Ash had given him, but no inspiration occurred to him.

"What do you think?" he asked Stella, then expanded his gaze to Jak and Gen. "All theories welcome."

A fraught silence fell, no one wanting to volunteer first. Finally, Jak shrugged. "Before Lena called out—or whatever Zeph heard—Zeph and I were looking at the lake and chatting.

She said there was something wrong. That the wind was blowing up here and not below. And that there should be birds and fish, even in winter, but she couldn't detect any of them."

Stella frowned. "Lena said something similar, that the weather was wrong. Like there were odd divisions that shouldn't be there."

Astar nodded encouragingly, projecting an aura of optimistic leadership he was far from feeling. "As if there are different realms crowded together, maybe? With different weather in each, and people—or lake creatures, even enormous ones—might seem to appear and disappear as they move back and forth."

Gen gave him an approving smile. "Good insight. That would explain why the lake creature disappeared for centuries when magic was isolated to Annfwn, then reappeared when magic returned to Carienne."

"It's moving back and forth between one realm and another," Jak mused. He'd sheathed his sword but idly spun the dagger between his fingers. "But what is this other place?"

"Or places," Gen put in, emphasizing the plural.

"Aunt Andi described the problem she foresaw as a magic rift," Stella said slowly, gray eyes focused on the far distance—or perhaps something not in this realm at all. "A rift is like a fissure. So what if these realms are meant to be separate, which must be the case, or there would be utter chaos with everything overlapping. If that's so, then magic might be a kind of physical force, like gravity, that either allows or denies passage between the realms. The presence of magic changes the normal rules that prevent moving back and forth. The rift then might bend those rules."

"Or break them," Gen concluded bleakly. "Possibly a rift like that could allow an intelligence unfamiliar with our world to reach through and animate a stone giant for fun, just to see what would happen."

"It makes sense," Astar concluded, battling the wave of hopelessness. He should come up with a plan. He had nothing. So, he looked to the people he trusted most in this world and asked them. "Though that doesn't give us much of a clue in what we should do next. Any ideas?"

Jak spun a dagger, the silver flashing bright. "Well, we could—"

The harsh call of a driver and the rattle of carriage wheels interrupted him, and they all spun to watch one of their two carriages speed away, making the turn so fast it went up on two wheels. Henk and Berendina were gone—presumably inside the fleeing carriage—along with both drivers.

"They left us," Gen said in disbelief, her indigo eyes wide. "What kind of person does that?"

"Scared people," Stella told her gently.

"People who don't think we count as people," Jak put in more cynically as Gen winced. "Sweet Gen, if you're about to apologize for the saber-cat display, don't. Henk isn't worth it, and it was a treat to watch you scramble his excuse for brains."

Gen combed her hands through her curling chestnut hair, scrubbing her scalp and looking pained. "I don't know what came over me."

"You had enough," Jak and Stella said as one, then exchanged bemused smiles. "He was an ass and you reached the end of your rope," Jak continued alone. "Well done, I say."

Stella nodded. "You are a lovely, kind, and generous person, Gen, but even you have your limits."

Gen shook her own head ruefully, then met Astar's gaze. "I have not been lovely, kind, and generous to you and Zeph," she said baldly. "I've been jealous, mean, and envious."

"Is there much difference between jealous and envious?" Jak asked, and Stella shushed him.

"Ugly, then," Gen retorted.

Astar had been staring after the rapidly disappearing carriage in consternation and building rage. Even if the decision had been Henk's alone, abandoning their crown prince and the high queen's appointed delegates came very near to treason.

"Willy?" Stella said quietly. "I have something to tell you."

She sounded so uncharacteristically hesitant that he had to stifle a groan. What next? "Oh?" he asked as neutrally as possible.

Briefly shapeshifting, she returned to human form with a glowing topaz sphere atop her outstretched palm. Perfectly smooth and round, the distinctive color depthless, the jewel was instantly recognizable, though Astar had only seen it once before. "The Star of Annfwn," he breathed, as Jak and Gen crowded close, equally rapt. Astar lifted his gaze to Stella's turbulent one. "Aunt Andi gave you the Star of Annfwn?"

Right away, he thought he should've tried not to sound so incredulous, but Stella only nodded somberly. "Just before we left. She said that I would need it, and that it should be mine now, since I bear the mark of the Tala."

Jak whistled low and long. "I wonder what that thing

would be worth on the open market?" When everyone glared at him, he widened his eyes in innocence. "A purely academic question."

"The Star's real value is in its ability to focus magic anyway," Gen said, studying the jewel intently. "Why didn't you tell us you had it?"

"Aunt Andi didn't want Rhy to know," Stella explained quietly. "She was concerned that he'd see her giving it to me as..."

"Tantamount to crowning you heir in Annfwn," Astar finished.

She nodded gravely. "Even though the rulership of Annfwn doesn't work that way, and even though the Star has nothing to do with it."

"Still," Gen replied thoughtfully, "it's a powerful vote of confidence in you as at least her heir in sorcery."

"She also said it would be best to keep it hidden unless I needed to use it." Stella glanced at Astar in apology. "Lena and I used it to combine our magic at Gieneke. That's how we vanquished the giant, and the intelligence behind it."

Astar nodded, understanding more how they'd managed that feat. "Can you use it to help Lena and Zephyr?"

"I don't know how I could," she admitted. "I thought maybe I should tell you I have the Star, in case you have ideas."

Unfortunately, he didn't. What he should've done was kept Lena safe to begin with. They were out here in the middle of nowhere, with no guides, two missing people, and the potential to be attacked at any moment. Clenching his hands into fists, he wanted to crush skulls. Which also would do nothing to solve their problems. Some leader he was.

Stella slipped her hand into his, thawing his frozen fist, her cool green presence flooding him. "It's not your fault."

He looked into her grave gray eyes, wishing that was the truth, the panic for Zephyr like frantic wing beats in his heart. *"I don't know what to do,"* he confessed subvocally.

"You're not supposed to always know."

"Ursula always does."

Stella shook her head slowly. *"Remember that I can sense Auntie Essla's heart the same as I can anyone's—and she is often afraid or angry or uncertain. She's simply learned to hide those feelings."*

That made sense. Though Harlan always knew how she felt—and he was the one she turned to when she needed to talk. Astar had seen that often enough, had stepped away to give them privacy. Zephyr could be that for him. Was that for him. He'd give anything at that moment for Zephyr's irreverent commentary and canny wisdom. But he didn't have her, so he could only wait for her to return with Lena.

Better to do something than nothing at all, Ursula said in his head. *When in doubt, making a decision—even a wrong one—is better than waffling. Fortune favors the bold, my boy.*

"All right, then," Astar announced. "None of us have the ability to follow Zephyr, which is why we sent her after Lena. We have to trust in that." *He* would have to trust her to return safely. "So we continue as we'd planned, down to the manse at the lake level. Stella and Gen, take wing, keep a sharp eye out for anything unusual, report it to me immediately, but stay in contact with each other, too. Jak and I will drive the carriage down."

Without protest, Gen took the form of a snowy owl, Stella a nighthawk—taking the Star with her—and they soared into the sky. Quickly, they formed a pattern of ever-widening and interlinking circles that allowed them to cover a large amount of territory, while putting them in regular, predictable contact. Astar silently blessed Gen's father, Marskal, who insisted on drilling all shapeshifters—at least the ones he could tempt, browbeat, or corral—in these tactical maneuvers. They'd all complained that they weren't soldiers and would never need to know... and look at them now.

Jak clapped him on the shoulder. "They'll be fine. Climb aboard—but I'm doing the driving."

Astar scowled at him. "I know how to drive horses."

Jak snorted. "Yeah, and I can shapeshift into a grizzly bear."

"Oh, now those are fighting words," Astar pretended to growl, seizing on the mock argument as a welcome diversion from worrying. The sun had nearly set, and shadows gathered at an alarming rate. Guiding the horses down that perilous, winding road to the bottom would be no picnic.

"Nevertheless, Your Highness," Jak replied cheerfully, climbing with agile grace to the high seat at the front of the covered carriage. "I'm trained in this. You're not."

"You're trained in steering a sailing ship, not a carriage," Astar pointed out, climbing up beside him. He was *not* going to ride inside the carriage.

"How different can it be?" Jak grinned and studied the long reins. "Now, where is the rudder..."

"Give those to me," Astar demanded.

"Kidding!" Jak protested, adjusting his grip expertly and clucking the nervous horses into motion. "Danu's tits—just trying for a bit of levity here."

"Yeah, but—"

A clap of wings had him jerking up his head, sword leaping to hand, the bear threatening to burst forth. Jak cursed in Dasnarian, fighting to control the horses as they reared in their traces. Astar recognized the raven barely in time to abort his swing—right as the huge bird became Rhyian, manifesting a slight bit above ground so he landed hard enough to send up a burst of dust and gravel from even that frozen ground. With wild eyes, Rhy leapt onto the carriage, seizing Astar by the collar of his furry cloak, his contorted face looming and spittle flying as he roared. "Where is she? What have you done with her?"

~ 27 ~

"COUSIN!" ASTAR ROARED back at Rhy, more than a little grizzly in it. "Calm your shit down!" Grasping Rhy's wrists, he wrenched the slighter man off of him.

Rhy fought back, his long body stronger than even most shapeshifters, freeing one arm to take a swing at Astar—who caught the incoming fist in one hand, holding and squeezing hard so the pain would penetrate Rhy's frenzy. "Stop the horses!" he yelled to Jak as the carriage jolted and bounced over the rougher ground off-road, careening perilously toward the cliff's edge.

"Trying," Jak gritted back.

Astar focused on quelling the frenzied Rhy, a problem he finally solved by essentially sitting on his cousin. Rhy might have that long-limbed slippery strength, but Astar still outweighed him. By then, Jak had control of the horses, steering them back toward the road, and Astar let out a breath of temporary relief. Very temporary, as one wheel gave with a mighty *crack!* and the carriage jounced once, twice—then abruptly capsized, throwing them all to the rocky ground and twisting the traces around the horses.

Winded—beyond dispirited—Astar lay there a moment

staring up at the purpling sky. Much the same shade as the bruises he'd have all over his body, no doubt. If he survived the night. Still pinned under him, Rhy groaned, so Astar shifted to the side and sat up. Jak was already with the horses, singing them a soothing song in Dasnarian—who knew the Dasnarians had lullabies?—and freeing the trapped steeds from the wreck of a carriage. He caught a few words, about baby birds and nests. Then, deciding Jak had the situation well in hand, Astar turned his attention to Rhy, who was sitting up also, but hunched over, gripping his skull in his hands like he was keeping it from coming apart.

"What the fuck, cuz?" Astar demanded.

Rhy's head snapped up, and he glared at Astar, still feral, his deep blue eyes catching the meager light and reflecting it like a cat's would. Or a wolf's. An odd combination of relief and trepidation washed over him. Rhy wasn't like Astar, limited only to his raven First Form, but he tended to cling to it, ever wary of attracting Moranu's attention by trying more forms. Not that there was any evidence that the goddess paid any more attention to Her children with multiple forms than She did to those with only First Form, or even the ones who couldn't shift at all, like Ash. Still, the Tala were a superstitious lot, and they tended to believe multitalented shapeshifters like Zephyr, Gen, and Stella were favored by the many-faced goddess.

Having qualities of alternate forms show up while Rhy was in human form was both good and bad. Good because it was about time Rhy quit worrying and hiding; bad because whatever was making him finally crack open didn't bode well.

And yes—Astar was grimly and fully aware of how similar his own situation was to his cousin's.

"Where is Salena?" Rhy demanded in return, sounding slightly more sane.

At least, until Astar told him the truth. "How are you even here?" he countered. "Did you fly from—"

In a flash, he was on his back again, Rhy pinning him to the ground with sheer fury and clawed hands around his throat, throttling the breath from him. With his black hair whipping in the biting wind, face harsh with fury and anguish, Rhy looked like a true avatar of Moranu, of the goddess in full vengeance. "Not. One. More. Word." Rhy nearly screamed it. "Until you explain why Salena isn't in this world anymore."

Astar tried to answer, but had no breath. He clawed at Rhy's hands, trying to free himself, but his cousin possessed a sudden and unexpected strength far beyond his usual. With no choice, Astar became the grizzly bear, throwing Rhy off him with the sheer change in size. Rhy whipped into wolf form, leaping for his throat with jaws snapping.

Then Jak arrived, hurling himself through the air with acrobatic ease, wrapping his arms around the snarling wolf and taking them both to the ground. Astar, knowing words would be needed more than brute strength, went back to human, helping to pin the wolf before it savaged Jak further. Kneeling with his full weight on Rhy, Astar grabbed the wolf's snapping jaws in both big hands, holding them closed with desperate determination and more than his own usual strength, too.

"Rhyian," he snarled. "Listen to me. Shift back and listen. Lena needs you. And she needs you rational. Shift back for

Salena."

The wolf stilled, then became Rhy in human form. "I know Salena needs me. That's why I'm here. Now stop fucking around and *tell me*."

Astar held up his palms in a peacemaking gesture. "Short answer is: We don't know, but Zephyr is looking for her. Let me make sure you didn't kill Jak, and I'll tell you the whole story."

Rhy tensed as if he might fight, and for a moment, Astar braced for it, but then Rhy sagged and ran a hand over his face. "Yeah. Sorry, man, I—See to Jak."

With a nod, Astar crawled off Rhy and over to Jak. "You all right?"

"A mere flesh wound," Jak replied, but his grin looked pained.

Rhy crawled over, too. "I'm sorry. Shit—I really tore you up."

"The nature of battle," Jak said, clapping a hand on Rhy's shoulder. "Sometimes you take friendly fire."

"I don't know as I'd call that attack friendly," Astar corrected sourly.

"I know, I know." Rhy raked his hands through his hair, rubbing his scalp. "I don't know what came over me."

Something about those words caught Astar's attention. Someone else had said that very thing, not long ago. *Gen*— when she'd become the saber cat. In fact, Astar had said the same thing to Zephyr, when he'd been so rough with her. And she'd been acting so aggressive and territorial—something he'd put down to her *gríobhth* nature and maybe congratulating himself that it was all about him, but what if it wasn't?

"Should I call Nilly down to heal you?" Astar asked.

"Nah. I got it." Jak began ripping strips of cloth from the bottom of his shirt. "If she's up to it later, she can catch anything that might leave an ugly scar. I'll keep the ones that add to my rakish good looks," he added with a cocky grin.

"Here's what we know about Lena," Astar said to Rhy, and related the events with neutral formality, much as he'd report to Ursula. "Now, how and why are you here?"

Rhy visibly struggled to contain himself, holding up a staying hand. "Salena is just ... gone?"

"Zephyr believes she can locate Lena, and I believe in Zephyr," Astar replied firmly, adding an internal prayer to any deity who might be listening to bring them back safely. "Gen and Nilly are aloft keeping an eye out. Meanwhile, we wait. Now: talk."

"Yeah, I saw the girls as I came in." Rhy cast a jaundiced eye at the sky. "I could join them, but ravens aren't great in the dark." At Astar's impatient movement, Rhy cocked his head. "Fine, I'll answer your questions. I know you don't want me here, but I couldn't stay away. I reported to Ordnung as ordered, then went back to Annfwn." He glared at Astar defiantly. "It was killing me," he ground out, "knowing you all were up here doing something important—"

Jak made a scoffing sound through his teeth, which were clenched around one end of a scrap of cloth he was tying over a bleeding wound on his upper arm. "If you count kicking our heels at the Elderhorst court important, though I did win some decent coin."

"You were doing that for a reason," Rhy insisted. "Whereas I was kicking my heels in paradise for no good reason at all. So, I flew to Elderhorst to find you, maybe try to make amends."

"*This* is how you make amends?" Astar asked incredulously, gesturing at Jak's wounds and his own.

Rhy shrugged in the elaborate Tala style and gave them a lopsided smile. "Mistakes were made?"

They all snorted with laughter at their standard excuse from boyhood to explain the many scrapes the three of them had gotten into.

"Let me help with that," Rhy said, taking another scrap of cloth from Jak and deftly tying it over another bleeding wound. "So, I flew to Elderhorst. Figured I might as well, since you'd made me memorize those bleeding *maps*. But when I arrived, I found out you'd all headed up here." He shook his head. "I was flying up here when... I don't know how to explain it, but I *felt* something. Like claws on the inside of my skull. And I... I heard Salena cry out for me, begging me for help. Then she..." His voice cracked, and he looked at them bleakly. "She disappeared from the world. I thought she was dead."

They sat in silence a moment, Moranu's crescent moon silvering over the shining black water of the lake below. "I didn't realize you and Lena were so connected," Astar finally said. If he had, would he have treated Rhy the same way? Probably.

Rhy made an incoherent sound of frustration and regret. "You didn't know? *I* didn't know! I don't know when or how that happened, but I can tell you that I spent seven long years apart from Salena without ever feeling her voice tug at me like that. And I feel sure Salena would tell you that I'm the last person she'd call out to for help," he finished bitterly.

"Zephyr heard her, too," Astar told him, musing over the puzzle pieces. "I'd say it was shapeshifters, but Lena isn't one, and Gen, Stella, and I didn't hear anything."

"Something is going on with you shapeshifters, though," Jak informed them. "Lena and I discussed it. You're all acting more animal than usual. I mean that in the nicest way," he added cheerfully.

Rhy threw Jak a vicious look. "You and Salena were discussing *me*, you mean."

Jak rolled his eyes, stood, and dusted himself off—without much effect, given how much frozen mud had been ground into his clothes. "You, my friend, have your head so far up your ass that you think you're the center of the universe because you can't see anything else."

With a growl, Rhy leapt for him, claws erupting from his human hands. Astar moved too late to stop him, but Jak needed no help. In an agile blur, he was behind Rhy, twin daggers crossed under Rhy's jaw, ready to slice. "Careful," Jak said in a lethal tone, all vestige of the jokester gone. "I went easy on you because I know you're out of your head, but you will be a good dog or I'll put you down. The moment I feel you shift, I'm cutting."

Rhy snarled, twisting—and subsided when one blade pierced his skin, a line of blood trickling down.

"You're not good at healing," Jak warned, "and Nilly is too

far away to help you if I cut too deep. Don't make me upset her."

"Jak," Astar said in a smooth voice. "Let him go."

Jak raised a brow at Astar, lifted one shoulder and let it fall, then withdrew his knives and planted a kick in the small of Rhy's back—all in one smooth movement—sending Rhy flying to his knees. Astar tensed, ready to shift and stop Rhy if he tried to attack again, but his cousin remained on hands and knees, spitting out dust and blood. "Fuck me, you Dasnarian lightweight—when did you get so freaking fast?" he gritted out.

Jak smiled thinly. "I may be a lowly mossback, but that doesn't mean I can't learn how to manage shapeshifters. All the more reason, in fact." He spun his twin blades and sheathed them. "Now, I may be able to kick shapeshifter ass, but I can't see in the dark like you two. What's the revised plan?"

Astar eyed the decimated carriage, decided it was a total loss. "Jak can ride one of the horses. My grizzly form sees well in the dark, so I'll guide us down the road to the manse. If we can find it quickly—since our guides abandoned us—we can be there in a couple of hours. Rhy—ride or fly, your call."

Rhy snorted. "You forget that these aren't shapeshifter horses or ones that have been tamed by Tala wizards to ignore big nasty predators. No way are these horses following a grizzly bear. We can take turns walking and riding, and I'll guide us. I saw the manse on the map, so I know where it is." Rhy glanced at Jak. "And that way we can keep Jak company."

Jak snorted. "You just want to know what Lena said about

you."

Unexpectedly, Rhy grinned and pounded Jak on the back. "So she *did* talk about me. Spill, bro."

"No way. I can keep a confidence."

"A *confidence*? Is that a euphemism for you seducing my woman?" Rhy demanded.

"Lena is not your woman," Jak returned hotly. "You had your chance there and blew it."

Astar sighed mentally as he shifted into bear form. It was going to be a long couple of hours.

~ 28 ~

THE MOMENT ZEPH found the gateway and slipped through, she marveled that she hadn't seen it before. Maybe it was being in gríobhth form—which, as Stella had pointed out, was more sensitive to half-states of all kinds and magic in general—but the threshold between one realm and the next stood out like a crease in a silk gown. Not a rift so much as a fold, and once she found it, the space between the upper edge and the bottom became markedly apparent.

As was the nothingness where they intersected.

If not for Lena's cries still echoing soundlessly in Zeph's head, she would've hesitated to enter that weird space that didn't seem to be anything at all. To her gríobhth senses, the narrow slit had no color or substance, no scent or feel. It was noticeable entirely because it defied rational explanation. In some ways, it reminded her of the fleeting sense of nonexistence that sometimes infiltrated her mind when she was shapeshifting. Though all shapeshifter children learned not to dwell on that non-space, lest they become trapped there.

Nobody with any sense would fling themselves into such a non-space. Fortunately, good sense wasn't high on the list of gríobhth virtues, so that made the decision even easier. With a deft maneuver of folded wings, she turned sideways and dove into the nothing.

For the space of three heartbeats, she seemed to hang there, formless and senseless.

Then the world burst into full scent, sound, and color. A warm and humid wind buoyed her wings, feeling far thicker than any wind she'd known. Below, a forest stretched, dense, unbroken, and primeval, with no evidence of human settlements. The cries and roars of strange creatures echoed up, her gríobhth instincts wary of them, though her human mind couldn't assign them to any animal she knew.

In the distance, a shape ascended into the sky—which had a greenish tint, all wrong for the world Zeph knew—and spread its enormous wings. A dragon. And a massive one, far larger than Zynda's shapeshifter version. Larger still than Kiraka or the other n'Andanan dragons. But then, those dragons had all once been shapeshifters, even if they'd settled into Final Form.

With every cell in her gríobhth body, Zeph knew this was a *real* dragon.

Though no one really understood the magic behind shapeshifting—and many superstitiously refused to think about it, lest Moranu become offended and withdraw Her gift—most thought of shapeshifting as a kind of swapping of one body for another. It wasn't as if her human body distorted to become the gríobhth, or vice versa, which was why size became irrelevant. Some irreverent types joked that shapeshifters must deposit their human forms in some other place while they used an alternate form.

Few cared to contemplate the implications of that for very long. Was the true owner of the gríobhth body forced to wear her human form at Zeph's whim? Or did her human body wait asleep for her to take it back again? What about those variations in dress and hairstyle she carefully cached? Perhaps each iteration of herself stood like a row of dolls on a shelf, glassy-eyed and deathly still, waiting to be donned again.

She shuddered internally. This was why she wasn't a philosopher.

Still, most Tala agreed that they couldn't simply make up a form. No becoming a horse with six legs, for example. The form had to have existed somewhere or somewhen for a shapeshifter to acquire it for their cache. With an uneasy turn of her stomach, Zeph contemplated that this place might be that where.

Keeping an eye on the dragon—which could and likely would eat her in a single gulp—Zeph *listened* for Lena. If she was somewhere below that dense canopy, Lena wouldn't be visible. Nor could Zeph smell or hear Lena, but the *sense* of her tickled at her mind, her friend's distress nearly painful. Following that tug, she decreased altitude, forcing herself to keep the glide slow and easy. No sudden movements or wing-flapping to attract the dragon's attention.

When Zeph ducked below the upper canopy and into the thick shadows, she released a bit of tension. Hopefully she and Lena could find a fold on the ground and go home that way, without risking the dragon's attention again. After all, flightless Lena had found the fold from the ground in their own world.

Unless the fold disappeared again, leaving her and Lena

trapped in this place forever. Well, they would deal with that if they had to.

Her relief at being out of sight didn't last long. She might've avoided the dragon—for now—but this forest was no more familiar than anything else in this world. The broad, waxy leaves big as the shields of the guards at Ordnung slapped at her with surprising rigidity, and they sprouted from gnarled limbs that grew together to make a nearly impassable barrier. Small creatures that looked part monkey, part reptile leapt about in droves, chattering through pointed teeth and hanging from prehensile tails. At least the monkey-lizards fled from the gríobhth—though not as far as Zeph would like, given their painfully high-pitched screeching.

She'd do better to switch to a smaller bird form to get through the tight network of branches. The peregrine would work, small, agile, but still possessing a sharp beak and talons, should she need to defend herself.

Except she couldn't shift.

The shock nearly had her crashing into a trunk, and she had to seize control of herself with a brisk mental shake. *Pay attention to the here and now.* The admonition came in her father's voice, and imagining his disappointment in her produced the cool state of alertness she needed.

Her wide wingspan would never make it through the resistant—and, it turned out, spiny—canopy. So she landed on a wide branch and clung with all four sets of claws, the hard wood equally as difficult to penetrate. Keeping her balance as she leapt ever downward from branch to branch forced her to concentrate on that, and not on the icy terror that she might never shift again. They'd all grown up on stories of Aunt Zynda's painful trial of being unable to shift for so long. Possibly the second-worst nightmare for a shapeshifter, next to botching a shift. But at least Aunt Zynda had been stuck in human form, with speech and thumbs.

Spending the rest of her life as the gríobhth, never able to kiss Astar again, or lay against him, skin to skin... the prospect turned her heart inside out.

Well, she wouldn't let it happen, no more than she'd give him up to another woman. In gríobhth form, there wasn't even a question. Astar was her mate, and only that mattered. Thrones and crowns and silly human ideas about honor and duty were like clothing to be donned and discarded. If she had to wear the costume of a queen so the rest of the world would acknowledge their mating, then so be it. She had no idea why that had ever seemed like an obstacle to her human mind. If Astar needed her to be a queen, then she would. Done.

With that epiphany, she finally burst through the dense canopy layer to the murky shadows beneath. The smooth trunks stood in straight and silent columns, the lowest branches easily ten times a human's height above the forest floor. But at least the space gave her room to spread her wings and glide to the forest floor, deeply layered with the dead leaves. She sank into them to nearly her belly, not unpleasant, except who knew what creatures might live beneath.

Given the apparent lack of life on the forest floor, she'd bet her beak that predators of some sort lay in wait below the thick detritus. No plant life seemed to live in the deep gloom. If the sense of Lena's increasing panic wasn't tugging so strongly at her, Zeph would've flown up and out. Better to take her chances with a dragon than an unknown and stealthy attacker that could come at her vulnerable belly from below.

Too bad her gríobhth couldn't hover, but she was way too heavy for that. A hummingbird would be ideal, though she'd never tried for that form, not wanting to encroach on Gen's First Form when Zeph had one Gen could never attain. Theoretically, anyway. Only she and Zyr could take gríobhth form, and they'd been more or less born to it, whatever that implied. Not that she could shift in this awful world anyway.

Wishing she could call Lena's name—she *felt* like she was nearby, but Zeph couldn't tell precisely where—she opened her beak and called softly, a gentle trill for a frightened chick. The sound drifted like fog in the crushing silence of the forest floor, eddying briefly, and then gone.

Something rustled under the leaf litter. Several of her lengths away, the still, musty surface *moved*.

Keeping one eye on the leaf movement, Zeph called again, more loudly. She'd already alerted one *thing*, so what was the worst that could happen?

Turned out the worst was awakening a dozen more of the *things*. In every direction, the creatures stirred under the deep detritus—and began arrowing toward her. The nearest, her first *thing*, moved stealthily enough that it was still a couple of lengths away. Legs tensed to leap away—she really needed to practice taking off from the ground in gríobhth form, though running through this leaf layer wouldn't happen—she called one last time, a roar of urgent summoning that ricocheted through the sentinel forest trunks and sent ripples of reaction through the canopy, the monkey-lizards screeching in an agonizing chorus.

The *things* under the leaf litter stilled, then moved toward her faster. Claws extended, tail at the ready, and wings unfurled, she prepared to escape—and to fight off what she couldn't elude.

"Zephyr!" Lena's scream, full of terrible hope, echoed through the forest. The first *thing*, still a length away, snaked slimy tentacles around Zeph's front paws. She didn't have to plan the leap—her feline instincts did that for her. With a *yowl* of horror, she did a snake jump that carried her well into the air, simultaneously slicing with her beak at one tentacle and using her tail like a whip to sever the other. Free for the moment, she pumped her wings furiously as more tentacles shot up to pursue her. The forest floor looked suddenly like a seabed full of tubificid worms, waving themselves in search of food.

She didn't like being food.

Twisting her body in midair, she changed her trajectory to land in a clear—and hopefully not easily predictable—spot. As soon as she hit ground, the *things* zoomed toward her, and she leapt again.

"Zephyr, if that's you, please help!"

I'm coming! Zeph thought at Lena, wishing she could actually send the thought. She roared, but was too busy leaping and avoiding tentacles to manage much more. Fuck her, she wished she could get a good glide going. Her wings throbbed with the strain, working to lift her heavy lion's body, which dragged her again and again to the deadly ground, the slippery leaves giving her next to no purchase to spring up again.

How had Lena evaded these tentacled *things*?

Gradually, she targeted Lena's voice, zigzagging her way there—and at last spotted her, crouched on an outcropping of black rock. How she'd found it in the otherwise featureless forest floor was nothing short of a miracle. Tentacles snaked up the rock around her on all sides, slapping at the stone wetly, flailing to reach her. Lena perched at the very top, bleeding from multiple lacerations, a dagger in each hand, mouth contorted in a soundless snarl as she stabbed the blades at any tentacle that came too near.

There wasn't really room for both of them on the rock, but Zeph didn't dare risk getting tentacled and dragged under by the *things*. With a roar of warning, she lunged for the top of the rock—an extra-long leap—and gave everything to her wings. She didn't quite reach the summit, but she landed with all claws extended, gouging the tentacles with big swipes of her hind paws as she clung to the rock with the front. It wasn't much different than trying to dig her claws into that iron-hard wood of the trees.

Lena seized her with a sob, wrapping her arms around Zeph's neck and burying her face in her feathers. Trying to be gentle with the frailer human, Zeph nudged Lena with the curve of her beak, then clacked urgently as a tentacle wrapped around a hind paw. She whipped it with her tail, severing the thing, but she couldn't fight all of them.

Fortunately, Lena was no shrinking violet—just imagine how Henk and Dina would fare in this situation!—and she quickly climbed onto Zeph's back. Good thing they'd at least practiced this much. "Go," Lena urged.

Zeph eyed the drop to the forest floor. Not nearly enough air for her wings to grab, even if she'd been fresh. Whipping two more tentacles away, she judged the height to the lowest and nearest branch. About three human heights.

Normally she'd say she couldn't do it, especially with a person on her back.

This wasn't normal, and she had no choice. Probably, too, this would be a good time to ask for help—she actually knew she needed it—but there was no help to be had. Except maybe Moranu.

Coiling down, winding herself into a spring, she prayed to Moranu for that help. If the goddess could even reach into this cursed world. Lena was chanting a prayer on her back, clinging hard. Maybe that would help too.

Zeph leapt into the air. Pumping her wings like never before in her life, she strained for the limb. Stretching to grab with at least her beak. She reached, reached... and felt herself begin to sink. It wouldn't be enough. If a gríobhth could cry, she'd be weeping in despair.

Then a gust of cold, wet wind buoyed her, giving her a lift. Turbulent and too gusty, the wind challenged her wings—but also gave her a boost and density to push against. With beak and then forepaws, she grabbed the limb, cursing the vile, stony stuff for being too hard to really dig into. Lena crawled up her neck, grabbing the limb and hauling herself onto it. "To the trunk!" she screamed at Zeph. "Kick up with back paws!"

Good idea. With nearly the last of her strength, Zeph lunged for the wide smooth trunk, splintering claws as she did her best to dig in, wings working to give her lift. With powerful back legs, she kicked herself up and landed on the limb belly down, aching wings furled, and all four paws dangling.

I eat you, she thought viciously at the futilely waving tentacles below. *Gríobhth wins.*

Lena seized her head on either side of the lethal beak and lifted Zeph's head. "You are the most incredible woman in the entire world," she vowed. "I don't know how you found me, but thank the Three that you did. I owe you for the rest of my life."

Zeph trilled a comforting sound, missing words more than ever. Lena frowned. "Can you shift—heal yourself and talk to me?"

Slowly shaking her head, Zeph realized her legs stung where the tentacles had grabbed her. Lifting one paw, she noted bleeding lacerations much like Lena's. Wonderful.

"You can't shift," Lena repeated. "But my weather magic works, much good *that* is."

Ah—that explained the fortuitous wind that saved their lives. She clacked her beak chidingly at Lena. "Well, yes. I did do that," Lena replied, "but you did all the real work. If only I could do something useful like call lightning. Or a flood! Then I'd drown those fucking *things*." She glared at the tentacles below, slowly slipping back into hiding, deprived of their prey. "All right," Lena continued, "I guess I do all the talking, and you can give me nods for yes, and so forth."

Zeph nodded encouragingly.

"I don't know how you got here, but I was walking along

the cliff's edge because I felt an odd juxtaposition in the atmosphere. Like it was one thing on this side and then—with a bit of overlap—something else on the other. In between the two sides was something like a pocket. I stepped closer and fell into nothingness." She wrapped her arms around herself, smearing the still freely flowing blood. "Horrible nothingness."

Zeph crooned comfortingly, adding a nod.

"Same for you? Sorry. I won't waste a lot of breath apologizing, but I'm so sorry. That's what I get for being curious. Anyway, then I burst through the nothing and was in this forest. I started wading through that *shit* and, well, you can guess the rest."

Zeph cocked her head in question, turning her head backward, hoping that got the message across.

"What do you see—oh! Did I try to go back through the gateway? Yes, I spent way too long circling trying to find it again. I'm afraid that... what if the portal doesn't open from this side? We'll be trapped here."

Zeph bobbed her head, trying to look like a sea monster.

"I have no idea what... Wait, the lake creature? I see! If it comes from here, then there *must* be a two-way doorway. Good thinking. But how to find it?"

Zeph pointed her beak at the sky, somewhere far above the solid-looking canopy.

"Fly?" Lena asked. "That's how you crossed over, I bet. Hmm. So, if you can fly us around, then I can feel for a change in atmosphere like I felt at Lake Sullivan. It could work."

Zeph nodded vigorously. It was their best chance—especially as she had zero intention of returning to tentacleland.

"I'm game," Lena agreed. "I sure don't have a better plan. But you need to rest."

Clacking her beak in disagreement, Zeph shook her head, then pointed her beak at one of Lena's bleeding wounds, holding up one of her own bleeding paws. Lena stared blankly, then blanched. "The blood isn't clotting. There must be some venin in there preventing it. You're right, if we stay here, we'll bleed to death."

Zeph rather thought they had a good chance of bleeding to death anyway, even if they made it back to their own world. Maybe Stella could heal alien venin. Maybe not. But it was worth a try.

Wearily, she climbed to all four feet, then leapt to the next branch up, then glanced back inquiringly at Lena.

"Climbing it is," Lena agreed, sounding as exhausted as Zeph felt. "No, I can do it. I learned how to climb trees in Aerron—a critical skill for escaping the desert lions—and you'll be carrying me soon enough. When we get to the top, I'll help you get aloft, and then I can rest like the dead weight I am!"

Trust Lena to be optimistic in the face of terrible odds. Still, Zeph would rather be on the wing and dodging dragons than being slowly reduced to strips in gloomy tentacleland.

~ 29 ~

THE GUYS REACHED the lakeside villa just inside of three hours. Gen and Stella, having been checking in with them regularly—and seeing no sign of Lena or Zephyr—had arrived ahead of them and had mobilized the resident staff into readiness.

The hot bath had been most welcome, as was the copious food and drink, though Astar had refused all liquor. He wanted to be alert and ready to help Zephyr. *If* he could do anything.

Rhy had eaten, then removed himself and his foul mood from their presence. He was probably out prowling the silent lakeshore. If not for the gleam of moonlight on the endless stretch of water, you'd hardly know the lake was there at all. No wind blew, no waves lapped the shore. It was uncanny, but the staff had assured them this was usual for the place.

Even they hadn't used the word "normal."

He sympathized with Rhy's restlessness, but Ursula had pounded into his head the value of resting when possible, to be in the best possible condition when the enemy finally attacked—or when rescue became possible. So, Astar stood on the balcony of his elaborate set of rooms, the ones Groningen occupied while in residence, and stared out over the water, spinning Zephyr's golden feather between his fingers. It was cold, yes, but oddly much less so than it had been up top. The lack of wind helped—and the air felt nearly balmy compared to the wintry chill they'd been enduring. Possibly that's why the lake didn't freeze.

Zephyr was right, though—the difference was uncanny.

A strange flaming color in the sky caught his attention, and he stared at it, wondering what it might be, hoping it heralded Zephyr's return. It looked like fire. Could something below be burning, casting the reflection into the night sky? If so, that would be a huge fire, devastating the landscape—and possibly settlements—in its path. That was all they needed.

His alarm began to bleed away, however, as the color changed, sifting into blues and greens that danced in ever-larger patterns across the sky. They were extraordinary, achingly beautiful, and his chest tightened with grief, wanting nothing more than to have Zephyr wrapped in his arms, watching too.

Stella eased through the doorway so quietly he didn't hear her at all—she had a knack for moving on silent cat's paws even in human form—but he sensed her approach. Slipping up against him, she ducked under the arm he lifted to put around her, and leaned her head against his chest.

"Jak's sky lights," she murmured. "We did get to see them."

Of course that's what they were. He'd kick himself for being a fool, but Jak's description hadn't captured the sheer otherworldly quality of the experience. "I didn't realize they'd move."

"Like flames, but cold," she agreed. "Lena and Zephyr will be all right."

He hugged her to him, taking a moment to choke down the surge of emotion at her words. "Foresight or optimism?"

"Some of both," she admitted. "In all honesty, I see futures with both possibilities."

Unable to speak, he nodded. That was what he got for asking.

"But I see them coming back more than not. Also, I believe in you, my brave Willy."

"What do I have to do with it?" he asked hoarsely.

She was quiet, her silence fraught with indecision, and he waited patiently. It wasn't easy for her and Aunt Andi, wrestling the dubious gift of seeing the possible futures. Saying too much, or even the slightest hint of the wrong thing, could twist fate into ugly turns.

"When the moment comes," she finally said, "take wing."

His already low spirits sank even lower. "You know I don't have a winged form."

"Yet."

"What do you—" He stopped when she shook him off.

"I can't say more. Just remember what I said. When the time comes..."

"Take wing," he murmured. *What kind of wings?* It must be possible, or Stella wouldn't suggest it. She'd seen that future, so he had it in him. Zephyr was certain of it. *You're so locked down, so determined to be a mossback prince in every way, that you stop yourself from embracing the ferocity of your nature—or of taking on any other form.* "How will I know the time has come?" he asked, more of himself than his sister.

"You'll know," she replied firmly, a wealth of unspoken significance there.

"Soon?" he ventured.

She looked up at the dancing colors in the sky, her eyes silver, blue, and green in the reflected light. "Very soon."

YOU KNOW YOU'RE tired *when giving yourself over to the tentacle things begins to sound like a good idea.* At least Zeph still had the spirit to be sarcastic, even if only in her own head, but she was nearing the phase of exhaustion where she'd begun to doubt her ability to stay aloft. She also really hated not being able to voice her caustic comments, or make suggestions aloud.

Aunt Zynda often remarked that she could stay in animal form for days if it wasn't unhealthy. Zeph—much as she enjoyed her various forms—had never quite understood her aunt's fascination that way. And now she knew, with absolute certainty, that she hated being voiceless.

She liked talking through problems. Circling the same argument in her head for the last several hours, much like her endless circling above the featureless forest canopy, had gotten her exactly nowhere.

She'd managed to get aloft—hooray!—but they hadn't found the fold. And she was tired. Had she mentioned being tired? No, because she couldn't *say* so. She had no voice. And there would come a point where she simply could no longer fly. The ongoing blood loss certainly didn't help. The branches of the upper canopy were too flimsy to hold her weight. The branches lower down were infested with the monkey-lizards, which had proved to be nasty little scavengers who'd watched them with uncomfortably avid hunger as she and Lena climbed.

Below, of course, was tentacleland.

And all of this meant she needed to fly somewhere that wasn't this horrible forest—if this world wasn't entirely covered with it, which was a distinct possibility—so that she and Lena could rest. But that meant flying away from the one location where they *knew* there was a fold to take them home. With the utter lack of distinctive landmarks, she might never find this place again.

In truth, a cold dread in her very empty stomach warned that she might've lost her point of entry anyway. Her brain had gone foggy—had she mentioned she was tired?—and she had no frame of reference for where she'd been.

Lena had tried to find the atmospheric fold, with no luck. For a while, Lena had kept up a steady monologue, describing what she was doing, trying different techniques, cheering and encouraging Zeph, speculating on the nature of the creatures beneath the detritus, but she'd long since fallen silent, rather grimly clinging to Zeph's back. Soon she would've lost too much blood to stay conscious. If she passed out and fell, what then?

Zeph had to confront that giving them both over to the tentacle things might be the best option. She'd rather be blood-sucked dry by a tentacle thing than nibbled to death by a horde of monkey-lizards. Though, really, being immolated or eaten in one gulp by a dragon would be the fastest death. At first, she'd been happy that she hadn't spotted any more dragons. Now she bitterly reflected that it just figured that the source of a quick, clean death would be withheld.

With death a looming inevitability, she just wanted to get it over with. Except that she'd promised Astar she'd return to him. What was he thinking at this moment? Though she knew he'd mourn her loss, maybe a part of him would be relieved. He'd be free to move on and marry a princess off his list. Maybe he'd keep her feather in a glass box, honorably and nobly mourning the love of his youth, and then be all pleased with himself for marrying the right woman instead.

Someone like *Dina*.

The thought made her burn with fury, giving her a short burst of energy. Not that it did them any good.

"Zeph," Lena said wearily. "You have to find somewhere to land. You're not bleeding as badly as I am. If you rest, eat something, you can keep searching for a way home."

Zeph shook her head, tired enough that the movement made her bobble midair.

"You know I'm right. Thank you for risking your life to come after me, but I'm soon going to be a literal dead weight." She sounded so sad. "You'll have a better chance without me."

Uh-oh. This did not sound good.

"If—*when* you make it home, would you tell Rhyian that…" She sighed heavily. "I don't even know what my last words to him should be. I wish I could say I forgive him, but I haven't yet. Maybe I never can, but now I won't get that time. Maybe just tell him that I never stopped loving him, and I'm sorry we didn't get a chance to... Something. Make it sound good. Whatever you think he needs to hear."

Zeph clacked her beak in what she hoped sounded like a bracing rhythm, then crooned comfortingly. She changed direction, too, flying in a straight line at random. Surely if she flew long enough in one direction, she'd reach something besides forest. Lena could still heal. Zeph would find a safe place for Lena to sleep, and she could hunt for them both. With food and rest, they'd feel better and could make a plan.

"Tell the others something good, too," Lena added, so quietly that even Zeph's sharp ears had to strain to hear her. "Make up some story about me going down fighting. Jak should know that his dagger lessons saved me."

Ah, so that's where she'd learned it. When had they been doing lessons?

"And tell Mom and Muku and Bethany I love them." She was quiet for so long that Zeph thought she'd passed out, which was good, since she still clung to Zeph's back. "I wish I'd gotten a chance to do at least one heroic thing," she said in a whisper. "Some Salena I turned out to be."

Except that the first Salena had sacrificed herself.

And Lena did, too, flinging herself to the side and off—too fast for Zeph to counterbalance. Folding her wings, she dove after Lena's falling body. Her caramel hair whipped like a banner in the wind of her fall, her eyes closed, expression almost peaceful as she gave herself over, arms outstretched.

Exhaustion forgotten, Zeph plummeted to catch Lena before she hit the canopy. Almost there.

And then Lena was gone. Vanished. Into a fold?

Hoping against hope, Zeph followed exactly. At the last moment, she saw the narrow slice of nothing. Too small for her gríobhth body to fit through. Too late to avoid it.

Hitting the nothing, she screamed, the edges of two realities tearing off her wings. Scraping her raw, turning her inside out, then nothing at all.

Tentacle things would have been better.

ASTAR HELD VIGIL, watching the dancing lights, the chill invading his bones. Stella had long since gone to bed, cryptically observing that she'd need her rest, but to wake her at once if anything happened.

So Astar waited for whatever was to happen. Every once in a while, he caught a glimpse of Rhy prowling the lakeshore in wolf form, occasionally pausing to sniff the air, then glumly resuming his rounds.

When the spark of light caught his eye, at first Astar thought it was part of the dazzling display of sky lights. But Rhy also noticed, the wolf's black silhouette freezing in a fierce attitude, followed by a long howl of urgent warning. Then he was the raven flying into the night sky, straight toward...

Lena. Falling through the sky like a shooting star.

And Zephyr, in human form, right behind her.

When the moment comes, take wing.

Stella was right: He knew the moment had come. With his gaze fixed on the two women tumbling through the sky—Rhy in raven form valiantly flying to reach them, as if he could do anything to stop their fall—Astar flung himself from the balcony with two thoughts in his mind.

Big wings.

Save Zephyr.

So intent was he on reaching her, that it never occurred to him to worry that he might fail, that he'd hit ground and die before she did. When his body exploded around him, massive wings grabbing the sky like claws to bark, he only climbed. Climbed the air like a tree, straight up to catch them.

He reached Lena first, catching her by tumbling her onto his broad back, trying to balance her there even as he stroked toward Zephyr. Rhy zoomed in, shifted to human form, and flattened himself over Lena. Shouting incoherently, Rhy nevertheless made it clear that he had her. Good to know, as Astar barely felt either of them. Whatever he'd become, he was enormous.

No time to think, he pumped toward Zephyr, tumbling in an uncontrolled fall, naked, bloody, and clearly unconscious or she would've shifted by now. Reaching for her, he found he had hands. Scaled and taloned, but good enough for catching.

He caught her in cupped hands—paws, whatever—as gently as possible, wheeling in midair back toward the manse. Lights once again blazed in the windows, people pouring out to point at him in wonder. Stella, in nighthawk form, shot out of a window, circling him. Finding a clear spot on the lakeshore, he flattened himself as much as possible so Rhy could jump off, Lena in his arms.

Astar laid Zephyr on the ground, then shifted to human form, picking her up again to hold against him. Then Stella was there, easing Zephyr away from him, her green healing energy swirling around them. "Lena, too," he muttered brokenly.

"Alive, and will stay that way," Stella muttered. "I gave her a jolt, and Rhy is taking her inside."

He was afraid to ask. He had to know. Zephyr was so cold. So still. "And Zephyr?"

"Hush. Let me work."

Stella was so rarely terse, and never with him, that he made himself be as still and quiet as possible. Zephyr looked so fragile. Even when she'd broken herself before, she hadn't looked so shattered, so pale and lifeless. *Is she dead?* The question rose relentlessly, pounded at his throat to be spoken, and only Stella's demand for silence kept him from asking. A good thing, as some deep instinct—Tala superstition, perhaps—warned that admitting the possibility aloud would seal her fate.

What would he do if Zephyr died? Go on, he supposed. Finish the quest. Eventually ascend to the high throne and rule to the best of his ability. Mourn Zephyr for the rest of his life.

He wouldn't marry, he realized. No power in all the realms—not even Ursula—could force him to do that. Just as she'd found another heir, he would, too. Stella's child, perhaps. Or Rhy's, if he managed to keep track of the children he sired.

But Astar would never take another woman to bed. Grizzly bears and gríobhths had that much in common—they mated for life. Did Zephyr realize that they'd mated? His bear knew. So did whatever winged creature he'd become.

He'd flown. And perhaps would never do that again, either.

In the still, dark, and cold hours before dawn, Astar sat on the shore of that ancient lake, watching the blue, green, and gold lights in the sky play over Zephyr's deathly still profile.

~ 30 ~

"YOU SHOULD TRY to sleep," Stella advised, stroking a hand over Astar's head.

Though his eyes felt like rocks in his head, Astar knew he'd never sleep. He stared hard at Zephyr's unmoving body in the bed. "I can't. Not until I know she'll wake up."

Stella sighed and came to crouch before him, careful not to obscure his view of Zephyr. Taking his hands in hers, she gazed at him with soft gray eyes. "She'll live. I promise that."

He risked looking at her, studying her face for clues. "But will she wake?"

Stella glanced away, confirming his worst fears. "Maybe," she admitted.

Taking a deep breath, he held it, forcing the need to rend and tear, to sob and scream, deep inside. "I'm in love with her," he said instead.

"I knew that."

"Probably before I did."

Stella cupped his cheek with one hand. "Yes. You always have loved her."

He tried to smile, couldn't manage it. "Why didn't you tell me?"

Rolling her eyes a little, she shook her head. "Some things you have discover for yourself."

"I won't marry anyone else," he said, declaring it aloud, so all the world would know.

"I know that, too," Stella replied, so somberly that he knew she must see a future where he was the lonely high king, solitary in his rule. "So, do you want to talk about how you took dragon form?"

"I don't have answers." A dragon. He'd shifted into dragon form without knowing the trick of it. All those times Gen and Zephyr had argued, debated, and analyzed how Zynda had done it, and he'd managed the feat without really trying. No—that wasn't true. A different sort of attempt, where only doing mattered, and nothing else.

"This might be a thing where we need to figure out the right question first."

"Nilly—I love you, but I can't think philosophy right now."

"No." She patted his cheek and rose. "I'm going to check on Lena."

"You said she'll be fine—and you need to sleep, too, after all that healing."

"She will be fine, but Rhy hasn't left her side either. I'll sleep, after I make sure you and Rhy do." She set a cool hand on the back of his neck.

"Rhy is stubborn," Astar replied, his gaze focused again on Zephyr. "And acting like a man possessed. I doubt you'll get him to budge."

"I have a few tricks up my sleeve," Stella replied.

Her smug tone should've warned him—in fact, did warn

him—but before he could escape her touch, the crash of sleep dragged him under.

ZEPH CAME AWAKE all at once—which was all wrong. She never woke up like that. Afraid to open her eyes, she searched her memory. Tentacles, monkey-lizards, or dragons? The image of a dragon zooming toward her through a night sky confirmed it. Death by dragon.

Well, it *had* been her first choice.

Though she didn't *feel* dead. In fact... that was Astar's scent, in the bedclothes around her, along with his living presence. And the heat of his body.

Rolling her head on the pillow, she cracked open one eye, terrified to hope. But there he was. Sound asleep on his back, mouth a little open as he snored in soft grizzly growls. And, for once, he slept peacefully, with none of his usual restless thrashing. Leaning up on one elbow, she gazed down at him, memorizing his face in repose, as it so rarely was. Astar. *Hers.*

Looking around the room, she wondered where they were. Not at Elderhorst. The scent of lake water edged around the corners of tapestries featuring Lake Sullivan's famous sea monster. All she remembered was diving after Lena, then that slice of nothing and scraping through the doorway too small to admit her gríobhth form.

With a stab of panic, she lifted a hand. Definitely in human form. And she felt good—like Nilly's brand of healing good—so they'd made it back. At least, she had. What about Lena?

Needing to know, she eased out of the bed, doing her best not to wake Astar. He didn't stir, which was so unlike him that she felt a stab of worry. He'd also fallen asleep fully dressed, though in the simple clothes he wore returning to human form.

She was naked. And, since there didn't seem to be anything for her to wear, she might as well attempt a shift and find out right now if the ability was gone forever. First Form would be easiest, but she couldn't bear to be the gríobhth right then. Instead, she went for a cat. Like sliding her hand into a glove, the form came to her. *Thank you, Moranu.*

Coming back to human form wearing a simple, black woolen gown, she realized she'd forgotten shoes. Clearly her shifting would need a bit of attention to get back up to par. Padding barefoot out the door, she tried sharpening her sense of smell, pleased when that ability came back easily enough. Following Lena's scent, Zeph found her friend in a smaller set of rooms a few doors down the way.

Lena, who'd been standing by a cheerful fire, warming her hands, whirled as Zeph slipped through the door. With a strangled cry, Lena flung herself at Zeph, catching her in a bone-crushing embrace. She was saying something—and crying at the same time—so her words made no sense.

Zeph opened her mouth and found salt water running down her own cheeks. So she clutched Lena in return, rocking her gently. Finally, Lena subsided, gulping back sobs and wiping her face. "I can't believe you saved us," she finally managed.

"*You* saved us," Zeph corrected. "You found the fold."

Remembering, she scowled and gripped Lena by the shoulders, anger rising. "Though you were trying to kill yourself, you gruntling idiot."

Lena smiled weakly. "I'd already put you in jeopardy by making you come to my rescue. I only wanted to give you a chance to live."

"Saying your goodbyes like that," Zeph growled, feeling a bit of the gríobhth's ferocity returning, beyond relieved that it didn't hurt.

"Speaking of which…" Lena jerked her chin at the other room. Zeph peeked through the open door—to see Rhy sprawled on the bed, fully clothed like Astar, and equally unconscious. "Nilly said she had to put him out because he wouldn't sleep, waiting for me to wake. She did the same with Astar."

Ah, that explained it. She frowned in confusion, though. "How is Rhy even here?"

"There are *many* questions," Lena agreed, then hesitated. "I'm in no position to ask a favor of you, but…"

"I am *not* taking you back to study the tentacle things," Zeph informed her decisively.

Lena grimaced in distaste. "Good name for them. But no, I was going to ask—would you *not* tell Rhy the things I said? In that place."

Zeph cocked her head. "Of course. Though, I feel I should point out that, when you thought you were going to die, he was the first person you thought of and wanted me to give a message to."

"I know." Lena rolled her shoulders, releasing a heavy sigh.

"And I meant what I said. The thing is—I love Rhyian, but I can't trust him. When I thought I was going to die, I could let him know I love him, without having to suffer the consequences of him breaking my trust again." Her pretty blue eyes filled with tears, making them all the more luminous.

Zeph embraced her again, gently this time. "I understand. Love should be easy, and it just isn't."

Lena held on. "Neither is trust. It should be, but... it just isn't," she finished wryly.

The roar of an enraged grizzly strained through a human throat had them startling and springing apart. Lena raised her brows. "Is that—?"

"Astar," Zeph confirmed with a grin, delight and joy bubbling up in her like Ordnung's finest sparkling wine.

The door flung open, banging hard on the frame, and both women shushed Astar, pointing at the other room where Rhy still slept. Zeph frowned to herself. She knew Rhy well, and something about the lines of his body made her wonder... was he only pretending to be asleep?

"Zephyr," Astar said hoarsely, seizing her attention and then—in three strides—seizing her and lifting her into the air to crush her against him. "You're awake," he breathed, like it was a miracle.

She pulled back a little to frame his face in her hands. "I am awake, and I'm just fine. I'm right here."

Cupping her head in his big hand, he pulled her down for a greedy kiss, the intensity of it melting her against him. "I thought you were gone forever," he finally said, leaning his forehead against hers. Remembering himself, he turned so he could see Lena, who watched them with fond amusement—and maybe a bit of wistfulness. "Both of you. I'm so glad you're back unharmed, and I want to hear everything."

"We'd like to hear your end, too," Lena replied. "There's much information to exchange, but for now..." She smiled at how Astar had yet to put Zeph down. "I think maybe you two need some time together. We can all convene to tell stories later."

"Good idea," Astar said. With no further comment, he tossed Zeph over his shoulder and carried her out of the room.

HOURS LATER, WHEN he thought he might have finally convinced his inner bear that his mate was alive and whole, Astar lay with his head pillowed on a folded arm, watching Zephyr sleep. Night had fallen, so they'd lit some candles, and the golden glow shimmered over her flawless skin. She lay on her side, too, facing him, which let him trace the long sinuous curve of her body, from slim shoulder down her delicate rib cage to narrow waist, then over the exquisite flare of her hip and down again the tapering slope of her elegant thigh.

As he drew his fingers back up the satiny path, he found her deep blue eyes open, watching him. "I didn't mean to wake you," he said quietly. "Go back to sleep."

She smiled sleepily, wriggling down into her nest like a contented kitten. "I've slept enough for a lifetime. I'd rather be awake to savor every moment with you." A line of pain formed between her brows. "I thought I was good at enjoying the moment, but that place…"

"Do you want to tell me about it now?" he asked gently. She hadn't before. In typical Zephyr style, she'd declared her own moratorium—on talking—and insisted their mouths be otherwise occupied.

She met his gaze with sober candor. "If it's all right, I'd rather tell the story once, with everyone there."

"Of course it's all right." He smoothed a hand over her hip, petting her the way she liked, and reining back his own impatience to know what had happened to spook her so.

"There will be decisions to be made," she warned darkly.

"Fortunately something I've been trained to do," he teased, happy to make her smile.

"Would you…" She hesitated, her fingers knotting the bedsheets. "It's not fair when I just said I only want to tell my story once, but will you tell me what happened on your end— how did we get back?"

He picked up her hand, kissing those narrow fingers. "You fell from the sky."

She winced, nodding. "My wings were broken?"

"No, you were in human form. First Lena appeared, falling, then you came after. Naked and unconscious." When she only listened, pressing her lips together, pain in her eyes, he continued, though he decided to leave out that she'd been as good as dead. "Nilly thinks that you went through some sort of portal as the gríobhth, perhaps with Lena on your back, and that it somehow stripped you of that form, throwing you into your human body."

"That makes sense," she mused. "I definitely didn't shift

back on my own. So, we fell—who caught us?"

He cleared his throat, embarrassed for no good reason. "Er... I did."

"As the grizzly?" She sounded justifiably dubious.

"Ah, no—I flew and caught you in the air."

Her eyes widened, a delighted expression replacing the haunted shadows. Extracting her fingers from his hand, she punched him lightly on the shoulder. "Really? Wings, Astar! That's wonderful news. What form did you find?"

He knew he must be blushing. "I didn't see myself, in truth. It all happened so fast, and I was focused on you."

She narrowed her eyes, suppressing a mirthful grin. "You're hedging. *And* you're blushing. What is it, Astar? Something big."

"I needed big," he said, sounding way too defensive. "To catch you both. Rhy was there, but as a raven and—"

Zephyr knotted her fingers in his chest hair and tugged hard. The mild pain went straight to his cock, renewing the constant hunger for her. "No more dodging. Tell me, or I'll take *steps*."

Tempting as it was to push her, to find out just what lengths she'd go to—and what sweet torments she'd employ in order to get the information out of him—he caved. "A, um, dragon," he admitted.

Her look of utter astonishment and admiration warmed his heart. "Truly?" she whispered.

"Nilly can verify. She saw everything. Well, so did a lot of people."

"So much for hiding the monsters from the nice mossbacks."

"You're not a monster, Zephyr." He untangled her fingers from his chest hair and kissed her. "You're a hero."

"And my mate is a dragon," she added with a grin. "I'll bet Gen is having a fit."

"I didn't plan it that way," he said. Zephyr was no doubt correct, as hard as Gen had worked to discover the secret of dragon form. "I'll talk to her, but I know she will be mostly happy that you and Lena made it back safely."

"True." Zephyr's smile took on a mischievous note. "I can always drive her crazy about it later."

"Do *you* mind?" he asked earnestly.

"That you attained dragon form without even trying?" She pushed him onto his back, straddling him and using her nails on his nipples. Unable to help himself, he arched under her, already breathless with wanting. "Yes, I mind. I'm horribly jealous, and I intend to make you pay."

He lifted his hands to her gorgeous breasts, kneading them just a little on the hard side, so her eyes blazed with answering arousal. She bent to kiss him, hot and long and lovingly. Then lifted her head to gaze into his eyes. "To be clear," she breathed. "I don't mind. I'm happy you found your wings. And I'm selfishly pleased that you bested Gen. I never really wanted to be a dragon—the gríobhth is plenty—I only tried for dragon to annoy Gen."

Laughing at her, he dragged his hands through her hair. "You're incorrigible."

She fluttered her lashes. "Why, thank you, Your Highness Crown Prince Astar."

The use of his title gave him pause. "I do want to talk to you about something."

"Oh?" She sobered, searching his face. "A bad something?"

"No." He ran his hands over her back. "You called me your mate."

"You are my mate," she replied bluntly, the ferocity of the gríobhth rising in her. "I thought I'd made that clear already."

"You did," he allowed, "but I need to tell you something."

She sat up, face going stony, invisible tail whipping in the air. "What?"

Smoothing his hands over her thighs, he smiled. "Don't look like that. It's a good thing. At least," he amended, feeling uncertain in the face of her fierce expression, "I think you'll be happy. About some parts. Maybe not all, but—"

"Astar, my only love," she replied silkily, not fooling him for a moment, "if you don't spit it out, I'm going to use my teeth on you."

He nearly choked on that threat—alarmed and aroused, as only Zephyr seemed able to do to him. "You're my mate, too," he informed her. "I won't marry anyone else. Ever." When she stared at him blankly, he forged on. "I decided, when I was afraid that you were gone forever, that I'd never be with anyone else. You are my one and only."

She considered that, head cocked like the gríobhth, but softening otherwise. "What about the high throne?"

"What about it?" he returned evenly.

"You need a queen."

"I don't, in fact. But the only way I'll have one is if she's you."

Zephyr smiled oddly, dropping her gaze and tracking one of his nipples with a sharp nail. "We both know I'm not queen material. Not who Ursula would choose."

"Ursula picked her own mate; I will, too. All I care about is that you love me," he answered with raw honesty. "Unless you don't love me enough to—"

She stopped his words with a kiss. "I love you enough to *anything*, Astar," she murmured into his mouth. "Everything that I am or will be is yours. Whatever you ask of me, I'll give. I thought of some things to tell you, too. If you need me to be your queen, then I'll figure out how to do that."

He felt the smile bloom across his face, the wonder filling his heart. "Truly?" he asked.

She shrugged, pretending to nonchalance. "How hard can it be?"

"Nothing is beyond your abilities," he replied with total honesty. "I'm so proud to be yours."

Smiling, she kissed him. "I promised you would be," she confided.

"You did?" he asked, not quite following.

Becoming the cat for a moment—and giving him a quick lick on the nose—she returned to human form with a folded piece of paper in her fingers. With a smile that looked almost shy, she handed it to him. The promise she'd given him on the Feast of Moranu, the one he'd given back to her, unread. Carefully unfolding it, for he knew he'd keep it all his life, he read the simple message.

You will be mine.

Once those words had sent him running. Now he exulted

in them. Catching her by the back of the neck, he drew Zephyr down for a long kiss. "I want to show you something," he said against her lips.

Pulling on his pants and draping her in a sapphire silk robe against the chill, he drew her out onto the balcony, closing the doors behind them. As he'd hoped, the sky lights danced with ethereal beauty, and Zephyr drew in her breath in a gasp of delight. Wrapping his arms around her, he savored that he'd gotten his wish from the night before. "I have something for you," he murmured into her ear. Digging the ring out of his pocket, he held it out to her.

"Salena's ring," she breathed.

"For you. Ursula gave it to me to give to my intended bride."

Taking it from his palm, she slipped it onto her finger. "I'll wear it with honor. And attempt to take the responsibility seriously," she added, leaning back against him.

"Not too seriously, I hope," he teased.

"Let's not ask for the impossible," she agreed pertly.

They stood there together, watching the lights. "I have only one question for you now," he said.

"Oh?"

He kissed her temple. "What next?"

She giggled. "I guess we'll find out together."

"For the rest of our lives."

"A good question to build a lifetime on," she agreed, turning in his arms, and this time, when she kissed him, they didn't use their mouths for words again for a very long time.

The story will continue in
The Sorceress Queen and the Pirate Rogue
Coming April 2021

TITLES BY JEFFE KENNEDY

FANTASY ROMANCES

HEIRS OF MAGIC

The Long Night of the Crystalline Moon
(in *Under a Winter Sky*)
The Golden Gryphon and the Bear Prince
The Sorceress Queen and the Pirate Rogue (April 2021)
The Winter Mage and the Dragon's Daughter (August 2021)
The Storm Princess and the Raven King (December 2021)

THE FORGOTTEN EMPIRES

The Orchid Throne
The Fiery Crown
The Promised Queen (May 2021)

THE TWELVE KINGDOMS

Negotiation
The Mark of the Tala
The Tears of the Rose
The Talon of the Hawk
Heart's Blood
The Crown of the Queen

THE UNCHARTED REALMS

The Pages of the Mind
The Edge of the Blade
The Snows of Windroven
The Shift of the Tide
The Arrows of the Heart
The Dragons of Summer
The Fate of the Tala
The Lost Princess Returns

THE CHRONICLES OF DASNARIA

Prisoner of the Crown
Exile of the Seas
Warrior of the World

SORCEROUS MOONS

Lonen's War
Oria's Gambit
The Tides of Bára
The Forests of Dru
Oria's Enchantment
Lonen's Reign

A COVENANT OF THORNS

Rogue's Pawn
Rogue's Possession
Rogue's Paradise

CONTEMPORARY ROMANCES

Shooting Star

MISSED CONNECTIONS
Last Dance
With a Prince
Since Last Christmas

CONTEMPORARY EROTIC ROMANCES

Exact Warm Unholy
The Devil's Doorbell

FACETS OF PASSION
Sapphire
Platinum
Ruby
Five Golden Rings

FALLING UNDER
Going Under
Under His Touch
Under Contract

EROTIC PARANORMAL

MASTER OF THE OPERA E-SERIAL
Master of the Opera, Act 1: Passionate Overture
Master of the Opera, Act 2: Ghost Aria
Master of the Opera, Act 3: Phantom Serenade
Master of the Opera, Act 4: Dark Interlude
Master of the Opera, Act 5: A Haunting Duet
Master of the Opera, Act 6: Crescendo
Master of the Opera

BLOOD CURRENCY

Blood Currency

BDSM FAIRYTALE ROMANCE

Petals and Thorns

Thank you for reading!

ABOUT JEFFE KENNEDY

Jeffe Kennedy is an award-winning, best-selling author who writes fantasy with romantic elements and fantasy romance. She is an RWA member and serves on the Board of Directors for SFWA as a Director at Large.

Books in her popular, long-running series, The Twelve Kingdoms and The Uncharted Realms, have won the RT Reviewers' Choice Best Fantasy Romance, been named Best Book of June 2014, and won RWA's prestigious RITA® Award, while more have been finalists for those awards. She's the author of the romantic fantasy trilogy with St. Martin's Press, The Forgotten Empires, which includes The Orchid Throne, The Fiery Crown, and The Promised Queen. She also self-publishes the romantic fantasy series Bonds of Magic, Heirs of Magic, and Sorcerous Moons.

Jeffe lives in Santa Fe, New Mexico, with two Maine coon cats, plentiful free-range lizards and a very handsome Doctor of Oriental Medicine.

Jeffe can be found online at her website: JeffeKennedy.com, every Sunday at the popular SFF Seven blog, on Facebook, on Goodreads, and pretty much constantly on Twitter @jeffekennedy. She is represented by Sarah Younger of Nancy Yost Literary Agency.

jeffekennedy.com

facebook.com/Author.Jeffe.Kennedy

twitter.com/jeffekennedy

goodreads.com/author/show/1014374.Jeffe_Kennedy

Sign up for her newsletter here.

jeffekennedy.com/sign-up-for-my-newsletter